The Mark and the Void

Paul Murray is the author of *An Evening of Long Goodbyes*, which was shortlisted for the Whitbread First Novel Award in 2003, and *Skippy Dies*, which was shortlisted for the Costa Novel Award in 2010 and (in the United States) the National Book Critics Circle Award. *The Mark and the Void* is his third novel. He lives in Dublin.

The Mark and the Void

PAUL MURRAY

HAMISH HAMILTON
an imprint of
PENGUIN BOOKS

HAMISH HAMILTON

UK | USA | Canada | Ireland | Australia
India | New Zealand | South Africa

Hamish Hamilton is part of the Penguin Random House group of companies
whose addresses can be found at global.penguinrandomhouse.com.

First published 2015

001

Copyright © Paul Murray, 2015

The moral right of the author has been asserted

This is a work of fiction. Names, characters, places, organizations, and
incidents are either products of the author's imagination or used
fictitiously. Any resemblance to actual events, places, organizations,
or persons, living or dead, is entirely coincidental.

Set in 11.88/14.27 pt Dante MT Std
Typeset by Jouve (UK), Milton Keynes
Printed in Great Britain by Clays Ltd, St Ives plc

A CIP catalogue record for this book is available from the British Library

BOXED SET ISBN: 978–0–241–14512–8
TRADE PAPERBACK ISBN: 978–0–241–14666–8

www.greenpenguin.co.uk

Penguin Random House is committed to a
sustainable future for our business, our readers
and our planet. This book is made from Forest
Stewardship Council® certified paper.

For my mother and father

Idea for a novel: we have a banker rob his own bank. He's working alone; at first, it'll look like a classic inside job. This man, however, is not what you'd call an insider. He's French, not Irish, and although initially he might look like a typical Parisian – black suit, expensive shoes, hair neat but worn slightly long – as the story unfolds and his past comes to light, we find out he never quite fitted in over there either. He didn't grow up in a leafy suburb, didn't attend a fancy *grande école* of the kind that bankers tend to come from; instead he spent his childhood in a run-down corner that the city prefers to disown, and his father's something blue-collar – a welder maybe, a veteran of 1968, a tough nut.

The family doesn't have much: the father's job is precarious, they're constantly resorting to moneylenders, bailiffs come to take the car away, all that. But the father's ambitious for the boy; the father's determined that he'll have a better life. So the son beavers away in his third-rate school and makes it into a second-rate university, and after graduating at the top of his class, he's offered a position in a prestigious French bank. It's dull work, mostly filing and admin, but he's diligent and quick and after a few months his manager takes note of him and recommends him for a start in the Research Department.

As a junior analyst, his official role is to dig up information on companies for the bank and its clients. In practice, he spends his time fixing paper jams, fetching coffees and listening politely while his boss describes his recent sexual adventures. When he gets to do his job, though, he finds that he likes it. More importantly, he's *good* at it. He watches money flow through the market, learns the secret influences at work on it, begins to understand how a speech made by an obscure politician in, say, Guangzhou can send stock prices soaring, while a rumour about a change in the interest rate can spark a worldwide panic. He works early mornings, late nights, hour after hour in the cold glow of the screen, developing models, monitoring trades, figuring out the best way to persuade a client that he and all of his competitors have got the value of a stock completely wrong. One morning, he checks his bank balance and sees he's got his first bonus: three times what his father would make in a year. That's when he knows he's made it.

But his father's not happy. Instead, he looks at the trophies of his son's success – the car, the suit, the unblemished hands – and despises them. It makes no sense – this is what he wanted for him! – yet the higher the boy climbs, the angrier the old man becomes. Everything the banker does to impress him has the opposite effect. He brings little gifts to the house, the father won't accept them. He takes them for dinner, the old man won't eat. They argue incessantly, the father berating the son for things he has nothing to do with – the neighbourhood changing, the rents going up, the President being elected. He calls him a deserter, a traitor. He looks at his son and sees the emissary of a world that no longer needs him.

What can the banker do? Does the old man genuinely want him to give up his job? That would be crazy, right? Besides, he likes it. He likes being wealthy and respected. He likes having a nice apartment in Auteuil and a nice new Mercedes to take him there; he likes nice meals in Le Grand Véfour and nice clothes from the Rue de Sèvres; he likes the beautiful girls who all of a sudden like him, and the micro-romances they squeeze in between the market's close on Friday evening and the Monday meeting at 7 a.m. And he's his father's son: he thrives on opposition. But it gets so bad that they can't even be in the same room together, and after his mother dies, he decides he's had enough. A headhunter calls him about a position at Bank of Torabundo, a rising investment bank with a European HQ in Dublin. They want an analyst to advise clients on financial institutions, domestic and Continental. His language skills make him perfect for the job; they're offering a significant increase on what he's making in Paris.

He doesn't think of it as flight, nor, exactly, as punishment. Yes, the old man is on his own now. But if they're ever to have a functional relationship, he needs to learn something about compromise. So the son takes the job, cutting off all contact with home, beyond monthly payments for the live-in nurse. He plans to return to Paris at Christmas and review the situation, only with the global crash he finds he's too busy to get away. Next Christmas, he thinks, without fail. But in April the nurse calls to tell him the old man has died in his sleep.

That's how we find him as our story begins. It's a couple of months later; he's back in Dublin, passing his days in the service of money; passing most of his nights that way too. He has no friends, no pastimes, no life outside of the bank. He works so hard he doesn't have a moment to himself, or, indeed, a self to have a moment. Someone observing might say he is depressed. He would say he wants only to be left alone. Certainly at this point he has no intention of committing a crime.

Here's the thing, though: someone *is* observing him. For a number of weeks, someone's been watching from a distance – a man, dressed all in black. He makes no effort to conceal himself, nor does he make any effort to communicate; he's simply *there*, a supernumerary presence imprinted on the scene. He never comes closer, just watches, eyes trained on the banker as if through a gunsight; but any day now, the banker knows he'll step out of the crowd and call him by his name; and at that moment everything will change.

That's the set-up. What do you think? Would people buy it?

I

A Boat Ride

As a remedy to life in society I would suggest the big city.
Nowadays, it is the only desert within our means.

Albert Camus

'Claude?'

'Yes?'

'What are you doing under your desk?'

'Me?'

'You're not hiding, are you?'

'Why would I be hiding?' I say. I wait a moment, hoping that this will satisfy her, but her feet remain where they are. 'I am looking for my stapler,' I add.

'Oh,' Ish says. On one ankle, between her patent-leather pumps and the hem of her skirt, I glimpse a slender chain from which several small animal charms dangle. Now a pair of brown brogues approaches over the fuzzy blue carpet tiles and comes to a halt beside Ish's pumps.

'What's happening?' I hear Jurgen say.

'Claude's looking for his stapler,' Ish says.

'Oh,' says Jurgen, and then, 'But here is his stapler, directly on the desk.'

'So it is,' Ish says. 'Claude, your stapler's right here on your desk!'

I clamber to my feet, and look down to where she is pointing. 'Ah!' I say, attempting to appear pleased and surprised.

'Are you coming for lunch?' Jurgen says. 'We are going to the hippie place.'

'I'm rather busy,' I say.

'It's Casual Day!' Ish exhorts me. 'You can't eat at your desk on Casual Day!'

'I have a meeting with Walter this afternoon.'

'Come on, Claude, you can't live on Carambars.' She grabs my arm and starts tugging me.

'All right, all right,' I say, reaching for my suit jacket, pretending not to notice the disapproving eye she casts over me as I put it on.

Ish studied anthropology back in Australia; Casual Day, one of the few rituals we have at Bank of Torabundo, is something she takes very seriously. For most of the staff a pair of well-pressed chinos and perhaps an undone top shirt-button will suffice, but Ish is wearing a low-cut top fringed with tassels, and a long, multicoloured skirt, also with tassels. She has even topped up her tan for the occasion, a deep greasy brown that makes it look like she has smeared her body with pâté. This image, when it occurs to me, immediately makes me nauseous, and as we descend in the lift my stomach dips and soars like a fairground ride. I dislike Casual Day at the best of times; today it spurs my paranoia to new and queasy heights.

'Is Kevin coming?' I say to distract myself.

'He went on ahead to try and get a table,' Ish says.

'This whole place goes mental on Casual Day,' Jurgen says.

At every floor the lift stops and we are joined by more people in pressed chinos with their top shirt-button undone, squeezing in beside us, sucking up the air. The crush makes my heart race: it's a relief to step through the double doors of Transaction House and into the fresh air – but only for a moment.

Pastel waves of identically clad bodies are converging on the plaza from every direction. I scan the approaching faces, the bland gazes that beat against mine. Amid all the smart-casualwear a figure in black should be easy to spot – but that means I too am an obvious target, and in a freezing flash I can picture him making his way through the sea of bodies, a cancerous cell swimming in the innocent blood.

'Thinking of getting a bidet,' Ish says.

'For the new apartment?' Jurgen says.

'Wasn't something I'd thought of initially, but the bloke from the showroom called up and said because I'm going for the full suite they can throw in a bidet for half price. The question is, do I *want* a bidet? You know, at this stage I've got my toilet routine pretty much worked out.'

'You do not want to feel like an alien in your own bathroom,' Jurgen agrees. 'I suppose Claude would be the expert. Claude, how much of a benefit do you think the addition of a bidet would be?'

'Do you think French people do nothing else but eat baguettes and sit on their bidets?' I snap. Out here I am finding it hard to hide my nerves.

Jurgen starts telling Ish about a special toilet he has had imported from Germany. I tune him out, return to my search. Above my head, monochrome birds wheel and swoop, like scraps torn from the overcast sky. How long has it been now? A week? Two? That's since I first became conscious of him, though when I think to before that, I seem to find him there too, posed unobtrusively at the back of my memories.

There's no discernible pattern to his appearances: he'll be here one day, somewhere else the next. In the gloom of morning, I might see him by the tram tracks as I make the brief, synaptic journey from my apartment building to the bank; later, bent over a pitchbook with Jurgen, I'll glance out the window and spot him seated on a bench, eating sunflower seeds from a packet. In the deli, in the bar – even at night, when I stand on my balcony and look out over the depopulated concourse – I will seem to glimpse him for an instant, his blank gaze the mirror image of my own.

The Ark is in sight now; inside, I can see the waitresses gliding back and forth, the customers eating, talking, toying with their phones. Of my pursuer there is no sign, yet with every step the dreadful certainty grows *that he is in there.* I stall, with a clammy mouth begin to mumble excuses, but too late, the door is opening and a figure coming straight for us –

'Full,' Kevin says.

'Balls,' Ish says.

'They're saying fifteen minutes,' Kevin says.

Jurgen looks at his watch. 'That would give us only twelve and a half minutes to eat.'

'Oh well,' I say, with a false sigh. 'I suppose we must go back to –'

'What about that new place?' Ish says, snapping her fingers. 'Over on the other side of the square? You'll like it, Claude, it's French.'

I shrug. So long as we are moving in the opposite direction to the Ark, I am happy.

The 'French place' is called Chomps Elysées. An image of the Eiffel Tower adorns the laminated sign, and on the walls inside are photographs of the Sacré-Cœur and the Moulin Rouge. Nothing about the menu seems especially Gallic; I order a moccachino and something called a 'panini fromage', and while Kevin the trainee offers his thoughts on Ish's lavatorial options, I sit back in my seat and try to relax. Be reasonable, I tell myself: who would be interested in following you? Nobody, is the answer. Nobody outside my department even knows I exist.

This thought doesn't cheer me quite as I intend it to; and the panini fromage, when it comes, only makes matters worse. It is not that the cheese tastes bad exactly; rather, that it tastes of *nothing*. I don't think I have ever tasted *nothing* quite so strongly before. It's like eating a tiny black hole wrapped in an Italian sandwich. There is no way food this bad would ever be served in Paris, I think to myself, and experience a sudden stab of homesickness. How far I have come! How much I have left behind! And for what? Now with every chew I feel the emptiness rising inside, as if, like a kind of anti-madeleine, the panini were erasing my past before my very eyes – severing every tie, leaving me only this grey moment, tasting of nothing . . .

I approach the counter. The waitress's scowl appears authentically Parisian, but her accent, when she speaks, denotes the more proactive hostility of the Slav.

'Yes?' she says, not pretending that my appearance has made her any less bored.

'I think there has been a mistake,' I say.

'Panini fromage,' she says. 'Is French cheese.'

'But it is not cheese,' I say. 'It's artificial.'

'Artificial?'

'Not real.' Prising apart the bread for her inspection, I point at the off-white slab sitting atop the melancholy lettuce. It resembles nothing so much as a blank piece of matter, featureless and opaque, before God's brush has painted it with the colour and shape of specificity. 'I am from France,' I tell her, as if this might clarify matters. 'And this is not French cheese.'

The girl looks at me with unconcealed contempt. You are not supposed to complain in restaurants like this one; you are not supposed to notice the food in restaurants like this one, any more than you notice the streets you hurry through, latte in hand, back to your computer. The screen, the phone, that disembodied world is the one we truly inhabit; the International Financial Services Centre is merely a frame for it, an outline, the equivalent of the chalk marks of a child's game on the pavement.

'You vant chench?' the girl taunts me. I raise my hands in surrender and, cheeks burning, turn away.

Only then do I realize the man in black is standing right behind me.

Around us, the café has returned to normal life; the sullen girl rings up another panini, the office workers drink their uniquely tailored coffees. I goggle at Ish at the nearby table, but she doesn't seem to notice – nor does anyone else, as if the stranger has cast some cloak of invisibility over us. Blinding white light pours through the open door; he gazes at me, his eyes a terrifying ice-blue.

'Claude,' he says. He knows my name, of course he does.

'What do you want from me?' I try to sound defiant, but my voice will not come in more than a whisper.

'Just to talk,' he says.

'You have the wrong man,' I say. 'I have not done anything.'

'That makes you the right man,' he says. A smile spreads slowly across his chops. 'That makes you exactly the right man.'

His name is Paul; he is a writer. 'I've been shadowing you for a project I'm working on. I had no idea you'd spotted me. I hope I didn't alarm you.'

'I was not alarmed,' I lie. 'Although these days one must be careful. There are a lot of people very angry at bankers.'

'Well, I can only apologize again. And lunch is definitely on me – ah, here we go.' The waitress appears, dark and genial as her counterpart in the fake French café was blonde and cold, and sets down two bowls of freshly made sorrel soup. We have crossed the plaza back to the Ark, and this time found a table.

'I can see why you like this place,' he says, dipping a hunk of bread into his soup. 'The food's fantastic. And I love all this nautical stuff,' nodding at the portholes, the great anchor by the door. 'It's like going on a boat ride.' He purses his lips and blows on the bread; he doesn't appear to be in any great hurry to tell me why we are here.

'So you are a writer,' I say. 'What kind of things do you write?'

'A few years back I wrote a novel,' he says, 'called *For Love of a Clown*.'

This prompts a faint ringing at the back of my mind – some kind of prize . . . ?

'You're thinking of *The Clowns of Sorrow* by Bimal Banerjee, which won the Raytheon. My novel came out around the same time, similar enough subject matter. It did all right, but when the time came to begin the next one, I found I'd hit a kind of wall. Started asking myself some really hard questions – what's the novel *for*, what place does it have in the modern world, all that. For a long time I was stuck, really and truly stuck. Then out of nowhere it came to me. Idea for a new book, the whole thing right there, like a baby left on the doorstep.'

'And what is it about?' I ask politely.

'What's it about?' Paul smiles. 'Well, it's about you, Claude. It's about you.'

I am too surprised to conceal it. 'Me?'

'I've been studying you and your daily routine for a number of weeks now. It seems to me that your life embodies certain values, certain fundamental features of our modern world. We're living in a time of great change, and a man like you is right at the coal-face of that change.'

'I do not think my life would make a very interesting book,' I say. 'I feel I can speak with a certain amount of authority here.'

He laughs. 'Well, in a way that's the point. The stories we read in books, what's presented to us as being interesting – they have very little to do with real life as it's lived today. I'm not talking about straight-up escapism, your vampires, serial killers, codes hidden in paintings, and so on. I mean so-called serious literature. A boy goes hunting with his emotionally volatile father, a bereaved woman befriends an asylum seeker, a composer with a rare neurological disorder walks around New York, thinking about the nature of art. People looking back over their lives, people having revelations, people discovering meaning. *Meaning*, that's the big thing. The way these books have it, you trip over a rock you'll find some hidden meaning waiting there. Everyone's constantly on the verge of some soul-shaking transformation. And it's – if you'll forgive my language – it's bull-shit. Modern people live in a state of distraction. They go from one distraction to the next, and that's how they like it. They don't transform, they don't stop to smell the roses, they don't sit around recollecting long passages of their childhood – Jesus, I can hardly remember what I was doing two days ago. My point is, people aren't waiting to be restored to some ineffable moment.

They're not looking for meaning. That whole idea of the novel – that's finished.'

'So you want to write a book that has no meaning,' I say.

'I want to write a book that isn't full of things that only ever happen in books,' he says. 'I want to write something that genuinely reflects how we live today. Real, actual life, not some ivory-tower palaver, not a whole load of *literature*. What's it like to be alive in the twenty-first century? Look at this place, for example.' He sweeps an arm at the window, the glass anonymity of the International Financial Services Centre. 'We're in the middle of Dublin, where Joyce set *Ulysses*. But it doesn't look like Dublin. We could be in London, or Frankfurt, or Kuala Lumpur. There are all these people, but nobody's speaking to each other, everyone's just looking at their phones. And that's what this place is *for*. It's a place for being somewhere else. Being here means not being here. And *that's* modern life.'

'I see,' I say, although I don't, quite.

'So the question is, how do you describe it? If James Joyce was writing *Ulysses* today, if he was writing not about some nineteenth-century backwater but about the capital of the most globalized country in the world – where would he begin? Who would his Bloom be? His Everyman?'

He looks at me pointedly, but it takes me a moment to realize the import of his words.

'You think I am an Everyman?'

He makes a *hey presto* gesture with his hands.

'But I'm not even Irish,' I protest. 'How can I be your typical Dubliner?'

He shakes his head vigorously. 'That's key. Like I said, *somewhere else* is what this place is all about. Think about it, in your work, you have colleagues from all over the place, right?'

'That's true.'

'And the cleaning staff are from all over the place, and the waitresses in this restaurant are from all over the place. Modern life is a centrifuge; it throws people in every direction. That's why you're so perfect for this book. The Everyman's uprooted, he's alone, he's separated from his friends and family. And the work that you do – you're a banker, isn't that so?'

'Yes, an analyst at Bank of Torabundo,' I say, before it occurs to me how strange it is that he knows this.

'Well.' He spreads his hands to signify self-evidence. 'I hardly need to say how representative that is. The story of the twenty-first century so far is the story of the banks. Look at the mess this country's in because of them.'

Ah. I begin to understand. 'So your book will be a kind of exposé.'

'No, no, no,' he says, waving his hands as if to dispel some evil-smelling smoke. 'I don't want to write a takedown. I'm not interested in demonizing an entire industry because of the actions of a minority. I want to get past the stereotypes, discover the humanity inside the corporate machine. I want to show what it's like to be a modern man. And this is where he lives, not on a fishing trawler, not in a coal mine, not on a ranch in Wyoming. This' – he gestures once again at the window, and we both turn in our seats to contemplate the reticular expanse of the Centre, the blank façades of the multinationals – 'is where modern life *comes from*. The feel of it, the look of it. Everything. What happens inside those buildings defines how we live our lives. Even if we only notice when it goes wrong. The banks are like the heart, the engine room, the world-within-the-world. The stuff that comes out of these places,' whirling a finger again at the Centre, 'the credit, the deals, that's what our reality is *made of*. So, with that in mind, can you think of a *better* subject for a book – than you?'

Essentially, he tells me, the process would be a more intensive version of what he has been doing already: following me around, observing at close quarters, focusing, as much as is possible, on my work for the bank.

'What would I have to do?'

'You wouldn't have to do anything,' Paul says. 'Just be yourself. Just be.' He glances at the bill, takes a note from his wallet and lays it on the plate. 'I don't expect you to make a decision like this on the spot. To lay yourself out for a perfect stranger – that's a big thing to ask. I wish I could say that you'd be handsomely rewarded, but right now all I can offer is the dubious honour of providing material for a book that might never get published.' He cracks a grin. 'Still, I bet the girls in the office'll be interested to find out you're a character in a work of fiction.'

'How do you mean?'

'Think about it – Heathcliff, Mr Darcy. Captain Ahab, even. Women go nuts for them.'

'Although those characters are imaginary,' I say slowly.

'Exactly. But *you'll* be real. Do you see? It's like you'll be getting the best of both worlds.'

As if to bear out his words, the beautiful dark-haired waitress flashes me a smile as she glides past.

My head is spinning, and it really is time for me to get back to the office. But there is still one question he has not answered. 'Why me? There are thirty thousand people working in the IFSC. Why did you choose me?'

'To be honest, that's what caught my eye initially,' he says.

'That? Oh.' I realize he's pointing at my jacket, which I am in the course of slipping back on.

'The black really stands out, especially with the tie. Most people here seem to go for grey. Must be a French thing, is it?'

Yes, I say, it's a French thing.

'Makes you look very literary,' he says. 'And when I got closer I could see you had a certain . . . I don't know, a sensibility. I got the impression that you were different from the others. That you weren't just going through the motions. That you were searching for something, maybe. It's hard to explain.' He rips a scrap of paper from a little red notebook and scribbles down his number. 'Look,' he says. 'I could be completely wrong, but I think there's a really important book to be written about this place. And I think you'd be perfect for it. If it doesn't feel right to you, for whatever reason, I promise I'll disappear from your life. But can I ask you at least to think about it?'

'Here he is!' Jurgen says as I enter the Research Department. 'We were beginning to think we must send out the search party!'

'Where d'you disappear to?' Ish inquires, through a mouthful of paper clips.

'Nowhere,' I shrug. 'I ran into someone and went for a coffee.'

'Casual Day.' Jurgen shakes his head. 'Anything can happen.'

Kimberlee comes in from Reception. 'Claude, Ryan Colchis called about some numbers on a Ukrainian outfit you were digging up for him.'

'Okay,' I say.

'And Walter's PA called to say he's coming in.'

'There goes your weekend,' Ish says.

I sit down at my terminal, confront the wall of fresh emails. Already the writer and his strange proposal are beginning to seem distant and unreal, one of those hazy episodes you can't be sure you didn't dream. And yet the familiar objects of the office have acquired a curious sheen – appear to *resonate* somehow, like enchanted furniture in a fairy tale that will dance around the room as soon as you turn your back.

'Hey, has Claude heard the news?' Kevin calls from his desk.

'What news?' I say, with a curious feeling of – what, synchronicity? As though someone is looking over my shoulder?

'Blankly's the new CEO,' Ish says. 'Rachael's office just sent down word.'

'Blankly got it,' I say. 'Well, well.'

'Things will be changing, Claude,' Jurgen says. 'This is the whole new beginning of the Bank of Torabundo story.'

'Yes,' I say, and then, 'I should call Colchis.'

'Are you feeling better?' Ish catches my arm. 'You looked a bit off earlier.'

'Yes, yes, I just needed some air,' I tell her, but she is not deterred: she continues to scrutinize me.

'Are you sure?' she says. 'You seem, I dunno, different somehow.'

'Claude is never different,' Jurgen says, clapping me on the shoulder. 'Claude is always the same.'

'Yeah . . .' Ish wrinkles her nose thoughtfully; and I turn my eyes to the screen, as if I have a secret to keep.

The Pareto principle, also known as the 80–20 rule, is one of the first things you learn in banking: for any given area of life, 80 per cent of the effects come from 20 per cent of the causes. Thus 80 per cent of your profits come from 20 per cent of your clients, 80 per cent of your socializing is with 20 per cent of your friends, 80 per cent of the music you listen to is from 20 per cent of your library, etc. The idea is to minimize the 'grey zone' that devours your day, the 80 per cent of your reading, for instance, that yields only 20 per cent of your information.

Walter Corless is very much aware what side of the rule he's on. He knows he is the wealthiest and most powerful man you have ever met, and as such he demands 100 per cent of your time and attention. A meeting with or even a call from Walter is like some supermassive planet materializing in your little patch of space – blocking the sun, overwhelming your gravitational field, so that you can only watch as the entire structure of your world goes hurtling off to rearrange itself on his. He started off selling turf from the back of a flatbed truck; thirty years later, he is chairman and CEO of one of the biggest construction companies in the British Isles. Even the worldwide slump hasn't hurt him: while his peers put all their chips into housing, Dublex diversified into transport, logistics and, most profitably, high-security developments – military compounds, fortifications, prisons – which, as unrest sweeps across Europe and Asia, constitute a rare growth area. That a company he named after his daughter now builds enhanced interrogation facilities in Belarus gives a good indication of the man's attitudes to business and life in general.

(That daughter, Lexi, now runs a string of nursing homes known informally as the Glue Factory.)

His driver calls me shortly after six; I go outside to find Walter's limo parked – in contravention of all of the Centre's rules – on the plaza in front of Transaction House. Walter is sprawled across the back seat. He stares at me as I squeeze into the fold-down seat opposite him, breathing heavily through his nose. He is a dour, grey-faced man, who looks like he was dug up from the same bog he got his first bags of turf. Newspaper profiles refer to his 'drive' and his 'focus', but these are euphemisms. What Walter has is the dead-eyed relentlessness of the killer in a horror movie, the kind that lumber after you inexorably, heedless of knives, bullets, flame-throwers. Though his fortune runs into the billions, and he employs a team of accountants in tax havens around the world, he still enjoys calling on his debtors personally, and the pockets of his coat are always full of cheques, bank drafts, rolls of notes in rubber bands. Sometimes he'll present me with a fistful, with instructions to invest them in this or that. This is not strictly my job, but then Walter doesn't care what my job is; or rather, as our biggest client, he knows that my job is whatever he says it is.

Tonight he wants to ask my thoughts on a tender. Dublex has been approached by the interior ministry of the Middle Eastern autocracy of Oran to fortify the private compound of the Caliph.

'They are expecting trouble?' I ask.

Walter just grunts. He knows, of course; he has specialists in every conceivable field, but he still likes to canvass opinions from as wide a spectrum as possible before making a decision, in order, Ish says, to maximize the number of people he can yell at if something goes wrong. 'Is there money in this fucker's pocket, is what I'm asking you,' he says.

'It's one of the biggest oil producers in the region. I imagine his credit is good,' I say.

Walter scowls. I tell him I'll look into it, and he signals his approval by changing the subject, launching into a familiar tirade about 'regulations'.

When we are done, I return to my apartment, where I can finally start investigating the mysterious writer in earnest. Searching online, I discover that the novel he mentioned, *For Love of a Clown*, is real; an image search confirms, in a picture that shows him shaking hands with a giant papaya at something called the Donard Exotic Fruits and Book Festival, that its author and the man who approached me are one and the same. His Apeiron page has two customer write-ups, both negative: the first compares his clown-themed novel unfavourably to Bimal Banerjee's *The Clowns of Sorrow*, and gives it a rating of two snakes and a cactus; the second offers no rating at all, and consists solely of the line 'On no account should you lend money to this man.' Beyond that, there is nothing. As far as the wider world is concerned, for the last seven years he might as well not have existed – which is consistent with what he told me about hitting a wall.

I go on to my balcony, try to look out with the eyes of a novelist. My apartment is in the International Financial Services Centre, a stone's throw from the bank. The city centre lies upriver; if I lean over the rail, I can glimpse the Spire, jutting into the darkness like a radio transmitter from the heart of things, but it's only on rare evenings, when the wind is blowing in a particular direction, that I hear its broadcasts – the whoops, the screams, the laughter and fights – and even then only faintly, like the revelry of ghosts. Usually, when night has fallen and only a few lights remain, chequering the dark slabs of the buildings, it is easy, looking over the deserted concourse, to believe the world has upped stakes and gone, followed the baton of trade west, leaving me here alone.

Before I came here I knew little about Dublin. I had an idea it was famous for its dead writers; I remembered the name of the river from arguments in school over whether it's *Liffey* or *Lethe*

22

the singer floats down in 'How to Disappear Completely'. I entertained vague notions about Guinness and authenticity.

It turned out to be very different from what I expected. At university, I had read about the *virtual*, the simulated world that abuts and interpenetrates our own – 'real without being actual, present without being there', in the words of the philosopher François Texier. I didn't think, after graduating, that I would require the concept again; I certainly never dreamed I'd find myself living in it.

That said, there is some argument as to whether the International Financial Services Centre is truly part of Dublin. It lies only a few minutes' walk from O'Connell Street, but the locals don't come here; many of them don't even seem to know it exists, in spite of the torrents of capital that flow into it every year. It was built twenty years ago as a kind of pacemaker, an ingenious piece of financial and legal technology embedded in Dublin's thousand-year-old body. A jumble of stumpy glass buildings, it stretches along the river like a pygmy Manhattan, on what used to be docklands. Its main function is to be a kind of legal elsewhere: multinationals send their profits here to avoid tax, banks conduct their more sensitive activities with the guarantee of a blind eye from the authorities. Many of the companies here have billions in assets but no employees; the foyer of Transaction House is crowded with brass nameplates, all leading to a single, permanently empty, office. They call this shadow-banking, and the IFSC is a shadow-place – an alibi that will say you are here when you are not, and cover your presence when you don't want to be seen.

Could you really set a book in such a place? In a city that is not a city? Filled with people who are paid not to be themselves? He says he wants to find the humanity inside the machine, to track down the particular amid the golden abstractions; he says he can see something different about me, and standing on the balcony I thrill at the thought that I might see it too. But what if he's wrong? What if he holds up the mirror, and nothing is there?

Jurgen shares none of my reservations. 'An author?' he exclaims, when I mention it casually after the Monday meeting. 'A real-life author? And he wants to put you in his book?'

'Yes,' I say.

'You?' Kevin the trainee says.

I shrug. 'It seems that I just . . . fit the bill, is that the phrase?' (In fact I know perfectly well it is the phrase.)

'Do you think he'll put us in it as well?'

'I don't know,' I say. 'I will ask him.'

'Doesn't it sound a bit weird?' Ish is more circumspect. 'Some bloke following you around, writing down everything you do?'

'What's *weird* is that it hasn't happened before,' Kevin says. 'When you think about it, there ought to be a lot more novelists wanting to write books about banks.'

'But he's not planning to slag us off, is he?' Ish says. 'You know, say we're all wankers and fat cats and so on.'

'He told me it was going to be a balanced account of life in a modern investment bank,' I tell her. 'He said he wanted to find our hidden humanity.'

'It is about time bankers were recognized by the art world,' Jurgen says. 'Given that we buy most of the actual art, it is frustrating to be continually misrepresented by it.'

'So are you going to do it?' Ish asks.

'I haven't decided,' I say.

'You have to do it!' Kevin expostulates. 'Tell him I'll do it if you don't want to.'

'As your superior, I think you should do it, Claude,' Jurgen agrees. 'Though of course the final decision remains with you.'

He adds that, while I am making up my mind, he will 'get the ball rolling' by running it by the Chief Operating Officer; before

I can protest, he has trundled away. Maybe Rachael will say no; I decide to put it out of my mind until I hear back.

I return to my desk, feel the familiar thrill in my viscera as I sit down in front of the terminal. Here is the market: the whole world represented in figures, a tesseract of pure information. The media like to portray bankers as motivated purely by greed, but this is not quite accurate. There are those who do it for the money, it's true – who like miners or deep-sea divers bury themselves miles below the surface of things, far from the light and everything they love, in order to return laden down with riches. But there are others who do it for the god's-eye view; those for whom the map has become the territory, for whom the market's operations as represented on the screen appear more complex than life itself, deeper and more intricate, bringing their own vertiginous intelligence to the brute facts of the world in the same way that a painting of a landscape magnifies its beauty by placing in a frame of consciousness the thoughtless doings of nature. For these latter sort, the highs of the best drugs are shadows next to the exhilaration they get from the shifting fields of numbers: rice growers in Henan, car manufacturers in Düsseldorf, pharmaceutical research firms in Cork and Montevideo, condensed, compressed, interacting with each other in ways of which they themselves have no conception, like molecules hurtling and dancing and colliding under a microscope.

Ish is an anomaly – not of the god's-eye-view sort, but not especially interested in money either, other than what she needs to pay for her apartment, which she bought off the plans during the boom at a price she now admits may have been extravagant even for an investment banker.

'Any word from the Uncanny Valley?' she asks me now.

'You are sitting here beside me, you know there is no word.'

'Oh, right.' A moment later she pipes up again. 'Hey, Claude?'

'If this is again a question about the book, the answer is "I don't know."'

'It's not about the book, it's about the movie of the book.'

'...'

'Well, if they make a film of it, will I get a say in who plays me? I mean, I don't want them to pick some old boot?'

The morning drags on with no response from Rachael. Shortly before noon, however, a shadow looms up behind me.

'Crazy Frog, what the cock are you telling custies about Tarmalat?'

'I am telling them that Tarmalat is carrying heavy exposure to Greek sovereign debt,' I reply, 'and there's no way they're going to hit their target.'

'I'm trying to *sell* them Tarmalat, you fucking dunce!' The muscles in his neck, which are extensive, bunch out like the mast lines of a ship at full sail. 'I've got two hundred of the cunts going at twelve and a quarter.'

'My source says their income's down nearly 30 per cent on this same period last year. A write-down of Greek debt can cost them a hundred million. Your customers will thank you for sparing them.'

'That's not going to get us commission, is it?' He scowls. 'Fucking Greek pricks,' he mutters. 'Why couldn't they stick to ... what is it Greeks are good at again?'

'Um, inventing democracy?' Ish suggests.

'They've been dining out on that one for a *long* time,' Howie retorts.

Howie Hogan does not look like a genius. Twenty-five, and hitting the gym hard every day, he still has a childish doughiness to his features, giving him the appearance of one of those over-fed, unimaginative rich boys who see the world as a kind of third-rate in-flight movie, to which they will pay attention only until they reach their real destination. This is, in fact, exactly what he is. But he is also BOT's star trader. Beside mathematical acuity, sharp reflexes, and an ability to get people to buy things they don't want, Howie is gifted with almost total emotional dissociation. Other traders freak out, crack up, crash and burn; Howie's only reaction, win or lose, is to smirk. I am fairly sure he smirks in his sleep. What is he doing here? He should be in London, at one of the bulge brackets, making ten times what he does at BOT; but some indiscretion in his past – details of which none of us has ever been able to establish – means he must get to the top the hard way.

Having chastised me for undermining sell-side, he would normally have lumbered off by now; instead he's still hovering. 'What's this fucking bullshit I'm hearing?' he says at last.

'Close & Coulthard's merger has been held up by the CMA,' I say. 'I IM'd you.'

'No, about someone writing your autobiography.'

'Oh, that.'

The smirk flickers. 'Who the fuck would want to write a book about you?' Howie says.

'An author,' I say expressionlessly.

'For your information, he thinks Claude would make the perfect Everyman,' Ish pitches in.

Howie laughs. 'Everyman!' he repeats. 'Who's that, the world's most boring superhero?'

'Isn't there a harassment hearing you need to be at?' Ish says.

'Look out, supervillains! Everyman's super-spreadsheet has the power to bore you to death!' Howie struts away, still cackling. 'Claude in a book! Who said the French have no sense of humour?'

'Don't mind him, Claude, he's just jealous,' Ish says.

'Do people say the French have no sense of humour?' I ask her.

'Of course not,' she says, patting my hand.

I return to my work, but this brief conversation has been enough to reawaken my fears. Howie is right. I don't have a story; I don't have time to have a story; I have organized my life here precisely in order not to have a story. Why would I want someone following me around, weighing me up, finding me lacking? I take

27

out my wallet, unfurl the scrap of paper on which Paul scrawled his number, but before I can call him and pass on my regrets, Jurgen approaches from the direction of the meeting rooms.

'Claude! Good news!' He grins at me with excitement. 'Rachael has given the okay for your book project.'

'Oh,' I say, surprised.

'You must call your author right away!' he exhorts me.

'I will,' I say.

'Right away,' he repeats.

'Yes,' I say.

He stands there, waiting. Without even wanting to, I see him as an outsider might: take in his pocket protector, his hideous tie, his strange plasticated hair that never seems to grow any longer. Is he happy? Lonely? Bored? Do any of these terms even apply?

'First I have a small errand to do,' I say. I go to the lift and hit the button for the ground floor. As I descend, I turn the decision over in my mind. He's not writing a book about me, I remind myself. He's shadowing me for research purposes. I am a highly successful employee at a highly successful bank. There is no reason to fear that he will find my life boring or empty.

The lift doors open. The security guards glance over, then away again almost immediately. Outside, the air is perfectly still. Workers clip back and forth in the windows of the buildings around me, a silent image of productivity. Yet across the river, the grey shell of Royal Irish Bank is populated only by seagulls, and just last week a German bank two floors below us imploded; we watched from above as the erstwhile employees filed out through the double doors – blinking in the light, clinging to cardboard boxes full of mouse mats and ficuses, casting up their eyes at the bright opaque windows as if to a land that was lost to them . . .

Paul answers on the second ring.

'It's me,' I say. 'Claude.'

There is a curious echo to the line, as if someone is listening in, and I have the strangest sense he already knows what I am going

28

to say . . . but the sound of his voice is warm and human, not the voice of a god or an omniscient overseer. 'How are you, buddy?'

'I am well, thank you. I'm calling to tell you that my boss has given the green light for your project.'

'Fantastic!' His delight sounds genuine, which produces a proportionally opposite effect in me, as I consider the fall for which he is setting himself up.

'So what exactly do you need me to do now?' I say.

'Like I told you, Claude, I don't need you to *do* anything. Just be yourself.'

'All right.'

'I promise, it won't be intrusive. You'll barely notice I'm there.'

'Very good.'

'You don't sound too excited.'

'No, no, I am,' I say; but then, impetuously, add, 'It is not very dramatic, you know.'

'What's that?'

'What we do in the bank, it is quite complex and technical. If you are looking for colourful characters, for exciting things to happen, it may seem rather . . . I do not know if it will give you what you need.'

Laughter comes back down the line. 'Don't you worry about that. I'm the artist, okay? It's my job to go in there and find the gold, wherever it's hidden.'

'You think there will be gold?' I say.

'I'm sure of it, Claude. I'm sure of it.'

To me, of course, it is unquestionably dramatic; to me, to anyone working in banking, the last two years have been like the Fall of Rome, the French Revolution, the South Sea Bubble and the moon landing, all rolled into one.

For half a decade – since, in fact, the previous financial crisis, which at that point represented the greatest destruction of capital in history – the world had been living on borrowed money. Wages went down, but credit was cheap; you were getting paid less, but borrowing the money to replace your car, take a holiday, buy a new house, was easy. The banks themselves were borrowing money at enormous rates, taking it from megabanks in Europe and lending it out again at a nice margin to you with your car, to the entrepreneur with his start-up, to the developer with his housing estate. As for the governments, they were content to let this happen, because everyone was so happy with their cars and holidays and houses; and of course the governments too were borrowing hugely to fund the services that workers' taxes no longer paid for.

In short, the whole world was massively in debt, but it didn't seem to matter; then, suddenly, almost overnight, it did. Someone, somewhere, realized that the global boom was in fact a pyramid scheme, a huge inflammable pyramid waiting to catch light. Investors panicked and began to pull their money out of the megabanks; the megabanks desperately began to call in loans from the regional banks, the regional banks called in loans from their customers, the customers called in loans from their trading partners, or tried to, though all of a sudden no one was answering their phones.

The consequences of this cataclysmic freeze-up of credit are still unfolding. Around the world, banks have been falling like ninepins, illustrious financial dynasties blown away like smoke. In the United States, Bear Stearns, Merrill Lynch, Lehman Brothers are among the major casualties, while in Ireland the high-street banks are still trading only after a government bailout. That bailout, in turn, has triggered a catastrophic series of events: factories shutting down, homes repossessed, mass emigration – nearly four hundred thousand people from a country with a population less than half the size of the Paris metropolitan area. Every day on the news there is another horror story: the pensioner who's been living on pigeons; the horses whose owners can no longer afford stable fees and have turned them loose to wander the byways, slowly starving to death. Nothing the politicians do seems to help; in Greece, in Spain, in Portugal, in Italy, public fury mounts, and revolution is in the air.

Buy to the sound of cannons, sell to the sound of trumpets, the saying goes. If you have positioned yourself correctly, there is a lot of money to be made.

At 4 a.m. I give up trying to sleep. I have a cup of coffee, then cross over to use the gym in the basement of Transaction House. Two traders on the Smith machines are anticipating how BOT strategy will change with the new CEO in charge – bragging about how much money they will make once they're 'off the chain', how ruthlessly they will 'fuck' rivals from other banks.

Upstairs, Thomas 'Yuan' McGregor and his Asian Markets team are already at their desks; I take advantage of the early start to read through the headlines, the latest prognostications of doom for Europe. The sun creeps through the window; faces appear in the lobby, still puffy with sleep. Slowly at first, then in a flurry, the day's small rituals begin: the tray of coffees delivered by the rain-speckled intern; the baffling jokes in the inbox amid endless emails flagged URGENT, HIGH PRIORITY, READ IMMEDIATELY; the collective groan at the sight of the courier with his package of amendments, redos, overnight changes of heart. As 8 a.m. approaches, the tension mounts. Positioning themselves for the market opening, traders call constantly, looking for updates, price-sensitive developments, anything that will give them the edge over the invisible hordes doing exactly the same thing, here and across the water. Soon the entire research floor is speaking intensely into phones, everyone completely oblivious to everyone else, eyes fixed instead on screens or on that empty point in mid-air where so much of life now takes place. It seems you can actually feel the market, straining like a dog on a leash for the moment trading begins.

The first couple of hours pass in a blur; after that, things begin to relax a little. I have arranged to meet Paul at ten. Ish and Jurgen want to come downstairs with me, but I prevail upon them to stay where they are. 'He wants to see my life as it is every day,' I say. 'Everything must be natural.'

'All right,' they say reluctantly, and slouch off in the direction of their desks.

Riding down in the lift, I am surprised at how nervous I feel. It's the same kind of anxiety that used to spring up years ago, as I made my way to a rendezvous with some girl I had fallen in love with, knowing that today was the day I had to make my feelings clear, knowing simultaneously that I wouldn't do it. And when the lift doors open and I find the foyer empty, the lurch of despair is familiar too.

I check my phone, but there is no word. Has he changed his mind? Was he merely having some fun at my expense? I hover by the doors, pretending I don't notice the security guards glare at me from their desk. And then I see him, hurrying over the rainy plaza, and just as it did at the appearance of Sylvie or Valou or Aimée or the others, I feel my heart soar.

He smiles at me brittlely, apologizes for being late; he looks almost as nervous as I am. I tell him not to worry, and bring him over to the security desk. There are various forms for him to fill in; then he is told to stand still while the guard photographs him, takes his fingerprints, scans his iris. For a long moment we wait in silence as the guard stares at a screen we cannot see. Then he sighs, and there is a clunking sound, and he reaches down to produce Paul's pass.

'Thought that guy was going to ask for a blood sample,' Paul says as we turn away for the lift.

'Ha ha, yes,' I say.

The lift takes a long time to arrive. Finally the doors part, and I press the button for the sixth floor. 'We are on the sixth floor,' I say, redundantly.

'Right,' Paul says.

We ascend. I search about for some fact or detail that might be useful to him, or at least break the silence.

'Otis,' I say.

'Excuse me?'

'The lift. It is manufactured by Otis. They are one of the most famous lift producers.'

'Yes.'

'That does not necessarily mean they are the best, of course. Still, this particular lift has in my experience always been very reliable.'

'That's good to know.'

'I presume that Otis was the name of the inventor. Though it might have been simply a name he made up . . . perhaps you know?'

'No, I can't say I do.'

'There is the option of the stairs also,' I add. 'But usually I take the lift.'

'Right,' he says.

Ah, *quel con*! I'm half-expecting that when we reach the sixth floor he'll thank me for my time and ride back down to the ground again. It's with some relief that I find Ish and Jurgen standing in the lobby, pretending to have an intense conversation about the potted plant by Reception.

'It's that fine line between watering it too much and not watering it enough,' Ish is saying; then a hush falls as we step inside. The two of them stare expectantly at the two of us, and my anxiety gives way to an upsurge of pride.

'Ish, Jurgen, this is Paul,' I say to them carelessly. 'He will be my shadow in the office for the next few weeks. Paul, may I introduce to you my colleague Ish, and Jurgen, the Financial Institutions team leader.'

'Hello,' Paul says.

We all smile at each other awkwardly for a minute – then, just as I am about to lead him away, Ish asks Paul quickly, as if she cannot help herself, 'Are you really a writer?'

'For my sins,' Paul says.

'Wow,' Ish murmurs.

I roll my eyes at Jurgen, only to see an identical expression of schoolgirlish reverence. 'A writer!' he says. 'It must be so exciting!'

'Beats working, I suppose,' Paul says.

'Ha ha, I hear *that*!' Jurgen says. He looks down at his shoes and then adds casually, 'In fact I am being a little disingenuous, as I know something about being a writer myself, from my work for *Florin Affairs*, the journal of medieval economics – perhaps you have heard of it?'

Paul makes a show of racking his brains.

'It is not to be confused with *Forint Affairs*, which is the journal of the Hungarian currency.'

'Right,' Paul says.

'If I may say so, you have made an excellent choice of subject,' Jurgen goes on. 'Bank of Torabundo is one of the most fascinating institutions in all of capital allocation. And Claude is one of its most valued employees.' He pauses, then turns to Ish. 'Though all our employees are valued,' he says.

'I'm Claude's best mate in this dump,' Ish volunteers. 'Which is funny, because people say that Frogs and Ozzies don't get on?

'Cos the Frogs are all, you know, *Shmuhh-shmuhh-shmuhh*, and the Ozzies are all, *Wa-hey*! But we get on like a house on fire, don't we, Claude?'

I picture the flames, the screaming. 'Yes,' I say.

'Anyway, if you want to know his secrets, you know who to come to!'

'Claude's got secrets?' Paul eyes me with a half-smile.

'There's his drawer of Carambars,' Ish says. 'That's the tip of the iceberg.'

'We should definitely talk,' Paul says.

'I will show Paul the rest of the office,' I tell them meaningfully.

'If you're writing about him, you have to put me in the book too, ha ha!' Ish calls after us. 'Only if you do, say I'm a size eight, ha ha!'

I tug him away. Eyes glance over at us with carefully pre-arranged expressions of indifference as we cross the room; it seems everyone has heard about the visitor. 'So this is the research floor,' I tell him, gesturing broadly at the clocks on the walls, the muted televisions, the cubicles crowded with screens, phones, paperwork.

'Where're all the guys shouting at each other?'

'The traders work upstairs, on the seventh floor, but we're in contact with them all day. Part of our job is to provide them with information on the securities they're trading in – the key drivers affecting share price, any relevant developments in the sector . . .'

'Is that Torabundo?' Paul points to a print hanging by one of the southerly windows, a verdant square of lush forests and effulgent sunshine. 'It's an island, right?'

'It is basically an extinct volcano in the middle of the Pacific Ocean,' I say. 'A big extinct volcano with an extremely benevolent tax climate.'

'Ever been?'

'No. The headquarters are registered there, but most of our operations are directed from New York. So, as I was saying, our role here is to study the market on behalf of our traders, and also to advise the clients of the best investment strategy –'

'Someone's got some pretty interesting desk ornaments,' Paul says, eyeing the cornucopia of shells, feathers, figurines and other relics that festoon the cubicle next to mine.

'Yes, those belong to Ish,' I say, experiencing simultaneously a flush of gratitude that he finds something in our environment interesting, and a pang of jealousy that it should be Ish. 'She spent a couple of years travelling around Oceania.'

'How'd she end up here?'

'I believe she started at the bank shortly after she split with her fiancé. She will no doubt tell you the story herself.'

'Came here to forget, eh?' Paul says, as he examines a shark's jawbone. 'Like the French Foreign Legion.' He turns to me. 'What about you, Claude? You here to forget too?'

I flinch inwardly, but keep my expression neutral. 'You can make the argument that we have all come here to forget,' I say. 'Although in most cases before anything has actually happened to us.'

'Nice,' he murmurs to himself, and taking from his back pocket his little red notebook, he jots down the line.

'So, if you look at this terminal here,' I say, pretending I have not noticed, 'you will see the very latest market information. And this one –'

'You know what, Claude, I don't want too much detail, it'll overload it. Why don't you just get back to what it is you do. I'll pick it up by watching you. It's better that way.'

'Are you sure?' I say dubiously.

'Please,' he says, with an ushering gesture towards my chair. 'Just forget I'm here.'

'Right,' I say, taking my seat and feeling, foolishly, as if I am an astronaut strapping himself into the cockpit of a rocket. Paul crosses the room and sits in an unoccupied chair; here – from a distance of about twenty feet away – he crosses his legs, lays the pad on his lap, affixes his eyes on me and waits.

'So I will continue with my morning call-around,' I turn to tell him. 'This is when we give our clients the state of play in the market and the movement we are expecting –'

'Honestly, I'll pick it up.'

'Yes, of course. Sorry.' I summon a deep breath. Just be, I tell myself.

Around me my colleagues are making their own calls, each passing on his own predictions for his own particular specialism – oil, utilities, telecoms. Clients pay tens of thousands for this daily service, but usually we go straight through to voicemail, so I'm taken aback when someone actually picks up.

'Hello?' he says.

'Hello? Ah –' I have forgotten who I called.

'Is that Claude?'

'Ah . . . oh, hello' – possibly it's Jim Chen? 'Hello, Jim?'

'Hello,' he says, not contradicting me. Relief courses through me, until I realize I have also forgotten what I wanted to say. 'It's about the market,' I say. That seems a safe bet.

'Yes,' Jim Chen says.

But what about the market? My mind has gone completely blank.

'Ah, I am just getting some news over the wires, I'll call you back,' I say.

'Okay, whatever,' Jim Chen says.

I put down the receiver. My shirt is soaked in sweat.

'Claude,' a voice calls across the room.

I revolve my head to see the silhouette of Paul against the window.

'You're trying too hard,' he says.

'I know,' I say.

'Stop *thinking* about it.'

'This is not so easy as it looks,' I say.

'Just pretend I'm not here. In fact, you know what, I'll go and roam around for a while, give you a chance to get into your stride. Is there a coffee machine around here somewhere?'

I give him directions to the canteen.

'Do you want anything?'

'No, thank you,' I say. Paul passes out of sight. Idiot! I chastise myself. Just be! Just be, can't you? Yet even when he's left the room the pressure is almost unbearable. I send an email to Ish and Jurgen, begging them to find time for lunch this afternoon. Then the phone rings. It is Geolyte, one of my clients. The board has called an emergency meeting for this afternoon after hearing rumours of an incipient takeover bid. How robust are its finances? Will it be able to fight off its attackers? For an hour and a half I am continuously on the phone, during which time I quite forget to be. Then, with a start, I remember. I look around hastily; from his chair, Paul nods at me, and toasts me with his paper cup.

Before we know it, it is lunchtime, and Paul and I are back in the lift, going down. 'Everything is all right?' I ask. 'You are not finding it too dull?'

'Are you joking? It's perfect.'

We push through the double doors.

'So many people,' Paul marvels.

'Yes, the spectacle can be a little overwhelming,' I agree. The plaza is a sea of suits and twinsets, identically dressed men and women milling about like the CGI crowd in some blockbusting movie, there to portray the mundane reality that will be shattered when Godzilla's foot comes down; although as the companies this particular crowd spends its days working for constitute some of the most powerful forces in the world, it's perhaps closer to the truth to say that *we* are Godzilla. This seems to me a rather clever thought; I try to think of some way of introducing it into the conversation. 'Have you seen the film *Godzilla*?' I ask.

'No,' Paul says.

Of course he hasn't! He is an artist! Why would he waste his time with such pabulum?

'Why do you ask?' he says.

'The lunchtime crowd here sometimes reminds me of Godzilla,' I say.

'Oh,' Paul says. The red notebook remains in his pocket.

Jurgen, Ish and Kevin are already in the Ark.

'You come here a lot,' Paul observes, taking his seat.

'It's the only restaurant in the whole Centre you can get freshly prepared organic food,' Ish says.

'That's why it's usually empty,' Kevin says. 'That, and the art.' He points to the canvas that hangs over our table, an enormous abstract that loosely resembles a crossword puzzle having sex with a pie chart.

'*Simulacrum 12*,' Paul reads from the label underneath. 'Ariadne Acheiropoietos – wow, what a name. You'd hardly need to actually paint at all with a name like that, it's like an artwork in itself.'

'I wouldn't call that painting anyway,' Kevin says.

'Right, and you'd know,' Ish says.

'*Simulacrum 40*,' Paul reads from the label of the painting at the next table, then leans back to squint at the adjacent alcove. '*Simulacrum 59* – are they all called *Simulacrum*? What's that about?'

'Obviously the work of someone with mental health issues,' Kevin says. 'Probably all the organic food. You can't eat that much quinoa and stay normal.'

There is a small throat-clearing noise: we look up to see the waitress has materialized at the table.

It's the same girl who served Paul and me on Friday, dark-haired, olive-skinned, rangy without quite being tall. 'Ready to order?'

'I'll have the quinoa,' Ish says. 'And so will he,' she adds, pointing to Kevin.

When the waitress has gone, Jurgen asks Paul if he is getting good material.

'I'm still finding my feet,' Paul says. 'It'll take a few days, I suppose.'

'The world of banking is full of complexity,' Jurgen agrees. 'But once you have understood the basics, you will find a story as exciting as any thriller. Look at Bank of Torabundo. Three years ago we were the little minnows. Now we have become the big fish on the block.'

'I read something about that,' Paul says. 'What happened?'

'A lot of our competitors were badly damaged by the financial crisis. Some collapsed entirely; others, judged too big to be allowed to fail, were given huge government bailouts. But BOT came through it untouched.'

'How come?'

'We managed to avoid exposure to toxic investments. Our CEO at the time was deeply suspicious of complex derivatives, and forbade us to take big positions in those markets.'

'Or property,' Ish said. 'He didn't like the look of the global property market, so that's another bullet we dodged.'

'The result, anyway, is that the bank has been, as one might say, "punching above its weight".'

'You must be pretty grateful to your CEO,' Paul says.

'Yes,' Jurgen says. 'Although he has just been fired.'

Paul looks surprised. 'Fired?'

'Yes, his conservative stance cost the bank a lot of investors.'

'Even though he was right?'

'There is a happy medium,' Jurgen says.

'Between right and wrong?'

'Sir Colin's a smart guy,' Kevin says, 'but definitely on the cautious side.'

'In some ways he belonged to an earlier era of banking,' Jurgen concurs. 'It is true that his sceptical attitude saved BOT from financial catastrophe. But once we *had* survived, the board felt a more audacious leader was needed in order to press home our advantage. The new chief executive was appointed only a few days ago. His name is Porter Blankly.'

Even speaking his name seems to quicken the atmosphere; our eyes glitter, as if we were sharing some magical secret.

'Sounds familiar,' Paul says, frowning.

'He is quite a celebrated figure,' Jurgen says. 'He joined BOT from Danforth Blaue, which you may remember was one of the biggest casualties of the crash.'

'It needed a fifty-billion rescue package from the US government,' Kevin chips in eagerly. 'Then it was bought for a dollar by Takahashi Group.'

'This is the guy you made your new CEO?' Paul appears confused. 'Isn't that like pulling the captain of the *Titanic* out of the water and asking him to skipper your catamaran?'

'He has proved he is a man not afraid to take chances,' Jurgen says seriously. 'Sir Colin was very much a traditionalist. He had the classic view of the merchant or investment bank as a go-between, bringing together companies and investors for a fee. But in recent years, many investment banks have begun trading for themselves. That is, instead of just acting in their customers' interests, they also bet on the market with their own money using complicated financial instruments called derivatives.'

'A derivative is a contract derived from an underlying asset,' I explain, seeing Paul's look of bewilderment. 'An asset being something you own – your house, your car, and so on. Instead of buying or selling the asset itself, a derivative allows you to do other kinds of deals based on it.

'For example, one simple kind of derivative is an *option*. This is a contract that gives me the right, but not the obligation, to buy something from you for an agreed price at an agreed date in the future. I am calculating that when that date comes, the price will be more than our agreed price.'

'Isn't that just a bet?' Paul says uncertainly.

'If you do it in the bookie's, it's a bet,' Ish says. 'If you pay some 23-year-old in an Armani suit two hundred grand to go to the window for you, it's a derivative.'

'Because there is no limit to how often derivatives can be sold back and forth, the market for them is astronomically bigger than the market for actual things. In fact, no one knows how big it is.'

'And these derivatives are what your Sir Colin didn't like the look of?'

'Exactly. Wall Street banks were using instruments so complex that almost nobody understood how they actually worked. When their bets turned bad, they lost literally trillions of dollars. Sir Colin's instincts were on that occasion proved right. However, the BOT board . . .'

'. . . wants to give it another shot,' Paul concludes, with a smile.

'There is a feeling that things are different this time,' Jurgen says.

'Our share price has jumped three points since the news came out about Blankly,' Kevin says. 'A lot of people in the office are talking about buying in now. Take out a loan, even; if the price keeps going up at this rate, you'd make it back in a couple of months.'

'Perhaps it is Fate that has brought you here at this time,' Jurgen tells Paul. 'To capture the bank at the moment of its metamorphosis from minor player into unstoppable banking force.'

'And nobody's worried about, say, history repeating itself?' Paul asks.

'History has already repeated with the last crisis,' Jurgen says firmly. 'We do not think there will be any more repeating.'

After the strangeness of that first day, we quickly find our rhythm. I learn to work unselfconsciously; Paul, for the most part, observes in silence. Often, in fact, he leaves me to my own devices, as he walks around the office, making notes in his pad, occasionally taking pictures with his phone. Whatever fears I had – that I would be required to perform, or emote, or any of the things I came here to avoid – are quickly banished; he is at pains not to intrude on me any more than he has to.

Unfortunately, not everyone is respectful of the artistic process.

'I have begun reading your book,' Jurgen says, adding, in case there is any confusion, '*For Love of a Clown.*'

'Aha,' Paul says.

'I am loving the character of Stacy. She is based on somebody you know?'

'No, I made her up.'

'Her little nephew Timmy, he is driving her crazy!' Jurgen laughs. 'Always he is getting into mischief. Stacy will be glad when her sister comes back from her research trip.'

'Yeah,' Paul says.

'I wonder if she will commit to her promise to bring Timmy to the circus,' Jurgen says, frowning. 'Always she is making excuses.'

'Obviously she is going to bring him to the circus,' I say scathingly, when Paul is out of earshot. 'How else are they going to meet the clown?'

'That is a good point,' Jurgen concedes.

'If they didn't go to the circus, there would be no book! It would end on page 15!'

'Yes,' Jurgen says, flicking through his copy as though to ascertain that it does, in fact, have words right up to the last page.

Ish is even worse. She gives Paul constant updates on her progress through the novel; sometimes I hear her reading chunks of it back to him. On other occasions, she will relate anecdotes from her life before the bank, cornering him in order to show him the innumerable pictures of her 'travels' with Tog, her awful ex-fiancé.

With me he speaks almost exclusively of the bank and its doings – the fees we charge, how much one of my research notes might sell for, the minimum assets a client must have in order to be taken on by BOT, and so on. He says he wants to understand my work completely before looking at any other aspects of my life.

This suits me perfectly well; when you work a hundred hours a week there are few other aspects to see. Even at the weekend, you remain on call; there might be a golf game with a customer, or a VP will dump a client on you at the last minute, needing analysis on a potential buyer for a Sunday board meeting. Occasionally I'll get a call from someone I knew in La Défense, visiting on business or posted here with one of the big French banks; I will go to a bar with them and listen to them complain about how bad the food is, how hard it is to sleep with Irish girls; I will find myself seeing them through my father's eyes – their slick hair, their pointed shoes – and wonder if this is what he saw when he looked at me. But in general, investment banking is not an industry that fosters close relationships. Friendship exists here in a purely contingent way, on the basis of a mutual coincidence of wants; even to people you like, it's best not to reveal anything that might be used against you.

'It sounds so cynical,' Paul says.

'As long as everyone understands those are the rules, it does not cause any issues.'

'And even of Ish you'd say this?'

'I'd say it's something she needs to learn.'

Paul watches me with a kind of veiled amusement, rocking gently in his chair.

'So what's the point of it?' he asks.

'The point?'

'Why put yourself through all this? Why starve yourself of a life? Just to make money, is that it?'

'Howie says that if you have to ask why, then you are in the wrong game.'

'But what do *you* say?'

He waits, notebook in his lap. It is dusk: fluorescent lights stud the darkening sky outside like imitation jewels.

'You're right,' I say. 'It's just to make money.'

'I wonder what he's like,' Ish says. 'You know, what his life is like.'

I don't reply. A couple of heavyweight Spanish banks, rumoured to be facing significant write-downs on non-performing property loans, are being aggressively targeted by speculators; the effect is rippling outwards to affect the entire sector, unravelling Europe's latest bid to stabilize itself.

'I bet he lives in a huge mansion,' Ish says. 'With a pool. And a Bentley. And in his garden, he's got those – you know those bushes, where they've shaped them into animals?'

'Topiary.'

'Topiary,' Ish repeats dreamily, as if pronouncing the name of some mythical land. 'What do you think, Claude? Has he said anything to you?'

'No.' I say it in a bored voice, but the truth is that I too yearn to learn more about Paul's life. He gets to work at eight, he leaves around six; beyond that I know almost nothing. 'Do you think Billy Budd knew where Melville lived?' he'll say if I press him. 'Do you think Emma Bovary knew what Flaubert did all day?'

'I suppose not,' I concede.

'I want you to act as if I'm not there. The less you know about my life, the easier that'll be.'

'Have you got to the part yet where the clown brings Stacy and Timmy backstage at the circus?' Ish says now.

'No,' I say.

'It's so beautiful,' she says. She sits smacking her gum for another minute. Then she gets up. 'I think I'll go and ask him how he thought of that scene.'

'I wish you would stop distracting him.'

'Who says I'm distracting him?'

'He is trying to work on his project. And you have a report to finish.'

Ish tiptoes around behind me, then crouches down and whispers into my ear, 'I think the real problem is that someone's jealous.'

'I don't know what you mean.'

'You're jealous!' she exclaims, straightening up.

'Who's jealous?' Jurgen says, passing by.

'Claude's jealous of me talking to his boyfriend,' Ish says.

'Paul is not my boyfriend,' I say.

'Look what I have,' Jurgen says, and takes from his briefcase a hardback copy of *For Love of a Clown*. 'A first edition. And it's signed!' I open it to the title page, where Paul has crossed out his name and written, 'For Jurgen . . . With irie, Paul.' I look up at him blankly. 'Irie?'

'It is a reggae reference,' Jurgen says. 'I have been telling Paul about my old reggae band.'

'I didn't know you had a band,' Ish says.

Jurgen nods. 'Back in Munich. Gerhardt and the Mergers. Mostly German-language covers, but we had original numbers too. We were regarded as being one of the best reggae and rock-steady crews on the Bavarian financial scene.'

'Were you the singer?' Ish asks.

'No, that was Gerhardt. He was at the time the number one risk analyst at Morgan Stanley. Our rhythm section came from the Credit Suisse Syndicated Lending Department. Then there was me, on guitar and mortgage-backed securities.'

Their conversation fades out; I remain entranced by the inscribed page. I have never seen Paul's handwriting before. It is sprawling, straggly, like briars over a tombstone. Unprompted, an image appears in my head: the author at a cherrywood table, his hand moving across the page, depicting the minutiae of our

47

lives in thickets of ink. For the first time it strikes me: we are being *narrated*.

Ish snaps her fingers. 'Let's bring Paul to Life tonight! That way we can find out more about him, and it'll give him a chance to see our crazy side!'

I groan and rub my eyes. 'There is work to do,' I say. 'Am I the only person who cares about work?'

'That's a great idea,' Jurgen says. 'Do you think he'll come?'

'Of course he'll come,' Ish says. Bending one foot up to her knee, she begins to hop around, arms upstretched to the ceiling tiles and the fluorescent lighting. 'Sorry, Claude!' she declaims. 'But no one person can own Paul! He belongs to everyone!'

'I will go and ask him now,' Jurgen says, and he walks away, singing to himself, *'Mach dir keine Sorgen, über die Dinge . . .'*

'Like the air!' Ish hops back towards her desk. 'Like birdsong! Like sunshine!'

To my surprise, Paul accepts the invitation. Now the issue becomes making it out of the office. It has been another bad day – a very, very bad day – for Ireland on the markets. The two ailing Spanish banks have caused a panic across the whole continent, with investors scrambling to pull their funds out of any bank felt to be vulnerable – which includes all the major Irish institutions. The worst hit, Royal Irish, lost a million for almost every minute of trading, and every time I put on my coat another frantic client calls, wanting to know if the government will step in to save it. But the Minister has yet to make a statement – in fact, no one seems to know where the Minister even is.

Just after six o'clock, I am summoned upstairs by the Chief Operating Officer; exiting the lift on the seventh floor I walk straight into an enormous Garda. My mind floods with a whole new order of panic. Have we been robbed? Is the building under siege?

The secretary appears in the doorway and motions me impatiently into the corner office.

'Ah, Claude, there you are.' Whatever turn of events has brought a policeman into her foyer doesn't seem to have bothered Rachael. But then, Rachael is imperturbable. No matter the time of day or state of the market, she always looks immaculate – streamlined, frictionless, like a virtual avatar of herself. Her hair is perfectly blonde, her skin perfectly white, her very presence has been buffed to a sheen as smooth as a mirror. People say she slept her way to the top, but it is literally impossible to imagine her having sex with Sir Colin or anyone else; others like to say she has a USB port instead of a vagina, and that her husband uses her to charge his phone, which seems marginally more plausible.

Four men are in her office, crowded uncomfortably on couch and chairs with cups and saucers balanced on their knees. 'Gentlemen,' Rachael says, 'allow me to introduce Claude Martingale, one of our most talented analysts.'

I turn to the seated men and experience one of those cognitive shocks specific to meeting in real life someone long familiar from a screen. For the last two years, ever since the collapse of Lehman Brothers finally ignited the bonfire that was the Irish economy, the Minister for Finance has appeared almost nightly on the TV news, where he has always seemed measured, controlled, on top of the situation. In the couple of seconds it takes him to half-rise and greet me, it is frighteningly clear that this confidence is a veneer no thicker than the film of make-up applied backstage. Up close, unmediated, he seems actually to embody the country's dire condition. Shadows devour his features, beads of moisture cling morbidly to the grey folds of his skin; his courtly, reasonable bearing is belied by great dark rings around his eyes. I had heard he was unwell: when I lean in to shake his hand I am hit by a stench so deathly I have to fight the instinct to recoil.

Rachael introduces the two men on either side of him as the Secretary General of the Department of Finance, and the Second Secretary at the Department in charge of banking policy. One is fat, one is thin; both wear glasses and the pursed, dismissive miens of civil-service lifers. Nearest the door is a fourth man, small with lugubrious eyes and a sallow complexion reminiscent of yellowing pages. He does not look Irish, but Continental – Portuguese, maybe, or Corsican. Rachael does not tell me his name, and he does not introduce himself; in fact he does not speak at all during the meeting, just remains in his corner, semi-translucent, staring at the Minister with those dolorous, unblinking eyes.

Rachael closes the door and turns to me brightly. 'The Minister has dropped by to speak to us –'

'Informally,' the fat secretary interjects.

'– to speak to us informally about the current, ah, uncertainty in the Irish banking sector.' Rachael cannot hide her delight at this coup; she is positively glowing. 'Minister, Claude has advised several major international investors in relation to Irish banks.'

The Minister opens his mouth into a strange gaping smile and wags it at me, like a grandfather who has had a stroke and is incapable of speaking. Then, as if this effort has caused some internal upset, he hastily brings a handkerchief to his mouth.

'Claude, perhaps you could explain a little more what it is you do,' Rachael prompts me.

'Certainly,' I reply, and begin to paint a broad picture of my role – namely, to dig through the loan books, deposit books and unexploded assets of distressed or defunct Irish banks, looking for anything ignored or undervalued that an external capital provider might take an interest in.

'Picking off the good stuff for the vultures,' the thin secretary translates.

I smile courteously. 'Even the vultures have to be persuaded to invest in Ireland at the moment.'

He sniffs; it is the fatter secretary who speaks next.

'Obviously the reason we're here is Royal Irish,' he says. 'We've sunk a lot of money into it, quite apart from the guarantee, and at this stage we thought things would be turning around.'

'They were turning around,' the thin man corrects him. 'Up until a couple of days ago. But now because of these bloody Spanish we've got investors pulling their money out again, and it's starting to look like it'll need another recapitalization.'

'Obviously there are very good reasons for keeping the bank open,' the fat man says, slinging a foot across his knee. 'It's of systemic importance, obviously. And we want to send the message to our international friends that Ireland's financial sector is in perfect health and ready to do business. At the same time, we can't just keep paying and paying.'

'So I suppose what we want,' the thin man says airily, 'is to get a fresh perspective on the situation vis-à-vis Royal Irish. Our advisers tell us core capital ratios have been returning to acceptable levels, and that once it gets over this, as it were, hump, it should be able to return to profitability without further government assistance. We'd like to know, beyond the current situation, where you might see the bank's position in six months, a year.'

The Minister grins mechanically and works his jaws by way of endorsing this, a blast of fetid air issuing as he does so.

All eyes are now on me, but I am not sure how to proceed. Things have not been turning around at Royal Irish; Royal Irish has been haemorrhaging money for months, first investors' money, then taxpayers' money. The general rule in banking is to tell the client what he wants to hear – that way, if you're wrong, he's less likely to hold you to blame. But to claim that Royal Irish can keep going for another week, let alone six months, would be like saying Louis XVI is alive and well and will shortly be resuming his kingly duties. It is finished as a going concern; surely they know that?

The men are waiting. I glance over to Rachael. She draws a thoughtful breath: a weirdly synthetic gesture, like a doll opening and shutting its sightless eyes. 'Maybe you could give us a broad idea of what a return to profitability might look like,' she says, with a meaningful nod.

I think for a moment, then start talking in vague terms about the volatility of the market, how nobody knows what will happen, how some Irish brands are certainly undervalued. It all depends, I say, on the wider recovery in Europe. If things stabilize, and if Royal genuinely do have capital reserves, and if they pursue a particular strategy, and divest themselves of their toxic assets, then yes, in that scenario they could get back on their feet. Each of those ifs would require a miracle, but the secretaries seem pleased with what they hear. They ask some follow-up questions, using financial jargon that makes no sense; the Minister, meanwhile, gazes down at his lap. He appears to be picking skin from his fingers; it comes away in loose white skeins, which flutter down to the floor. Then he leans over to the thin secretary and gurgles something in his ear.

'Yes,' the secretary says, and turns to Rachael. 'There's a new man in charge here? This fellow Blankly?'

'Porter Blankly, that's correct. He's based in New York, of course.' She addresses this to the Minister, who is gazing up at her with a kind of prayerful desperation. 'But I speak to him almost every day. Porter is – well, I'm sure I don't need to tell you he's an inspirational figure. He believes that if you can get the market on your side, anything is possible.'

The secretaries seem pleased with this too. They whisper together a moment. The Minister grins at us, a crunching sound issuing from his mouth along with a fresh gust of fetor – he is eating raw garlic, I realize; he has been peeling skin from a clove he clutches in his left hand.

'Thank you, Claude,' Rachael says. Taking my cue, I stand up and shake hands with the visitors again. The Minister has his handkerchief pressed to his mouth again; above it his shell-blue eyes roll wetly at me, as if signalling desperately, *There is a man trapped in here!*

'I don't get it. What did he want you to do?'

It's Friday night; we are leaving the building at last.

'Reassure him. Make him feel he has made the right decision to recapitalize Royal Irish. Tell him they can still get back on their feet.'

'And they can't?'

'At this stage Royal Irish doesn't even have feet.'

'Just an arsehole,' Ish grumbles.

'You mean Miles?' Paul says. If any one person can be held

responsible for Ireland's current state, it is Royal Irish's CEO, Miles O'Connor, who made some forty billion euros of loans to property developers that then went bust – although next on the list would be the Minister himself, who has committed the country to paying off all of the money that Royal and the other banks owe. It's hard to understand. In France, where if someone misses a coffee break there is a national strike, a scandal like this would have shut down the streets. Yet the Irish seem able to absorb any amount of punishment without complaint – like the drunk at the bar you expect any moment to topple off his stool, who instead keeps throwing back shots, his massive inebriation having become a kind of self-perpetuating system, a kind of replacement gravity . . .

Just as I am thinking this, I hear Ish say, with a note of alarm, 'Whoa! That guy looks a bit the worse for wear!'

That's putting it mildly: the gentleman in question, wearing a dark wool suit, has a bloody red socket where his left eye ought to be and a withered claw instead of a hand. We stop and watch as he lurches over the plaza and across the bridge, where he is greeted by five or six other similarly cadaverous figures.

'Zombies,' Jurgen says.

The zombies have raised a tent on the riverbank opposite, around which they stagger, gesticulating at the traffic with authentically decomposing hands.

'What's this about?' Paul says.

'That building there was supposed to be Royal Irish's new headquarters,' I tell him, pointing to the concrete shell on the far side of the river. 'They had just started construction when the crisis hit.'

'Why the costumes, though?'

'A zombie is what you call a bank that's still trading even though it's insolvent.' The first revenant has produced a placard that reads DO NOT FEED THE ZOMBIES and is waving it about.

'They're saying that if the bank is finished, the government shouldn't be giving it any more taxpayer money.'

'But why would they give it more money?' Paul asks. 'If it's dead in the water?'

'They're in denial. They still think it can be saved.'

'Huh,' Paul says, as one of the zombies' arms falls off and under the wheels of a truck.

'The Financial Services Centre brings in a lot of money,' Ish says. 'But the reason it does is that all of these international banks and funds and special purpose vehicles and God knows what else can come here and do whatever it is they want to do and they know they'll be left alone. It's a bit like a red-light zone, see?'

'So . . .' Paul is not quite making the connection.

'So if a bank goes bust, it's like if a hooker dropped dead. Suddenly there's ambulances coming in, health authorities wanting to do blood tests, news crews demanding to know what's happened. Even if you, Mr Sex Tourist, aren't worried about catching whatever it is killed her, still, it's not feeling so private any more. So you quietly pack your bag, and the next day you're off to Luxembourg or Liechtenstein or the British Virgin Islands, or wherever it might be.'

'You mean the Irish government want to cover it up because it's bad for business.'

'Who knows? Maybe they genuinely think Royal Irish is salvageable. Stick a few more billion in there, close your eyes and hope for the best.'

'It is what in the bank we call "magical thinking",' I add. 'It is more prevalent than you might expect.'

Paul gazes at the cavorting zombies, the great financial memento mori that is the unbuilt bank hanging over the grey river. 'They're going to need it,' he says.

And here is Life, dark and full of strangers, yelling at each other from their private intoxications like monkeys screeching through the bars of their cage. Music booms all around, prohibiting conversation at anything less than a shout; battalions of drones, haircuts modelled after the heroes of the day, neck their fizzy lagers, their syrupy alcopops, and perform the minimal courting rituals required before they have sex with each other. The bar's style is classic Celtic Tiger – white armchairs with zebra throws, ubiquitous mirrors, large unseated area, palpable air of incipient violence – like a cross between a hairdresser's and the Stanford Prison Experiment. Nevertheless, Life is the closest thing the Financial Services Centre has to a local. This is where the real information is exchanged: who's getting paid what, who's hiring, who's on the way up/down/out; tips for good schools, good builders, good mechanics, good tailors, good divorce lawyers.

The name is a pun – *Life* is Gaelic for Liffey, the river that splits the city into north and south (and, broadly, rich and poor) – and gives rise to many more puns ('I hate Life', 'After a few drinks Life won't seem so bad', and so on), which we make instead of finding somewhere less repugnant. On Friday nights, patrons will typically skip dinner in order to start drinking sooner – unthinkable in Paris; get stuck beside Ish and you will first be treated to what seems an unending series of humorous cat videos, then, as the hysterical laughter dies away, find yourself attempting fruitlessly to comfort her as she rehearses yet again the break-up of her relationship, before lurching off into the night with whichever opportunist has bought her last drink.

Tonight the turbulence on the markets has lent an extra edge of mania to the proceedings, as employees of the many banks not currently punching above their weights contemplate the idea that this time next week they may be out of a job, and reach desperately for a lifebelt.

'Think the brunette there's taken a shine to you, Kev,' Gary McCrum, Utilities analyst, says.

Kevin turns to look. The dark-haired girl at the end of the adjoining table glances up and away again. She has delicate hands, eyes with a little too much white in them, a disorientating air of weightlessness, like a dress on a clothes line flapping in the wind.

'Totally checking you out,' Dave Davison, Commodities, confirms.

Kevin scrutinizes the brunette dubiously, like a diner in a restaurant examining the lobsters in the tank. 'Is she hot?'

'Is she hot? She's right there in front of you!'

'I've looked at so much porn I can't tell any more if IRL women are good-looking or not,' Kevin confesses. 'I have to imagine if I saw her on a screen would I click on her.'

'IRL?' I ask Dave Davison. 'This means Ireland? Irish women?'

'*In real life*, Grandad – here, Kev, look at her through my phone. See? She's an eight, easy.'

'Well, a seven,' Gary says.

'Maybe she is more of a seven,' Dave concedes.

'Pff, I'm not wasting a drink on a seven,' Kevin says, and turns his back on the brunette, who dips her eyes woundedly into her lap, then reaffixes herself to her friends' conversation, throwing her toothy smile about the room betimes like a cracked whip.

'I used to feel that way about sevens,' Dave says sadly. 'Then I got married.'

'Those two are really hitting it off,' Jurgen says to me, nodding over to where for the last half an hour Paul and Ish have been deep in conversation.

'I hope she is not telling him anything too personal,' I say.

'Such as her theories about where it all went wrong with Tog?'
Jurgen says.

'Yes.'

'Or the time she got diarrhoea in China?'

My eyes widen. 'You think she's telling him the Yangtze river-boat story?'

Maybe I should go and check, I decide; but someone is blocking my path. It's Howie, arriving with Tom Cremins, Brian O'Brien and a couple of other traders, all carrying glasses of single malt whiskey. They crowd in beside us; the girls at the next table swivel their heads towards ours once more, like lovely, money-tropic flowers.

'Hear you had a little chat with the government today,' Howie says to me. 'What'd he tell you? Are they going to recap Royal?'

'He didn't say.'

'He must have said something.'

'He actually didn't,' I say, recalling with a twinge of horror the Minister's grinning, terrorized aphasia. 'Anyway, even if I knew, I couldn't tell you – you *know* I couldn't tell you,' raising my voice as he starts swearing at me, 'it'd be insider trading.'

'Crazy Frog, if they locked up everyone in this town who's insider trading, there'd be no one left on the fucking inside.' Howie plonks his glass down on the table, making the ice cubes jingle. '*Someone* ought to be making money out of this eurozone shit-show. This whole fucking week has been a disaster on every conceivable level, like getting raped by a guy with a tiny cock.' The eavesdropping girls flinch, but don't stop staring; Howie's attention, however, is already elsewhere. 'Is that the writer?' Pushing past me he taps on Paul's shoulder and asks him the same question. Paul turns with a slightly confused smile. 'What the fuck are you doing writing a book about this guy?' Howie demands, gesturing at me.

'Ah –' Paul says, looking startled.

'He's not a player. He's a research analyst. It's like you've gone to Silverstone and you're watching the mechanics. I mean, do what you want,' Howie sniffs. 'It just sounds like a boring book, that's all.'

'Well, you see, in a way that's the –'

'There is crazy shit going down right now,' Howie interrupts. 'I mean world-historical craziness. You should be speaking to the traders. Or the hedge funds. If I had a hedge fund, I'd be shorting the shit out of the whole of Europe. And in six months I'd be a billionaire.'

'You're talking about the –?'

'The whole continent's fucked. The politicians don't know what to do. All that can save it now is a war.'

'A war?' Kevin hiccups.

'That's the way it's heading. France, Italy, Spain are all watching their economies go down the tube, Germany's there with its arms folded, saying, "Don't expect anything from us." There's all the ingredients for a war, right? And it would stop all the, you know, the bollocks.'

'*War*,' Paul repeats, scribbling in his red notebook.

'War's a good thing. What stopped the Great Depression? World War Two. Or look at the Baghdad Bounce. NASDAQ crashes, the economy's assholed, till the US invades Iraq and the stock market goes up 80 per cent. Capitalism needs war. Besides, war's what made Europe great. The whole reason their currency's in the toilet is you've got a bunch of bureaucrats in charge, trying to pretend the last thousand years of history never happened. Acting like Europe's all just one big happy family, singing and holding hands like a bunch of fucking Smurfs. And they wonder why everyone's lining up to short them! Would you invest in a Smurf economy?'

'*I* wouldn't,' Kevin says.

'No way,' Howie says, but his eyes are suddenly vacant and he peers back and forth as if he can't remember what he's doing here.

At that moment, Tom Cremins pulls his sleeve. 'We're going,' he says.

'Yeah,' Howie says, and drains his glass. He turns to Paul once more. 'When you get tired talking to this joker, come and see me,' he says. 'I'll show you stuff that'll have you haemorrhaging from every orifice.'

With that, he and the traders bounce off, their conversation a blizzard of acronyms and stomach-turning sexual references, like a Scrabble game at a gang bang.

'Interesting guy,' Paul says thoughtfully. I watch him watch Howie barge his way through the drunken, suited bodies, feeling the same pang I might have at a school dance, seeing the girl I adored bloom at the attentions of some handsome delinquent. Then, as if he senses my unhappiness, Paul turns to me, and with an enthusiasm that strikes me as false says, 'But then, you're all interesting! I just had a great conversation with your friend here. Did you know she studied anthropology? I thought you bankers were all rocket scientists.'

'That's just the traders,' I say. 'My background is philosophy – François Texier, do you know him?'

Paul shakes his head.

'In fact he might be a useful person to think about for your book,' I say. 'He had many fascinating ideas about simulacra, and the derealization of modern life.'

'Derealization?' Paul repeats, with a half-smile.

'Yes. He was interested in a Buddhist concept called *sunyata*, or voidness. According to this *sunyata*, reality as we perceive it is an illusion. We see the world as divided up into objects – this glass, this table, this person. But in fact, these are merely snapshots of processes that are in a constant state of change, all parts of a great intermingling flux.'

'That does sound pretty derealizing,' Paul admits.

'Actually, the derealizing comes as an attempt to cover over this notion of flux,' I say, excited to feel these thoughts coming to life in my mind again. 'To a culture centred on the individual, the idea that we are all just transitory surface effects on some great sea of emptiness has not been popular. Texier's argument is that most of Western civilization has been an attempt to build over the void with huge, static systems of thought, religious, economic, scientific, that divide everything into facts, each with its own specific place. We call it analysis, but really it is escape. Or as he puts it, "We write the encyclopedia to explain the world, and then we leave the world to live in the encyclopedia." The simulacrum is a kind of a derivative of these –'

'Oi! What's going on here?' Ish arrives with a tray of drinks. 'You know the rules, Claude. Friday night – no Frenchness!'

'I'm just explaining that we have all come to banking from different disciplines,' I say.

'Kevin here was halfway through a medical degree,' Ish says. 'Imagine, he could actually have been useful to somebody.'

'Doctors don't make shit these days,' Kevin says.

'It used to be the smartest people didn't always want to be the richest people,' Paul says.

'Maybe the smartest people got smarter,' Kevin returns.

'*I'm* not going to spend the rest of my life at it,' Ish says. 'I've still got a box of my old clothes at home. As soon as I get my next bonus, I'm going to chuck my whole wardrobe of daggy work shit straight into a skip and fuck off to the Pacific. It'll be like Corporate Ish never existed.'

'What about your apartment?' I say.

'Oh yeah.' Her face falls. Turning to Kevin she says, 'Here, want to buy an apartment? It's got a bidet.'

'Property's finished,' Kevin says. 'I'm putting all my money into global pandemics.'

As midnight approaches, I see Paul put on his coat.

'The end of your first week,' I say. 'It is all going well?'

'Sure,' he says – but I detect a hesitation.

'Only . . . ?'

'It's nothing,' he reassures me. 'I'm just trying to figure out how it all hangs together.'

'If you have questions, maybe I can help.'

At first he blusters nothings, then he pauses, looks at me, as if deciding whether to take me into his confidence: 'I feel like I'm *missing* something,' he says. 'I've got the characters, what you do, the rhythm of the day. But I still – I feel like I'm not getting to the *heart* of things, you know?' I must look very worried, because he claps me on the shoulder. 'It'll come. Maybe I just need to change my focus a little bit.'

'We will see you on Monday?' I say.

'Of course.' He grins. 'Have a good weekend. You're off-camera! Let your hair down.'

Not long after, the lights come up; Life begins to empty, its pinchbeck promises having slipped away, as always, through the cracks of the night.

We gather our things and make our way outside. I am deep in thought: what Paul said about missing something bothers me, and as if picking up on that, Jurgen says, 'So he has told you what's going to happen?'

'Happen?'

'In the book.'

'We know what is going to happen in the book,' I say. 'It is about me, a modern Everyman, experiencing a typical day.'

'Yes, but there will be some kind of story also?'

'That is the story,' I say.

'That is the story?'

'Yes.'

'You, sitting at your computer, writing research notes about banks.'

'That's right.'

Jurgen says nothing to this.

'It's not supposed to be one of those books where things happen,' I explain. 'It's about discovering the humanity in ordinary lives.'

'Oh,' Jurgen says.

There is another silence.

'It's not going to be boring,' I say.

'Of course not,' he says.

Around us the Centre looms, darkened and empty like a Perspex necropolis. I think again of Paul's parting words, and anxiety quickens in my sinews once more. 'Did he say anything to you?' I turn to Ish. 'What were you talking to him about for so long?'

'He was asking about the Torabundo archipelago. I travelled around there a bit with Tog back in the day. She pauses, then says, '*I* reckon he's got something planned for you.'

'Like what?'

'Like . . . I don't know . . . maybe you fall in love.'

'I'm not going to fall in love,' I say categorically.

'In a book this is exactly the kind of thing the main character will say right before he falls in love,' Jurgen says.

'Yeah,' says Ish. 'Plus, you're French. You lot practically invented love. French kissing. French letters. It's the whole French thing.'

'How would you feel if I said the "whole Australian thing" was kangaroos and tinnies and daytime soap operas?'

'That *is* the whole Australian thing, Claude. Why do you think I left?'

'Yes, well, then you will understand that not everyone fits into the national stereotype.'

'I certainly do not think that when people speak of the "typical German",' Jurgen chuckles, 'they are imagining a crazy man who loves reggae music, and writes articles about medieval economics while listening to reggae music on his computer!'

'My point is that adventures, escapades, dramatic reversals, falling in love – these are the hackneyed tropes that Paul's trying to get away from,' I tell Ish, though I am perhaps trying to persuade myself as much as her. 'He wants to depict modernity as it genuinely is.'

'Love's not hackneyed,' Ish says obstinately.

'What does love have to do with this place?' I throw my arms up at our surroundings, great glass panopticons surveying all the other panopticons. 'I am serious, what does love have to do with anything we do all day long?'

'Well, that's what he'd better work out,' Ish says. 'If he wants anyone to read his book.'

'There are plenty of good stories without love.'

'Like what?'

I think for a moment. '20,000 *Leagues Under the Sea*.'

We have emerged on to the quay. Over the river, beneath the concrete skull of the unfinished headquarters, the zombies sleep in silence.

'Just because you don't have it doesn't mean you don't need it,' Ish says, staring into the dark water. 'Every story needs love. Even at the bottom of the sea.'

Over the weekend, *Forbes* publishes a long article about our new chief executive, Porter Blankly. The accompanying photographs show a man in his sixties, with the craggy, portentous good looks of the star of a Hollywood Bible epic, and white hair in a sculpted wave, like a roll of ice cream caught mid-scoop. In every picture he is shaking hands with someone, as if that's all he does for a living; anyone in the industry will know that each of those handshakes represents a game-changing new synergy, a market stampede, and a multimillion-dollar windfall for his shareholders. The piece is titled *Blank to the future*, and it runs as follows:

Four years ago this summer, Porter Blankly achieved a dream he had cherished since childhood: He became a billionaire. Subprime mortgages were booming, and Danforth Blaue, a bank once perceived as a starchy also-ran, was thanks to his leadership right at the heart of the action. The day stock options took his wealth on paper to the magical ten figures, Blankly celebrated with a quiet dinner at home with his wife and legal team. Then he bought eight stories of the Empire State Building.

Porter Blankly has always dreamed big. Hailing from a hardscrabble town of blue-collar laborers, many of them employed on his father's private railroad, he was spotted as a teenager by a scout for Harvard's varsity golf team. He dropped out of 'Old Crimson' after only a year to play full-time, and although a shoulder injury cut short his professional career, his experiences on the courses of the 1960s were formative. This was a time of ferment in the Massachusetts golf scene. Ideas and books by the young firebrands of the new conservative movement were being passed around – as well as other material. '[US Ryder Cup team captain Don] Hartford turned up one day with a sheet of blotter acid,' Blankly recalled later, 'and everything changed. The fairways were rainbows, the holes were mouths, speaking to you. You've heard about crazy golf – at that time all golf was crazy. People were showing up in sunglasses, without ties . . . everything was being questioned.'

The potent cocktail of fiscal conservatism and perception-altering drugs would shape an entire generation. Many of the figures Blankly encountered at that time went on to become key figures in politics, banking, and in the nascent world of computing, into which they carried the revolutionary concept they had learned on the fairways – that reality was plastic and could be molded as they saw fit.

Though he never completed his degree and had no training in finance, arriving in Wall Street Blankly found his +2 handicap much in demand. He was taken under the wing of the legendary Walter Wriston of Citibank, and, as he quickly came to dominate in inter-bank and pro-am tournaments, effectively given an open brief. At the time the major banks were plowing money into Latin American dictatorships, but Blankly, never one to follow the crowd, instead staked his money on a then little-known warlord in the Middle East. The bet paid off: While Wall Street lost a fortune when their dictators were deposed, Ahmed bin-Ahmed, as he was then known, went on to become the Caliph of the oil-rich state of Oran, and today remains one of Blankly's biggest financial backers and closest personal friends.

Tragedy was to strike at the end of the 1970s, when his wife of only six months, heiress Cressida Heinz-Boeing, committed suicide, but Blankly bounced back, taking a position at Drexel Burnham as the junk bond boom began. This was the age of the so-called 'Masters of the Universe,' when traders made millions from peddling mountains of practically worthless bonds; Blankly soon became famous for his aggressive acquisitions strategy and his colorful private life, dating a string of models, and being photographed in New York's hottest nightspots.

Yet behind the scenes, he was under considerable pressure. The collapse of the junk bond market following the indictment of his boss and close personal friend Michael Milken left him with personal losses of over ten million dollars. A greater loss was soon to follow with the suicide of his second wife, Caspian Dupont. Reeling from this double blow, Blankly spent some time in the financial wilderness. According to friends, he thought seriously about leaving banking and beginning a new career, possibly in restoring old boats. However, the dearth of professional-level golfers in the major houses soon had Wall Street beating a path to his door. He returned to Citi in the early 1990s, where he remained a divisive figure – beloved among employees for his inspirational memos, but attracting controversy for his refusal to indulge what he called the 'mania' of that time for political correctness. He drew fire for remarking to a reporter that, with regard to Wall Street management structure, 'women on top [was his] least favorite position'; less than a week later, he found himself in hot water again after accusing African-American golfer Tiger Woods of stealing his wallet at a fundraising event.

This was a challenging time for Blankly, one which in later years he would refer to as 'the toughest hole.' His venture capital firm, Tourniquet, which had invested over a billion dollars in websites aimed directly at dogs, cats, and other pets, was wiped out by the Internet crash, while on the home front his third wife, Fanfarla Pinochet, survived only 'by a miracle' after accidentally dropping a toaster into her bath (the couple divorced later that year).

But he was to bounce back with the September 11 attacks on the World Trade Center. Now with hedge fund Elite Capital Partnership, Blankly is widely believed to have put in a huge order for gold in the seconds after the first plane hit. By the time the second tower fell two hours later, the price of gold had already risen almost 20%. In the chaos that followed, this single transaction is believed to have resulted in almost unthinkable profits for a small number of investors, including Blankly's long-time friend the Caliph of Oran; although no records of the trade exist, Blankly was very soon headhunted by

Danforth Blaue, where he became the most highly remunerated CEO in the world. Within a year he was delivering record profits through heavy investment in subprime mortgages. He featured on the cover of *Fortune*, and in the accompanying interview told the reporter that 'we are in a new paradigm of growth now that cannot be stopped.'

This paradigm did stop shortly afterwards, however, and with the collapse of the subprime housing market, the subsequent 'credit crunch,' and worldwide losses of trillions of dollars, Danforth Blaue was saved from annihilation only by a last-second government bail-out. Public anger toward industry chiefs like Blankly, who throughout his career had criticized politicians for any attempts to regulate Wall Street's activities, was exacerbated by the discovery that Danforth had in fact been betting heavily against the toxic subprime assets they sold their clients. It then emerged that billions of dollars of taxpayers' money handed over to rescue the firm had been used not only to pay huge bonuses to the failed bank's executives, but also for a Hawaiian-themed 'rescue party,' which featured a live performance from rapper Fugly B of his 2008 hit 'Bag It and $plit (F*** you B*****s)' as well as a swimming pool filled with banknotes. Worse, not long after the bailout a lifesize bronze statue of himself that Blankly was having delivered by crane to his office was dropped onto a bus of special-needs students visiting Wall Street for the day. While none was injured, Blankly's job was felt to be untenable and he stepped down, with a further 'leaving bonus' of $33 million and a replacement bronze statue.

Though Blankly had been pilloried by some for 'turning reality into a fruit machine' via complex financial instruments of which he himself had little understanding (cf. the leak of his highly embarrassing memo re 'hoosits' and 'whatsits' for collateralized debt obligations and synthetic collateralized debt obligations respectively), others took a more nuanced view. Following his departure from Danforth, Blankly – still a 'scratch' golfer with famously soft hands – was approached with several different job offers, including Special Advisor to the Treasury, Chair of Professional Ethics at

Harvard University, and President of the World Bank. It is no surprise, however, that the man who once said he had 'capital allocation in his blood' opted in the end to return to investment banking. Previously helmed by Sir Colin Shred, best known for his outspoken views on the Windsor knot, Bank of Torabundo emerged from the crisis punching above its weight and hungry for fresh ideas on loan portfolio management. A statement to shareholders said that Blankly's brief was to radicalize the bank's MO and leverage its sound financial fundamentals into market share. Potential joint ventures or other strategic combinations have not been ruled out, though Blankly has refused to comment on rumors that the bank will begin trading on its own account, or that he is seeking to set up a hedge fund within the firm itself.

About his own role in a financial collapse which in the US alone has cost more than the New Deal, the Marshall Plan, the Korean War, the Vietnam War, the 1980s Savings and Loan Crisis, the invasion of Iraq, and the total cost of NASA including the moon landings, all added together and adjusted for inflation, Blankly is unrepentant. 'We were wrong about a lot of things. But don't forget about all we got right. We helped people to borrow more money than anyone ever thought possible, and with that borrowed money, they went out and bought their dreams. Yes, they fell far, but only because they had soared so high – higher than the human race had ever gone before, high enough, almost, to touch the face of God.'

'One thing's for certain,' Jurgen says, putting down the magazine. 'The days of thinking inside the box are over.'

'He sounds like a nutter,' Ish says.

'They are not paying him to be sane,' Jurgen says. 'They are paying him to innovate solutions and then monetize them.'

'He sounds like my Uncle Nick,' Ish says.

'Excuse me,' Jurgen says. 'But having heard several stories about your Uncle Nick, I am satisfied that he and Porter Blankly bear no resemblance to each other.'

'Have I told you about the time he bought the bag of ferrets?' Ish says.

'Doesn't sound like he's a big fan of lady bosses,' Jocelyn Lockhart says. 'Bet Rachael's shitting it.'

'You'd better watch your back too, Ish,' Gary McCrum advises.

'I wonder if he'll send *us* an inspirational memo,' Kevin says. 'It's so exciting!'

Paul hasn't arrived yet, but I set the Blankly article aside for him. That's not the only thing awaiting his attention this Monday morning. Jurgen plays a song for us on his phone, which he tells us he recorded with his old reggae band, Gerhardt and the Mergers.

'As the lyrics are in German, I will give you a synopsis. The song is called "Banking Babylon". It tells the story of a Rastafarian who comes to the big city in order to look for a loan. However, the bank manager, who is white, turns down his application.'

'Why?' Ish says. 'He's a racist?'

'At first it appears a straightforward case of racism. However, as the song goes on, we discover there is more to it than meets the eye. The bank manager has legitimate concerns about the Rastafarian's ability to repay the loan. Specifically, he believes the Rasta wants to use the money to buy "ganja", and not as start-up capital for a small business as he is claiming on his application form. So you see, it is overturning your preconceived notions.'

Ish and I agree that this is a very unusual angle.

'That was the unique selling point of our band, the Mergers,' Jurgen says. 'As four white men working in highly paid private-sector jobs, we were able to give both sides of the story. This is evident in the very title of the song. In Rastafarianism, "Babylon", which according to the Bible has enslaved the Jews for many centuries, is regarded as the site of all evil. But in fact, ancient Babylonian society was highly sophisticated. Indeed, with the Hammurabi Code, the Babylonians could be regarded as the forefathers of modern banking. That is something few reggae songs give credit for.'

Ish, for her part, has brought in some anthropological material about the island of Torabundo. 'Turns out to be pretty interesting,' she says. 'So, the Polynesians have been there for thousands of years, just minding their own business, canoeing back and forth between the other islands in the archipelago. Then, in the seventeenth century, the British arrive and start raiding the islands and carrying people off to use as slaves. The building that eventually became Bank of Torabundo, that was the headquarters of the whole operation.'

'It was quite common for empires to station their slave trade in the New World,' Jurgen says. 'As it was no longer tolerated in Europe. It became a sort of offshore industry.'

'Could be pretty good for the book, though, eh?' Ish says. 'Like this big fancy bank's origins are sending slaves off to dig up pigeon shit.'

'Scratch beneath the surface of any great power and you will find slavery,' Jurgen says equanimously. 'The Romans. Alexander the Great. This very city, in Viking times, was the biggest slave market in Europe. In fact, Irish slave girls became units of currency for a time.'

'They used girls as *money*?' Ish says, horrified.

'Ireland did not have any precious materials – gold, silver – for export,' Jurgen says. 'So for international trade they used slave girls, or *cumals*. I believe one *cumal* was worth approximately three cows.'

'That explains a lot about Irish men,' Ish says, looking darkly at Jocelyn Lockhart, who's taking a call on the other side of the cubicle. 'A *lot*.'

'My point is that slavery has always been a part of the business world,' Jurgen says. 'But what is to be gained by dwelling on the past, or unpleasant aspects of the present? Most people would prefer to think about happy, upbeat things that reflect our twenty-first-century outlook, such as smartphones, or casual sex with attractive strangers.'

'Yes, but Paul wants to show what's beneath all that,' Ish says. 'Such as slaves.'

Jurgen taps his pen against his teeth. 'Hmm, I do not think it will be necessary to bring this particular detail to Paul's attention.'

Ish squints at him. 'You're not *censoring* me?'

'Of course not. I am simply advising you, as your superior, that this is not the kind of information the average Joe Bloggs reader is interested in. I know, because I have asked myself, as the average reader, if I am interested in reading about the bank's origins in slavery, and the answer I have come back with is a resounding "No".' He issues a decalorized smile. 'Now, time to work. Claude, please review this report for Mellon. The statistical information seems underdeveloped.'

He tosses a heavy folder on to my desk. I wait till he's gone, then hand it to Ish, who hands it to Kevin. 'Put in more pictures,' she tells him.

Seven o'clock becomes eight becomes nine, with no sign of Paul. I try to work, but find it hard to concentrate; in fact, I have been fretting all weekend. What did he mean when he said he wasn't getting to the heart of things? The bank's whole purpose is to get *away* from the heart of things – to turn things into numbers, then those numbers into imaginary things, then to divide up the imaginary things into pieces to be bought or sold, swapped or hedged, back and forth, again and again, until the underlying reality they emerged from is entirely forgotten. He knows that; it's what drew him to the subject in the first place. So what's the real issue? If he thinks something's missing – does he mean me?

His eventual appearance, shortly before eleven, does nothing to reassure me. He is pale, tired, preoccupied; I give him the *Forbes* article, but he puts it aside with barely a glance.

'Something is bothering you.' There is no sense ignoring it.

'It's just a little more complicated than I expected,' he says. His smile, meant to put me at ease, only flags his own frustration. What can I do? I offer to make him a flow chart showing the different departments and their various tasks; I ask if he wants to go over the analysts' assessment methods again, price/earnings ratios, free cash flow, and so on. No, no, he shakes his head, it's not that.

'So what is it?' I ask, with my heart in my mouth.

'It's the money,' he says at last.

'The money?'

'If it's a book about banking, ultimately it has to be about money, right? But I don't . . .' he trails off, knits his brows. 'I don't *see* anything. You do all these deals, you get paid all these fees, and it's all just . . .' He makes a *poof! g*esture with his hands.

'Ah,' I say. 'Maybe you need to visit the back office.'

'Back office?'

'The administrative part of the bank. It's where they do the paperwork, record into the system all of the trades, underwritings, bond issues, and so on, put the actual money into the accounts.'

This seems to awaken his interest. 'How come I haven't heard of it till now?'

'There is a Chinese wall between it and the rest of the bank.' Seeing his blank look, I clarify: 'That just means that access is barred to us. In case someone is tempted to sneak in during the night and change the records, cover up a bad trade or losing ticket, even re-route funds into an unauthorized account.'

'Right, right,' Paul says, frowning again and opening his red notebook to jot this down. 'So you can't go in there?'

'From our side, no. The doors are locked. But I'm sure you can get clearance, if you are looking around only for your book.'

He asks me if I will make the arrangements. This turns out to be difficult, and not just for reasons of security. There is a strict hierarchy to investment banking, of which back office lies at the very bottom, below even lawyers. Suspecting, accurately, that the analysts and traders look down on them (just as the M&A bankers look down on us), back office are notoriously unsympathetic to requests for help. My banking career started in the back office, however, and this gives me a certain amount of currency among them. Eventually, Paul gets his tour.

When he returns, however, his mood seems even worse. He takes out his notebook and sits by the window, but he writes nothing, instead just stares balefully out over the river. Then, though it's not even 4 p.m., he gets up and leaves. He doesn't say goodbye.

That evening, the Minister gives a press conference to announce further exceptional liquidity assistance, that is to say, money, for Royal Irish Bank. On the TV screen, he has regained his air of command, though he grips the lectern with both hands, as if anticipating the torrent of fury that will come back at him; sitting on the dais behind him I spot the little sallow man, staring at the Minister as before, like some horror-movie psychic demonstrating mind control.

'I don't get it,' Kevin says.

'You're not the only one.' Since the news came out, the zombies have been beating a drum by the unfinished HQ, with motorists honking their horns in solidarity.

Not long after the announcement, we discover the reason for the Minister's clandestine visit the previous week. He has commissioned BOT to write a special report on Royal Irish Bank.

'Essentially, they are worried that more recapitalization will be needed,' Jurgen says. 'A lot of taxpayers' money has been put into the bank. Now they are getting nervous that the bank's executives have misrepresented its return to health.'

'Fucking right,' Ish says. 'Talk about make-up on a corpse.'

'They don't have advisers already?' I ask.

'Up until last week they were being advised by Gerson Clay,' Jurgen says. 'However, as you are aware, Gerson have gone bust.' He pauses to allow himself a brief moment of gloating. 'I need hardly tell you that this is a highly prestigious commission.'

'Good job, Claude!' Ish ruffles my hair.

'Is it going to be a lot of work?' Kevin says.

'Most of the work'll be deciding how much we can get away

with charging them,' Ish says. 'Poor old Minister, he hasn't got a clue. If we told him to buy a really big mattress and stuff all the country's money in it, he'd go and do it.'

'We will not be advising the government to put the country's money in a mattress,' Jurgen says. 'Rachael is keen that we find a positive angle. A way forward which will produce the most favourable outcomes for the major players.'

News of the government commission, as well as our rival Gerson Clay's demise, buoys the whole office. I have my own reasons to be glad. Royal Irish was the centre of the great Ponzi scheme that was Ireland's property market, with one hand doling out money to the developers who built the apartments, housing estates and mansions, and the other doling it out to the people who wanted to live there, neglecting, at every point, to establish whether anyone was in a position to pay it back. This report, directed right into the heart of the national folly, will surely give Paul what he needs to root his novel.

When the writer arrives at the office next morning, however, he is not alone. A man is with him: a great, hulking creature almost seven foot tall, with a sloping forehead and brawny, knotted forearms that extend from an ill-fitting nylon shirt. Paul introduces him as Igor Struma, poet, professor of contemporary art and member of the celebrated Vladivostok Circle.

'He's going to be helping me with some of the more conceptual stuff,' Paul explains. What exactly this means I am not sure, but for the rest of the day, instead of observing me and my colleagues, the two of them spend their time muttering in secluded corners, or slinking around the office, making inscrutable gestures – knocking on walls, poking at ceiling tiles, tracing with their fingers mysterious vectors from the floor, behind computers, up to the power supply.

I have a bad feeling about this Igor. One cannot say what a poet ought to look like, of course, any more than one can say what a murderer ought to look like – but he definitely looks more like a murderer than a poet. He smells bad in several different ways at once, like curdled milk in a public lavatory, and when I type his name into the search engine, a red VIRUS WARNING!!! sign flashes up immediately on the screen, and a moment later a member of the IT team bursts into the office, demanding to know what I've done.

The others do not seem to share my reservations. Jurgen, on the contrary, is positively ecstatic. '*Two* famous writers! We have almost enough to start the salon!'

'But what is he doing here? Has anyone checked his credentials?'

'Paul asked him to help out with the book,' Ish says. 'You said yourself he was having a few problems. This is a good sign. You don't want him to pull the plug on the whole thing, do you?'

'Of course not. I am just confused. If Paul is writing a book about me and my work here, why is he spending all his time with some poet?'

'This is the artistic process,' Jurgen says, with a shrug. 'Who are we to question it?'

I do not want to obstruct the artistic process, but when I see Igor, under Paul's supervision, making a gun-shape with his thumb and finger and boring an imaginary hole into the wall, it is hard not to think the novel is being dismantled before my very eyes.

Later that day, Paul invites me to the Ark for lunch, with his helpmeet nowhere to be seen. 'I thought I should fill you in a little on Igor's role,' he says, as the waitress guides us to a table. 'You're probably wondering what he's doing here. I'm writing the book, you're the subject, what am I doing bringing a third party into it?'

I make a stock gesture of innocence, as if the thought had never crossed my mind.

'The fact is that while the romantic image is of the writer working away in solitude, it's often much more of a collaborative activity. Every writer has his strengths and weaknesses. It's quite common to draft in a colleague to help out with elements you're less sure about.'

I have heard about such practices in other art forms, but I confess that I had not encountered it in literature before.

'It's kind of a trade secret,' Paul says.

'Can you give me an example?'

'An example . . . well, I suppose the most famous partnership would be J. R. R. Tolkien and Ian Fleming.'

'Really?'

'Oh yes. When Tolkien was putting *Lord of the Rings* together he was great at working out, you know, the ancestral backgrounds of the elves and so forth, but in terms of *plot*, he was hopeless. So he brought in someone who did know about plot: his old friend Ian Fleming, creator of James Bond. The whole magic-ring thing was Fleming's idea. In the original version Tolkien was just going to have the hobbits and the elves reciting poems to each other.'

'I didn't know that,' I say.

'Similarly Tolstoy, when he was writing *War and Peace*, found the Peace parts no problem, but he really got stuck when it came to War. So he got in touch with an up-and-coming young naval officer called Winston Churchill.'

'Winston Churchill co-wrote *War and Peace*?'

'Just little bits here and there. Details. Like I say, writers generally prefer not to talk about it.'

'And what is Igor's specialism?'

'Places. He's a master. Big places, small places, indoors, outdoors. He can do mountain ranges and lakes; he could write a paragraph about a broom cupboard that would have you bawling your eyes out. I suppose you could say he has an intuitive grasp of *structure*.'

'Which you feel has evaded you in the bank,' I say.

'Exactly. It's an unfamiliar environment – to be frank, not one that readily yields up its inner poetry.'

'That's true,' I concede.

'So I thought, okay, time to call in the expert. Given that I have this incredible access – which I am so, so grateful for – I might as well take advantage of it. So Igor's going to be concentrating on the location details. The character stuff, plot, all that will still be me.'

This does make sense. 'And you have known Professor Struma for long?'

'That man taught me everything I know,' he says simply.

'Oh . . .' I say, struggling to conceal my surprise. Perhaps I have misjudged him.

At that moment the door opens; Paul waves and Igor lumbers, creaking, towards us. He takes off his ancient rain mac, releasing a cloud of pungent inner odours, and gives the waitress his order with a dry, smacking mouth; he stares after her as she leaves, like a cat watching a pigeon.

'So I was just telling Claude something about the collaborative process,' Paul says.

'There is nothing wrong with collaborating,' Igor says, rather confrontationally.

'I mean in the book. You're going to help me out with the book.'

'Eh?' Igor says.

'The book,' Paul repeats. 'Set in the bank. The tale of the Everyman.'

'Oh yes, yes,' Igor says. 'Everyman, James Joyce, real life.' His bloodshot eyes swivel over to me. 'You are the Frenchman,' he says. 'Paris.'

'That's right,' I say uncomfortably.

Igor stares at me without speaking, his head weaving ever so slightly from side to side. 'Lately I have watch excellent film about Paris,' he says. 'In this film, three horny guys are going there and diddle many French prostitutes. Title of film is, *Ass Menagerie II: French Connection*. You have seen?'

'No, I don't think so.'

'Is sequel to first *Ass Menagerie*.' He thinks about this, then adds, 'Though story is very similar.' He retreats into a prolonged, cacophonous cough, a sound like shovelling coal.

'So Igor was wondering whether he might be able to see some floor plans of the bank,' Paul says.

'Floor plans?' I say, surprised.

'To help him with his descriptive passages,' Paul says.

I glance over at Igor. He glares back at me with his basilisk eyes. I don't know what to say; then, to my relief, the waitress comes along with his coffee, and he is distracted once again by her departing posterior. 'Very nice,' he comments, and then asks Paul a question I don't quite catch, but which sounds something like, 'Have we got a file on her?'

Paul clears his throat in a way that might or might not be artificial, then says, 'So maybe I should explain a little more about Igor's process –'

'I am sorry,' Igor cuts in, 'I must move seats. I cannot look at this fucking painting any longer.'

With much clattering, he rises and drags his chair to the opposite side of the table, so that his back is to the offending artwork.

'*Simulacrum 18*,' I read from the label. 'Our friend Ariadne Acheiropoietos again.'

'So the way Igor likes to work –' Paul persists.

'Oh, Jesus Christ, this one is even worse!' Igor says, discovering he has moved seats only to find himself staring directly at *Simulacrum 33*.

'Is everything all right?' the waitress asks, hurrying over.

'He's just having a strong reaction to the art,' Paul explains.

'I feel like I have fingers in my brain,' Igor laments, rubbing his eyes.

'Oh,' the waitress says. 'Well, let me know if you need anything.' She beats a retreat to the kitchen.

'So about these floor plans,' Paul says.

But Igor has turned his gaze to me again. 'What does this mean, this *simulacrum*?' he demands. Is he serious? Didn't Paul say he was a professor of contemporary art? Or is he trying to catch me out?

'It is a term from philosophy,' I say reluctantly. 'It means a bad copy or false image of something.'

'Why are they covering the wall with fucking simulacrums, in this place where people are trying to eat?' The reptilian stare bores into me again.

'Ah,' I stammer, 'well, I imagine the artist is making some comment about fakes and counterfeits. Maybe by calling her painting *Simulacrum* she is pointing to some much bigger falseness in the world around us. "Art is the lie that shows us the truth", didn't someone say this? Though I am sure you know more about it than I do.'

For a moment I think I have satisfied him. Slowly he sets down his cup and appears lost in contemplation. Then he leans over the table. 'Are you calling me a liar?' he says, in a low, guttural voice.

And I see he has curled his fingers into a fist.

Back at the bank the situation only gets worse. 'He keeps poking at the ceiling,' Gary McCrum complains. 'Prodding at it with some sort of a rod, right over my head.'

Joe Peston storms over. 'That fucking Russian of yours unplugged my terminal!'

'He's researching a novel,' I tell them both.

Computers are interfered with, files misplaced. Kimberlee approaches me in a state of disquiet to report that she sat down at her computer only to find Igor under her desk, apparently sniffing her seat. 'He is examining the structure,' I say. But the truth is that I have no idea what he is doing. As for Paul, he barely speaks to me; he is too busy lifting furniture, pulling up floor tiles, taking paintings from the walls and staring at the blank pale spaces that are revealed. When I approach him, he snaps at me, or nods without listening. Whatever has eluded him about BOT until now, Igor's appearance hasn't helped find. In the short time he has been here, he has aged visibly.

'It's not your fault,' Ish says. It's the next morning; we are in the canteen with the door closed, eating cereal bars. It feels strange to be hiding from our own narrator. 'It's what Jurgen said. The artistic process. Writing a book is hard. That's all.'

'Maybe a bank isn't the right setting for a novel.'

'Well, he's got to make it the right setting, hasn't he?' Ish says. 'That's his job, not yours.'

'I keep thinking he should've written about Howie. Cocaine, hookers, multimillion-dollar trades.'

'He didn't want that, Claude. He wanted an Everyman.'

'It could be that he has not found the right one.'

82

'You're crazy!' Ish exclaims. 'You're a brilliant Everyman.'

'You think so?'

'Definitely.' She nods. 'I've been watching you, Claude, and you're doing a great job.' She squeezes my hand in hers. 'Just be yourself,' she says. 'Anyone would want to read a book about you.'

I am touched by her words, but it is increasingly clear that my non-life in Dublin has defeated Paul's powers of representation – that there is simply not enough here for his art to gain a foothold. And when I emerge from the canteen, the final blow descends. Liam English, the head of the department, calls me over. 'Look at this,' he says. On the other side of the room, Igor is holding the water cooler steady while Paul balances on top of it, unscrewing the vent over the air conditioning, apparently with the intention of inserting some kind of camera into the interior. I try to make light of it, remarking on the incredible concentration that artists bring to bear on things that we take for granted, such as air vents. 'Wrap it up,' Liam English says.

I wait until Igor is not around, then approach Paul at the desk he has commandeered. He is scribbling in the red notebook, which he now shuts and covers with his hand. 'Yes?' he says.

'Lunchtime,' I say.

He casts about him, looking for an excuse to refuse me, but he can't find one and reluctantly rises from the desk.

I don't know how significant it is that the very same waitress seats us at the very same table where we had our first conversation. It mightn't necessarily mean that we have come full circle. Yet how changed he is from the ebullient, garrulous figure who stepped into my life that day! Now he barely speaks; when our food comes, he merely picks at it.

'You are not happy,' I say.

'What?'

'You are not happy with the project.'

'I'm perfectly happy,' he says. 'I'm deliriously happy.'

'You have not said a word to me all day.'

'Maybe I just don't feel like talking.'

'I don't believe that is why.'

'Oh, you can read my mind now?'

'It's obvious things are not working.'

Paul puts his hands on top of his head and lets out a long, slow, whistling sound. 'I told you, there's a structural issue. We'll figure it out, if you'll just get off my case.'

'My boss wants you to finish your research.'

This at least produces a reaction. He bangs his palms on the table. 'What?'

'He says it's becoming disruptive.'

'That's crazy!' Paul protests. 'Who are we disrupting?'

'Everyone,' I say with a trace of sadistic pleasure, then regret it. He is beyond crestfallen; he looks utterly sick. 'Maybe I can talk to him, win you an extra day or two,' I say. 'But only you. Igor must go.'

'Okay,' he mutters. 'Thanks.'

I watch him for a moment, his thoughts visibly in disarray. 'What happened?' I ask.

Something in him seems to give: he sets down his fork, gazes back at me starkly. 'There's nothing there, Claude,' he says. 'I can't find anything there.'

Now it is my turn to feel sick.

'I knew it wouldn't work,' he reflects. 'Deep down I knew it.'

'There must be something we can do,' I say. 'Some way to salvage it.'

'I don't see what, if your boss is kicking me out,' he says.

'There must be something.'

He sighs, puts his head in his hands. He stays like that for a long time. Then he lifts his head again. 'Unless,' he says.

'Unless what?'

'Unless . . .' He stares at me, studying my face, as if trying to read something there. 'Unless we change the angle,' he says at last.

'Change it?'

'Right now I'm seeing two serious, two very serious problems with the book. The first is that *nothing happens*. There's no story there. In the past a novel didn't always need a story. You could just make it about a day in somebody's life. But that was when life meant people, movement, *activity*. You guys in front of your screens all day long, selling each other little bits of debt – it's a whole different order of nothing. I know there's a big story behind it, I know the bank is expanding and growing and so on, but I can't *see* any of that. It's like a hurricane, you know? It's this incredibly powerful entity, storming all over the world, levelling everything in its path, but at the eye of it, where *you* are, it's just . . . it's just a void. A dead space.'

I nod bleakly; this does not seem an unreasonable assessment.

'And obviously that affects our Everyman,' he says. 'Which is problem two. Readers like to feel a connection with the characters they're reading about. Visit a book club, that's all they talk about. I loved Pip, I adored Daisy, Yossarian is so funny, we all hated Snowball. But with you – there's just not enough showing up on the page.'

'Oh,' I say.

'I know there's more to you than some anonymous salaryman. But from the reader's perspective, it's not so clear. Unless they see some evidence to the contrary, my fear is they'll see a banker and immediately think the worst.'

'Yes,' I say, seething with embarrassment.

'Look,' he says, 'it's not irremediable. We just need to give your character more agency. We need to get him *doing* something.'

'Like what?'

'Something dramatic,' he says. He looks down at his coffee, stirs it but doesn't drink. 'Everybody,' he says slowly, 'even the guy with the most boring job in the world, at some point finds himself in a situation where he has to make a choice. A choice between good and bad. That moment – when the clock strikes thirteen, when everything else drops away – that's where we need to put you.'

Is it me, or as he says this does the air seem to tauten, to take on some tremulous energy? A cloud's shadow rolls over the plaza; the dark-haired waitress stops at the window with her hands on her hips as the pigeons take flight.

'For example,' he says. He strokes his chin. 'Okay, how about this. Rather than the Everyman just *working* in the bank, instead we have him *rob* the bank.'

'Rob the bank?' I repeat.

'That's right,' Paul says, nodding.

'Rob it?' I say again, in case I have misheard.

'Yes, rob it,' Paul says.

'This is Igor's idea?'

'No, it's my idea. You can see where I'm coming from, right? It spices things up, gives the story momentum, as well as making your character a bit more attractive. Now you're an outlaw, sticking it to the man!'

'Yes, yes, I understand that.' I dab my mouth with my napkin in case my expression gives me away. 'But robbing a bank – is this really something that our Everyman would do?'

'Why wouldn't he?' Paul returns. 'Who hasn't thought about robbing a bank?'

'But nobody actually does it,' I say. 'It just doesn't seem realistic.'

'It's not like I'm saying we send him back in time,' Paul says testily. 'He's not breaking the laws of physics or anything.'

'Nevertheless, it takes us far away from the authentic picture of modern life you wanted to create originally,' I point out. 'In fact it turns the story into exactly the kind of cliché you told me you wanted to escape. I am not trying to be negative,' I say, seeing his face darken, 'only, I don't understand what kind of motivation our Everyman can have to do something as non-universal as rob a bank.'

'Well, he'll have motivation,' he says. 'I'm going to give him motivation, if you'd just let me finish.'

'I'm sorry, please continue.'

Paul begins to speak and then stops, staring furiously into his coffee cup.

'Because already the Everyman is paid very well for work that is quite legal,' I clarify. 'So it is difficult to imagine what will make him do something very risky like this.'

'What if he wants something his money can't buy,' Paul says.

'He wants to rob the bank to get something money can't buy?'

Paul swears under his breath. 'Okay, how about – how about he falls in love.'

'In love?'

'Yeah, with a . . . with a waitress. That girl there, for instance.'

We both turn to look. The dark-haired waitress is on the other side of the café, placing dirty crockery on to a tray; her long ebony tresses are tied up in a bun, from which a ballpoint pen pokes.

'See, we need to be making better use of the resources we have. Fictionally speaking, someone like her is pure gold. She's sultry, she's exotic, she's a struggling artist. A woman like that, as soon as she appears the story's bumped up a couple of gears.'

'She's an artist?'

'Well, yeah.' He stares at me as if I am an imbecile, then points around the room at the various *Simulacra*.

'Those are hers?' I look over at the waitress again, then back at him. 'She's Ariadne Acheiropoietos? How do you know?'

'Because I asked her.'

'Oh.' I sit back dizzily.

'See? It's a good twist, isn't it?'

I am thinking of the many uncomplimentary things my colleagues and I have said about her paintings while she was standing right beside us.

'So our lonely, bored, overpaid banker runs up against this

beautiful but impoverished painter,' he goes on, warming to his new theme. 'He finds they have something or other in common – it doesn't matter what it is, French philosophy, say. Next thing he knows, he's fallen head over heels in love with her. He's breaking out of his sterile world of numbers, experiencing feelings he hasn't had in years. But how's he going to win her heart?'

I find I am gripped in spite of myself. 'How?'

Paul spreads his hands summatively. 'By robbing the bank.'

The intrigue dies away again. 'I am not sure I see the connection.'

'You don't think robbing a bank will get her attention?'

'There must be easier ways to do it,' I say. 'What about their shared interest in French philosophy?'

Paul rolls his eyes heavily. 'Jesus, Claude, a woman like that, every dude who comes in here is going to be hitting on her. He needs to bring out the big guns. So how about this? He finds out her father – her father's going to die unless he gets a vital operation. But it's an extremely expensive operation, so expensive that even the banker doesn't have enough money to pay for it. So he robs the bank. I know it sounds unrealistic on the face of it,' he continues, before I can object. 'But in terms of showing his inner life, it's actually *more* realistic, do you see what I mean? She *inspires* him. She's everything he's not. She believes in things, in art, in love, in life! He looks at her, and he sees a chance to begin again!' He's gazing across the room at the waitress, his cheeks flushed, as if it is he, in fact, who's being brought back to life. 'From talking to her – because she's Greek, so we can put in all the stuff about the financial crisis, what it's done to her home and her family – the Everyman begins to become aware of all the injustice he's part of. He's not going to take it any more! He'd rather rob the bank and risk going to prison than see the woman he loves suffer another minute. Suddenly we've got a hero we can get behind!'

He falls silent, poring happily over the empty space of the café as if seeing the story enact itself in front of his eyes, until at last I clear my throat; he looks up, startled, then waves his hand. 'Well, anyway, those are just the broad strokes,' he says. 'The real question,' his voice lowers; resting his elbows on the table he clasps his hands tightly together, as if warding something away, 'is how he robs the bank.'

He looks at me expectantly.

'How?' I repeat.

'If you were in that position, where you wanted to pay for an operation for Ariadne's dying father, what would you do?'

'Probably I would speak to the head of department about an advance on my bonus.'

Paul exhales sharply. 'No, if you were *robbing the bank*, Claude.'

I give the question some thought. 'I don't know.'

'You don't know?'

'If I can be honest, since he decided to rob the bank, I have felt more and more estranged from our Everyman.'

'Claude –' With a murderous expression, Paul lifts his arms above his head, like an orchestra conductor at the thunderous apex of some violent symphony; then he lowers them again and slumps back in his chair, and he says, in a wan, tired voice, 'I'm not going to lie to you. I need this. It's been a long time since *Clown*. I need this book, and this book needs a story, and right now it doesn't have one.'

I blink back at him. I want to help him, but his story no longer makes sense to me.

'It doesn't have to be your character, even,' Paul says with a touch of desperation. 'Say there's a very wicked banker in there. That guy, what's his name, the arsehole from the bar, he wants to rob the bank. What does he do?' He is pale now, and his voice has a dry, prickly quality, like a fabric charged with static electricity. 'I suppose what I'm asking you is, where's the safe in this place?'

'The safe?'

'The safe.' His eyes are locked on mine; his fingertips bounce up and down on the tabletop.

'Well, there is no safe,' I say.

'What?' He puts his hand to his ear, as if he were a long way away.

'There is no safe,' I repeat, louder.

'There's no safe?'

'No,' I say.

Paul stares at me for a long moment. Then he glances over his shoulder to the table by the window where Jurgen has just sat down with one of the senior managers. 'I get it,' he smiles, giving me a wink. 'Classified information. Okay, put it this way, then: Where isn't the safe?'

This ontological riddle throws me. I contemplate it for a long time, before replying slowly, 'Well, I suppose it isn't everywhere.'

Paul stops smiling and kneads his brow. 'Look, when I ask where isn't the safe, I mean where is the safe. When you say there is no safe, what is it exactly that you mean?'

'I mean there is no safe,' I say.

He exhales a long, thin breath, his body at the same time seeming to drift a little to the side. 'So where,' he says softly, 'do you keep the money?'

'There is no money,' I say.

'There is no money,' Paul repeats, nodding. And then, 'What kind of bank has no money?'

'A merchant or investment bank,' I say.

Paul goes very quiet. He lifts his coffee cup to his mouth, but his hand is trembling so hard that he lowers it again without it reaching his lips. 'Oh,' he says.

'You must remember that unlike a high-street bank, an investment bank does not take deposits from customers. Instead we fund our operations primarily with short-term or even overnight borrowings.'

'Right,' Paul whispers.

'Of course, we don't like to talk about this, because it means that we're a lot less secure than we pretend. In fact we are all just twenty-four hours away from a funding crisis! This is investment banking's "dirty little secret"!'

'Ha ha,' Paul's laughter is low and hoarse, as if he had a rope around his neck. 'So now the question we have to ask ourselves is, given that it's an investment bank, with no money on the premises, how is he going to rob it?' He looks at me with eyes half-dazed and half-desperate. 'That's the question we have to ask, isn't it?'

I chew on my knuckles thoughtfully. 'I fear it will be difficult for our Everyman,' I say.

'It will?'

'Very difficult.'

'Right,' Paul says. For a long moment he doesn't say anything else or even look at me; he merely sits in his chair, twitching.

'But there are other ways for you to spice up the story,' I say, realizing that I have made him even more discouraged than he was already. 'For example, maybe there is a fire in Transaction House, and I am the Bank of Torabundo fire warden, so I must make sure everyone escapes.'

'That's a good idea,' Paul agrees, rising unsteadily to his feet. 'A very good idea.'

'Or we could keep the love story with the waitress and the French philosophy, but leave out the robbery.'

'Yes,' Paul says. 'That's worth looking at.'

'And meanwhile my character is dealing with the ongoing crisis in the eurozone – nobody knows how much the currency will depreciate, it is a very tense situation –'

'Yes, there's certainly a lot to think about,' Paul interrupts in the oddly wispy voice into which he has lapsed. I have the strange impression there is less of him, as if over the course of the lunch little pieces of him have been stolen away, like twigs taken by birds as they build their nest, one by one by one . . . 'Sounds like

I'd better get back to the drawing board! Tell you what, I'm going to take the rest of the afternoon off to think about these suggestions of yours.'

'Frankly, I think the book will be much better this way,' I say. 'The bank robbery idea was perhaps a little *de trop*, like we say in French.'

'It probably was,' he says. 'I don't know what I was thinking. Well – see you tomorrow.'

'See you tomorrow,' I say.

But Paul does not come in tomorrow; nor does he appear the next day. The weekend goes by without word from him; Monday morning turns into Monday afternoon and still there is no sign.

'Maybe he has writer's block,' Kevin says.

'Maybe his muse has deserted him,' Jurgen says. 'This is what happened to Gerhardt, the leader of my reggae band, Gerhardt and the Mergers. After his receptionist transferred to head office in Frankfurt he did not write a single song.'

'I am his muse,' I point out. 'I have not deserted him. I am waiting for him right here.'

'Yes, it is perhaps the less familiar situation of the artist deserting his muse,' Jurgen says, frowning.

'I wouldn't worry about it, Claude,' Ish says. 'Didn't you say he was doing plot changes?'

'He was trying to think up new directions for the book.'

'There you go then,' she says. 'These things take their own time. You can't push the river, that's what my Uncle Nick always tells the people in the dole office.'

In fact, Ish is almost as eager to see Paul herself, in order to share a discovery she has made about the island of Torabundo. 'Today it's basically the Financial Services Centre, only on a beach and with bigger spiders – but it used to be part of this really famous kula ring.' She looks at our blank faces. 'The gift economy? Malinowski, Marcel Mauss, all that?'

'Are you having an acid flashback?' Kevin says.

'Gift economies are how everything worked before we had markets,' she explains. 'Instead of buying things from each other, people would just give each other what they needed. You give me a calabash of milk, I give you a shell adze, you pass the adze on to my cousin, I share the milk with your grandmother, and so on, and so on.'

'You are talking about barter,' Jurgen says. 'The system that existed before money was invented and people no longer had to carry around adzes looking for someone to swap them with.'

'Not barter. They didn't exchange things. They gave things. Whenever anthropologists travelled to places where people still lived like that – without markets, I mean – instead of barter they found these gift circles. And one of the most famous examples was this island about a hundred miles from Torabundo, called Kokomoko. I actually went there with Tog a few years back, after we studied it in uni. A French anthropologist wrote a book about it. What she found was that people on Kokomoko didn't hold on to anything. No one *owned* anything. Instead everything just cycled around constantly. Small things, like tools and food and clothes, but big things too. Kokomoko was famous for these beautiful necklaces, for instance, and they'd give them to the tribes on the neighbouring islands. Like, they'd sail over to Torabundo and there'd be a gifting ceremony with a big feast. But the Torabundans wouldn't keep them, they'd sail on to the next island a few months later and pass the necklaces along to the tribe there. And that tribe would pass them on again, to the next island. And meanwhile there were other gifts from other tribes – cowries or arrowheads or whatever it might be – going from island to island in the opposite direction. That's the kula ring. All of these islands, hundreds of miles apart, brought together by gifts.'

'What was the point of that?' Kevin says.

'What was the point of what?'

'Of just randomly giving each other things for no reason.'

'Well, why do you buy a round of drinks in the pub?' Ish says. 'Why doesn't everyone go up and buy their own drink?'

'I have often wondered this very same thing,' Jurgen says.

94

'Financially speaking, the Irish mania for "rounds" makes no sense. Particularly if I am drinking a relatively inexpensive Pilsner lager, and I must be forking out for someone else's costly whiskey and Coke. Even if they then buy me a beer, I still incur a net loss.'

'Yeah, but that's the point,' Ish says.

'That I incur a net loss?'

'If I buy something from you, you hand it over and we both walk away and that's the end of our relationship. That's the market economy in a nutshell. But if I *give* you something, even if it's just a drink that I know you're going to get me back, then there's a bond created between us that carries on into the future. Like, a social bond. So on these islands, gifts were a way of tying everybody together, like the different families, the different tribes, and so on. Not just them either, but the dead and the living too, because they believed that when you give a gift, a part of your soul goes with it, and joins with whoever else's soul that gave it before. And at these feasts they'd recite the histories of the arm shells or the necklaces or the cowries or whatever it might be, and the stories of their ancestors who were still present in these magical objects. So instead of just walking out of the shop, they stayed connected, over generations.'

'What if you didn't want to stay connected?' Kevin says.

'Why wouldn't you want to be connected?'

'Because you don't feel like handing over all your stuff.'

'Look, say you're living on an island in the Pacific, and your next-door neighbour needs an awl to tool some leather, and you've got an awl, you're not going to keep it from him, are you? Because you know some time down the line you'll need something from him, like food or a knife or a pair of shoes. Or just a friendly word, someone to look in on you if you're sick. You know it's important to preserve that relationship, in short.'

'I'd just tell him to go to the awl shop and get his own,' Kevin says.

'Right, and for the rest of your life you wouldn't talk to anyone around you and you'd just curl up every night alone with your awl, would you?'

'I'd have a really good one,' Kevin says.

'I think what Kevin is saying,' I interject, 'is that we can see what they are trying to do with these networks of exchange. But they do seem to introduce a lot of unnecessary complication.'

'Claude, we're working in, like, the epicentre of unnecessary complication.' She waves a hand at the glass towers, their thirty thousand inhabitants. 'And what's it all for?'

'It is precisely to ensure that moneyed individuals can continue to stockpile wealth in peace,' Jurgen says. 'Without constantly being interrupted by neighbours and similar nuisances looking for awls and other goods.'

'I wish you could see this place,' Ish says wistfully. 'Then it'd all make sense to you.' She looks out the window, and for a moment her face takes on a radiance quite different from the cold grey early-morning light lifting in from the river. 'Anyway the point is Torabundo dropped out of the kula ring to be an offshore tax haven, so now you've got the gift economy and its absolute dia- metrical opposite side by side. That's bound to be something Paul can use, right? Like he could contrast the simple tribal island ways on Kokomoko with our miserable complex affluent ways. That sort of thing.'

Is that the kind of spicing up he meant? I keep coming back to our conversation in the café. At the time it made me angry (he spends weeks poring over my life, then tells me there's nothing there?) but I'm starting to see the problem from his point of view. He wants to give an honest account of life in the International Financial Services Centre; but he also has a duty to frame some sort of a narrative, to tell a story with a beginning, middle and end. In a way, we face a similar dilemma with our clients. On the one hand, we commit to giving them an accurate account of what's happening in the market. On the other, we know that an accurate account is too complicated to be of any use to them. And so instead we tell stories: turn companies into characters, quarterly reports into events, the chaos of global business into a few simple fables ending with a buy or sell recommendation which, if followed, will hopefully result in a profit. The truth is fine in principle, but stories are what sell.

The robbery is unfeasible on any number of levels (although he is not the first to suggest it: my father had often proposed a bank heist, though he also suggested I go in with a machine gun and 'just shoot everyone'.) But the love story? On its own that would show the banker's rich inner life, without requiring any major changes to the rest of the plot. Waiting for a client one morning, I watch Ariadne from behind a menu and weigh her up. Her limbs are long, her movements, as she glides down the narrow aisles of the restaurant, fluid and graceful; she carries herself with a sort of gladiatorial kindness, smiling implacably at all comers. And her eyes: from her complexion, I expect them to be brown, but instead they are a startlingly vivid green, like a storm-lit sea, restive and electric. They continue to wrongfoot me every time I catch a glimpse of them – until she notices me staring, and smiles, and I blush and pretend I wanted to order another coffee.

Then something happens that puts the book out of everyone's mind. A little after midday – 7.05 a.m., New York time – Ish jumps out of her seat. 'I just got an email from Porter Blankly!'

A moment later, similar exclamations can be heard about the room. I look at my inbox. 'I've got one too.'

Kevin comes rushing up. 'Porter Blankly's sent us all emails,' he says.

'It must be one of his inspirational memos,' Gary McCrum says.

'Fuck!' Ish says.

'Have you read it yet?' Kevin asks.

'I'm too excited,' Ish says. 'Claude, you open it.'

Tentatively, as if handling a live wire, I move the cursor over the envelope icon and click on it. The email consists of two words. ' "Think counterintuitive," ' I read aloud.

' "Think counterintuitive," ' Ish says.

' "Think counterintuitive," ' Kevin mutters to himself.

Around the office the phrase can be heard repeated over and over, like a murmurous breeze circulating between the cubicles.

'Is that inspirational?' Ish asks. 'Do you feel inspired?'

'I definitely feel *something*,' Kevin says, frowning and assuming an odd posture, as though searching for his keys. Before there can be any further discussion, however, Jurgen appears to tell us that a very important email has just come in from Porter Blankly.

'We know,' Ish says.

'Good,' Jurgen says. 'Rachael has been in touch to say that each department must submit one major counterintuitive strategy by the end of the week. Until further notice, counterintuitiveness should be considered your top priority.' He is on the point of bustling off again, but Ish calls him back.

'What does it mean?' she says.

Jurgen pushes his glasses up his nose, surprised. 'I have received only the same memo as you, but I am guessing it means that instead of bowing to the prevailing wisdom and following the herd, we will now be innovating exciting new outside-the-box-type alternatives.'

'Oh,' says Ish.

'How counterintuitive does he want us to be, exactly?' Jocelyn Lockhart asks.

'How counterintuitive?' Jurgen says.

'Well, say if my intuition is telling me it would be a bad idea to punch you in the face. Does that mean I *should* punch you in the face?'

'Or set fire to the computers?' Gary McCrum chips in.

'Or stop working now and go to the pub? You know?'

Jurgen strokes his chin thoughtfully. 'These are good questions. Porter has not specified his parameters. Perhaps we should limit the counterintuitiveness to our respective fields for now, and later, if we find we are still bogged down in conventional, mainstream thinking, we can experiment with more radical options, such as face-punching.'

Initially the response to the new imperative is not entirely serious: free pizza is mooted, paid naptime, daily meetings before the markets open in order to study staff dreams for potentially important data. A couple of days later, however, the strategy becomes less abstract. That morning, Kimberlee the receptionist comes hurtling into the Research Department to tell us that a tramp is asleep in the supply cupboard. She wants to call security; the analysts, however, see an opportunity to demonstrate their machismo, and an Armed Response Unit is quickly put together in the shape of the Oil team leader, Brent 'Crude' Kelleher, and his mountain-biking cronies, Andrew O'Connor and Dwayne McGuckian. 'How are you "armed"?' Ish asks. In unison, the Armed Response Unit roll up their sleeves and begin copious flexing of biceps.

Not long after, though, they hurry back in, looking decidedly less intrepid. There *is* a tramp on the premises, they confirm; however, he is no longer asleep, or, for that matter, in the supply cupboard. A moment later, with a guttural roar, a ragged figure lurches in. He is tall and spindly, with blazing eyes and a voluminous thicket of black beard that gives him the look of a medieval mendicant, flagellating himself around Europe. Long streamers of duct tape hang from his shoulders; I can't understand what he's saying, but it is clear that he is very, very angry. He charges down the aisle between the cubicles in pursuit of the Armed Response Unit, who career out of Research into Sales; a moment later they reappear in the lobby, frantically jabbing the button for the lift, when its doors open and two enormous security guards jump out and dash after the tramp, who turns and speeds back towards his supply cupboard. Too late! We watch from our cubicles as the guards rugby-tackle him, bringing him crashing to the ground; then one of them springs up to kneel on his back, while the other one prepares to hit him with his baton. The tramp howls out some kind of unintelligible imprecation – and the guard stops, baton frozen in the air.

'*Deystvitelno?*' he says.

The tramp issues another screed.

The security guard climbs off his back and says something apologetic. Now the tramp rises to his feet and straightens himself. The first security guard says something to the second security guard. Then both the security guards start obsequiously dusting down the tramp, who stares away into the middle distance with an imperial hauteur. Through the glass of the lobby we see Liam English coming in our direction, fists clenched by his side; the Armed Response Unit follow after him, looking chastened. Liam English dispatches the security guards with a single jab of his thumb. Then he embraces the tramp.

BOT has a new employee. Grigory Erofeev, or Grisha as he prefers to be called, although he makes it clear that ideally no one would speak to him at all, has been flown in directly from Moscow's Institute of Advanced Mathematics to head our new Structured Products Department, where he will come up with mind-bending combinations of currencies, futures, swaptions and other such entities, which the bank can sell on to clients and use on its own account.

This constitutes a major change in BOT's direction.

Before the crash, every bank had to have at least one Russian physicist on its payroll. The bulge brackets would go on safari to St Petersburg and return with whole university departments, setting them up in grim dorms to remind them of home, where they would sit gloomily eating pirogi and scrawling in refill pads.

Sir Colin, our former CEO, saw this, as he saw so much of the twenty-first, twentieth and indeed nineteenth century, as so much modern flim-flam. He didn't believe investment banks ought to be trading for themselves at all – how could that not lead to a conflict of interest? – and the idea of betting the house on equations which nobody in the entire operation understood except for some depressed-looking Vlad in a pirogi-stained vest he thought simply unhinged.

'But that's what makes it counterintuitive, see?' Howie is particularly excited by the new arrival. 'Nobody's doing this stuff right now.'

'They're not doing it because it didn't work,' I point out.

'Crazy Frog, you think the first aeroplane worked? You think the first telephone worked? The first shot of penicillin –'

'I get the point.'

'This guy is a visionary, Claude. He's out there, out in the fucking Siberian tundra, staring at the fucking sun and seeing – seeing –'

'Seeing what?'

'Seeing the shit that's going to take us to the next level.' Howie leans closer, lowers his voice. 'He's been telling me about his PhD. Providential antinomies. Ever heard of them? Of course you haven't, they haven't been used for three hundred years. But guess what, Grisha here's discovered some way of applying them to bond yields.'

'To do what?'

Howie flaps his hand in irritation. '*I* don't know. What they do isn't the point. The point is that this time *we're* the ones doing the crazy paradoxical rocket-science shit. This tiny, insignificant little bank has, through a fluke of history, got a split-second start on the big boys. That's what Porter's counterintuitive strategy's about, see? If we wait for them to grow their balls back, they'll wipe us out. But if we take advantage of that head start, and do all the things that right now they're afraid to do – who knows how far we can go?'

Grisha has been given his own office, a small, cramped box room behind the Sales Department with just a desk and a whiteboard – no TV, no Bloomberg, not even a phone. He doesn't seem to mind; he spends most of his time out on the plaza, apparently talking to the pigeons.

'Look at that,' Howie says approvingly, gazing down from the window. 'Mad as a nail. How can he *not* make us a fortune?'

Porter's memo coincides with a golden streak for the bank such as I have never experienced before. Every call we make, every pitch, every trade, every merger, buyout, bond issue, comes off as smoothly as a case study in an economics textbook. Europe teeters ever closer to the brink of some unimaginable financial apocalypse, whole streets in Greece burn, and here the zombies by the riverside grow in number as the Royal Irish recapitalization, as predicted, fails completely, the fresh infusion stripped away by international speculators – but our share price leaps up, and up again; the whole world is long BOT.

Yet to me these successes seem somehow insubstantial. Without Paul there, everything has begun to slide out of focus; and the longer he is gone, the worse it gets. Figures blur on the screen, clients' voices merge into one another. I'm waylaid by memories, things I haven't thought about in years, a game of tarot in my aunt's kitchen, my mother taking my hand as we cross the Pont des Arts.

Perhaps it's to combat this that I find myself returning again and again to the Ark to watch Ariadne dance her *pas de seul* between the tables. How alive she is, how embedded in her day! Even when she's daydreaming, standing still, she seems to throw off energy, invisible waves that ripple outwards to catch up the people around her. Will she catch me up too? If the two strands of our story come together, might the writer come back in order to tie the knot?

'Doing some reading?'

'What? Oh – yes – beginning the Royal Irish accounts.'

'But this is not accounts.' Jurgen fishes out the book stuffed under the stack of ledgers. '*De Part et d'Autre*, François Texier. Another novel?'

'Philosophy,' I say gruffly, cheeks crimsoning. 'It's . . . I thought it would be useful, for something I am planning to do.'

'Very good,' Jurgen says. But he does not leave; instead he parks himself upon the adjoining desk, gazes out for a moment at the rain and then says, 'You know, Claude, an artist is not like a banker.'

I open a folder, highlight a raft of redundant files.

'It is in an artist's nature to be mercurial,' Jurgen continues. 'Do you know this word, "mercurial"? It means prone to rapid and unexpected change, as liquid mercury is in the barometer.'

'I am familiar with it,' I say. The files yield up pale blue, translucent images of themselves, as if I am extracting their ghosts and transporting them to some electronic afterlife.

'It is a good word,' Jurgen says. 'Mer-cur-i-al. It is what Stacy calls Bobo the clown in Paul's book – have you reached this part, where Stacy breaks up with Bobo?'

'Of course,' I mutter.

'Bobo, as a clown, is constantly searching for new jokes and new sensations. Stacy, as a health and safety officer, wants order and regularity. Their two lifestyles are completely different. This is why she terminates their relationship.'

'She does that in Chapter 5,' I object. 'But then at the end she realizes she's still in love with him.'

'I stopped reading after Chapter 5,' Jurgen says. He broods over his folded arms for a moment. The recycling bin flashes indigo as the files are subsumed and resurrected as empty space. 'I suppose the thing to remember is that it is only a book,' he says, getting up. 'Not real life.'

On Tuesday morning, my team has a meeting with Cornerstone, one of several American private equity firms currently occupying the city's five-star hotels. The market believes Ireland will soon go the same way as Greece: bankruptcy, riots, decades of national bondage. Value investors like Cornerstone are gambling the opposite. Operating on the principle that the moment of maximum pessimism is the best time to buy, they sift through the wreckage of Irish society, checking out shopping malls, stud farms, golf courses, whole estates of houses, businesses that can't stay afloat and, of course, the loan books of faltering Irish banks.

We meet them at the hotel. There are three of them, tanned, sockless, in open-necked shirts and Patek Philippe watches, exuding an air of amused, joshing serenity. I do a surreptitious check for any giveaway tattoos. Many American bankers are ex-military – bland-faced, blue-eyed, faultlessly courteous men who went directly from their tour of Iraq or Afghanistan to MBAs in Wharton and Harvard. Indeed, the head of Cornerstone, General John Perseus, was one of the top commanders of the original invasion of Iraq; I suppose when you have seen an entire country being shelled to oblivion, holding your nerve during a bear run on the stock market does not present a major challenge.

Cornerstone are interested in Royal Irish. That they have chosen to consult us about them is quite a feather in our cap. This morning, though, I cannot get the pitch straight in my head. 'Excuse me – let me just, ah . . .' I awaken my laptop screen, squint at the spreadsheet. Numbers swim between the columns, decimal points dancing about like fleas. 'Ah . . .'

The three private equity bros gaze at me amusedly, serenely, hands draped loosely between their legs in the enormous leather armchairs.

'Of course, the pertinent data has already been set out for you in the accompanying file,' Jurgen says, stepping in. 'If you will turn to page four . . .'

'Fail to prepare, prepare to fail,' Kevin says philosophically as we are leaving.

'What are you on about, pipsqueak? Claude had them eating out of his hand,' Ish says.

Jurgen does not say anything, but when our car pulls up at the IFSC he waits for the others to climb out and then turns to me. 'You know that as a managerial policy I do not believe in issuing threats or warnings,' he says.

'Yes,' I say guiltily.

But there is no more; with that he gets out of the car, closing the door in my face.

'Maybe you need someone observing you,' Ish hypothesizes. 'You know, like electrons.'

'Electrons?'

'What's that thing about electrons? You know, that unless someone's there looking at them they don't stay in the one spot? Instead they're just sort of spread out all over the place?'

'I have been working as an analyst for years without anyone observing me,' I say.

'Maybe you didn't know you were an electron.'

'I'm not an electron,' I say.

It is late; we are among the last ones left in the office. Outside, arrayed in the darkness, the buildings with their sparse panes of light look like monolithic dominoes waiting to fall.

'You've tried calling him?'

'Hundreds of times.'

Ish tocks a pencil against her teeth. 'I wonder what happened,' she says.

'It is obvious what happened,' I snap. 'He realized the novel wasn't going to work.'

'Why wouldn't it work?'

'Why?' I can't contain my anger any longer. 'Because what we do is – empty! Meaningless! No one in the world could find it interesting, unless they were being paid!'

'You don't *know* that's what happened. Wouldn't he have said something, if he was just going to drop the whole thing? Like, why would he just disappear?'

I limit myself to another glower, push my brain to engage with the wall of numbers on the screen.

'Those new directions you said he was thinking about,' Ish says. 'What were they, exactly?'

'What were they?' I repeat.

'Like, maybe there's a clue there. To what might have happened to him.'

She gazes at me ingenuously. I have a momentary vision of Ariadne stepping towards me, cupping my face in her hands, bringing her lips to mine, and experience a brief stab of pain.

'He didn't have anything concrete,' I say.

She falls silent again. On her desk sits an ever-growing mountain of papers she's waiting to show to the writer – articles about her gift-island, photocopies from textbooks, Polaroids of her younger self, skinny, smudged, beaming, with her arm around various stocky topless tribespeople – like ingredients for a spell, as if she believes he might be able to summon her up out of her own past.

'Could it be,' she says at last, 'he wants you to find him?'

'I told you, he does not answer his phone.'

'No, I mean, track him down. You said he was thinking up new directions for the book. Maybe this is it. This is what happens.'

'The writer is in the book?'

'Yeah, and the banker has to help him. Like in that film, you know, with that guy.'

Find him: for some reason, the idea has never occurred to me before, as if the traffic between his life and mine could only ever be one way. It has, I must admit, a certain resonance. But how would we find him? He projected himself into our world without betraying any hint of his own, in spite of our best efforts.

'Maybe there's a clue in here.' Diving into her bag, she pulls out *For Love of a Clown* and starts flicking through it. 'Does he mention any neighbourhoods? Can you remember?'

I frown. Mostly the clown is travelling around in a caravan, or pitched up in a field with the rest of the circus, though there is a memorable scene near the end, when the clown comes to Stacy's house and honks his nose outside her window –

'Wait a minute,' Ish says, opening the book up again to the very first pages. 'Of course there's a clue in it. Look, the publisher's address is right here. Asterisk Press, Cromwell Road, London. They'll know where he is.'

Genius! I seize the phone there and then, but Ish reminds me that it's the middle of the night. 'Right, right,' I agree, setting it down again but remaining on my feet, full of nervous energy. I look at Ish, swivelling gently in her chair. 'Well. I suppose we should go home.'

'I suppose so,' Ish agrees.

'Thank you for helping,' I say.

'I'm in the book too, don't forget,' she says. 'I want to find out what happens.'

That night sees the worst riots yet in Athens. While the new Greek government huddles inside the Old Royal Palace, Zegna Square is alight. Cars burn like pagan fires, gunshots streak through the black sky; masked protestors and masked police come together with a thunderclap that can be felt in the chest even thousands of miles away. Next morning, I have nervous clients on the line as soon as I turn on my phone, and at 10 a.m. I see Walter's limousine pull up outside. Nobody from his office calls me; they just assume I will know he is there, which, to my embarrassment, I do.

In the back seat, Walter is livid. What are those gobshites doing over there? Will their fucking shambles of a government last the week? If it falls, and Greece tells its creditors to go to fuck, what then? I tell him that his investments have been spread across a wide portfolio precisely to protect them from this kind of shock, and that in fact Dublex will most likely benefit from the increased volatility in terms of security contracts. It's the same speech I gave him a few weeks ago when the Spanish banks teetered, and a few weeks before that when it was Portugal on the brink. Every time his fears are harder to dislodge, as if he can see the flaming torches massed outside his house.

'I don't see what he's so worried about,' Kevin comments when I return. 'It's not like he's going to run out of money, whatever happens.'

'The more you have, the greater your fears of losing it,' Jocelyn Lockhart says. 'Classic human psychology.'

'In Somalia, you worry about an empty rice bowl,' Gary McCrum concurs. 'In the suburbs, you worry about burglars running off with your flat-screen TV. But if you're a billionaire – what would it take for a billionaire to lose everything?'

'I don't know,' Kevin says.

'Well, Walter fucking knows. I guarantee you, Walter lies awake every night, conjuring up whatever kind of Boschian nightmare you'd need to make any serious dent in his fortune. Defaulting Greeks are just one pixel of the fucking IMAX screen of unrelenting carnage that's the inside of that man's head.'

'That's why serious players never quit while they're ahead,' Jocelyn says. 'They're always rushing off to make more billions to protect the billions they have already. Looking for that little bit more that'll make them bulletproof. But then that's just more for them to worry about. It's a vicious circle, see?'

'So . . .' Kevin looks deeply troubled by this information. 'Are you saying . . . they shouldn't bother? They'd be better off not being rich?'

'No, I'm saying they need to tighten their focus,' Jocelyn says. 'If you're worried about the apocalypse, you want to be investing in two things and two things only: weapons and gold. And by gold I mean actual bullion you can hold in your hand, not some certificate. Then, when it all goes tits up, you're ready. Fortress in the Swiss Alps with an underground generator and its own water supply, maybe three hundred mercenaries to take out any fammos who come looking to get in – sorted.'

' "Fammos"?'

'Yeah, from the famine, you know.'

'An island would be better,' Gary McCrum asserts. 'With a self-sustaining farm.'

'Oh, yeah, an island's the ideal,' Jocelyn says. 'Though you're probably going to have to cut back on your mercenaries a bit.'

'Or get robot mercenaries?' Kevin says.

'Nice,' Jocelyn says. 'You should say that to Walter. He'd be well impressed.'

'You think?' Kevin says.

'Might even sign you up for a place in the fortress,' Jocelyn says. 'You could look out the window and watch us all burn.'

Kevin beams, as though he would like this very much indeed.

At last a quiet moment presents itself. I use my mobile so the bank won't record the call; the line is poor, and the girl who answers doesn't seem to know anything about Paul. 'You published his novel,' I tell her. '*For Love of a Clown*, surely you know it?'

The girl tells me, rather peevishly, that it must have been before her time, then puts me on hold. A moment later a second voice, a man's, comes on the line. He introduces himself as Paul's editor. Warily, as if he suspects some kind of scam, he tells me that while Asterisk Press did indeed publish Paul's first novel, they have had no contact with him for some time.

'Really?' This strikes me as strange. 'He has not been in touch regarding his new book, the story of an Everyman working in a mid-tier investment bank?'

'No,' the editor replies. 'We haven't heard anything from him at all.'

'Hmm,' I say, and then, 'perhaps you have an address where I can contact him?'

'Sorry,' he says. 'We can't give that information out to strangers.'

'Yes, but I am not really a stranger,' I explain. 'You see, I am the Everyman whose adventures will appear in his next novel.'

He apologizes again, invites me to leave a message which he can pass on, though he adds that Paul has not replied to any correspondence for several years, so they don't know even if the address they have is the right one.

A series of phone calls to literary magazines and institutions in Dublin proves scarcely more informative; of the few people who remember him, one insists that he is dead, and refuses to be persuaded otherwise even when I tell him I recently had lunch with him. Nevertheless, a picture begins to emerge. One acquaintance makes reference to the writer's disappointment over the reception of *Clown*; several speak about a hostile review in the national press.

Once I retrieve this review, which is hidden behind a paywall, his retreat from the literary world becomes considerably less of a mystery.

' "How can something so trivial feel so exhausting? Reading this deeply unfunny, unintentionally depressing book, one might be tempted to conclude that the novel, like the circus, has simply had its day, and that novelists have come to inhabit the same territory as the clown chosen here as protagonist – once-beloved figures so outmoded that they now inspire only pity and incomprehension." '

'Fucking hell,' Ish says.

' "Yet this book comes on the heels of Bimal Banerjee's masterful *The Clowns of Sorrow*, in which the obsolescence of these forgotten jokers gives them a tragic grandeur, confronting us with the unbreachable gulf between ourselves and the past . . ." '

I fall silent, skimming down the page. Ish nudges me. 'What else?'

'There is a lot of stuff here about Banerjee continuing Joyce's great hermeneutic project.'

'What about Paul?'

Frowning, I read down to the last paragraph. 'She thinks he should not write any more novels.'

'Right, I got that.'

And it seems that, for many years, he took her advice. I think back to that first conversation, the 'wall' he said he'd hit with his work; now it appears in quite a different light. Yet these discoveries have brought him no closer, and we must resort to desperate measures.

'What the fuck is that thing?' Kevin says.

'Telephone directory,' I say.

'Landlines?' Kevin says. 'Who still has a landline?'

'I keep a landline for when I need to find my mobile,' Jocelyn says.

'We've got a maid to do that,' Gary says.

There are ten men listed who have the same name as the writer. Whenever Jurgen isn't within earshot, I go through them one by one. Over the course of the evening, I manage to make contact with a butcher, an upholsterer, a sound engineer, a data miner, and a retired army captain who served with the United Nations in the Biafran War. They know nothing about my Paul, yet I can't shake the sense of them as facets of a crystal, different aspects of the same entity – the men he might have become in different circumstances, at a different time, with different choices.

As I put down the phone for the last time, I have one of those dizzy moments, the vertigo that comes when just for an instant you get an inkling of how vast the world is, how populous and unknowable . . . Then it recedes again and is gone.

'What about that number there?' Ish points to an uncrossed name at the top of the list.

'It's disconnected.'

'That doesn't mean there's no one there. Think about it. If this was a book, where would the person you were looking for turn out to be? It's always the place with the disconnected phone, right?'

She keeps prodding me until I look the address up. It turns out that 323 Superbia is only ten minutes' walk from the Centre, and so, mostly to mollify her, I agree to pay it a visit.

'When?' she says.

'Soon,' I promise.

'I can't wait that long! The suspense is killing me!'

'All right, all right.'

Taking the lift down to the plaza, I follow the tram tracks in the direction of the train station until I pass out of the Centre. And here, on the teeming road, are the Irish: blanched, pocked, pitted, sleep-deprived, burnished, beaming, snaggle-toothed, bald-ing, rouged, raddled, beaky, exophthalmic; the Irish, with their demon priests, their cellulite, their bus queues and beer bellies, their foreign football teams, betting slips, smartphones and online deals, their dyed hair, white jeans, colossal mortgages, miraculous medals, ill-fitting suits, enormous televisions, sto-ical laughter, wavering camaraderie, their flinty austerity and seeping corruption, their narrow minds and broad hearts, their drunken speeches, drunken fights, drunken weddings, drunken sex, their books, saints, tickets to Australia, their building-site countryside, their radioactive sea, their crisps, bars, Lucozade, their tattoos, their overpriced wine and mediocre restaurants, their dreams, their children, their mistakes, their punchbag his-tory, their bankrupt state and their inveterate difference. Every face is a compendium of singularities, unadulterated by the smooth-ing toxins of wealth and privilege; to walk among them is to be plunged into a sea of stories, a human comedy so rich it seems on the point of writing itself. For a moment I wonder, hopelessly, what the International Financial Services Centre can offer to compare – then I remember that this was his very point, that the storyless, faceless banks are the underwriters of all this humanity, that we are the Fates who weave the fabric of the day . . .

Coming from the Centre, with its clean lines and ubiquitous dress code, the chaos of detail is almost overwhelming; I take ref-uge in the map on my phone. It takes me off the thoroughfare and into a warren of flats and terraced houses. There are no cars, no people, just boarded-up windows, incoherent graffiti, detritus so random it seems deliberate. The further I go, the worse it gets, till the very molecules of the air and brickwork seem on the point of fraying, drifting apart to leave yawning rents of pure nothing-ness. And then, in the midst of this desolation, I come upon a large, glittering tower.

To say it appears out of place would be an understatement. It looks like a five-star hotel that has been stolen from some exclusive neighbourhood of Shanghai or Los Angeles and then dumped here. Gilt filigree gleams from the railings of the balconies; mosaics twinkle on the dark stone of the façade; a majestic eagle peers down from the distant rooftop. From one side of the building hangs an enormous hoarding. Beneath the marks of rain and dust, it shows in black and white two willowy girls with kohl-ringed eyes, gazing hungrily over basketball-sized wine glasses at a smirking young man in very tight jeans who has hoisted himself up to sit on the kitchen counter, car keys flung in some obscure invitation on to the table in front of him. All three figures balance sunglasses in their hair, as if life could, at any moment, become too radiant to behold. The strapline below them reads, *SUPERBIA: ENTER BEAUTY.*

The entrance door to the lobby is flanked by two stone effigies, one of which holds an intercom. There is no response from 323, or indeed anything to indicate the intercom is working. Impulsively, I try the door – and it gives way.

The lobby is full of silence and dust. Nymphs bathe in dust in an ornate fountain; dust cloaks the tall mirrors along the walls. Gaps have appeared in the Moorish tiling, and the nameplates of the metal letterboxes are empty.

The lift is not working so I mount the stairs in intermittent light. No sounds can be heard anywhere. Reaching the third floor, I make a left, but after a short distance run into a thick plastic sheet that hangs like a filthy veil from ceiling to floor. Pushing it aside, I can just make out a lightless corridor studded by pockets of deeper darkness, doorways to rooms, or the shells of rooms. From somewhere a sharp, scurrying noise issues. I hurry back the way I came, turn a corner, then another, then stop and try to orient myself – and realize I am standing outside apartment no. 323. Mostly as a formality, I lift my hand to knock, and then I hear a voice.

'You pawned it?' it says. And then again, 'You *pawned* it?'

'That's right,' says another voice, a woman's.

'Jesus, Clizia!' The man sounds very like Paul, though his tone is different from any I have heard him use. 'What am I supposed to work on?'

'Work!' the woman's voice, fierce and heavily accented, crows. 'You tell me the day you want to work, I go out and buy you brand-new one. Work, this is the big joke! Ha ha, I am laughing!'

His tone hardens. 'Well, where's the money, so?'

'What money?'

'The money from my damn writing desk, that's what money.'

'Is gone.'

'Gone? You spent it? All of it?' Heavy footsteps pound the floor. 'On what? Lottery tickets?'

'I bought *food*, idiot! I bought *food*, so we don't *starve!*'

'That's great! And what are we going to do tomorrow? What are we going to do tomorrow, when the food's gone and my desk is gone?'

'Oh yes, tomorrow is when you were going to make the big moneys, I forgot.'

'Well, what's your plan, exactly? Pawn the floorboards? Pawn the, the damn oxygen in the air?'

'I leave you, that's what! I leave you!'

'I wish you *would* leave me,' the man roars back. 'I wish you would leave me, then I could get some peace and quiet! I wish one of us had the courage to bring this nightmare to an end, so I could at least look forward to dying al— oh, hello, Claude.'

Somewhere around 'nightmare', the storming footsteps rapidly increased in volume, and now the door has been flung open and Paul and I find ourselves looking at each other. I don't know which of us is more surprised, although he works quickly to compose his features, transforming swiftly from conjugal fury to boggling horror to mild bemusement. 'I didn't expect to see you,' he says, in a tone of strained jollity.

'I was just in the neighbourhood,' I say, in a similar tone. For a moment we stare at each other through the masks of our untruths: then, realizing he has no choice, Paul makes an ushering gesture. 'Won't you come in?'

'I don't want to intrude.'

'Don't be silly – please!'

He ushers me into a lavishly appointed room, something like Tutankhamen's tomb might have looked like if they had decided to bury him in a modern kitchen. Every inch abounds with design features – spotlights, LED displays, gold-plated knobs and rails and switches – that so bedazzle me it takes me a moment to register the young woman who stands behind the island. She has platinum-blonde hair and a simmering expression; her left hand is curled around a mug, in the manner of one about to lob a grenade. From the wall, the silenced television throws violently jumping light over her face.

'Claude, this is my wife, Clizia,' Paul says. 'Darling, this is Claude, the man who's been very kindly helping me out with my project these last few weeks.'

'Charmed,' the woman says sullenly.

'You never told me you had a wife,' I say to Paul in the joshing, avuncular tone we established a moment ago, though in the claustrophobic atmosphere it is fighting for its life.

'And you,' Paul says, wagging his finger at me humorously, 'are not supposed to be here! I thought we'd agreed you didn't need to know anything about my life.'

'Yes, that's true, but for the last couple of weeks you have not come to work –'

'Ha,' the woman says.

Paul turns to her. 'Darling, do you mind?'

She shrugs, tosses her platinum locks, and then, with deliberate slowness, slouches over to the sink, where she pours herself a glass of water and, raising her chin over her long white neck, slowly drinks it, continuing to gaze at me as she does so. She is almost extremely beautiful. Her features, from a formal point of view, are perfect – large, oceanic eyes, exquisite cheekbones, a mouth that, though I have never seen a pomegranate, irresistibly recalls pomegranates, or some epic, perfect work of pornography. Yet there is a hardness to them, as though they had been carved from some material whose first allegiance was not to beauty – adamantine, titanium, industrial diamond. The same might be said for the aggressive curves of her body, today squeezed into an old-fashioned floral dress whose pastoral innocence they mock so relentlessly it seems almost cruel.

'You did not come to work,' I repeat, 'and so I started to worry that . . . that – I'm sorry, something is watching me from under the table.'

'Under the – oh, for God's sake.' Paul crouches down and addresses the owner of the eyes: 'Damn it, Remington, what are you doing down there? Why aren't you in bed?'

'I am in bed,' a high-pitched voice replies.

'You're not in bed, you're under the table. I can see you quite clearly.'

'This is my bed,' the voice explains. 'Because I'm a dog.'

'You're not a – just get out of there.' Paul stretches his hand between the chairs and extricates a small boy with grubby knees. 'How long have you been down there? Were you listening to Mummy and Daddy's private conversation?'

'Dogs hear things people don't hear,' the child says mysteriously.

'Go to bed,' Paul says. 'Your human bed.'

'Who is this?' I ask.

'This is my son, Remington,' Paul says. The boy is slight and resembles his mother, though in a softer, more benign way, the sharp edges rounded out and the porcelain skin spangled with amber freckles.

'I'm four,' Remington says to me. And then, 'Dogs can't talk.'

'Very nice to meet you,' I say, shaking his diminutive hand.

'Do you have any bones?'

'I'm afraid not.'

'Bow-wow-wow-wow!' Remington exclaims. 'Dogs like bones!'

'That's enough, Remington – now, as to the novel, I've had some very –'

'Dogs like barking! Bow-wow-wow!'

Paul turns to his wife with a pained expression. 'Can't you do something with him?'

'Certainly, darling,' Clizia says. 'You want I take him to nursery? Or bring him for stroll around garden?'

'Bow-wow-wow!' barks Remington, tearing around the limited floor space. 'Bow-wow-wow-wow-wow!'

Paul pulls his hands down his face. 'I'm losing my fucking mind here.'

'Why don't I just ring for Nanny?' Clizia says brightly. Her husband responds with an expletive, and in an instant, while I stand there in a paroxysm of embarrassment, the argument begins all over again.

'Mum and Dad are always fighting,' Remington whispers to me confidentially. 'It's because I'm bad.'

'I'm sure you're not bad,' I say.

Remington pauses a moment, contemplating this; then he slaps his two hands over his eyes and will not reappear, no matter how I cajole.

Clearly the best thing is for me to go. But as I make my way out of the apartment – picking my way past Louis Quatorze chairs, black chandeliers, other signature excesses of the Celtic Tiger – something catches my eye. On a stack of loose papers scattered over an approximately desk-sized area of floor sits the red notebook. I flinch: it's like seeing Excalibur resting in the umbrella stand, or the Maltese Falcon propping up a lowboy.

I glance over my shoulder. Clizia is issuing a torrent of foreign words that sound vaguely like backwards French; Paul is shouting that he will have her deported. I look back. The notebook calls to me like a siren from a rock, enjoining me to turn its pages.

I know I shouldn't; yet something is not right here, and it may hold the answer. Nobody pays any attention to me as I edge over and lift it from the floor. With a dizzying sense of anticipation and dread, I go to the first page.

It is blank.

I turn to the next page.

It is blank.

I begin to feel a queer sort of chill, like a draught blowing down the hallways of my being. Fuck you, Clizia is bellowing at Paul. Fuuuuuuuckkkk youuuu!

The next page, the one after, and the one after that – blank. The page following is filled with handwritten text: a single word, *blahblahblahblahblahblahblahblahblahblah*, repeated to take up the whole page. Opposite it is a crude cartoon, a stick-man in the basket of a hot-air balloon. The stick-man wears a crown and holds a bag marked with a euro symbol in either hand. On the page after that, a doodle of a camel, then more pages featuring similar doodles, either of breasts or of erect penises, or of erect penises defiling the breasts in one way or another. Then I come to a sequence of what seem to be measurements. Measurements, diagrams that seem ominously familiar, and a few pages later, a heading in capitals: WHO'S OUR MARK?

'Whoa-ho-ho, what are you doing with that?' Before I can read any further, Paul has appeared and snatched the book out of my hand.

My head snaps back; my vision swims. WHO'S OUR MARK? The question jigs mockingly before me.

'You know you're not allowed to see that,' Paul scolds, stowing the notebook in a drawer.

'It's empty,' I say, though my voice seems to come from elsewhere.

'Well, it's just rough notes,' Paul says. 'A word here and there, aides-memoires, as you'd call them.'

'Our conversations, our stories, the time you spent with us . . .'

'All up here.' He taps his head with an index finger. 'Locked away in the vault, don't you worry.'

I barely hear him. I feel like I've been drugged, and that line keeps flashing up at me. 'Who is Mark?'

'I'm sorry?'

'You have written, WHO'S OUR MARK? What does this mean?'

'Oh, that – that's nothing, just an old idea I didn't end up using –'

'Perhaps you thought it might be a good name for the Everyman, before you met me,' I reason faintly.

'Yes, that's exactly it,' he agrees, guiding me towards the door. And it sounds plausible; yet I can still feel the question descending through me, WHO'S OUR MARK?, rearranging everything, like some powerful agaric hidden in a plate of food.

'Now why don't you head back home' – he reaches for the door handle – 'and first thing tomorrow I'll come in and tell you all about this new direction I've thought up –'

WHO'S OUR MARK? Fragments whirl before my eyes, snatches of old films, Humphrey Bogart, Jimmy Cagney – what are they saying to each other? I lean in to read the subtitles . . .

'Claude?'

Rather than just working in the bank, instead we have him rob *the bank.*

'Claude, is everything . . . ?'

And up from the dark depths, silent and swift as a shark, the truth now surges into view. The mark: the patsy, the mug, the sucker. '*Le gogo*,' I hear myself whisper.

'What?'

'*C'est bon pour les gogos.*' The words come out without me knowing why; and as if I'd uttered a magic spell, or whatever is the exact opposite of a magic spell, in an instant I understand everything. 'There's no novel,' I say.

'What?' He seems baffled. 'What are you talking about? Of course there's a novel!'

How I yearn to believe him! Yet even as I look at him he seems changed: the artist of the last weeks vanished, his place taken by this other man, furtive, contingent, mired in the trash of the everyday. It's like when you find out your lover has been unfaithful: in one horrible instant everything she was to you, the whole beautiful enchantment, falls away, and you see her as she really is – mortal, machinating, tethered like everyone else to a little patch of space and time. And the worst of it is that you knew all along.

He is still making protestations of innocence. I let them wash over me. Everything is clear now, terribly, unforgivingly clear. The novel was simply a ploy, to win my trust and get him into the bank. From there he would have free rein to plan his theft. 'And Igor – or whatever his name is – he is not an experimental poet.'

'Well, I mean, not precisely –'

'He's a pest exterminator,' Clizia says. 'He is the brains of the operation,' she adds sardonically.

'You're not helping – Claude, listen, we can still make this happen. Nothing has changed!'

He goes on: he entreats and implores, he issues a myriad offers and possibilities. But the words have become meaningless, as if he were speaking another language. For a moment I watch his mouth gobble, without hearing what it says; then I rise to my feet. 'I have to go.'

'You don't know what it's been like for me these last years – the pressure I'm under . . .'

I trudge heavily back around the table. He lays a hand on my arm. 'Look – it's true, I needed something to tide us over. But just so I can finish what I'm working on. I've got something up my sleeve so big it'll make all of us rich. Rich!'

I shake him loose and open the door, walk through the darkness to the stairwell.

'There's no need to involve the authorities!' Paul cries after me, as I begin my descent.

2

In the Abyss

Life is something so hideous that the only way to endure it is to escape it. And one escapes by living in art.

Gustave Flaubert

'Wow.' Ish sits back in her chair, fingering the chain around her neck.

'Mercurial,' Jurgen says. 'Very, very mercurial.'

'And you're sure about all this?' Ish says. 'You couldn't just have – I don't know, got your wires crossed?'

'Perhaps this is just another part of his research,' Jurgen suggests. 'Perhaps he is now working on the story of a novelist who tries to rob a bank.'

'It was a scam,' I say. The monotonous sound of my own voice infuriates me. 'All of it.'

'Just like a man!' Ish, with a sudden access of fierceness, gets to her feet, setting her earrings a-jingle. 'They promise you the moon and the stars, but they're only after the one bloody thing.'

'They are seeking to burgle your safebox?' Jurgen says.

'Too bloody right,' Ish says.

'I am wondering now what is the next step,' I say. 'I suppose we must tell the police.'

Jurgen pulls thoughtfully on the end of his pen. 'I am not so sure. On one hand, it seems clear that Paul's plan was a failure. On the other – did you take the notebook with you?'

I shake my head.

'Yes – I suspect in that case his plot will be difficult to prove. Without hard evidence, it will come down to his word against yours. Furthermore, the negative publicity for the bank would be significant. The idea that BOT's top analysts were fooled by such an obvious trick, that they sat idly by while prospective bank robbers measured the walls, is not one shareholders will enjoy. My preference would be to keep the incident to ourselves. I will have the small word with security to make sure everything is in order. If it is, we will drop the entire matter. Anyone asks, we can simply tell them the project did not work out.' His calm surprises me. I expected him to be apoplectic – to hurl office equipment across the room, to plot revenge using the whole mighty legal machinery at our disposal, to express all the rage that I, consumed by shame, cannot.

'I know that Paul has done a terrible thing,' he says. 'Taking advantage of our trust, manipulating us for his own ends, to say nothing of attempted robbery – these are undeniably heinous acts. At the same time, we must remember that artists are not bound by our conventional morality. To a bourgeois sensibility, trying to rob a bank is plainly wrong. But for an artist it is different. In fact, didn't a famous poet once say, "Bad artists borrow, great artists steal"?'

'I don't think he was talking about stealing money,' I point out.

'Perhaps not. Nevertheless, we cannot condemn the panther for killing the gazelle. That is simply its nature. The artist is fundamentally a transgressive figure. Michelangelo, Bob Marley, in fact the entire original line-up of the Wailers: these were all men censured by their times. In banking too there are moments when we must act in ways that ordinary Johns would condemn as dishonest or unethical in order to succeed. So let us not rush to judge. Maybe he came among us under false pretences. Maybe he lied to us about putting us in a novel. But Paul changed us, and because of him life will never be the same again.'

'My life hasn't changed one bit,' Ish says.

'Mine neither,' I say. 'It is exactly the same.'

'A plant does a lot of its growing underground,' Jurgen says mysteriously. 'Anyway, as soon as one story ends, a new one is beginning. This morning I have heard from Rachael's office that an extremely powerful private investor has taken an interest in the Irish financial sector. Apparently, BOT is near the top of the list of investment banks under consideration to be his agent.'

And with that, Paul and his book are put back on the shelf; the oddity, the intrigue of the past weeks, simply dissolves, as if it had been merely a *divertissement*, like a juggler on the plaza whom the temps observe as they eat their panini, before the security guards arrive to chase him away.

Normality returns. I send emails and study reports; I attend meetings and write notes; I pay my credit-card bill and upgrade my broadband speed. At night, I put myself on the rack, demand to know how I let myself be taken in. Yet there is no mystery to it. My life is interesting; my life has meaning; other people, strangers, will want to know about my life. He told me what I wanted to hear: it's the same trick we use with clients every day. They prefer buying to selling. They prefer gaining a little to losing a lot. They want to invest in Apple because they like their iPhone. And we say, 'That's just what you should do,' and take their money. People will believe anything, if it's what they want to hear.

The 'extremely powerful private investor' turns out to be none other than Porter Blankly's old friend the Caliph of Oran – or, to be exact, Tordale, his sovereign wealth fund.

'The Caliph of Oran,' Ish frowns. 'Isn't he some sort of dictator?'

'That's right,' Jurgen says. 'He is one of the most successful dictators in the world. His personal wealth is believed to be in the tens of billions, and in the current situation that is growing by the hour.'

'What's the current situation?' Ish says.

'Unrest,' I say. 'Uprisings.'

'Indeed,' Jurgen says. 'Anti-government demonstrations throughout the Arab world have had a highly disruptive effect on oil production. Oran's capacity, however, has not been affected. Instead the hike in prices has brought the Caliphate spectacular profits. Now his sovereign wealth fund is seeking to diversify.'

'How'd he find us?' Ish says. 'Blankly?'

'I think on this occasion we may have Walter to thank,' Jurgen says.

'Walter Corless?'

'He's doing some construction work out there,' I remember.

'Yes, the Caliph is taking measures to fortify his oilfields and private city in case the unrest spreads,' Jurgen says. 'My surmise is that Walter may have spoken informally to his finance people. Officially they are interested in investing in the Irish banking sector. Unofficially, I hear that they are considering shifting their entire operation to Dublin. The light regulatory regime may suit their needs. A delegation is coming over at the end of the week to hear presentations.'

'They're not giving us much time to prepare, are they?' Ish says.

'No doubt this is a part of their evaluation process. Consequently it is very important that we –'

But his words are drowned out by a tremendous pounding. What could it be? Construction work in the plaza? A controlled explosion on a nearby building? I look about for an explanation and then find it poised, sculpturally, in front of me. Ariadne has come to our table; the sound is the beating of my own idiotic heart.

'You are ready to order?'

The others go first; I pretend to study the menu, in order to hide my blushes.

'And for you?'

I start to speak, but it turns into a cough. Finally I struggle out, 'Nothing for me, thank you.'

'Very good.' She smiles, sashays away.

'Not having anything, Claude? Are you feeling okay?'

'I'm fine. Just not very hungry.' I sink back into my chair, attempting to conceal my laboured breathing. 'So, this presentation . . . ?'

'Yes – so Liam wants them to meet Rachael first, and then our team. Afterwards . . .'

I concentrate as best I can, but talking about investment with Ariadne in the room is like trying to read the business news by the light of a meteor shower. Finding out the novel was a fake hasn't dimmed her appeal. On the contrary, every day as lunchtime approaches I find myself getting giddy; I turn brick-red when she greets me, then squeak like an adolescent when she asks for my order. What is happening? It's as if, simply by making the suggestion, Paul had set something in motion – as if the story had taken on a life of its own, like a genie freed from a lamp. It makes no sense; I've spent many hours patiently talking myself out of it. Still the feelings refuse to leave me.

And I keep coming back to the fact that this is where Paul said the story should *go*. True, he said it in the course of trying to rob the bank. But could it be that his instincts remained sound, even when used to deceive? Could he have picked up on something between us, a latent connection waiting to be made? Is it my imagination or has Ariadne noticed it too? Does she look at me now with a clouded sort of a frown, as though there's some fact about me that she can't quite lay her hands on? On some unconscious level, is she too waiting for our story to begin?

As the meeting with Tordale draws closer, though, it squeezes out everything else. No more lunches, no staying up late, reading philosophy; we are in the office till the small hours, making calls, talking to the number-crunchers, pulling together every available scrap of information on the Irish banking system.

Most of our meetings are pedestrian affairs, quibbling over financial models with pension managers, fund managers, treasury people. This is different. The Caliphate's fund is worth several billion dollars. The day before the presentation, Rachael calls me to her office and promises me a guaranteed bonus if Tordale signs up with BOT. The figure she names is astronomical; she makes it sound like a threat.

'These guys are not messing around.' Howie, who finds most of our work laughably dull, has taken an interest in this particular encounter. 'They're averaging a 13 per cent annual return on a fund bigger than some countries' GDP. You need to go into that conference room and slaughter them. You need to literally take your figures and stab them in the eyes with them, and when they scream, reach down their throats and yank out their hearts. Then you can start talking.'

'Where will we put their bodies, Howie?'

'I'm not kidding. I know these types of guys. They're cannibals. They're not going to hire the team with the nicest biscuits.'

I am in the gym at five the next morning, trying to work off some of my nervous energy. Ish arrives at half six with her hair newly and spectacularly blonded. For the next couple of hours we swivel in our chairs, drink endless coffee, leaf unseeingly through documents like students before a final exam.

I'm talking to Brent 'Crude' Kelleher, trying to get a read on the latest shifts in the oil market, when there is a groan. A group of analysts is gathered in front of the TV, where the German chancellor is making an announcement. Even without hearing her, I can tell the news is bad. 'Look at that fucking face,' Dwayne McGuckian says. 'She looks like she just ate a bag of dicks.'

It had been hoped that at the latest summit Germany, as the only country in Europe with any money, would come forward with a plan to stabilize the teetering banks and the increasingly rickety-looking governments holding them up. Instead the Chancellor is giving a lecture on responsibility. *Committed as we are to the European project, we cannot endorse reckless fiscal behaviour . . .*

'Switch it off,' Gary McCrum says.

'Spread's already gone up half a point,' Jocelyn Lockhart reads off his terminal.

'*Scheisse*,' Jurgen mutters.

'What's going on?' Kevin says, arriving on the scene. Ish explains that Germany is refusing to step in to cover the losses of the weaker nations; even before the press conference has ended, the amount of interest investors are demanding before they'll lend any more money to Ireland has jumped. Some of the ratings agencies are now publicly doubting the country will be able to pay its bills for much longer.

'What happens then? If it can't pay its bills?'

'Someone else takes over. Probably someone with a German accent.'

'Maybe they could send 'em a few slave girls,' Kevin says. 'Till they get the accounts sorted out.'

No one laughs. This is not good news: not even a high-risk investor wants to put his money in a country about to go belly-up. Eleven o'clock comes and goes with no word from Tordale. Ish sits tentatively prodding her hair, as if it were a wild and unpredictable animal. Jurgen paces up and down, flipping a pen between his fingers. Kevin alone is oblivious, calculating in a spreadsheet what he might do with his bonus. 'We'll be promoted too,' he tells me. 'You should go for MD.'

Losing patience, I'm about to snap that they aren't coming, when Kimberlee rings through from Reception to say they've just arrived. Ten minutes later, they are on their way down from Rachael's office; we put on our best smiles.

I had imagined the fund would be staffed by Arabs, but the four men who step out of the lift are white and English. The eldest is maybe twenty-five. The others are barely more than boys, slight-framed, tender-skinned; with their braces and slicked-back hair, they resemble corporate hobbits, on their way to do a deal with Sauron. Their eyes are bloodshot and their faces pale, and one of them has skinned the knuckles on his right hand. The leader introduces himself as James Harper. The others, who all seem to be called Olly, eye Ish and nudge each other. Rachael's expression as she hands them over to us is unreadable.

Jurgen takes the party to the meeting room. The delegation doesn't reply to his questions with anything more than monosyllables. Their suits reek of cigarette smoke and I can see a murky brown sweat-line ringing the collar of the boy walking ahead of me.

'You had a chance to see the city yesterday?' I ask him, when he catches me looking.

He turns away again and says loudly, 'This bloke wants to know if we saw the city yesterday.' The other three emit low, lurchy laughter. 'We saw a bit of it,' he says to me, with a leer.

'You boys have been "on the tear", as we are saying here in Ireland,' Jurgen says. 'Maybe you are drinking a few Guinnesses, ha ha?'

Ish shoots me a look that says, *We are doomed.*

In the conference room we're joined by Chris Kane from Sales, who makes a brief speech about Bank of Torabundo punching above its weight post-crash, adding that as our new CEO is a good friend of the Caliph's, he looks forward to BOT and

Tordale becoming friends too. Then we crack open our laptops and begin the presentation, a concise but forensic breakdown of the major and minor Irish banks and their prospects in this volatile environment. The visitors aren't listening. They fiddle with their BlackBerrys, they smirk into space. It's only when one of his team actually falls asleep and starts to snore that James Harper confesses – though this is not quite the right word, as his tone is more smug than contrite – that they didn't get much sleep. 'The lads from Danske Bank took us out for a pint last night,' he says. 'Though it ended up bein' a lot more than one.' He hooks an extremely expensive leather brogue over his knee and draws himself back in a yawn. 'Those boys know how to 'ave fun,' he says.

'But do they know how free cash flow will bear on future share performance?' Jurgen asks.

I lean over to Kevin and mutter in his ear, 'Get Howie.'

What's the difference between a dead prostitute and a Ferrari? Did you hear about the Irish prostitute? What do you call a prostitute on a fishing expedition?

Around the table, shiny pink faces grin at us. Howie snaps his fingers at the waitress; a minute later a fresh tray of lagers with single-malt chasers appears. 'Now that's the kind of woman I would love to have dead in my garage,' Howie says as the waitress walks away.

We are in Life Bar, treating the Londoners to 'hair of the dog'. I am not used to drinking this early in the day, and already the room is swimming slightly. The Tordale delegation, however, look decidedly more lively.

'Now I'll tell you who you don't want near your kids,' Howie says, and proceeds to give a libellous but extremely well-informed account of a British cabinet minister's private activities. Kevin gazes at him with naked adoration; James Harper punches him matily on the arm; the room revolves on its hitherto unused axis.

No one has mentioned caliphs, banks or investment opportunities since the presentation. What time is it? Three? Four? Ish's face has taken on a greenish look, either from the whiskey or the prostitute jokes; more of both keep arriving, like gatecrashers to an already oversubscribed house party, as well as a man Howie refers to only as 'the Bulgarian', who has made two visits to our table, on both occasions performing an elaborate handshake with the trader and then leaving again, without taking off his sunglasses. On the way to the bathroom I notice the floor canting to the left, as though tipping me towards the exit. Inside I find Howie and James Harper huddled in conversation by the cubicle doors. As soon as they see me come in they break apart.

'Claude!' Howie exclaims, as if I am a long-lost friend, or any kind of friend. 'I was just telling James about you. This guy,' turning to James, 'is the best wingman you'll ever have.'

'Oh yeah?' James squints at me sceptically.

'Women go crazy for him. 'Cos he's French, see? They're light years ahead of us over there. In France they actually teach you how to eat pussy in school.'

'That's exactly the kind of fing they ought to be doin' in England,' James Harper says seriously, regarding me now with a certain amount of appreciation.

'Claude, we're thinking about going somewhere a bit more lively, what do you say? How about VD's?'

My heart sinks. 'Fantastic,' I say.

'Jimbo, why don't you go and round up your troops and we'll get a taxi,' Howie says. When the Londoner is gone he puts his arm around my shoulder and leans in to me. It seems I can feel heat blasting from his face. 'We're going to nail these bitches, Claude,' he says in a low voice. 'We're going to rape them and cut off their heads and bury them in the forest.'

'Very good,' I say uncertainly.

'Do a line, it'll keep you sharp. Do it,' he commands, shuttling powder out on to the cistern.

Now as I walk back the floor is trying to flip me up towards the ceiling. But I'm too smart for it! How brilliant and talented I am! Of course this deal is going to come off! There is no way anyone could resist our intelligence and charm. I put on my coat, wink at one of the hobbits. But as soon as the door opens, everything begins to slide again. Outside? Do we really have to go outside? Outside is *not* inside. A rash of oily sweat breaks out on my forehead. Fresh panics crowd in on the initial outside/inside scare. Howie couldn't actually be planning to rape and murder the Caliphate's sovereign wealth fund, could he? Sometimes with traders it is hard to tell.

People are hurrying back and forth across the plaza with their briefcases and box files. We step between their grey insubstantial bodies as if through a sea of wraiths. The sounds of the city, the sky, the river, all of these things seem at one remove.

'You've got these twunts too, 'ave you?' James Harper flicks a hand at the sagging tents and wayward signage of the zombies encamped outside Royal Irish. 'They're all over the Square Mile. Facking waste of space.' Putting his hands together, he bellows at them, 'No one cares, you twunts!'

Chris Kane grabs my arm. 'This is going great,' he mutters. 'Those pie charts really got their attention.'

I grin back at him as one might at a figment of one's imagination one doesn't want to offend. The hobbit beside me elbows my ribs. 'Ten o'clock, mate,' he says. I turn my head, my all-purpose false grin at the ready – and then see he is pointing to the window of the Ark, where Ariadne is on her hands and knees cleaning up a spill and inadvertently revealing most of her cleavage. The hobbit launches into an impressively comprehensive list of things he would like to do to Ariadne. I pretend I have not heard, step quickly ahead to the kerb.

Glowing yellow roof-signs swim like radioactive clots down the artery of the traffic. Howie holds out a hand, and one cab, then a second, pull up to us. 'Why don't you ride with these two boys,' Howie suggests to Ish, nodding to the two younger delegates, who gaze out of the cab's dark interior like baby owls.

'Actually I thought I might head home,' Ish says.

Howie is dumbfounded. 'What?'

'You're going to VD's!' Ish protests. 'You don't want me there! I'd be cramping your style!'

Gripping her shoulder, Howie takes her aside and hisses to her, 'That's the whole point! We've got gash coming to the club with us! That's what makes us cool, and Danske squares!'

'Gash?' Ish repeats.

'Do I have to tell you your job? Just get in the car. When you get home you can wipe the tears away with your big fat fucking bonus.'

With her mouth tight shut, Ish climbs into the back of the cab. 'I will ride in this car too,' Jurgen says judiciously, and goes to the passenger door.

The rest of us set off in the other taxi. Traffic is heavy: we move at a crawl past sparkling new office blocks, others barely begun, cranes that have not moved an inch in two years. 'So free years ago this was the fird-richest country on the planet,' James Harper observes. 'And now it's facked.'

'Property bubble,' Howie says. 'Crashed the banks.'

'They didn't actually crash,' Chris Kane interjects hurriedly. 'The Minister guaranteed them.'

'I 'eard about that,' James Harper says. 'Not just the deposits, right? He said they'd cover every fackin' bond and loan and dodgy deal wiv the Russian mafia the banks was into. Why'd he do that then?'

Howie shrugs. 'Stupidity.'

'The banks lied to him,' I qualify. 'About the size of their debts.'

'And now Paddy's got to pay for it, and the whole place is in the shitter, just like Greece.'

'It's different,' Howie counters. 'The Irish aren't going to cause trouble. They'll do what they're told. Anyway, the problem here is the banks. In Greece, the problem is Greece.'

'Yeah, but your Minister's made the banks and Ireland the same fing, 'asn't 'e, wiv 'is magic fackin' wand of incompetence.'

Howie shakes his head. 'Greece is finished. This place will recover. In the meantime, there's a lot of money to be made. It's a national fire sale. You can get the whole water grid for half nothing. What's that going to be worth in twenty years?'

'Wawter's been pushin' us to get into Royal Irish.' James Harper is silent for a moment.

Howie glances at me. 'Don't know that that's the first call I'd make. Word is they're sitting on a black hole.'

'Don' tell Wawter that,' James Harper says. ''E's in 'em up to 'is tits.'

I turn in my seat. It is very important, at a meeting like this, never to show your ignorance. But in my many conversations with Walter Corless I have never heard him mention Royal Irish, let alone seen any of their stock in his portfolio. Is he keeping secrets? Or is James Harper simply misinformed?

Howie is telling him about other investment possibilities, retail banks with a million depositors available for 2 or 3 per cent of what they were worth two years ago. But the Londoner is hard to impress.

'We've 'eard all the 'ard-luck stories. Every sodding bank in Europe's been over looking for a few quid from the Gaffer. Most of the Yanks as well.'

'But he could do very well out of it. Real estate, too.' Howie gestures out the window at the pristine rows of empty buildings. 'What is it they say? When there's blood on the streets, buy property?'

'Don' tell me about blood on the streets, mate,' James Harper says. 'Oran, you put on a bulletproof vest before you get off the plane.'

I turn again. 'I thought the unrest hadn't reached Oran.'

'They keep it ou' of the papers, don' they. But the las' time I was over there, they'd 'anged a load of revolutionaries across the road from my 'otel. Eleven geezers lined up along the street like We Are Fackin' Dead FC. Fackin' dogs barkin' all night, tryin' to chew their shoes off.'

'Terrorists?'

'Some bunch of ragheads comin' ou' of the deser'. You know the type, Koran in one 'and, AK in the uvver. Makin' a big bleedin' hullaballoo that the Caliph's a blasphemer and not a proper caliph and all tha'.'

'But he's got things under control?'

''E's got nuffink to worry about. Seen 'is bleedin' Imperial Guard? Fifty fackin' sand niggers seven foot tall that can kill a man wiv one blow. 'E's all right. It's every uvver cunt who's shittin' it.' He shifts his weight, making his buttocks squeak against the vinyl. 'Once Wawter's got this wall finished, it'll be easier. 'Opefully the Gaffer can keep a lid on fings till then.'

As he speaks, we pull up at our destination; the suddenly sombre mood is lifted by the other Tordale delegates, who haul their leader from the cab with the happy news that they mooned a policeman en route. James Harper brightens immediately.

Two bald, Puffa-jacketed sentinels are guarding a stairwell. Over their heads, a neon sign spells out VELVET DREAM'S. A deep, pulmonary thrum issues from the subterranean entrance; the four brilliantined visitors hasten boisterously down the steps towards it. Following after them, Ish momentarily catches my eye; I give her a sympathetic pat on the elbow.

At the door we are met by a svelte girl wearing a kind of heart-shaped velvet bustier that covers half of her breasts and some legal minimum of her genitals. She leads us to a table; Chris Kane conspicuously passes her a credit card, and our guests, as if at a signal, start shouting drinks orders. Around us, girls glide constantly through the red-tinged murk. Some carry trays of drinks, others plastic gourds, which they shake like tambourines, soliciting 'tips for the dancers'; others carry nothing at all, but bend in close to the men on the banquettes and whisper in their ears. Now and then one will get to his feet, as if he's been fingered by the thought police, and be led away into the darkness. At the top of the room is a stage, where a girl with long blonde hair and enormous, unreal breasts is spinning around a pole in metallic hot pants; as she pivots, faster and faster, hair and pants become interweaving rings of light, like some electrical phenomenon.

'Busy,' Chris Kane observes.

'Recession-proof, innit?' one of the hobbits says. 'People'll always want to watch a fit bird get her ganny out, good times and bad.'

'Structurally, sex industry's very robust,' another hobbit agrees.

'Look at the flamin' structure on that,' the third hobbit says, nodding at a statuesque girl in a thong who has arrived at our table. Her vampish maquillage and stupendous bosom cannot quite counteract a callow, bumpkin quality – perhaps it is in the way she stands, her shoulders squared as if ready to carry a hay bale.

'Myou vont privet dents?' she inquires.

The Tordale delegation crack up. 'You wot, darlin'?'

'Privet dents?' the girl repeats, shifting uncertainly. Ersatz gemstones glitter blankly from her thong.

'A *privet* dance?'

'You got a musical bush, love?'

She is blushing now, the colour visible even in the degraded light.

'Only teasin' yer, sweetheart.' The youngest hobbit pats her hand. 'I'd love a dents.'

The girl smiles uncertainly and performs a clumsy back step as the hobbit gets to his feet. Chris Kane hurriedly passes him the credit card; the hobbit takes it without even looking at him. As she leads him away, he gives his comrades a rascally grin. 'I'm goin' to put a great big dent in 'er privates!'

'No touchin', mate,' his colleague reminds him. 'Remember Birmingham.'

Howie and James Harper are at one end of the banquette, deep in talk. Jurgen begins telling us how many *Weissbiers* on the market are strictly speaking not *Weissbiers*. One of the hobbits slides over to Ish. 'Ow'igh'?' he says.

A famous banker once said that the key to gaining a client is to become his friend. People give their business to people they like; in banking, where what we actually do with the money becomes ever harder to explain – indeed, where a client half-expects his own bank to rip him off – a strong bond between you and your account is paramount. Hence the fortunes spent on 'entertaining': the rugby matches and Grand Prix and golf tournaments, the lavish dinners and *premiers crus* and trips to Venice, the girls who appear at the door of your client's hotel bedroom at 2 a.m. just in case he needs anything. Obviously, the system turned into a racket long ago; nowadays the best salesman is the one who can make his client believe that he is his friend *in spite of* the ostentatious gifts and luxuries he bears.

For me this has always been a lie too far: at these events I usually limit myself to making sure the glasses stay full. Looking for a waitress, I see that a fresh dancer has come onstage. She has long dark hair and a tawny complexion and looks enough like Ariadne that I experience a pang; as she cavorts naked around the pole, I clothe her in a black Airtex T-shirt and jeans, give her a tray, and a smile, and a smudge of cinnamon on her apron . . .

Then something else catches my eye: a silhouette at one of the tables girdling the stage. I stare at it without knowing why; then I realize who it belongs to. 'Excuse me one moment,' I say to our guests.

He is alone, gazing up at the stage, so fixed on the dancer's performance he doesn't notice me until I tap his shoulder. He turns;

I see the drowsy swim and swoon of his pupils as his eyes attempt to focus, then recognition dawns at last and an expression of horror crosses his face. He springs or rather staggers to his feet, staying upright for only a moment before falling backwards over his stool, from which position he warns me not to try anything.

'I'm not going to try anything,' I say.

'That's good,' Paul says, pulling himself back on to his stool. 'For you.' He lifts a shot glass from the table and brings it to his lips, not seeming to notice that it is empty. The dancer smacks her buttock, leaving a bright pink handprint glowing on her skin.

'What are you doing here?' I ask him.

'What are you doing here?' he retorts, eyes trained on the dancer, who has stalked over to the end of the stage so that another solitary spectator can tuck a note into her G-string, which has evidently remained on for that purpose. 'If you're looking for an apology, you're wasting your time.'

'I'm not looking for an apology.'

'Oh, you want to have me arrested, is that it? Well, go right ahead. There's not a judge in the land who'd convict me. They'd probably give me a medal.'

'I don't want to have you arrested.'

'Well, what do you want, so?'

I am at a loss. I came over on impulse, without thinking why; only now does it occur to me that we have nothing to say to one another. Onstage, the dancer shucks down her knickers to reveal a finger of carefully trimmed pubic hair, then reaches between her legs to spread her labia. To a rising chorus of hoots, wolf whistles, catcalls, she slowly begins to arch her torso backwards.

'Was it always a scam?' I hear myself say.

'What?' he says irritably.

'The book. Your book. Did you ever intend to write it?' Even as I speak the words I know the question is futile, irrelevant, like asking the person breaking up with you whether they ever really loved you.

Paul looks up at me, suitably disgusted. 'Seriously?'

'I thought maybe in the beginning . . .'

He waves a hand, cutting me off. 'I don't do that shit any more,' he says.

'What shit?' I say. 'You mean writing?'

Paul shrugs, returns his attention to the floor show. Inch by inch, thighs quivering, the dancer has bent back so that her dark hair sweeps the floor and the spotlight shines directly athwart the sad little heart she holds between her fingers; from behind, the noise of the unseen crowd breaks over us, cheers and applause as if the vagina were a famous diva hitting a high C.

'You don't write at all?'

Paul casts about him and signals to a passing girl, pale with a mane of chestnut hair.

'Private dance?' she says, coming over.

'I have to go,' he says to me.

'Wait.' I reach out, grab his arm. 'Why me?' I say.

Paul looks back at me with a mixture of pity and guilt and exhaustion. 'I have to go,' he says again.

I release him; the chestnut-haired girl takes his hand; I watch him follow her away towards the honeycomb of rooms at the back. Onstage, the dancer takes a bow; a moment later, a dolorous attendant trudges out with a spray and a flannel, with which he wipes down the pole and the dance floor.

'There 'e is!' One of the hobbits grabs me in a loose headlock as I slide back into our table. 'You 'orny little fucker, I fough' you was goin' to crawl righ' up that bird's minge!'

I smile, take a sip from my repulsive fluorescent drink and put the encounter out of my mind. Glancing around the table, I gauge our progress. The smallest and most earnest hobbit is speaking animatedly to Chris Kane, whose face exhibits the mixture of fascination and panic characteristic of one whose efforts to feign interest are undermined by his inability to hear what's being said. The burly boy who put me in a headlock rambles to

Jurgen and Kevin about football; his curly-haired colleague, now wearing his tie wrapped around his head Rambo-style, is talking to Ish in a low intense voice that requires her to lean ever closer. Of Howie and James Harper there is no sign, but I spot Howie's Bulgarian friend from earlier moving through the crowd in the direction of the toilets. That is where the deal will happen, if there is one; our job now is to run interference, keep the others happy so Howie can work uninterrupted.

I order a fresh round of drinks, take a surreptitious look at my watch. The next dancer has come on, a synthetic blonde with breasts like warheads who humps the pole slowly and then, as if at the flick of a switch, at double speed. Her siliconized body and its clumsy imitations of love put me in mind of an early iteration of a new technology, those first, oxymoronic mobile phones the size and weight of breeze blocks.

'So' – with a suddenly businesslike air, the burly boy now places his elbows on the table and leans in – 'BOT's based in Dublin a good while now?'

'Almost ten years,' Jurgen says. 'The regulatory climate here gives our clients many options not available to London banks.'

'Ten years,' the burly boy considers. 'And in that time' – he looks around at each of us in turn – ''ave you ever seen . . . a leprechaun?'

Hilarity engulfs the visiting party. Their faces are rubicund and sloppy with drink, and looking at them I have the incontrovertible certainty – as if it were inscribed over the scene, like the motto of a Hogarth print – that we are being taken for a ride . . .

And then a shadow falls across the table.

A girl is standing there: a black girl, easily six foot tall, lithe and muscular and making no pretence at affability. 'Private dance,' she says. She pronounces it like a death sentence. The visitors look at each other; we look at them looking at each other. Chris Kane readies the credit card.

'You ge' off wiv 'er,' the curly-haired boy says.

It takes a moment for Ish to realize he is talking to her. 'Excuse me?'

He nods up at the lap dancer. 'Go on, give her a snog,' he says.

Ish, for once, is speechless; she stares back at him agape.

'Why not, she's gorgeous,' he persists. 'You been givin' me the brush-off all night, maybe this bird's more your flavour. Come on, I'll pay.' He reaches into his jacket pocket and takes out his wallet. From the fold he removes a wad of bills and counts them out on to the table. Ish turns to Jurgen, but he sits there as if frozen, grinning glassily at thin air.

'Go on! Go on!' the boy's comrades urge Ish, laughing. The lap dancer waits motionlessly at the tableside, her face utterly blank.

'Fuck off,' Ish says. The other two make mock-appalled *Oo!* sounds, but the curly-haired boy is undaunted. 'I'm not saying you have to lick her out, just give her a kiss. "Ow much to kiss 'er, wiv tongues?' This latter is directed at the lap dancer.

'Come on, don't be an old biddy,' the burly boy joshes Ish. 'Walter told us you lads knew how to have a laugh!'

I get to my feet. 'I am afraid we have another appointment.'

Jurgen's eyes flash at me from the banquette; I ignore them, reach for Ish's hand, which she gives me dazedly, though she remains in her seat.

'Wait,' the curly-haired boy says. He has stopped laughing. The others stop too and look at him. He licks his lips and says slowly to Ish, 'If you get off wiv her, we'll sign wiv BOT.'

Over our table, in the midst of the thudding music and the barracking laughter, a dome of silence falls. Ish hunches miserably in her chair; Jurgen carefully examines his cufflinks; Kevin gawps as if he's watching the Wimbledon final; and the lap dancer continues to look on, impassive as a Japanese mask. Then some kind of fracas starts up at the top of the room, a man and a woman shouting. Everyone turns to look; I take advantage of the distraction to tug Ish to her feet and drag her away. She appears conflicted: at the door, she turns to me. 'Maybe –'

'Go,' I say, hustling her up the stairs.

The shouting voices get louder. Craning my neck as I make my way through the crowd, I can see the chestnut-haired girl from earlier berating a punter. His back is turned, but there is no doubt who it is. A bouncer storms past me to intervene; I find myself hurrying after him.

'What's going on?' the bouncer demands.

'He take my money!' the dancer says accusingly.

'I didn't!' Paul protests.

'You take!'

'It was a simple misunderstanding,' Paul says to the bouncer.

'I no misunderstand!' the dancer counters, in a voice like a circular saw. 'I understand very well! This man is thief!'

'Would you just let me explain? What happened was, I wanted to tip her, but I only had a twenty, so I put the twenty in her G-string, and then I took out a ten as change –'

'He take my money!'

'As *change* – what, I can't take change?'

'Right, mate, you're out,' the bouncer says.

'But I'm a regular!' Paul cries. 'I have a loyalty card!' This does not sway the bouncer, who twists his arm behind his back and shoves him down a gauntlet of jeering drinkers towards the exit. I give chase, reaching street level just in time to see Paul propelled over the asphalt to land in a heap on the kerb opposite.

'You're barred!' the bouncer shouts after him.

Crossing the road, I help him sit up. 'Are you all right?'

'Oh, sure.' He examines his front teeth with a finger and thumb. 'They say you're barred, but then in a week they've forgotten all about it.'

By the stairwell, the bouncer is laughing with his cronies; now they step aside to allow in a stag party.

'So this is what you do instead of writing,' I say.

'When I can afford it,' Paul replies tersely. He drags himself to his feet and spits.

'I think that is a great shame,' I say.

'You're one of a very small number.' He takes his wallet from his pocket, peers into it fatalistically, then replaces it.

'You never answered my question.'

'What question?'

'Why did you pick me? For your . . . plan?'

He shrugs, looks away. 'I told you before. You were different. You had qualities.'

'What qualities?'

'Loneliness. Desperation.'

This stings; to cover it up I spit out another question. 'And the book? Did you ever intend to write it?'

'Oh Jesus, Claude, what does it matter?' he exclaims, jumping to his feet. 'Okay, I never intended to write a book. Happy?'

I don't reply, look down at the cracked asphalt instead.

'And I'll tell you what else, if I did through some calamity start a new book, I wouldn't write about you and your friends in a hundred years. A bunch of people with one character attribute between them, Mr Greedy, Mr Greedy, Mr Greedy and Mr Greedy, like something out of Roger Hargreaves' nightmares? Who's going to want to read about that?'

He stares at me with blazing eyes, as if expecting an answer. I say nothing; I feel a huge rent has been slashed in the canvas of my soul, and blackness is billowing out.

'Look,' he says, maybe regretting his candour. 'You're not the worst of them. I'm sorry I did this to you. But my God, man. You don't even live in the world. You don't breathe the air, you don't eat the food. You're up in your strange little satellite, placing bets on all of us down below like kids racing beetles. How could you think, how did you ever possibly think that you were an Everyman?'

I can't speak; what can I possibly say? Paul waits a moment, with his hand on my shoulder; and then he turns and walks away, leaving me in the shadow of the club, from which the music booms so loud that even out on the street I experience it not in my ears but in my chest – pounding between my ribs, like some-one else's heart.

I meet Chris Kane in the gym the next morning; he tells me that he stayed out with the Tordale team till three. He appears aglow with health, in spite of his long, debauched night and minimal sleep; this is often the way with my banking colleagues, even the older men, as though they had a picture of themselves moulder-ing in the attic, or, more likely these days, had outsourced the disintegration of their bodies to some proxy in the Third World, some Manuel or Cho or Pradeep who wakes up one day with shattered capillaries, clogged lungs, a fissiparous liver that are none of his doing. 'Great bunch of lads,' Chris Kane says, and then, 'I just hope Ish didn't damage our chances.'

'That guy was out of line.'

'He wasn't serious! Fuck's sake, you have to show you're able to take a joke!'

Upstairs, Ish is already at her desk. I can feel the resentment directed at her from around the room – as can she, to judge by her posture, crouched behind her terminal.

'Thanks, Claude,' she says in a low voice when she sees me.

'Thanks for what?'

'For sticking up for me.'

I blush, as our pusillanimous show comes back to me; if Tor-dale were testing our moral fibre – though they almost definitely weren't – we failed with flying colours.

'What a night,' Ish says.

'Just business.'

'I bet Rachael's bulling.'

'They never intended to take us on.'

'Howie said they did. Howie said that when we were having our argument he was in the jacks doing rails with the main guy, and the main guy started telling him he was thinking of leaving his wife.'

'So?'

'He said it showed we'd got to the next level.'

'It didn't show anything. They're not going to take us on. They won't take on Danske either. They came here to drink, that's all.'

I find Jurgen standing at the window, peering out at the zombies with his binoculars. They are just beginning to stir: one heats a saucepan of water on a gas burner, another eats a bowl of cereal in the opening of his tent. They are not wearing their costumes yet: you can see how young they are.

'Have we heard anything?' I say, keeping my tone neutral.

'They will revert to us by the end of the week,' he replies in the same clipped, mechanical tone. A pretty girl with a heap of tousled brown hair emerges from a tent and turns on a string of fairy lights; adjusting his focus wheel, Jurgen says, 'You have completed your report on Royal?'

'It's not due for two more weeks.'

'That is not what I asked you.'

'No, it's not finished,' I say, and then, feeling rebellious, 'but I can tell you now that I would not recommend Royal Irish to any client.' Jurgen says nothing to this, just continues to stare out. I am about to step away, then I stop. 'What happened last night,' I say.

'Yes.'

'We are supposed to be a team.'

'Yes, we are supposed to be a team,' he returns.

'A team looks after its members.'

He remains silent, stares out at the zombies. Then he says, 'A team exists to achieve goals. If there were no goals, there would be no team. Therefore goals take priority over members. And members who do not achieve the team's goals will be replaced.'

The report is going slowly, very slowly. Financial institutions are chimerical creatures at the best of times, but Royal's books are like nothing I've ever seen. Every figure is a door into a world of illusion – of shapeshifting, duplication, disappearing acts. Deals are buried or recorded more than once; borrowers are split into two or lumped together; mysterious sums arrive and depart without explanation, like ships full of toxic waste that pull into a harbour in the middle of the night and the next day are gone again.

Royal Irish: the name sounds like a bad poker hand, one that looks unbeatable until it capsizes and you lose your shirt. After everything that's happened, it's sometimes hard to remember that until quite recently it *did* look unbeatable. When I first arrived at BOT, only a couple of years ago, Royal was being described as 'the best bank in the world'.

Across the ocean, the subprime market was just beginning to turn, but Ireland was still booming. Coming from Paris, which for several years had been in the doldrums, I felt like I had stepped through the looking glass. Every day was like Christmas Eve: the shops, the pubs, the restaurants were all full, all of the time. In the beginning, the boom was fuelled by IT and pharmaceuticals. Now it was construction. Dublin was undergoing its very own Haussmannization. Cranes cluttered the skyline, new builds were everywhere; the old architecture, meanwhile, was being transformed, hospitals becoming shopping malls, churches becoming superpubs, Ascendancy manors becoming five-star golf resorts.

And at the heart of it all was Royal. They were the developers' bank of choice, spinning out the credit from which the new city would be built. In the fevered boomtown climate, the value of property could double every six months; already several of these developers had become billionaires. But they didn't rest on their laurels. Instead, they used what they'd made on their last project to borrow more for their next one. Royal were happy to pay out: they had a steady stream of cheap credit from European investors, eager to gain exposure to the turbocharged Irish economy.

Only Bank of Torabundo stayed away. Our chief executive, Sir Colin Shred, was deeply sceptical about Royal. He thought they were over-invested in a single sector, he thought that sector was heading for a crash. But Royal's share price had risen astronomically – 2,000 per cent in seven years – and our clients were howling at the fortunes they were missing out on. It was clear to me within a few weeks of starting at BOT that if I could change Sir Colin's mind, many people would be grateful to me.

I decided to set up a meeting with Royal's CEO, Miles O'Connor, to talk through his figures and long-term strategy. But this proved far from easy. As head of the best bank in the world, Miles was a man much in demand. Businessmen and governments alike clamoured to learn his secrets; he was flying all over the world, dispensing wisdom. I had almost given up hope when Bruce Gaffney, a salesman I knew at Royal, called to tell me that if I came to the Shelbourne Hotel that night he could get me five minutes – no more.

Royal's AGM had been that morning and an air of jubilation filled the hotel lobby, along with wafts of cigar smoke that drifted in through the revolving doors. When he began at Royal, then an inconsequential boutique, Miles had targeted the rugby clubs both for staff and for clients; the atmosphere tonight was that of a locker room, loud with backslapping and hur-hur-hurring; the waitresses were having a hard time. I spent what seemed like many hours on the margins of things, having the same desultory conversation about the French scrum over and over again. Any time I caught a glimpse of Miles, he was at the centre of a cluster of men who hung on his every word like barfly apostles. Then, out of the blue (or had Bruce, unbeknownst to me, intervened?), I found myself thrust up against him.

I had not expected to like him, but I did. Moments after meeting me, the leader of one of the world's most successful banks was calling me a 'sound cunt' and asking what I was drinking! After working in Paris, where everything was swamped in protocol and 23-year-old men conducted themselves like mouldering dukes, I found this refreshing to say the least. He was slight, silver-haired, foxy, quite unlike the meaty second-row types he liked to surround himself with; he was smoking a fat cigar, which in the reception room of one of Dublin's oldest and costliest hotels was even more against the rules than it was elsewhere. He had a mischievous sense of humour.

'Take a look, Claude,' he said, pulling his phone from his pocket. 'What do you make of this fella, eh?' I looked at the phone. On the screen was a picture of a glossy black stallion. 'His name's Turbolot,' Miles said. 'We're thinking of appointing him to the board.' His frank black eyes regarded mine. I gazed back at him dumbly. Slapping my stomach with the back of his hand, he hooted with laughter. 'Your face! Jesus Christ!'

He knew Sir Colin didn't care for him. He didn't seem to mind; instead he found it quite natural. 'He's a Brit. He hates to see the Paddies getting ahead. To him, that's the lunatics taking over the fucking asylum. But the tide has turned, Claude, that's what he needs to accept. Do you know what we did last week? Bankrolled a consortium to buy the Chichester Hotel from the Duke of Edinburgh. The Irish are buying up the Queen's fucking back garden! Of course the old guard don't like it.'

'He thinks you've taken on too much risk,' I told him; I realized that with him I could speak directly. 'He thinks you've left yourself exposed if the market turns.'

Miles dismissed this with a wave of his cigar. 'Look, Claude, he's your boss, I don't want to speak ill of him. But Sir Colin's a fossil. He's the remnant of an empire that's spent the last hundred fucking years slowly sinking into the sea. Ireland is different. It's small, it's young, it's versatile. And because in Ireland we're not wedded to a whole lot of empty protocol, we understand that when change happens, it's big! And it's fast! There isn't time to run all your decisions past Risk and Treasury and whoever else. Your job is to get the money out to the fella who's going to use it, ASA-fucking-P, and there's an end to it. *He* doesn't want to be hassled by some prat with a diploma looking for fucking pie charts and breakdowns and all that. He wants to make something happen. He wants to do a fucking deal. Now the question is, are you going to help him?'

He looked me straight in the eye, smoke pumping from his mouth in industrial quantities, sweat beading on his brow, his bow tie slightly askew. 'Listen,' he said, 'you're here to ask me how it all works, and I'm just going to tell you the truth, which is that I don't have the faintest fucking notion. Sometimes I feel like the dog that woke up with two mickeys – I know it's a good thing, but I'm fucked if I know how it happened. I'll tell you this, though: the Irish have been everybody's bloody slave long enough. It used to be whenever I'd go to the airport it'd be full of young people shipping off to Australia or New York for whatever gammy bit of work they could get. Now when I go the airport I see them coming back. Coming home, because they can have a better life here. I know it's all supposed to be about the bottom line. But I'm proud of that, I'm bloody proud. You'll have another?'

He pointed at the half-empty glass in my hand; before I could reply, he had disappeared and a fresh pint materialized. It took me a moment to realize that was the end of the interview. But when I thought about it, what more analysis did I need? He was right, wasn't he? Maybe on paper the bank looked vulnerable – but that was only if you believed in the old way of doing things. The world was changing. Switch on the television, you saw ordinary people being turned into superstars overnight. Why shouldn't Miles and his developers do the same for Ireland? Why should they be weighed down by the relics of the past? History was being rolled back, ancient oppressions undone; did it matter if the bank's loan book outweighed its deposits?

To Sir Colin it did. He rejected my request to issue a 'Buy' recommend for Royal; he declined to hear the presentation I'd put together. Later I heard that was when the board of directors began to mass themselves against him. But of course he was right. Looking through Royal's loan book now is like swimming through a drowned world, the numerical ruins of hotels and houses, of malls and towers and temples, all buried under blue-tinged, airless fathoms of debt; the city is being sold off piece by piece, for bargain-basement rates, and the airports are full of people saying goodbye.

'You are ready to order?'

'Not yet, thank you, I am waiting for someone.' I speak off-handedly, without quite looking at her.

'Okay,' Ariadne says gaily. 'Call when you want me.'

I watch her glide away, divert her course at a raised finger, lavish her smile on two men in iron-grey suits who don't know quite what to do with it. Outside, a steam of ricocheting droplets hovers over the plaza. For the last week the rain has been almost continuous; in the office we have all become experts in its different personae and gradations – can predict the worst of downpours, gauge the gaps that will allow us a coffee run. More than once I have dreamed that the Ark has come unmoored and floated away with me in it.

'Checking out the arses, eh?'

I look up. Bruce Gaffney, my Royal Irish contact, is grinning down at me, emitting his familiar emphysemic-dog laugh, *hcchh hcchh hcchh*. He peels off his raincoat, parks himself across the table from me. 'I wondered why you wanted to meet in this kip. Now I get it. How's tricks, Claudius? What can I do you for?'

I tell him the government has commissioned a report from us on Royal. He issues a comical huff of exasperation. 'Reports,' he says. 'They can't get enough of those things, can they?'

'The last recapitalization didn't work. You're running out of money faster than they can replace it. They're wondering if there's any point giving you more.'

'Well, if they don't want to see yours truly fed to the sharks by a bunch of very fucking unhappy bondholders they'll keep the taps on,' he says. 'You're French, Claude, you know the famous German bonhomie doesn't stretch all that far.'

Ariadne returns with her order pad; I ask for two coffees. The instant she turns away, Bruce goes into a routine, boggling, winking, panting in fake agony. 'The point is, soon there won't be any money left to give you,' I say, ignoring this. 'They can't raise those kinds of funds any more.'

'Dark times, Claudius, dark times,' Bruce Gaffney says, and shakes his head, as if I have been telling him about some other bank in some other country very, very far away. 'Aha!' He brightens, as Ariadne returns with our coffee. 'The goddess of the grounds. The Beatrice of the bean. Thank you, darling.'

I try again. 'Can you survive without another recap?'

'What, nothing at all?' he says, as if affronted, then, seeing my expression, changes tack: 'What I mean is, we're almost over the hump! If we could get another, say, seven billion, we'd definitely be able to hold our own till this all blows over.'

'You said that the last time.'

'Yeah, but last time we should have said we needed fourteen billion. I don't know where we got seven, frankly. Some trainee probably just made it up.'

'But you see' – I am struggling to keep my patience – 'that's exactly why they've asked me to write this report. They don't trust the figures you're giving them.'

'Right, right,' he says, his attention wandering across the plaza again; then, as I open a folder and pass a spreadsheet over to him,

'Ah, here, don't be dumping this stuff on me, not on a bloody Friday afternoon.'

'I just wanted to know if you can clarify some things.'

He rolls his eyes, presses his lips, as if I had brought him to lunch and then tried to sell him a watch.

'This figure here, do you know what it relates to?'

'What, off the top of my head?'

'It's fifty million euro.'

'I don't know,' he says. 'Gandon.'

'Gandon is here. Whitcroft is here. Dreyer's, Gane International, all those are accounted for. But this money here, there's no indication where it's going. Instead someone's tried to bury it by hiding it inside another transaction.'

Bruce Gaffney flicks his teeth with his fingers to produce the first two bars of 'La Marseillaise'. 'Must be one of those things, then, mustn't it?'

'What things?'

'The things they have on aeroplanes. That they dig up when it crashes. What do you call it? A black box.'

'A black box?'

'Yeah, a black box.'

'You are telling me nobody knows what this fifty million might relate to.'

He shrugs, looks me full on. The plaza passes translucent in his glasses, veiling his eyes.

'I'm trying to help you,' I say.

'Oh Jesus!' He throws up an exasperated hand. 'Maybe Miles took a few quid out to invest or something. It's a bank, Claude, it's a highly complicated fucking, you know, operation. I mean, are you going to put every single rubber fucking band into this bloody report?'

'With so many irregularities it will be hard to find a buyer.'

'Fine, fuck the buyers. It'll sort itself out. Like I've told you for the last two fucking years, what Royal has is a minor cash-flow problem. The real issue is that we're being made the scapegoats. We're carrying the can for the whole country turning to shit. Well, fuck that, Claude. Fuck that. It's not like we went around putting a gun to people's heads and telling them to take out a second mortgage. Everybody partied. Now they're blaming us for their hangover.' The flare of temper is quickly damped down; he becomes affable again, solicitous. He leans in closer to the table. 'Look, I know the books are a bit of a mess. It's fucking Royal, what do you expect? But the fact of the matter is the place is *sound*. I'm in there every day. I can tell you with my hand on my heart, it's sound. Now I know you're a straight shooter, I'm not going to tell you what to put in your report. But I would ask, as a colleague, that you give the full story. Don't just be banging on exclusively about anomalies or black boxes or whatever the fucking secretary dropped behind the radiator.'

As he gets up I ask him about Dublex.

'What about Dublex?' he says.

'Do they have a holding in Royal?'

This time his ignorance seems genuine. 'First I've heard of it. Walter crawls out of his gravel pit the odd time for a round of golf with the board, but that's about the size of it.' Now a smile crosses his face. 'Here, have you seen these lads dressed as zombies outside the new HQ? It's fucking classic, there's a zombie Miles and everything, this little lad with a silver wig and this suit covered in shit? Hilarious.' He pauses judiciously at the door. 'See, that's the kind of protest they should have in Greece instead of chucking petrol bombs. They're making their point but at the same time giving everyone a bit of a laugh. Fuck knows we could use one. Good to see you, Claude. If there's anything else I can do for you, you know where to ask.' He points at his bottom, then hurries ('Fuck's sake!') back into the rain.

I gather the documents spread over the table, tap them straight, set them down again. There is nothing I can do that will make them make sense; they are not a black box, but a black hole, into which time, trust, meaning, other people's money, disappear endlessly.

'Another coffee?' Ariadne has reappeared at my shoulder.

I smile stiffly. 'I should go back to work.'

'You can wait till rain stops,' she says, and then, 'Hey – you want to try something?' Before I can reply she has whisked away, and then whisked back again with a plate. 'Baklava. It's my grandmother's recipe.'

She hovers as I lift a forkful to my mouth. The cake is sweet and sticky, with crunches of almond and cinnamon. It's hard to eat with her watching me, and also hard to swallow, and speak. Nevertheless, I am able to declare, mostly honestly, that I like it.

'My grandmother makes it much better. I think it's maybe the honey she use.'

'No, it's good,' I say, taking another bite. 'Savoureux, as we say in France.'

'In Greek, we say nostimo. Which means, hmm, something you want to come back to. You know, like nostalgia, the pain to want to return home.' She laughs. 'That's Greece, you cannot even eat a cake without the past come looking for you.'

I smile. How green her eyes are, and bright; looking into them is like walking through an enchanted forest. It strikes me that I am alone with her; I feel an odd sense of unburdenment, as if we are two characters in a play meeting in the wings while the scenery is changed.

'So, you are from Greece?' I say, wincing internally at my accent, the dinosaur-clomp of the words. 'What has made you come to Ireland?'

'Ha ha, you watch the news?'

'It has not always been like this.'

'No, until this year we cover it up. And you, you're from France?'

'Yes,' I say. There is a pause; I realize in horror that I have exhausted my entire conversational repertoire.

'And your friend too?' She nods at the empty seat.

'He is not my friend.'

'Not the man, today. The other one. Doesn't wear a suit, always in black.'

'Oh, him. No, he is Irish.'

'Why doesn't he come here any more?'

'He, ah . . . well, he lost his job.'

'Ah, that's a shame.' She appears genuinely dismayed. 'I always liked to see you two talking. It look like you are coming up with a secret plan. I thought someday maybe you'd call me over, make me a part of it. "Okay, Ariadne, here's what we're gonna do." '

'We almost did,' I say.

'Well, if you ever make another, let me tell you I am a very good person to be included.'

'Is that right,' I say levelly, though I feel like I'm in a car that is spinning out of control.

'Yes, because, for a beginning, I can make special cake with magical powers of returning the past. I can paint the abstract paintings with magical powers of not selling. And, hmm, I can use my Greekness to give the etymologies of many words, very useful quality.'

'Give me an example.'

She draws herself up straight, knits her brows, takes a moment. 'So,' she says. 'This word *psyche*, that means your mind or your soul or your spirit. In Greece, in ancient times, *psyche* was the word for a butterfly. And in those times they think, when you are nervous about something, or you feel something intensely, you have inside you a *psyche*. And then slowly the meaning changed, and this *psyche* becomes something immortal that is essential to you.'

'But that's how the idea of the soul began? From butterflies in the stomach?'

'Or you can look at it the other way round,' she says, fixing me in her green gaze. 'You can say these moments when inside you is jumping – like when you're talking to somebody you like – that's how you know you have a soul.'

And she smiles, and I smile, and her eyes glow at me, and with a flurry of heartbeats I have the indescribable but irrefutable sense that I am back in the story again, or that life and story have somehow come together in one impossibly fragile moment, like a *psyche*, a butterfly lighting on my palm . . .

Raised voices can be heard as I approach the door, but this time I resist the urge to eavesdrop. I knock stoutly; after a series of rattles and chunks it opens a fraction. Paul's beleaguered face falls further when he sees me.

'Oh God, you again? I told you I was sorry, can't you just leave me alone?'

'Wait!' I jam my foot in the door. 'I need to talk to you.'

'There's nothing to talk about!'

'Just for a minute. Please. You owe me that much.'

He begins to speak, then relents. 'Okay, come on.'

Clizia is by the refrigerator, brandishing, for reasons I do not inquire into, a frying pan. The air is decidedly fraught, and a repetitive croaking issues from the next room.

'I hope I am not interrupting . . .'

'Haven't interrupted anything, Claude. Just enjoying a peaceful, non-violent breakfast here with my totally functional family. Can I get you something? A coffee, maybe? Clizia, would you mind fixing our guest a coffee?'

'We don't have coffee,' she says.

'Well, how about tea then? Tea all right with you, Claude?'

'Whatever is convenient,' I say.

'No tea either,' Clizia says. Her accent makes everything she says sound contemptuous, as if every statement were preceded by a long pull on a cigarette and a defiant billow of smoke. Paul half-turns in his chair. 'We don't have tea or coffee?'

'You vant me to steal some?' she says.

'A glass of water would be perfect,' I say.

Remington wanders through the bedroom door, burping.

Paul pours a glass of brownish water and plonks it down in front of me. 'It tastes a bit strange, but we think it's basically okay,' he says. 'Okay, so what do you want to talk to me about? Remington, for God's sake, stop burping.'

'It's my *burp*-day.'

'It's incredibly annoying,' Paul says. 'Sorry, Claude, go on.'

'I want to ask you about Ariadne.'

'The waitress? What about her?'

I tell him about our conversation in the café yesterday, its strangely pregnant undertone.

'Okay,' he says. 'But what's that got to do with me?'

'That time in the Ark you said she would be the perfect love interest for the Everyman.'

'Yes.'

'So I want to know – what happens next?'

'Next?'

'In the story.'

Paul looks mystified. 'I don't understand what you're getting at,' he says.

'What I'm getting at is, I have somehow found myself in the plot of your novel. And I want to know what I should do.'

'You're asking me for love advice, is that it?'

'I'm asking what you think will happen next in the novel of the Everyman.'

'There is no novel,' he says, with a touch of desperation. 'We've been through this.'

'What if I asked you to write it,' I say.

There is a long silence; even Remington stops his burping. 'Is this some kind of joke?' Paul says.

'No joke. When we spoke in the café you told me my life lacked a story. Obviously you had your own agenda. Nevertheless you were right. What I am asking you now is to write that story.'

He glances back at his wife, as if to assure himself he isn't dreaming. Leaned against the fridge, Clizia stares down at me impassively. In the morning light, the apartment's veneer of opulence is thinner, and I can see signs of decay all around: drawers off their runners, nails poking jaggedly from floorboards, a long silver split in the obsidian countertop.

Paul gets up, backs away to the sink, looks at the floor. 'I'm very flattered that you should ask me,' he says slowly. 'But I don't write books any more. I told you that.'

'I'm not talking about a book.' I take a sip of brackish water, lean forward on my chair. 'You said that what the Everyman needed was a love story. Now I want you to help me plot that story.'

'In real life?'

'In real life. Move the narrative forward, create scenes, maybe some dialogue. Essentially, nothing different from what you have done before, only that, instead of putting my life into your book, you would, so to speak, put your book into my life.'

Remington burps thoughtfully. Paul pulls his hands through his hair and down his face, as if I have set him some fiendish mathematical problem. 'Claude – look – I don't want to hurt your feelings, but that is a really fucking weird idea.'

'It's unusual,' I agree. 'But it is quite rational. When we want medical advice, we go to our doctor. When we want financial advice, we speak to our broker. We are happy to delegate many areas of our lives to people better qualified. Why should relationships be any different? When we fall in love, why not have a specialist to advise us? Someone who understands human nature, who can help us to express the right feelings?'

'Pff, is crazy talk,' Clizia says.

'Of course, I would be willing to pay whatever you feel such a service merited,' I add.

'Not interested,' Clizia says.

'Hold on,' Paul intervenes. 'Didn't you hear him? He says he's going to pay!'

'It will never work,' she says. 'No one falls in love with a disguise.'

'On the contrary,' I say, 'people fall in love with disguises all the time.'

'And what happens when this woman finds out truth? You want this man make you scripts for the rest of your life? He is not even any longer writer!'

'Well, hold on a second,' Paul objects. 'I can write if I want. If someone's going to pay me, then I'll write.'

'Ha, you have not written word in seven years!'

'Look, would you please just – Jesus, Remington, what are you doing to that rug?'

'I want to see if the grey bits taste different from the blue bits.'

With a gurgle of exasperation, his father picks him up and carries him to the sink, where he begins wiping fluff from his tongue.

'If you want to become close to this woman, you bring her a nice bunch of flowers,' Clizia says to me. 'Not idiot conspiracy.'

'It's his money, isn't it? He can do what he wants with it,' Paul says, over his shoulder. 'Look, this is impossible. Come on, Claude, let's go somewhere we can talk about this in peace.'

'Wait!' With a swift sidestep, Clizia blocks his passage. 'Bring the boy!'

'But we're trying to have a meeting!'

'He needs fresh air.'

'Clizia, the whole reason we're going somewhere else is that neither of you will be there!'

Clizia folds her arms.

'Can we go to the park, Dad?' Remington tugs his sleeve. 'Can we feed the ducks?'

'Oh Christ,' Paul says. 'Sorry about this, Claude.'

'Not at all,' I say. 'The park is a perfectly good place for a meeting.'

Remington runs to the fridge and comes back with a bag which he presents to his father. Paul looks displeased.

'We have no tea or coffee, but we've got a whole loaf of stale bread?' he says. 'We've nothing for the humans, but a fridge full of food for the ducks?'

Clizia chooses not to hear this.

Scowling, Paul puts Remington's coat on and leads us out to the hall. 'Let me give you a piece of advice, Claude,' he says, pulling the door closed. 'Never marry a lap dancer.'

'Right,' I say uncertainly, and follow them down the dimly lit corridor.

The lift is still broken, and on the landing the plastic sheeting that covers the portal to the unfinished wing whispers and sways. 'Are there other people living here?' I ask.

'That depends what you mean by *living*,' he says, starting down the stairs. 'And by *people*.'

'Oh,' I say.

'Ours is the only apartment they actually managed to sell. We bought it off the plans.' He laughs. 'That was the boom for you. A first-time novelist and an ex-stripper could get half a million from the bank for an apartment that didn't exist yet. Now we're in so much negative equity we'll probably be stuck here for the rest of our lives.'

'It's a nice apartment.'

'It's a classic Celtic Tiger piece of shit. There's a Jacuzzi, but the water's brown. There's a heated towel-rail in every room, but the radiators don't work. That's not the worst of it, either.' He pushes through a heavy metal door, to a vast, inky space; at first I have the bizarre notion that we are underwater, then in the distance I spy a car. 'Look at that.' He points to the wall. A long, ragged crack stretches all the way from the ground to the ceiling. 'And there's another one, on that side. And another one there.'

'What happened?' It looks as if there has been an earthquake.

'Pyrite. In the walls, in the foundations. It expands when it gets wet. They might as well have built the place with icing sugar.'

'So . . .' I frown, not wanting to draw the obvious conclusion.

'The whole building's worthless. Totally worthless. Ten years

165

or so it'll probably fall down with us in it. Until then, of course, the bank still wants its mortgage repayments.'

'Dad, can I have the keys?'

Remington runs off to a point right in the centre of the grey morass, where he raises his arm stiffly, like an orchestra conductor; in its corner, the car bleeps and flashes obediently. He scurries over to it and opens the door.

'There's nothing you can do?'

'Not much. The builder's gone bust. The insurance say they're not liable. We don't have the money to bring it to court.' He climbs into the car. Remington has already belted himself in at the back. 'It could be worse,' he says. 'As a former novelist, I do get some enjoyment out of living in a giant metaphor. Pyrite. Fool's fucking gold. If you put it in a book, no one would believe it.'

He starts the engine; we pull out into the wan sunshine. The neighbourhood doesn't look much better by day. A new selection of garbage lines the footpath; the street is deserted, but in the heavily graffitied playground a succession of cadaverous figures shuffles up to a man in a leather jacket, while a solitary child amuses itself on the broken merry-go-round.

'Dad, how many ducks are there in the park?'

'Twenty-six.'

'Do you think there was ever a boy who had a pet duck and he kept it in his bedroom?'

'No, I don't think there was.' He cranes his head around. 'Now, Daddy and Claude have important things to talk about, so I want you to play at being quiet, okay?'

'Okay. Dad?'

'Yes?'

'Who would win in a battle between Aslan and a dinosaur?'

'Aslan would win.'

'Even if the dinosaur was really big?'

'Yes.'

'Even if he was bigger than the universe?'

'Is this you being quiet?'

'Oh yeah,' Remington remembers.

The car noses on to a bridge; the river glints sullenly below us.

'So your wife,' I say.

'What about her?'

I want to ask him about what he said in the hallway about marrying a lap dancer, but can't quite summon the courage. 'She is from Eastern Europe?'

'That's right. Little place called Ectovia. Used to be part of Makhtovia, then when Transvolga seceded from Makhtovia it became a subdistrict of Transvolga. Then it seceded from Transvolga, to become the Ectovian Free Democratic Republic. Though "Free" is a bit of a stretch, they've had the same president for the last fifteen years. He used to be a carpet salesman. In fact, he sold us the rug in the living room, the one Remington was licking, I don't know if you saw it?'

'And how did she come to be in Ireland?'

'Well, the Ectovian economy's been in a bad way for a long time now. No jobs, no money, young people queuing up to leave. Clizia was one of the lucky ones, she was recruited to come here and work as a waitress. But then when she arrived, she found out she'd actually been contracted to a lap-dancing club. She couldn't get out of it till she'd paid off the people who brought her over.'

'And is that . . . how you met?'

He laughs. 'I'm afraid so. I was out celebrating my book deal with some friends; Velvet Dream's is where we ended up. My friends got me a lap dance with Clizia as a joke. You can't imagine how embarrassed I was, this woman who looked like she'd just come down from Mount Olympus, and she's stuck in this little cubicle with me, doing this ridiculous . . . Anyway, I was so nervous I started jabbering away to her about my book, and then *she*, who's standing there in her underwear, starts telling me about Dostoyevsky and the dialogic imagination. I didn't even know what the dialogic imagination was. I still don't. But by the time I left that cubicle I was head-over-heels in love with her.'

We come off the bridge and nose our way slowly along the quay, in the opposite direction to the river.

'In Ectovia, they take literature very seriously, that's what I found out later. They used to have a special firing squad just for novelists.'

'And does she still work there? In Velvet Dream's?' Thinking this might explain my bizarre encounter with him last week.

'No, she hasn't done that stuff for a long time. A couple of weeks after I met her I bought her out of her contract. Took half my advance, probably the most romantic thing I've ever done.' He pauses, and then says, 'I'm not sure she ever forgave me.'

I study his face, but in profile it's hard to read his expression. 'She works as a cleaner now,' he continues. 'Offices, private residences.'

'Does she like it?'

'Like it?' He turns to me as we pull up at a traffic light. 'Getting up at 5 a.m. to clean toilets for minimum wage?'

'Sorry, silly question.'

'Clizia's got two degrees, Claude. She's read more books than anyone I've ever met.'

'Sorry.'

The light turns green. To the left, the tanks and towers and vats of the Guinness factory loom zanily over a high stone wall, like something from an alcoholic fairy tale. 'It could be worse,' he says. 'At least as a cleaner she doesn't have people looking at her. She's basically paid to be invisible. Although it's not nearly as much as she got paid for taking her clothes off.'

'And you?'

'Me what?'

'You are working too?'

'I have a few irons in the fire.'

'A book?'

He wags his head. 'That ship has sailed. Maybe in a country like Clizia's, where they've only got three hours of electricity a day, you can still make a living writing books. Here people don't want them any more. They've got other things. Phones. Games. Porn. Horse tranquillizers. I'm not complaining, I'm just saying, these are the market realities.'

'And it is these market realities that persuaded you to stop writing?' I say.

'Pretty much.'

'It was not, for example, because of the review?'

'What review?' His head snaps round.

'The Mary Cutlass review of *For Love of a Clown*.'

'Oh, that,' he says. His tone is indifferent, but his face has turned the colour of a London bus. 'I didn't pay much attention to it.'

'Really?'

'All that woman likes to read about is genocide,' he says. 'The Holocaust, Rwanda, Cambodia, Srebrenica, if you're writing about some soul-harrowing nadir of human depravity you get a big gold star. My book is about a girl who falls in love with a clown. How could she not hate it? It was like sending a dog to review *Cats*.'

He still hasn't explained what he meant by irons in the fire, but before I can ask him an enormous peal of thunder shakes the sky; a moment later, water sluices down with a kind of exultancy.

'Dad, it's raining.'

'I can see that.'

'Are we going home?'

'No, we're not.'

Signalling right, he brings us back over the river and up through an imposing gate. On either side of a long avenue, behind cascading veils of rain, the park materializes as a damp shimmer of colours, viridian, jade, ochre and crimson bleeding into one another and pulsating weakly as if through static. 'A duck!'

Remington cries. He is right: between a pond and a bed of rose bushes stands a lone mallard, his motionless beak pointed proudly skywards. The car pulls up; grabbing his bread, Remington makes a bid for the door. His father yanks him back by the hood of his coat.

'It's pouring rain! What's your mother going to say if I bring you home soaking wet?'

'We could tell her I fell into the pond?' Remington says hopefully.

'We'll just have to wait till it stops,' Paul says. As he speaks another peal of thunder cracks through the sky.

'Jesus Christ,' Remington says in the back seat.

'Remington.'

'I'm just saying what you say,' Remington replies innocently.

Paul mumbles darkly to himself.

'Christ, what a country,' Remington says.

'That's enough.'

'Jesus fucking Christ, this fucking country.'

'Okay, look' – Paul unbuckles his seat belt, then opens the door to extricate Remington – 'try and find a dry part to play in, will you?'

With an exclamation of pure joy, Remington tears away across the grass, throwing fistfuls of bread at the surprised duck.

'He is a very energetic little boy,' I say.

'He certainly is.'

'*Remington*,' I repeat. 'Is that a family name? Or from your wife's homeland, perhaps?'

'Not exactly, Claude,' he replies, with false pleasantness. 'Tell me, have you ever heard of a TV detective called Remington cocksmoking Steele?'

'Of course, although in France he is just called Remington Steele.'

'Well, it turns out that in a certain corner of the former Soviet Union old *Remington Steele* is still very popular. In fact, it's the number one show over there, bigger even than *Celebrity Gulag* and *Top Ten Interrogation Bloopers*. I thought it was a ludicrous name for a boy. But I was overruled.'

Out on the lawn, the duck has escaped; Remington entertains himself by running around in long, uneven ellipses, making quacking noises. He seems not to notice the rain. Looking out at him, Paul folds his hands atop the steering wheel. 'Okay, Claude. This proposal of yours. I'm presuming it's some kind of revenge, right? Some kind of sting or hidden-camera-type deal, where you can show my web of lies to the world?'

'No,' I say, disconcerted. 'It is just as I said to you in the apartment. I have developed feelings for Ariadne, but it's been a long time since I've had any kind of relationship, and I fear that, as you said, there is not enough of me showing up on the page.'

'So you want me to help you.'

'That's right.'

'You want me to rewrite your character, so it'll click with this girl in the café, like *Pretty Woman* or something.'

'Yes, or *Cyrano de Bergerac*. You have diagnosed very accurately the emptiness of my life. Now I want you to help me to fill it.'

He puffs out his cheeks, watches a busload of ponchoed tourists alight into the rain.

'You don't like it. You think it is an impossible idea.'

'It's not that I don't like it,' he says. 'Frankly, I'm so broke that if you were proposing I dress up as your nanny and spank you I'd give it serious consideration. But I don't *get* it. You're not a bad-looking guy. You have a ton of money, you've got your whole French thing going on. What do you need me for? There must be lots of women out there just dying to jump in the sack with you.'

'They are all the wrong women.'

'And Ariadne, who you barely know, you're certain is the right woman.'

'Yes. But I don't think she will be impressed by my money. Or my Frenchness.'

'It's always the one you can't have, eh?'

'I don't know. It is this time.'

'And why ask me?'

'I liked your novel. It seems to me that it too is a story of opposites attracting.'

'Okay, sure, but the fact remains I tried to rip you off, Claude. Why would you trust me after that?'

I consider this. 'Your plan was very stupid. Yet your intuitions were strong. First, to pick me out as the subject for your scam – to find someone, as you say, who feels something is missing from his life and so can be manipulated. The next thing, you discover Ariadne. From all the women you could have chosen, you find exactly the one I will fall in love with.'

'I picked her out because she happened to be in my line of vision. If it had been the blonde one I would have said her.'

'I disagree. These split-second decisions are a matter of pure instinct. It's the same thing that makes the great trader. He can see the story before anyone else – not all of it, just the first lines, the edges, as they are coming out of the future. But that is enough.'

Paul does not react to this, just continues to gaze at the shifting silver-grey mosaic of the rain on the windscreen. 'You don't have to literally write the words in my mouth,' I tell him. 'What I want is a consultant. Someone who understands this world of the heart that has become foreign to me and can advise me what to do. If you agree, then I propose to pay you –'

I name a sum; I feel it is generous. But he seems unmoved. I don't understand.

'There is no downside here. Even if you think it's a waste of time, you'll still get paid. It isn't exactly writing, but at the very least it'll pay for you to reclaim your desk from the pawn shop.' At the mention of the desk he flinches, but before he can speak there comes a cry from outside. From the top of an incline,

Remington is shouting that he has found something. His father rolls down the window.

'What is it?'

'I found an ant!' the boy shrieks. 'Look, Dad, look!'

He hurtles down the hill and over to the car, holding out his cupped hands. A tiny black shape scurries back and forth over the pink dunes of his palms – antennae flailing, all its landmarks stripped away in an instant. I feel a surge of pity and recognition.

'Can I keep him, Dad?'

'What do you want an ant for?'

'To be my friend.'

'Hmm, I don't know if we've got room in the apartment for pets.'

'Please?'

'All right, all right. Now shake off some of that water, we're going home.'

'Where will I put my ant?'

'I don't know, stick him in your pocket.'

'I have a box,' I interject hastily, and dig around in my coat. Emptying out a heap of breath mints, I present the plastic case to Remington, who tips the bewildered ant inside.

Paul gets out to put the boy into his seat, then climbs back into his own. But he doesn't start the engine; he just sits there, contemplating the rain. Then at last he turns to me. 'I'll do it,' he says. 'But it'll cost you —'

The figure he names is double what I proposed. His audacity makes me laugh. 'Maybe you should be working for BOT.'

'Maybe I shouldn't have got in half a million euros' worth of debt,' he says without smiling. 'Then I wouldn't have had to start thinking like a banker.'

'I think I'll call him Roland,' Remington says, dangling the breath-mints box before his nose in the back seat. 'Sit, Roland. Stay, Roland. Play dead, Roland.'

'What kind of name is Roland for an ant?' Paul objects. 'Think of something else.'

'Hmm . . . Roland?' Remington says.

Paul turns around in his seat. 'Jesus Christ, Remington, the name you just thought of was Roland.'

'What's a good name for an ant, Dad?'

Paul thinks for a minute. 'Anthony,' he says.

Remington and I are forced to concede that this is a good name.

'See, that's what you're paying for,' Paul says.

I mean to keep it to myself, but am so excited that in a moment of weakness I let slip to Ish that I have engaged the writer's services. She is not impressed.

'I can't believe you're even talking to that slimeball,' she says.

'There didn't seem any point in holding a grudge,' I say. 'After all, he didn't actually do anything.'

'He did plenty,' Ish says. 'Imagine if his plan had come off, where would we be then?'

'Now I have seen how he lives I can understand it a lot better,' I tell her. 'He has a young family. He's deeply in debt. He bought an apartment during the boom that is now worth a fraction of its original price.'

'Join the club,' Ish comments mordantly.

'He's stopped writing.'

'Completely?' This takes her by surprise.

'He hasn't written anything for seven years.'

'So what does he do all day?'

'Nothing. Drinks, goes to strip clubs.'

'So you're going to give him another crack at robbing the bank, is that it?'

I don't answer. Ariadne has arrived with our orders. She smiles at me as she sets down the plate, I smile back at her . . .

'Claude?'

'Ah, yes, so . . .' Without mentioning Ariadne, I give Ish the barest sketch of the plan, the idea of continuing the next months of my life 'as if they were in a book'.

'What's the point of that?' she says.

'I suppose it's a kind of life coaching. Embracing the moment, that kind of thing. Discovering my humanity.'

'That chancer, what does he know about humanity? When's the last time anyone saw *his* blimmin' humanity?'

'Well, this is only a pretext,' I say. 'My real hope is that if I ask him to create the scenarios for me, after a while he may be inspired actually to write the book.'

'The book about the banking Everyman?'

'That book. Any book. It seems to me that if he has a regular income, maybe he will no longer feel so disillusioned. He will remember he is happier as a working writer than as an unemployed con man. This is my – what do you say, ulterior motive?'

'Be careful, Claude,' she says gloomily. 'You can't try and change someone. My online psychic's always telling me that.' She chomps down on a stick of celery. 'Are we going to be in these, whatyoucall, scenarios as well?'

'Ha, I think I will keep him away from the bank this time. To avoid any temptation, you know.'

'Probably right,' Ish agrees. She crunches her food morosely for a moment, then says, 'The more I thought about it, the more I wondered if I wanted to be in a book anyway. You know, what if I turned out to be one of those characters nobody likes? And they skip all the bits with me in them, and they complain on Apeiron about how boring I am?'

'You're not boring.'

'If he was going to put me in a book, I'd much prefer it was the me from a few years ago. When I was travelling with Tog, going to all those amazing places.' She twirls the celery vacantly in the air, lost in some sad dream, then suddenly brightens. 'Oh, here, though. Did I show you my necklace? My mum just sent it over.'

She hooks the string with her finger, pulling it free of her neck so I can see it better. The necklace is composed of shells; they all appear white at first, but when I lean closer I see that they are very subtly graded, running from blue to pink.

'It's from Kokomoko?'

'Yeah, one of the tribal elders gave it to me. Here, I'll show you a picture.' She takes her tablet from her bag and pulls up an image of an extremely wizened old woman. 'Her name's Kavitatni. She's a king.'

'Not a queen?'

'No. She's a king from about three centuries ago, called Viri the Fierce.'

I am confused.

'Well, like I was telling you, on the island, everything and everyone's all bound up together.'

'In the gifts.'

'Yeah. Everything circulates, which means nobody really dies. Instead, all the ancestors are still floating around. They're in the gifts, they're on the fishing boat, they're at the feasts. And whenever there's an important decision to be made, the dead kings speak through their chosen mouthpiece.'

'So your friend here is . . . possessed by this King Viri?'

'Well, she channels him. It's quite funny when you've got some bigwig from Shell or whatever coming over wanting to talk about mining rights, and they find themselves having to make their presentation to the ghost of a king in the body of an old lady.'

There are more pictures, semi-naked people in coracles, or daubed in spirals, brandishing spears; I make appreciative noises, all the while watching Ariadne from the corner of my eye as she circulates between the tables.

Was Clizia right? Is my plan insane? Many of my colleagues have attended weekend seminars on picking up women, the kind that advise you to begin by insulting whoever it is you want to sleep with; others are signed up to Internet dating agencies that promise 'perfect love without suffering' by feeding your personal data into a computer to find your optimal match. Hiring a writer to mastermind my courtship does not seem significantly madder than these. And I wasn't lying to Ish: I do nourish hopes that I can coax Paul back to writing. If his debts didn't weigh so heavily, if he had time and space to think, why shouldn't his creativity flourish once more?

In the meantime, however, there is work, where the mood is less buoyant. We have been holding out hope that Tordale will come back to us, but today on the news we see the former British Prime Minister being welcomed by the Caliph of Oran to his magnificent palace. 'That's that, then,' Ish says.

Kevin doesn't follow. 'He's there with the UN,' he says. 'Setting up a ceasefire with the rebels.'

'That's just the cover story,' Ish says.

I explain that as soon as the Prime Minister left office, he had signed up as a consultant to one of the Big Three banks; that's the real reason he's in Oran.

'What would a politician know about banking?' Kevin asks.

'He doesn't need to know anything,' Ish says. 'His phone's got every head of state in it from the White House to Beijing. Think about it. You're a genocidal tyrant facing down a hundred thousand Islamic fundamentalists. Who do you want as your financial adviser? A bunch of nerds with four-colour pie charts? Or the guy with the back door to every nuclear missile silo in the Western world?'

It's just business; these things happen all the time. Still, the news casts a pall of gloom over the whole office. Then, as if he has sensed, from across the blue expanse of the Atlantic, his acolytes losing faith –

'Inspirational memo!' Kevin exclaims. 'A new one!'

'Holy shit!' Around the office people jump up from their cubicles, jack-in-the-box fashion, the better to contemplate the message.

' "All that glitters is not gold," ' Ish reads.

'What does it mean?' Kevin says. 'Why's he telling us all that glitters is not gold?'

'It's a riddle,' Ish decides.

'Are you talking about the Blankly email?' Joe Peston from TTM says, coming in from the lobby.

'Did you get it too?'

'Everybody got it.'

'What do you think it means?'

'Not sure,' Joe says, rubbing his jaw. 'It seems to operate on a number of different levels.'

'I imagine it means all that glitters is not gold,' I say. 'That is, be careful of overvalued stock.'

'What are we, four-year-olds?' Joe says. 'Everyone knows all that glitters isn't gold.'

'This guy's paid twenty-eight million dollars basic a year,' Jocelyn Lockhart concurs from across the divider. 'He's not getting that just to send his staff proverbs. There's a whatdoyoumacall. A subtext.'

'Maybe he wants us to short gold,' Kevin suggests. 'Like, when he says all that glitters isn't gold, he means gold is overvalued.'

'The price of gold has risen for the last six months,' Joe muses. 'Could be time for a correction.'

'If he wanted us to short gold, wouldn't he just tell us to short gold?' I say.

'What kind of a riddle would that be?'

'Yeah, Claude, don't be stupid.'

'The memo says all that glitters is *not* gold,' I point out. 'His issue is not with gold itself. He's talking about other, misleadingly glittering substances.'

The others agree that this is a good point. 'But if all that glitters *isn't* gold,' Jocelyn says slowly, raising a finger, 'then all that *doesn't* glitter isn't necessarily *not* gold. Right?'

There is a silence as we struggle to establish whether this

makes sense or not, and are still doing so when Jurgen clips in and tells us summarily that the Minister's office has been in touch again about the Royal Irish report, and that they do not think they can wait till the end of the week.

Ish and I look at each other. 'When do they want it?'

'Tomorrow,' Jurgen says.

'Tomorrow?' We boggle in unison.

'What's the rush?' Kevin says.

Jurgen wiggles a finger in his ear. 'My conjecture is that Royal Irish has run out of money again. If so the Minister will have to decide in the next few days whether to infuse yet more funds, or whether the time has at last come for a wind-down.'

'That's all very well, but how can we possibly get the report done by tomorrow?' Ish says. 'Do they have any idea how much information there is to go through?'

'There is a series of black boxes within the accounts,' I explain. 'I am beginning to think an anonymous investor has used them to build up a holding in the bank. Either way, it is very hard to get a clear picture of its status.'

Jurgen considers this. 'But you have a general idea?'

'Oh, we've got a general idea, all right,' Ish chimes in. 'It's fucked, that's the general idea.'

'My professional opinion would be that the bank is fucked,' I concur.

'They're facing litigation left and right,' Ish goes on. 'Their collateral's going up in flames. Their brand has become an international byword for corporate malfeasance. There's literally no telling how much they owe. The Minister can pour in as much money as he likes, it'll never be enough. They'll bleed him until there's nothing left.'

'And there is no positive spin we can put on this?' Jurgen says.

'That is the positive spin,' I say.

'Believe me, they don't want to see this report any sooner than they have to,' Ish says.

'What about the idea that the bank is of systemic importance? Too big to fail?'

'Not true,' I say. 'The bank's business is all in one small sector, commercial property. If the government decides to wind it down, the losses will be contained.'

'And the creditors?'

'Will face significant write-downs. But they will be expecting that.'

'Mmm.' Jurgen stalls momentarily in that way he has, as if encountering a glitch in his coding. Then he nods assent. 'Very good. Get as much done as you can before tomorrow. Rachael wants to see it before you sign off. And remember,' he says, pausing on his way back to the office, 'keep all this information confidential until the report is published.'

He turns to go, and is almost knocked down by Gary McCrum, who comes barrelling into the room in a state of extreme agitation. 'He solved the riddle!' he exclaims. 'He solved it and he's made a bloody fortune!'

'What?'

'Who did?'

'Howie! It was so simple! So simple!' For what seems like a long time he is too excited to tell us anything more; he just bounds around, hooting, like an ape that has won some banana lottery.

'What's the safest bet for an investor?' he says when we manage to calm him down. 'Better than gold, even?' He looks manically from one face to another. 'T-bills, right?'

'T-bills?' Kevin says, curiosity overcoming embarrassment.

'US Treasury bonds,' I tell him. 'Essentially IOUs issued by the American government. They are regarded as practically risk-free.'

'Oh, right, I knew that,' Kevin says.

'What's that got to do with Howie?' Ish asks.

'Don't you see?' Gary exclaims, partially reverting to ape mode. 'That's what Porter's email meant! T-bills are shakier than they look!'

'Howie bet against US Treasury bonds?' Joe Peston says, somewhat scandalized.

'It was him and Grisha. Some crazy fucking rocket-science deal using those weird antinomy things. But it came down to shorting T-bills. And then on the news – wait, have you heard the news?'

We turn to the TV, where the crawl tells us that a few minutes ago a Texan congressman, protesting government threats to take away the oil industry's billion-dollar subsidies, doused himself in gasoline in the House of Representatives and set himself on fire. A brief, almost unprocessable image flicks on screen, a writhing, suited silhouette at the centre of a ball of incandescent light, while horrified figures with tans and elaborate hairstyles clamber around him powerlessly.

'The Texans are talking about seceding from the Union,' Gary McCrum says happily. 'The dollar's sunk like a stone.'

And not just the dollar. In the resulting turmoil, Dexter's, the ratings agency, has downgraded the investment rating of the world's safest security from AAA to AA. What the repercussions for the rest of the world will be, no one can tell; but for BOT, it means one very, very, very lucrative trade.

'Betting against T-bills.' Joe Peston shakes his head in admiration.

'Extremely counterintuitive,' Jurgen notes. 'Essentially, Howie has combined two inspirational memos into one unstoppable supermemo.'

'But how did Blankly know?' Kevin asks. 'How did he *know* all this stuff was going to happen?'

'That's why they're paying him the big bucks,' Gary says, clapping him on the shoulder.

'Yeah,' Kevin says, turning towards the window and gazing up, as if Porter Blankly might be circling among the clouds out there, like Superman.

Official celebrations are scheduled for the following evening; tonight Kevin, Ish and I are trapped in the office, labouring to finish the report on time. The sixth floor empties and the lights in the buildings around us wink out one by one; the inky near-black of the sky only adds to the sense that we are literally submerged in Royal's accounts, a labyrinth of debt with some terrible wrongness at the centre of it that at times I catch a glimpse of but never for long enough to lay hold of . . .

'He'll get the idea,' Ish says, meaning the Minister. 'No way he'll chuck any more money at them after reading this. Best thing at this stage'd be just to shove them off a cliff.'

At 4 a.m. I mail the completed document to Rachael and Jurgen, then go back to my apartment to sleep for a couple of hours before returning to the office. Thankfully, the next day is relatively quiet, apart from a mid-morning meeting with Walter, most of which he spends complaining about the cost of port capacity in Belgium, where Dublex is shipping the cement they can no longer use in Ireland after the collapse of the construction industry. As I'm about to leave I ask him whether he has money in Royal Irish. He stares at me a moment, then says, deliberately, 'I have no holding in that bank.' I tell him that's good news, as it's about to lose whatever minimal value it still has. He doesn't respond to this; he's hiding something, but then businessmen are always hiding something, particularly at his level, where the meticulous world of contracts and accounts and due diligence dissolves, and international commerce reveals itself to be an ethereal matter of nods, winks, unspoken understandings.

As soon as evening falls, I set off for Paul's apartment to hear his initial 'plot outline'.

A commotion is issuing from inside. He answers the door as soon as I knock, his expression grave. 'Remington's ant escaped,' he tells me.

'Oh,' I say.

'Come on, come on,' he says, chivvying me over the threshold, 'we don't want it getting out.'

Obligingly I step in –

'Stop!' Paul shouts, frantically waving his arms and staring at my feet. I do as I am told, waiting on the spot for further instructions.

The scene in the apartment is chaotic. Cupboard doors have been flung open, tins emptied, drawers pulled out, hideous Ectovian rugs overturned. Clizia, dressed only in a towel, is on her hands and knees, calling 'Roland! Roland!' into the darkness under the couch. The ant's owner, meanwhile, is standing in the doorway opposite, a stubby, bellowing fountain of grief.

'It's the damnedest thing,' Paul says, getting down on all fours. 'That ant lived like a king. A nice cosy breath-mint box. A delicious sugar cube all to himself. Why would he run away?'

'I suppose a cage is a cage, no matter how opulent,' I reflect.

'In retrospect I may have made the air holes too big,' Paul reflects. 'Well, I hope he's happy, breaking a little boy's heart like that. The poor kid's been crying for so long I'm worried his body's going to run out of liquids. Here, I'll go this way, why don't you check in there.'

The bathroom is clouded with fragrant, Clizia-inflected steam, which makes it both hard to see anything and rather disconcertingly intimate. The small space is dominated by a Jacuzzi, black and gargantuan, like a hippopotamus backed into a broom closet; cluttering the damp rim are tubes of creams and lotions, many with the ends cut off so the remnants can be scraped out. A toilet, also black, looms menacingly out of the mist. I cannot see any ants, but reaching for the door handle I find myself grasping instead a pair of knickers that hang from it. They are sheer and stringy, almost to the point of dissolving in my hand; I feel embarrassed even being in the same room as them, and hurry out again, only to discover the way back blocked by Clizia, her towelled rear pointed up to me and her nose pressed to the floorboards in the manner of some impossibly sexual aardvark. 'I'll just take a look in here,' I say in a high voice, and push through the door on my left.

I am in the master bedroom. It features the same Babylonian trappings as the rest of the apartment – velour drapes, gilt sconces, ornate architrave – but here they are almost invisible, because everywhere I look, there are books: stacked double on shelves, crammed into cases, piled in towers that reach almost to the ceiling, resembling nothing so much as the walls of a child's fort, a meticulously constructed and intrinsically doomed attempt to keep the world at bay. A laptop sits on a desk by the window, the manufacturer's logo rotating and distending anamorphically; I regard it with a certain degree of temptation, wondering whether my story may already be taking shape there. Then I notice something on the desk itself – a numbered sticker in the corner. This must be the writing desk that Clizia pawned! Paul has redeemed it! My heart leaps. For why would he do that, unless he intended to write?

The thought that my plan for him is already having an effect gives me high hopes for his plan for me. I look again at the laptop. Surely under the circumstances it wouldn't be wrong to have a very quick glance at what he's doing? Given that I'm providing the material and the financing? Just a peep, a sneak preview as it w—

'Oh God!' Reeling back from the computer, I slip on a paperback and fall backwards on to the floor; a tower of books pounces gleefully on top of me.

'Research! Research!' cries Paul, running in from the next room and diving between me and the computer screen, although the image has already seared itself indelibly into my brain. 'That's a separate matter I've been looking into,' he tells me, clearing fallen books from my chest, 'for a potential – hey!'

'What's going on in there?' Clizia yells from the next room.

'I've found him!' Paul calls, crouching down in a corner.

'You found him?' Remington comes rushing in, with Clizia behind him; she levels a single, reductive glance at me, still prone on the floor, then looks away.

'See for yourself.' Paul rises to his feet and opens his cupped hands. 'Look, Remington. Who do we have here?'

Remington glances down into his hands and snuffles. 'I don't know.'

'Well, it's Roland, see? Look, he's waving his little leg at you. *Hi, Remington!*'

'That isn't him.'

'What do you mean? Who else would it be?'

'A different ant.'

'It's not a different ant, take a listen – Roland, is that you?' Paul brings the conched hands to his ear, then says, in a high-pitched voice, '*Yes, it's me all right.*' He lowers his hands again to address the ant. 'We've all been very worried about you, Roland, where have you been? *I went away to see my AUNT!* That's very funny, Roland, but next time let us know in advance, okay?'

'It's not him,' Remington gurgles through incipient tears.

'It is him!' Paul remonstrates. 'Of course it's him!'

'It's not,' Clizia chimes in.

'Whose side are you on?' Paul says.

'It's not even an ant,' she says exasperatedly. 'It's a spider.'

Paul examines the tiny creature crouched in his palm. 'So it is,' he says. 'Actually it looks a little bit like your mother.'

'My mother would cry bitter tears if she knew that I have shackled myself to a man who cannot even tell an ant from a spider,' Clizia attests.

'Let's try and think positively about this,' Paul says. 'Remington, how would you like a brand-new pet spider?'

From his wails it is evident that Remington would not like this very much.

'What if we pull a couple of its legs off?' Paul says in an undertone to me. 'Think that'd fool him?'

'Wouldn't it be better just to find Roland?'

'Forget it,' Paul says. 'That ant is history.' Hearing this, Remington's howls double in volume.

Clizia gazes from one of us to the other in utter disgust, then, picking up her son, 'Come on, Remington, you help Mama dry her hair,' she says, and carries him, still bawling, to his bedroom. The door slams behind her. Paul and I find ourselves in silence.

'So,' I say.

'Yeah,' Paul says. 'Well, look, thanks again for helping with the search. I'll let you know if there are any new developments.'

'You're welcome,' I say. 'But while I am here, maybe we should have a quick discussion of the plan.'

'The plan?'

'The plan you were devising – for me and Ariadne?'

'Oh, that,' he says, face clouding.

'We had arranged to talk about it tonight, if you remember.'

'Right, right, of course – I'll be perfectly honest, Claude, what with the whole Roland situation, this place has been kind of a madhouse.'

I do not follow. 'When did Roland escape?'

'About half an hour ago. But it's been brewing for a couple of days now.'

'I see,' I say, though this is not quite true. 'So we are slightly behind schedule.'

'Slightly,' Paul says.

'Well, perhaps we should review what we have so far.'

'Yeah, you know, as an artist, I'm not entirely comfortable with showing work before it's ready. But rest assured, I'm making serious headway with your story.'

'Ha,' Clizia comments, sweeping out of the nursery like a svelte, ironical bush fire.

'Pay no attention to my wife. I'm giving this my fullest attention.'

'If you are paying him to look at whores on the computer, then I can confirm that he gives it his full attention,' Clizia says. She looks at the clock, swears, then clips off into the bathroom.

'Are you going somewhere?' Paul asks. Clizia barks something fierce but unintelligible from the other room. 'What?' he shouts back.

She reappears in a tracksuit with a nylon sports bag on her shoulder. 'Volleyball try-outs.'

Paul looks nonplussed.

'I have told you twenty times,' Clizia says. 'There is try-out tonight for volleyball team. Cleaners' league.'

'I don't remember you mentioning –'

'That's because you don't listen to anythink I say!' she shouts back, with surprising vehemence. 'Too busy wasting time with the idiot plans!'

'It's not an idiot plan,' he says. 'Jesus, Clizia, you complain when I'm not working, then when I am working you're standing around all the time making sarcastic remarks –'

'Working, ha,' she says, taking a hairbrush and furiously attacking her hair.

'Yes, working, we're not in Ectovia now, people have jobs other than peeling potatoes and digging mass graves –'

A whimper emerges from Remington's room; she throws her arms up. 'I'm going to be late!'

'I'll take care of him,' Paul says. 'Go to your try-out.' She stomps off without saying goodbye. 'Sorry about that,' he says to me as the door slams shut. 'She's been kind of tense lately.'

'She doesn't approve of our arrangement.'

'She doesn't approve of much that I do, Claude. I wouldn't worry about it.'

The nursery door opens and Remington pads out. 'Dad, can we play *Rainbow Mystery Epic*?'

'Aren't you supposed to be asleep?'

'Just for a minute? I'll be Pikaboom, Number One Rainbow Collector. You be Purple Aqualing.'

'Okay, okay.'

'Now steal my rainbows.'

'I'm going to steal your rainbows!' Paul roars. Remington shrieks, and runs off behind the couch. His father turns to me wearily. 'So anyhow, there's the progress report.'

'I see.' I stroke my chin. 'Well, I imagine it takes a little while to find your way into a project. Let's meet again in a few days' time, when you've had more time to think. Why don't you come over to my apartment? We can have dinner, and afterwards we will be able to talk undisturbed.'

'That'd be great, Claude. I'll have everything locked down by then, I promise.'

I suppose I should be disappointed, but as I let myself out I am tingling with excitement. The symbolism of the redeemed writing desk seems to me incontrovertible; I make my way down the hall, lost in happy fantasies of rescuing his career (and quite possibly his marriage).

And then something calls me from them. It is so subtle that at first I can't tell what it is or even which sense has perceived it, but with every onward step it grows stronger. Perfume: the same heady scent that gilded the edges of the steam in the bathroom now dances languorously through the stale air of the hallway. On the landing, it becomes denser, more insistent, directing me to follow it down the stairwell . . . but then I notice something else. In the dust beneath the plastic sheeting that closes off the unfinished rooms are fresh footprints – two different kinds, one set (trainers?) going in, another set (heels?) going out.

189

I push aside the plastic sheet, step on to bare planks. Everything is dark; perfume pours from the doorless entrance to the right. I follow it, stepping through the frame into the shell of an apartment. The light of the city moon shines through the window to bleach the unsanded floorboards. In a corner lies the nylon sports bag, inside it the tracksuit, trainers and top that Clizia wore when she left the apartment. I'm sure there is a perfectly reasonable explanation, but I can't think of it. Nor can I think why she would bathe, or wash her hair, or put on those scandalous knickers before a volleyball game. I stand by the window for what seems a long time, but the answers don't present themselves; there is only the opaque shimmer of the night and the city, and her perfume wrapping itself round and round me, purring like a cat.

Life is so loud that it takes a few moments to realize it is almost empty. Everyone is packed into one little corner where the BOT celebrations are in full swing. 'Rachael's started a tab,' Ish explains, pointing to where the Chief Operating Officer stands deep in conversation with Howie. Outside the bank, she appears even more like a hologram, the digital reprise of something happening far, far away.

'If I was Howie, I wouldn't drink anything that she'd bought me,' Joe Peston says.

'Rachael doesn't see him as a threat,' I say. 'A deal like that makes everyone look good.'

'I don't know, Claude,' Gary McCrum says. 'If Porter wants to keep him at BOT he'd better come up with something pretty special. And Rachael'd better hope it's not her head on a plate.'

Word of Howie's spectacular coup has passed beyond BOT and into the greater financial world. Trading forums are alight with it, investment bloggers ballyhoo it, Howie's name bounces through time zones from one continent to the next. Many commentators see the trade as a vindication of Porter Blankly's controversial counterintuitive approach: in an article entitled 'Wrong about Wrong?', Bloomberg praises Blankly's discounting of data and logic as 'a Copernican revolution in active credit management'. Today saw a whole series of similarly counterintuitive positions around the world, traders betting against the market, common sense, their own best instincts.

'Such bullshit,' Ish grumbles.

'What are you talking about?'

'The whole thing was a fluke. It's totally obvious.'

'A fluke?' Kevin squeaks. 'He solved the riddle, Ish!'

'I don't think that even was a riddle,' Ish says. 'What do you think, Claude? Do you think Porter Blankly genuinely knew what was going to happen with the guy setting himself on fire? Or was it all one big coincidence?'

I shrug. 'I know what we'll be telling our shareholders.'

Jurgen appears with a fresh bottle of champagne. He tops up our glasses, then raises his own. 'Exciting times,' he says, 'and more is on the way.'

'Word is that Agron is happening,' Joe Peston says to Jurgen.

'Agron is happening?' I say.

'Agron is on,' Jurgen confirms.

'What?' Ish says.

'Barely here a month, and already he's moving on Agron,' Gary McCrum says. 'Now that's a chief executive.'

'Look, people keep saying "Agron" over and over and I have no idea what it means,' Ish says.

'That is unusual,' Jurgen says, 'as the potential Agron bid has been mooted in the last two issues of *Torabundo Times*, the in-house bulletin that is printed out weekly for your personal consumption.'

'You read that thing?' Ish says.

'What do you do with it?' Jurgen says,

'I use it to line the parakeet's cage,' Ish says.

Jurgen takes a tiny pad from his shirt pocket and makes a note.

Agron is the Agronomical Bank of Wisconsin. It began life in the 1930s as a small savings and loan, offering succour to farmers affected by the Dust Bowl. However, in the 1990s it began a series of mergers and takeovers, beginning with US investment bank Close Weintraub, then spreading its tentacles across both oceans to devour a Belgian commercial bank, a Swiss reinsurance firm, an Australian gold mine, as well as a host of other, more esoteric investments.

'However, many of these acquisitions were not as robust as

they had thought,' I tell Ish. 'The gold mine is the subject of an enormous lawsuit for environmental damage, the Belgians have been hurt by the collapse of the national government, et cetera, et cetera. Agron does not have the reserves to ride out all of these disasters.'

'The board is looking for a white knight,' Jurgen says. 'Porter believes he can convince the market to back us.'

'Wait a second,' Ish says. 'Let me get this straight. Agron was doing famously, until it bought a whole load of dodgy banks and overextended itself and now it's broke, right?'

'That's right.'

'And now Porter wants us to go and do exactly the same thing?'

'In a sense,' Jurgen says. 'But BOT is in a very different position from Agron.'

'Wasn't *Agron* in a very different position from Agron before it bought all these dodgy banks?'

'That's what makes this deal so counterintuitive,' Jurgen says. 'No one is doing insanely risky takeovers like this at the moment.'

'Can we raise that kind of capital?' Joe asks.

'That remains to be seen. But Porter is determined to expand, one way or the other.' Jurgen pauses, weighing his words, and then says, 'What I hear from New York is that Porter was very disappointed not to get the Caliph's sovereign wealth business. Given his long-standing personal relationship with him.'

'Business is business,' Gary McCrum says.

'Yeah, the guy's trying to put down an uprising, after all,' says Joe.

'This is exactly the point. The Tordale episode has made Porter realize that BOT does not yet carry sufficient weight to be a major force at the geopolitical level. It is still affected by global events, instead of setting its own agenda, reality-wise.'

' "Reality-wise"?' Ish says.

'A sufficiently large bank would create its own reality as opposed to simply reacting to consensus,' Jurgen explains.

'What the –' Ish shrieks as the man of the hour seizes her from behind. 'What the fuck, Howie?'

'I'm creating my own reality,' Howie says. 'Can you feel it? Just there against your thigh?'

'You're a fucking child,' Ish says, furiously swiping whiskey off her top.

'Congratulations on your trade,' I tell him.

Howie just shrugs. 'I figured somebody in this operation ought to be making some money.'

Clearing his throat, Jurgen remarks modestly that actually his team has made some money for the bank also, in that we have just submitted BOT's first ever government-commissioned report. 'It does not compare to your trade, of course. Nevertheless, from what I hear the Minister is very happy.'

'Maybe he'll put you in his will,' Howie says; then, seeing our blank looks, 'You haven't heard? He's dying. It's just come out.'

We check our phones in case this is one of Howie's dubious jokes. It's not. The Minister has been diagnosed with terminal cancer; somehow a newspaper got hold of it, and broke the news before he even had time to tell his family.

'Fucking journalists,' Joe says, shaking his head. 'Fucking vultures.'

'It was bloody Royal Irish that did for him,' Ish states. 'He turned the whole country inside out trying to keep it going, and himself with it. And for what? No investor's going to go near that place with a ten-foot pole.'

'I've got a ten-foot pole you might be interested in,' Howie says.

'What is *wrong* with you?' Ish says.

Howie just laughs and swaggers away.

'Seriously, what is that guy's problem?' she asks.

'He likes you,' Kevin says.

'Fuck off.'

'He does.'

'He does like you, Ish,' I confirm.

'Howie doesn't *like* anyone,' Ish says. 'I bet he just wants an I for his creepy BOT sex-alphabet.'

'I was his K!' Kimberlee exclaims in passing.

'Looks like you missed your chance, Kevin,' Joe Peston says.

The news the following day is dominated by the Minister's bleak prognosis. Messages of support pour in from allies and opposition alike, as well as conjecture as to who will replace him. One name that keeps cropping up is Walter Corless.

'Walter?'

'Well, why not?'

'Aren't you supposed to have an ideology to be a politician? Like, believe in something?'

'He believes in money.'

More importantly, money believes in him. As CEO of a major multinational, Walter has the financial acumen to steer the nation through the present economic cataract – or such is the hope.

'A BOT client as head of Finance, I like the sound of that,' Jocelyn muses. 'Plenty more sweet consultancy work.'

'Walter's a fucking nutcase,' Ish says. 'Put him in charge and he'll turn the whole country into a rendition site and sell it to the CIA.'

'Gotta make the money somewhere,' Jocelyn says, shrugging.

It seems that the revelation of his illness has pushed the Minister past some point of no return. In his press conferences now he looks not merely sick but, for the first time, defeated. 'The fundamentals are sound,' he keeps saying, the same blanket denial to every question, in the same leaden, exhausted tone. His face is suddenly gaunt, wasted. I can't work out quite what it reminds me of; then I look out and see the grey hulk of the unfinished Royal Irish headquarters, rain lashing in through the empty sockets of the windows.

The international news is even worse. The Germans are

castigating the Greeks; the Greeks are burning German cars. In Texas the blackened husk of the self-immolated congressman has made a speech from his hospital bed, declaring that he might not have any skin left but he can still shoot a gun (at least that's what his press officer says he says; the croaking is to my ears unintelligible); hordes of elderly people storm the streets of El Paso, his home town, waving Confederate flags and flaming torches. In Oran the Caliph's new fleet of British-made bombers, bought in an oil-for-weapons deal brokered by the ex-Prime Minister, raze what is being called a rebel stronghold, though it looks, in the 'before' photos, like a village harbouring nothing more dangerous than goats.

The whole world is becoming angrier and angrier – but not me. Paul is coming over tomorrow night to lay out his initial plans, and already it seems I can feel Ariadne's warmth stealing into my life, like the first rays of light creeping into a room as outside the sun wheels into view.

On the day of the dinner, however, he calls to tell me there's a problem. 'Remember that volleyball try-out Clizia went to the other night? Well, she made the team.'

'Oh,' I say neutrally. 'That's good.'

'Yeah, only the thing is, she's got a game tonight, so I have to babysit Remington.'

'Oh,' I say again.

'You know, make him his food and so on.'

I realize he's angling for something. 'I would be happy to prepare something for Remington too.'

'Why, Claude, that's very kind of you,' Paul says, with painfully false surprise. 'But I don't want to impose on you.'

'No imposition, I don't very often have the chance to cook for others.'

'Fantastic – listen though, Igor's probably going to come over too –'

'Igor?'

'Yeah, but don't worry about him, he'll eat anything. Except fish. He *hates* fish. And chicken. But don't go to any trouble.' He tells me he will see me at seven, then ten minutes later calls again to say that it might be closer to half seven, and also that Igor doesn't eat beef but does eat veal.

I put the phone down, not sure what to do. A part of me wants to tell him about the perfume in the stairwell, the clothes stuffed in the bag. But what business is it of mine? Anyway, it's not impossible that there really is a volleyball game. Isn't it?

They arrive at 7.45. Paul apologizes again for the change in plan. 'This whole Cleaners' Volleyball League is all a bit out of the blue.'

'Of course,' I say. 'And how are you, Remington?'

'Remington's got a joke, haven't you, Remington?' Paul prompts him.

'Will you tell me your joke?' I ask, bending down to the boy.

'What do you call a man who's been attacked by a cat?' Remington mumbles.

'I don't know, what do you call a man who's been attacked by a cat?'

Remington sways shyly back and forth a moment, then goes to hide himself behind his father's leg.

'It's funnier when he does the punchline,' Paul says.

'Not to worry,' I say, and then to Remington, 'Do you like hamburgers?'

He nods solemnly, then tugs his father's trouser and whispers in his ear. 'Oh, right – Claude, we're wondering if it would be possible to watch a little *Rainbow Mystery Epic*?'

A minute later Remington is installed on the sofa, the serenity of his attention in almost exactly inverse proportion to the blizzard of lightning flashes, screeching robo-animals and epileptic scene shifts issuing from the TV screen.

'Jeez, Claude, where's all your stuff?' Paul says, gazing around the apartment at the abundance of white surfaces.

'I left most of my things in Paris.' In fact it had been a relief to get away from them – the artworks, antiques, juicers and coffee-makers, the shelves of unread books, unwatched DVDs, unlistened-to compact discs, all carefully arranged in alphabetical order: everything that had promised to be the final piece of the jigsaw, and then wasn't. Now, apart from one or two *objets*, I just download everything; it sits unseen and forgotten on my hard drive, an alternative life I can own instead of living or even needing to think about.

'These your parents?' Paul flashes a photograph at me.

'Yes,' I say. 'I have been putting the family pictures on computer – how do you say, making an archive?'

'Your father looks like a pretty serious individual,' he says, leafing through a stack of old Polaroids. 'Look at those arms. What did he do?'

'He was a blacksmith.'

'You're joking.'

'Does it seem funny?' I strip the foil away from the neck of the bottle he has brought.

'No, no, it's just . . .' He looks down at the picture again. 'I mean, talk about a dying art. Can't be many of those left.'

'No, there are not many,' I say.

'So what was it like?'

'What was what like?'

'Being the son of a blacksmith?'

I shrug. 'It was just his job. I didn't pay so much attention. I was busy with my studies.'

'Of course. You were his greatest creation.'

'I don't think he saw it that way.'

'Old father, old artificer,' he says obscurely, gazing at the picture. 'Maybe there's a book in you after all.'

'That's his story, not mine,' I say, handing him a glass of wine, delicately taking the photographs with the same movement and replacing them on the shelf. 'So, you have had a chance to think of some ideas?'

'I sure have. But I'd rather wait till the big guy gets here.'

'About that,' I say. 'Why are we involving Igor, exactly?'

'Well, he could really use the money,' Paul says. 'I mean, he's having a hard time getting by at the moment. By the way, I told him to invoice you separately, is that okay? He's going to put it down as a termite infestation.'

'I don't intend to be rude,' I say, going to the hob and rattling pots to cover up any trace of anger in my voice, 'but I am not sure that Igor has something to contribute to this project.'

'I fully understand what you're saying. You don't need to worry. Igor's an extra pair of hands, that's all. Also, he's the one who knows how to use all the equipment.'

'Equipment?'

'The surveillance equipment. He's got a real knack for it. Back in the Communist days, he did quite a bit of work in that field. Say what you like about the Soviets, in terms of surveillance, those guys were the gold standard.'

I stare at him in mystification, but before I can ask for clarification, the intercom sounds.

'That must be him!' Paul says.

With great reluctance, I go to the speaker.

'Hello! Hello!' shouts Igor's voice.

'Push the door,' I tell him.

'Hello! Hello! Can you hear? Igor calling!'

Eventually he manages to get in. I have not seen him since his plot with Paul was exposed, and it seems to me a guilty look crosses his face as I open the door; but then, he may have many other things to be guilty about. His furtive appearance is accentuated tonight by a large, clinking bag and a beige rain mac of the kind favoured by perverts in films; he enters the apartment shoulders hunched, head bowed, legs taking long, loping strides, as though stealing down an alleyway.

'There you are!' Paul greets him. 'You remember Claude?'

Igor brandishes his stained teeth at me in the kind of

duplicitous smile one might employ while secretly installing surveillance equipment in the home of a friend in the former Soviet Union.

'You are very welcome,' I say coldly.

'Make yourself at home, Igor,' Paul encourages. 'There's wine on the counter, and some really nice cheese. Hey, Remington, look who's here! Say hello to your Uncle Igor!'

'Hello, little Remington!' Igor crooks his knees and spreads his arms out wide, like a degenerate bear. On the couch, Remington starts to cry. Igor, unhugged, creaks to his feet again. 'Well!' he says to me. I do not reply. He hovers uneasily between couch and kitchen; I sense that he wants to say something about the bank deception, but he just shifts from foot to foot, as if suppressing a bowel movement. Then he asks me where the bathroom is, and I realize with horror that he *is* suppressing a bowel movement.

I hurriedly point him in the right direction.

'The flush, in this house, she is good?' he asks urgently.

'What?' I say, but he doesn't expand, instead hastening away.

'That Igor,' Paul says fondly, shaking his head. 'I could tell you some stories.'

'There is no need,' I say, and remove myself to the safety of the cooker.

Not long after, the bathroom door opens and Igor saunters back into the room with an unconcealed air of unburdenment. 'Very nice facility! Toilet roll soft like velvet! I feel like it should be wiping its ass with *me*!' He stretches, then sets himself down on the couch. Remington edges in the opposite direction. 'Why you bring the boy, eh?' Igor says.

Paul explains that Clizia has gone to play volleyball.

Igor makes a *tsk* noise, and wags his finger. 'You are playing a dangerous game, my friend,' he says. 'Sports can give these womens crazy notions, as well as unsafe muscle mass.'

'She's never been the sporty type,' Paul concurs. 'But she's been so damn angry lately. I'm hoping this'll help her relax.'

'In old days of Ectovia, no sport for the women,' Igor reflects. 'Unless incest! Ha ha! If incest is Olympic sport, Ectovian womens win every gold medal!'

'I told you before, Igor, I don't like you spouting all that Soviet BS about Ectovia. There was no more incest there than anywhere else.'

'Ach, you are right. Incest is everywhere, and it is just the political correctness gone mad that peoples must say they do not incest, when everyone is incesting all the time.'

'Dad, what's incest?'

'Dinner is served,' I say quickly, even though it is not, quite. The television is silenced and Remington reluctantly seats himself at the table; it feels odd to hope that a four-year-old boy will have a civilizing effect on the conversation.

'Sorry, Claude, I should explain. Igor's from Transvolga, and when the Ectovians seceded, they took most of the carpet manufacturing business with them.'

'Ha!' booms Igor, pounding his meaty hand on the table. 'We do not want them or their shitty carpets! What is Ectovia, only the shithole city of Karakel, and a few crappy fields where the fey menfolk practise their gymnastics and the women walk their dogs that are like little furry gays!'

'As you can see, it's still something of a sore point.'

'They are short bastards too, these Ectovians,' Igor adds judiciously.

'Bastards,' Remington repeats.

'That's right, little one!' Igor chuckles, reaching over to stroke the boy's cheek.

'This looks fantastic, Claude,' Paul says, as I deliver the plates.

'*Escalopes de veau cordon bleu,*' I say. 'It is the characteristic French dish.'

'I'll tell you what, if you ever get as far as cooking a meal for Ariadne, you'll be home free.'

'So,' I say, seating myself, and ignoring Remington's mistrustful stare from under the bun of his burger, 'your plan.'

'Okay. Well, without blowing my own trumpet, I think I've had a breakthrough. What happened was, I looked up that play you mentioned, *Cyrano de Bergerac*. And it turned out to have all these great ideas! What happens is, there's this guy who likes this girl, but he's shy, so he gets this *other* guy –'

'I am familiar with the story.'

'Right – so what I'm thinking is, *we* do a Cyrano of our own! Like, I give you the lines, and you say them to Ariadne!'

'This is your breakthrough?'

'You don't like it?'

'It just sounds very similar to what I proposed to you already.'

'Well, superficially, maybe, but see, with the surveillance equipment I can not only give you lines, I can also monitor her response to – what's up, buddy?'

Now Remington needs the toilet. Apologizing, Paul goes to escort him, leaving me alone at the table with Igor, who fixes me with a silent, ghoulish smile. I try to think of something to say but the smile is too disturbing, so instead I get up from the table on the pretext of fetching something from the fridge – only for Igor to rise too and stroll around the living room, appraising my sparse possessions with a nakedly avaricious eye.

'Nice place,' he says, picking up a conch shell from the dresser. 'Very nice.'

'Thank you,' I reply, cracking open the oven.

'Nice, expensive objects,' he muses, moving closer. 'They are pay you many moneys at this bank, eh?'

I pretend I haven't heard him, and hunker down, bustling about meaninglessly with the racks.

'I think I will go over here and cut some more cheese,' Igor declares, and I am just wondering why he felt the need to announce this, when my arm is twisted behind my back and a blade pressed to my throat.

'Don't move, dog!' Igor hisses, his rancid breath in my nostrils like an encyclopedia of stenches.

'What are you doing?' I hear Paul cry in horror from behind him.

'Quick, tie his hands!' Igor commands. And then, to me, 'Talk, pig!'

'Talk about what?' I am genuinely at a loss.

'The safe, where is it?'

'What safe?'

'What the hell are you doing?' Paul shouts.

'I am trying to find out where the safe is.'

'Jesus, Igor, would you let it go? There is no safe, I explained that to you a month ago.'

'But . . . you say we come here for the plan,' Igor says. He sounds confused, though he keeps the blade to my throat.

'The *new* plan, Igor! The *new* plan! I told you, we're helping Claude to get with the waitress, remember?'

'Oh,' Igor says. He lays the knife down on the counter. There is what may be safely described as an awkward silence.

'Why was Igor killing Claude?' Remington whispers to his father.

'It was a joke,' Paul tells him, and then, inspired, says, 'Right, Igor? It was a practical joke!'

Igor hoists his lips into an unconvincing grin. 'Look, not even sharp!' He waggles the cheese knife at me with what is meant to be a comical expression. 'No way to cut a man's throat with this! Only child's throat!'

'Ha ha ha!' laughs Paul.

'Ha ha ha!' laughs Igor.

'Ha ha!' Remington joins in. Now all three of them are laughing.

'I think it might be better if Igor left now,' I say.

'No more veal?' Igor's eyes well with disappointment.

Paul shakes his head. Igor turns to me for clemency. With a gasp of disgust, I look away.

'May I use bathroom once more before I go?' he asks humbly.

'You may,' I reply, still without looking at him.

Igor trudges to the bathroom. The awkward silence prevails again.

'Dad, was Uncle Igor ever a person?' Remington asks.

The toilet flushes, and Igor shambles sheepishly back into the room. His rain mac is on again and has been buttoned right up to the throat; with difficulty he stoops and picks up his bag. At the door he turns. 'No hard feelings,' he says, and lifts his hand in farewell. Four fresh toilet rolls and a veal cutlet tumble from under his coat. The four of us look at them on the ground. 'Okay,' Igor says, and lets himself out.

I make coffee, and Remington returns to the television.

'So, all's well that ends well,' Paul says.

'From now on, I prefer if it is just you and me working together,' I tell him.

'What are you saying?'

'I am saying, no more Igor.'

'What? Why? Because he came at you with a cheese knife?' Paul attempts to work up a plausible tone of incredulity. 'We're trying to make art here, Claude! It's not going to be like working in the bank! Some days you'll feel inspired, some days you won't! Some days Igor will come at you with a cheese knife, some days he won't! That's the creative process!'

I confine myself to pouring the coffee.

'Look, I don't want to pull rank, but I would respectfully remind you that I'm the artist here. You commissioned me to direct your life artistically and now I must respectfully ask you to let me do my job.'

'I am not stopping you from doing your job. I would love to see any evidence at all of you doing your job.'

He gasps, then there is a silence. I glance over my shoulder, but he is not looking at me. Instead, he seems to be staring at something on the far side of the room.

'Claude, what is that?' he says.

'What is what?'

'That, on the table there.'

'That is a novel by Bimal Banerjee, called *The Clowns of Sorrow*.'

'I can see that. What I'm asking is what it's doing in your *house*.' His tone is that of a wronged lover who has discovered traces of a rival in his mistress's boudoir.

'I am reading it,' I say, feeling apologetic all of a sudden without knowing quite why. 'It's about circuses,' I add, thinking this might endear the book to him.

'I know that, Claude. I know because that fucker *completely ripped me off*.'

He is genuinely angry; it surprises me, especially as Banerjee's book has only very superficial similarities to his own.

'Are you kidding? They're both about circuses! They both have clowns in the title, for God's sake!'

'Yes, but your novel is a bittersweet romance about a clown and a starchy office worker, for which the circus provides an occasional backdrop. *The Clowns of Sorrow* is' – I turn to the back of the book for assistance here – ' "both an allegory for the poverty and wonder of the India of the early twenty-first century, and a brilliantly constructed arena in which language itself is set to perform breathtaking feats of daring and imagination." '

Paul listens to this with his head bowed and his hands on his hips, like a truculent footballer receiving a telling-off from the referee. 'You don't get it, Claude,' he says. 'This is a writer thing. I spent years putting together the first serious clown novel – breaking down that wall, opening people up to the idea of a book about that world. And then he sweeps in and takes all the glory!'

It is true that Banerjee's novel received praise and prizes that Paul's did not; however, both books came out at the same time, so it is difficult to see how the Indian could have deliberately stolen Paul's idea.

'Exactly!' Paul pounds his fist into his palm. 'How?'

'What I meant was, it seems more likely that he *didn't* steal your idea.'

'Oh, he stole it all right. He stole it, he sold it, and then he disappeared with a big pile of money before anyone got wise. And nobody's seen him since.'

'Mmm.' I am not sure whether I should tell him or not; but I suppose he will find out sooner or later. 'Of course, he hasn't actually disappeared. He has a new book coming out.'

'What?' Paul goggles, flushes, goggles some more, until he looks rather like one of the creatures in *Rainbow Mystery Epic*.

'There was an interview only a few days ago – you didn't see it?' I wake my laptop, and a moment later a caramel-skinned man with thinning hair and opalescent gold eyes is glowering out at me. 'Here we are – Mary Cutlass meets the award-winning novelist Bimal Banerjee.'

'Mary fucking Cutlass,' Paul says disgustedly. 'That's the witch who slaughtered my book.'

'This is what she says: "After seven long years, the most brilliant writer of his generation has made his triumphant return. His new novel, *Ararat Rat Rap*, is a work so masterful and compendious as to make everything else written in the last twenty years seem redundant –"'

'Oh Christ,' Paul says.

' "– with the exception, that is, of his own *The Clowns of Sorrow*, a groundbreaking imagining of India and the originator of the 'circus-novel' genre, subsequently much imitated –"'

'What!'

' "The new book, to whose scale and ambition only the work of Tolstoy comes close, presents both a pulverizing denunciation of the last three thousand years of civilization, and, in its inexorable beauty, its jocundity and its breadth of emotion, a glimmer of hope –"'

' "Jocundity"? What the fuck is "jocundity"?'

' "I travelled to London –" '

'This woman writes like a fucking hernia,' he expostulates. 'It's like they gave a fucking hernia a weekly column and told it to be as excruciating as possible until all of their readers have hernias too.'

' "I travelled to London last week," ' I read again, then stop. 'Well, that is not technically how hernias work.'

'What?' Paul says.

'Reading a hernia's column could not possibly give one a hernia. Perhaps a better likening might be to a virus, which passes itself on to everyone it comes into contact with.'

'Everyone's a critic!' Paul declares to the ceiling.

' "I travelled to London last week to meet the writer. Still a young man, Banerjee is exotically handsome, his leviathan intellect complemented by the looks of a Bollywood idol and a surprisingly powerful frame. I asked him how he had spent the past seven years." Banerjee replies: "Writing, writing. People ask, how can it take seven years to write a book, but to me, clock time, calendar time, is mere shadow play. The true marker of time is the creation of the novel. Each is as it were an oak-ring in the tree-trunk of my soul." '

'Aaagh!'

'Do you want me to keep going?'

He gurgles; I take it as a yes.

'Mary Cutlass: "*Ararat Rat Rap* takes as its starting point the Armenian genocide of 1915 –" '

'Oh, so that's what's got her so excited,' Paul chimes in sardonically. 'Genocide, that's what she most loves to read about as she chomps on her croissant in her enormous fucking mansion in genocide-free Killiney –'

' "– travelling forward in time to the present-day follies in the Middle East, and backwards to the days of the Old Testament – all of it seen through the eyes of an uncommonly talented rat. Did you find it difficult to keep so many disparate strands together?" Banerjee: "No." '

'That's all he says? "No"?'

' "*Difficult* is not the word. It was agonizing, heartbreaking. So many pages were lost because my tears made them illegible. Yet, even then, the novel continued to sing to me, and by listening closely I found I could go on, just as by following his own song Jephot finds his way through the maze of history." '

'Well, that's just meaningless,' Paul says. 'That just doesn't make any sense.'

'Mary Cutlass: "Jephot is the narrator and hero of the novel, a rat with a gift for rapping who becomes a hip-hop superstar. His voice is brilliantly achieved. Like Banerjee himself, Jephot the rat is charismatic yet unknowable, seductive and at the same time capable, one feels, of brutal force –" '

'Jesus, just give him your knickers, why don't you?' Paul, who is now lying on the floor, exclaims. 'Stop, Claude, I can't take any more of this.'

This irrational hostility to a fellow author's success does not seem to me the attitude of a man who has turned his back on writing for ever. I don't draw attention to it, just note ingenuously, 'According to this, the new book is published by Asterisk Press – didn't they publish your book too?'

From the floor comes a short, ironic laugh. 'Sure did. Daresay my old editor's behind this one. He always was a sucker for a fast-talking Indian with a novel about a singing rat.'

'It says here that Banerjee is reading in Dublin next week. Do you want to go along?'

'Why would I want to go to that?'

'Maybe your editor will be there. You could catch up on old times.'

Paul is silent for a spell; then he says, in a quieter tone, 'No, I don't think that'd be such a good idea.'

'You don't think he would be glad to see you?'

'We had a sort of falling-out.'

'Artistic differences?'

Paul waves his hand vaguely. 'Who knows? It could have been anything. These publishing people are totally inscrutable. But anyway,' he says, rolling up into a sitting position and rapping on the floor, 'why are we even talking about this stuff? We've got work to do.'

The fact that the Minister is not going to get better, unavoidably apparent every time he speaks on camera, seems to have woken the Irish from their state of denial regarding the future of the country. Now they have gone to the opposite extreme: rumours are circulating that the government will very soon run out of money and require an intervention.

'What does that mean, intervention?' Yet another panicked investor on the line.

'If Ireland can't pay its bills, the International Monetary Fund will step in as they have done in Greece. They'll take over all major political and economic decisions until the books are balanced again.'

Most of my clients, whose patriotism doesn't extend beyond the bounds of their golf club, quite like the sound of this, although if they turn on their televisions they will see the IMF's current project is not running so smoothly: another day, another riot in Athens, thousands of citizens waving banners, hurling projectiles, collapsing to the ground in paroxysms as canisters of tear gas clatter around them. Though for me, this footage has taken on a romantic light, sparking fantasies of Ariadne and me running hand-in-hand from a masked and baton-wielding policeman . . .

'Claude? You there?'

'Oh. Yes. We don't think the IMF'll need to come here. Ireland's not Greece. The Minister's issued a robust denial. Seemed plausible.'

I have arranged to meet Paul at lunchtime for what he terms 'initial blocking'. It's only when I let him into my apartment that I discover this means he wants me to go and talk to Ariadne.

'Now? Today? But we have not prepared,' I remonstrate, following him into my bedroom, where he starts rifling through the wardrobe.

'Of course we've prepared! What were we doing last night? Jesus, Claude, how many black suits can one man own?'

'But we have not decided – I have not thought this through . . .'

'You don't need to think it through! That's why I'm here, remember?' Paul turns, places his hands on my shoulders and in a sonorous voice says, ' "Claude adjusted his stylish black suit in the mirror and smiled. The moment had come, and he was ready. Striding across the plaza, he threw open the door. The beautiful waitress started, then blushed. Taking her hand, he said –" ' The doorbell sounds. 'That'll be Igor.'

' "He said that'll . . ."? Oh,' I say, as he bustles past me to the door, and then, 'Wait, what's Igor doing here?'

'I ran into him last night in Private Desires – come on up!' he shouts into the intercom.

'Private Desires?'

'Yeah, it's a little lap-dancing club on Capel Street.'

'What were you doing there?'

'I'm barred from Velvet Dream's, remember? Don't look at me like that, Claude. Getting a lap dance helps me think.'

'You told me you had no money.'

'It's one of the cheaper places. Mostly Romanians. Anyway, while I was there I ran into Igor, who had also come there to think, and we agreed that we shouldn't let some silly misunderstanding get in the way of the three of us working together.'

'Oh, I am very glad you agreed that.'

'I promise, he's got it all straight this time,' he says. A moment later, Igor lurches in with his clinking bag. If he is feeling remorse or embarrassment about last night's events, he does not show it. Placing the bag on the coffee table, he unzips it and removes a series of grey objects, rather like bleak industrial flowers with long metallic stamens. I presume this is the surveillance equipment he talked about.

'I asked you to do this because I wanted an artist's perspective,' I tell Paul quietly. 'Not all this technology.'

'This is the artist's perspective,' Paul insists. 'It's the twenty-first century, you think writers are still running around with inkwells and quills?'

'I think you are introducing a lot of unnecessary complication to give Igor something to do.'

'Listen, maybe hiding behind a bush and whispering to his buddy worked for Cyrano in the seventeenth century, but if your girl, or for that matter any of the numerous security guards patrolling this place, catch sight of me hissing at you from under a table it's not going to look good for either of us. Look, relax, this time out I won't even speak. I just want to get a read on how the two of you interact. Think of it as a dry run.'

'Hold still,' Igor says. He leans in to affix a bulky plastic earpiece. Paul says something unintelligible about radio signals; Igor responds with something opaque about transmitters, and goes to tap on an antediluvian laptop.

'Now remember,' Paul says, clasping my shoulders, 'you're the hero. The whole story flows from you. Plot is just the illustration of character, your character. You're the guy making it happen.'

'What am I going to say?'

'It doesn't matter what you say. What matters is that she knows you're in charge. Women don't want some wishy-washy type who doesn't know his own mind. They want someone authoritative, manly, who's not afraid to take control.'

'Are you sure an authoritative, manly man is what Ariadne is looking for? Given that she works in a feminist cooperative.'

'Pff, this feminism is all an illusion,' Igor rumbles. 'Only for depressed womans who cannot find man, and so must dress like lesbian, and not the good kind of lesbian.'

'What Igor's saying is that a strong narrative appeals to every-one, no matter what their politics or persuasion. I'm not suggesting you go in there and hit her over the head with a club. Just be direct, confident. Own the scene.'

I try to break into my new masterful persona by squinting manfully into the middle distance. Spots dance before my eyes.

'Testing.' As he speaks, Igor's voice is fuzzily replicated in my earpiece. 'Can you hear me?'

'Yes, I can hear you, you are standing right beside me.'

'And I can hear you,' Paul confirms, cupping his hand around his own earpiece. 'Okay, looks like we're ready to go.'

'Are you sure that thing is safe?' I look dubiously at the ancient transmitter humming ominously on the balcony. 'Wouldn't it be easier just to use my Bluetooth?'

'Stop delaying,' Paul says. 'Let's do this.'

It must be said that as I make my way towards the café, I feel even less authoritative than usual. Out here, away from my mod-els and spreadsheets, everything feels flimsy and contingent, at the mercy of riptides and crosswinds, the random vicissitudes of nature.

'How are you getting on there?' Paul's voice sounds in my ear.

'Fine,' I say tightly.

'That's great. Now you just keep cool. Remember, she's a character in *your* story. She's there for you. And we'll be with you too, every step of the way.'

I turn and look back up at my balcony. Two figures wave down at me, like mocking, malefic insects. What am I doing? Am I really going to go up to her and just start talking? It feels so crude and anachronistic! To my left, Transaction House croons to me seductively. I could go back to my desk, think this through prop-erly; maybe I could friend her online, find out her likes and dislikes, then in six months or so take the next step, it wouldn't be so dramatic in terms of the story, of course, but realistically –

'Keep going, Claude.'

The door of the Ark. I push it open, a ton weight. Happy diners gabbing to each other, the compressed bedlam of the coffee machine, the clank of cutlery on porcelain. 'Claude strode into the café,' a voice – Paul's? My own? – urges inside my head. My body feels alien, unwieldy, like an enormous robot that I am controlling with levers from a tiny chamber behind the eyes. As I lurch over the floor all sound disappears, save for the industrial suck and *hoosh* of my breathing; I stumble through a forest of disconnected sense-impressions until, like a beacon, Ariadne comes into view.

'Hello,' I say, but it comes out as a cough.

'Hi you!' she says, sliding a tress as rich and dark as coffee back behind her ear. 'You want a table?'

'Yes,' I say, though this is not what I want at all – already the narration is slipping out of my grip! Ariadne turns away to find me a seat, my cheeks flame with failure, it's all gone wrong – and then something distracts me. 'New painting?'

Ariadne glances behind her to where the canvas hangs, I imagine illegally, on the fire door. 'Yes,' she says, lowering her green eyes bashfully. 'I just finish this weekend. I don't know if it works, or what.'

The painting features a series of warped helices knotted into each other, like the DNA of some painfully malformed beast: it seems to protrude bulkily out of space itself. 'I like it,' I say.

She laughs. 'This morning, I heard a customer say it's like a zebra ate a whole load of fractals and got sick.'

'*Bof*, they said the same thing about Van Gogh's *Sunflowers*,' I tell her.

'Maybe,' she says, and she smiles – not her usual waitress smile, it seems to me, but a deeper one, incorporating her whole being. A sudden wave of joy wells up in me. Here I am! This is happening! How did I ever believe there was anything to fear? Ariadne is everything that is good, therefore only good things can come of this. 'What's it called?' I ask her.

'*Simulacrum 122.*'

I nod, tapping my nose thoughtfully. Out of nowhere, Paul's old idea has popped into my head: that we bond over French philosophy. 'I wonder, by any chance are you familiar with –' I begin. But at that moment there is a loud and painful buzzing in my ear, and then Paul's voice says, 'Sorry, Claude, we lost the connection for a minute there. Are you in the café?'

'Yes,' I say, trying to incorporate it into my question for Ariadne, 'yes, I wondered if –'

'Okay, Claude, you're doing great. Now, are you ready to approach the subject?'

'I have always wondered,' I repeat, trying to dig the earpiece out of my ear without calling attention to it, 'whether, ah –'

'Wait, were you talking to her already?'

I cough deliberately.

'What was that? The connection's not that good here.' In the background there is a popping sound, rather like a cork from a bottle.

'What do you wonder?' Ariadne cocks her head and regards me bemusedly.

'Just stay calm, Claude, and remember you're in charge. I'm going to go out on the balcony and see if I can fix this transmitter. Igor, you take over here for a second.'

'I wondered if you have ever read –'

'You have great big dick,' a gravelly voice booms in my ear.

'What?' I can't stop myself blurting.

'I didn't say anything,' Ariadne says, surprised.

'You have biggest dick in world, you are striking her with your firmness.'

Frantically I pull at the earpiece, but it is wedged in tightly by its many points. Ariadne's beautiful forest-green eyes cloud with concern.

'Is everything all right?' she says.

'Your wood is so hard, you are the master.'

'Yes, yes,' I tell her, desperately poking myself in the ear.

'You are lion between the sheets with your mighty length.'

'Please stop,' I whisper.

Ariadne flinches, ever so slightly. 'I have to take an order,' she decides. 'I come back to you.'

I watch in agony as she hurries away, and at that moment it seems to me as if the whole café were merely a stage set after all, now collapsing and disintegrating before my very eyes. I reach after her – but before I can speak, a tremendous peal of static explodes in my ear. Just barely managing to suppress a scream, I turn and flee, offstage, out of the theatre, into the null space of the outside.

Paul is on the sofa in my living room, leafing through a magazine. He gets up when I come in. 'There he is! There's the hero!'

I do not give him the acknowledgement even of a snort of exasperation, simply wrestle off my jacket, now soaked with rain, and throw it over a chair.

'Igor had to leave,' he says. 'He had a big exterminating gig. Beetles.'

I go into the kitchen area, where cupboard doors have been flung open and the counter littered with tartine and cookie wrappers. 'What is this?'

'Oh, yeah, we got hungry, so we made a snack.'

'And drank two bottles of Brouilly?' I say, finding the empties upended in a bin.

'Yeah, we were thirsty, also, it turned out.'

'How did you drink two bottles of wine in twenty minutes?'

'Well, we didn't drink both of them, we –'

'My rug!'

'Yeah, see that's most of bottle one there.'

Clenching my jaw, I slam the cupboards shut, bundle up the debris and wipe down the surfaces.

'So I think we made some important headway there,' he says.

'We made some important headway in the wrong direction.'

'Mmm,' he says ambiguously, and then, 'Look, I'll be perfectly honest with you. That didn't go 100 per cent according to plan.'

'I know it didn't go 100 per cent according to plan,' I say. 'I was very well placed to see it not going according to plan.'

'Igor and I have been discussing it,' he says. 'We both feel we may have taken a slightly wrong turn with the whole virile, masterful thing.'

I stamp back into the living room, strew salt over the wine-stained rug. 'Maybe this whole idea was a wrong turn.'

'Don't say that. It was just a dry run, remember? And at least she knows who you are now, right? You've put yourself on the map, so to speak.'

'I have put myself on the map as a gibbering psychopath,' I say.

'You're blowing it out of proportion. Try and see it from the perspective of a novel. When do these things ever work out the first time round? There have to be a few comic mishaps, right?'

I replace the salt in the cupboard and dust my hands.

'And anyway, there was a positive outcome.' Paul follows me back into the kitchen. 'By listening to your conversation, I was able to work out something that you had in common: a shared love of modern art. That's something we can build on.'

At the present moment I don't want to build on anything; I am damp and hungry, and desire nothing more than to go back to the office, putting this misconceived episode behind me. But Paul, no doubt sensing a threat to his pay cheque, keeps buzzing about me. 'Look, if you're really feeling bad about it, we can start over.'

'How can we start over? This is reality, not typing. We can't just throw it in the bin.'

'Ariadne's not the only beautiful waitress in town. I've got a whole folder full of them, brunettes, blondes, redheads . . .' He falls silent, realizing he has said too much.

'You have a folder full of waitresses?'

'Of course not. It's a figure of speech, that's all.'

'A figure of speech meaning what?'

'Nothing, forget I said it.'

Cogs begin to turn in my mind. 'Has the folder of waitresses . . . has it got something to do with all this bizarre surveillance equipment?'

'It's got nothing to do with anything,' he says impatiently. 'Can we just drop the subject?'

'Not if I'm being implicated in one of your scams.'

'It's not a scam, it's a totally legitimate business venture, and anyway, it's over, it's all in the past . . . oh, for God's sake.' He rolls his eyes. 'I'll tell you, all right? But you have to promise to keep it secret.'

He glances over his shoulders; then, bringing his hands together and pulling them apart, as though unfurling an imaginary banner in the space over his head, says, 'Hotwaitress.com.'

'Hotwaitress.com?'

'That's right.'

'What is Hotwaitress.com?'

'Right now it isn't anything.'

'But it was a business venture? Some Internet thing?'

He sighs. 'Well, really I should go back to the beginning. To seven years ago, when *For Love of a Clown* came out. I was young and naïve, I had the usual fantasies – everyone would stop what they were doing to read it, I'd become famous, it'd usher in a new era of peace and harmony, all that. Instead it got one terrible review and then vanished without a trace. Look, the world is full of books. Moaning because no one wants to read yours is like complaining that you've been standing on the street corner with your dick out for an hour and nobody's stopped to give you a blowjob. Still, it hurt me. And when I sat down and tried to start book number two, I had problems.'

'You were blocked?'

'I was blocked, I'd lost faith – whatever the reason, nothing was happening. And meanwhile, of course, I'd got married, we'd taken out this huge mortgage to buy the apartment, Remington was on the way, I had no idea how I was going to pay for it all.

'I didn't tell Clizia because I didn't want to worry her. I acted like the new book was coming along fine, and I kept heading out to work every morning. But at this stage I wasn't even trying to write,

I was just sitting in cafés, looking out the window, wondering if everyone would be better off if I just jumped off a bridge.'

'Seriously?'

'Clearly you've never been in debt, Claude. After a while it's all you can see. And it's a vicious circle, because the more I worried about it, the less chance there was that I'd ever come up with an idea for a book. Anyway, there I was, being depressed in various cafés. There were maybe three or four I'd go to at different times of the day. Over time I got to know a few of the waitresses quite well, and if it was quiet we'd have these long, philosophical talks. They were young, they had all these hopes and dreams, and though I couldn't exactly share their optimism, still, it was a way out of this endless despairing conversation I was having with myself the rest of the time. In fact, I realized after a while that talking to the waitresses was actually the high point of my day. And then it hit me – *that* was the idea.'

'What? Become a waiter?'

'No, no, I mean that relationship. Waitress and customer.'

'I don't understand.'

'You think you're the first man to fall in love with a waitress, Claude? This is a growing phenomenon. And it's no mystery. Think about how we live now, packed off in our digital eyries. Yes, we have phones, we have email, but we might not speak to an actual flesh-and-blood person all day. And then we go to a café, and suddenly in the midst of our fully networked isolation there's a pretty girl who smiles at us and asks how we are. She's actually there, not just a face on a screen. And she's bringing us cake! Is it any wonder we form attachments?'

'That sounds plausible,' I say gruffly, embarrassed at having my own situation so unsparingly detailed. 'But how does your business venture relate to it?'

'Okay. So you've developed these feelings, which are very natural and human. What happens when you sit down in a café or restaurant only to find that your favourite waitress isn't there? On the one hand, it doesn't sound like a big deal. But seeing her was literally the only thing you had to look forward to all day! And it actually feels pretty crushing. That's the kind of scenario Hot-waitress is designed to eliminate. What we proposed –'

' "We" – this means you and . . . ?' I ask with a sinking feeling.

'Me and Igor. What we proposed was a comprehensive guide to waitresses in cafés and restaurants all over the city. When they're on, when they're off, what sections they're working, their likes, dislikes, hobbies and pastimes, the latest gossip as well as plenty of pic—'

'Wait, wait,' I interject. 'Are you serious? This was a genuine business venture?'

'Well, yeah,' he says, looking slightly offended. 'What's the problem?'

There are so many problems I have difficulty focusing on one. 'How exactly would you find out all these personal details? The waitresses are just going to tell you?'

'No, of course not. We'd have a dedicated data-collection team deployed across the city. And we'd also repackage whatever the waitresses have uploaded themselves, on to Facebook and so on.'

The surveillance equipment: at last the pieces fall into place. I feel a kind of deep and distressing pang within, a sort of moral headache. 'Surely this can't be legal.'

'It's an information service, that's all,' Paul says. 'How can information be bad?'

He sits down opposite me and leans earnestly over the table. 'Imagine being able to tap into a resource like that for Ariadne. Think what a comfort that would be.'

'I wouldn't be comforted by the knowledge that countless others were out there, stalking her online.'

'It's not stalking,' Paul says.

'It is,' I say.

'It's not.'

'It is practically the definition of stalking,' I say.

Paul throws his hands in the air. 'It's the twenty-first century! People expect to be spied on! For a good-looking woman it'd probably be more upsetting if she found out she *wasn't* being spied on.'

'And your wife, what did she think about this business venture?'

'Oh, Clizia,' he says impatiently.

'Well? You told me before how much she hated being stared at by men in the club. What did she think of you keeping waitresses under surveillance?'

'Clizia's living in a fool's paradise. We have to eat, don't we? This is what people want now. They don't want novels. They want reality, up close and personal.'

'Someone else's reality, turned into entertainment.'

'You might not like it. But I'll tell you this, the response to Hotwaitress was the polar opposite of the response to *Clown*. We had investors queuing out the door! Venture capital, private equity! We had a pre-launch party with an elephant – an elephant!'

'So what happened? Why aren't you an Internet millionaire?'

His face clouds. 'There were legal issues. You know how it goes – it got tied up in court, all our funding went on solicitors' fees.'

'Maybe for the best,' I say.

'It could have been big. Loneliness is one of the few growth areas these days. And it's self-perpetuating, you know? Because the more people pay to stop feeling lonely, the lonelier they tend to get.'

'Is that why you spend all your money on lap dances?' I say.

He purses his lips, lowers his eyes. 'About that,' he says. 'I'm going to need another advance.'

ELEPHANT RUNS AMOK AT CITY CENTRE EVENT

A man was seriously injured last night and the ground floor of a Dublin hotel badly damaged when a hired elephant went on the rampage at the launch of a new Internet dating service. Witnesses reported that the animal became enraged when an intern employed by the service attempted to dress it in a 'French maid' costume. After trampling the man, who remains in hospital, the elephant overturned a number of tables in the reception room and charged at hotel guests. A zookeeper who arrived to sedate the animal described it as 'extremely agitated'. The hotel manager, Mr Wallace Willis, said that the event had been 'a fiasco' at which 'basic safety had been thrown out the window'. The company's director, Mr Igor Struma, was not available for comment last night. Mr Struma, described in the company's press release as an entrepreneur and bounty hunter, is wanted for questioning by authorities in Ukraine in connection with the robbery five years ago of a consignment of gynaecological equipment. The company's president, Mr Paul

'Whatcha readin' there, Claude?'

'Nothing. Old news.'

'I saw you in the Ark.' Ish is chewing one of their home-made cookies. 'I was waving at you, but you didn't notice.'

'Ah-um . . .' I swivel my chair away, busy myself shuffling documents.

'You were talking to that waitress, and then you just took off, like a streak of lightning! What happened, she catch you sneaking a peek down her top?'

'Mmm.' I stare at the screen and batter a random series of keys.

'Like a streak of lightning.' She chuckles to herself, and then, abruptly, she stops. 'Wait a second . . . are you after her? Were you in there trying to chat her up?'

'I am not "after" anybody,' I say irritably.

'Is that what all this put-my-life-in-a-book stuff is about?' she asks. 'You're trying to get with Ariadne? That's her name, isn't it? Ariadne?'

'I have no idea what you're talking about.'

'Ariadne,' Ish repeats, as if she's talking to herself, and then, 'There's nothing to be embarrassed about, Claude. She's gorgeous. And she seems really cool too, like a real free-spirit type.' She notes this with a kind of sadness, as though she were watching Ariadne through the bars of a cage. 'Though I wouldn't have thought she'd be the kind of girl *you'd* go for.'

'I'm not "going" for anyone,' I snap; I experience a sudden, vehement wish for her to go away, because now I too can see the bars of the prison we are both incarcerated in, and my plan to escape seems foolhardy, laughable, like trying to dig your way out of a cell with the stirrer from a semi-skimmed latte.

'Okay, whatever you say,' she shrugs. 'Anyway, FYI, I have a date tomorrow night.'

'What are you telling me for?'

'No reason,' she concedes, and turns to her computer.

This afternoon's episode has left me with serious doubts. Paul's intervention not only ruined a promising conversation with Ariadne, but I can't even console myself with the thought that it might have inspired him to write; instead, it seems only to have reawoken memories of his hare-brained business plan.

Now I find myself torn. After today's demonstration, the wisest course of action is surely to cut my losses and abandon the project. At the same time, the more I find out about Paul's life, the more responsible I feel for him. Clizia's permanent fury now makes perfect sense. To marry an artist and find yourself chained instead to a professional lost cause, whose efforts range from monetizing isolation to outright theft – isn't that a betrayal just as bad as the one that brought her here? When she signed up to work as a waitress and instead found herself contracted to a lap-dancing club? Would it be any great surprise if she were looking for a way out?

The rain comes down all day, and the next morning it is heavier still, turning the plaza into a dismal game of hopscotch, figures in black shoes and trench coats leaping and splashing their way to shelter. At the zombie encampment, one of the tents has collapsed, and the undead scurry about with tape and buckets.

'What's going to happen to them when Royal Irish gets shut down?' Gary McCrum says, looking out the window. 'Will they all just leave?'

'I suppose. Royal's the zombie bank, after all.'

'Shame.' Gary McCrum scratches his belly. 'They bring a bit of life to the place.'

'They're zombies, Gary.'

'You know what I mean.'

The government has had a number of days to digest our report, but so far no action has been taken on Royal. The Minister gives a brief statement this afternoon, but it's just the same threadbare phrases again: Royal is open for business, Ireland's fundamentals are sound, the IMF is not moving in. Behind him stands the little Portuguese man I saw in Rachael's office; he listens to the Minister with lowered eyes, as if to a eulogy at a funeral.

Dark days for Ireland, and Greece, and almost everybody else; but at BOT the good times continue to roll. The market has responded positively to our quixotic takeover bid for Agron; the American bank's board of directors is reportedly receptive, as, no doubt, a beached whale would be receptive to being put back in the sea; an underwriter has been found, and Porter Blankly's old friend the Caliph has offered BOT a line of credit to the tune of several billion.

'I still don't understand how this is supposed to work,' Ish says. 'Agron is huge. We're small. If we borrow all this money to buy it – won't we be over-leveraged? Like, massively?'

'This is in fact the whole point,' Jurgen says. 'Porter's strategy is to distribute BOT's connections so widely across the global marketplace that we become systemically necessary, that is, too big to fail.'

'So they can't let us go down, because then all of the people we've borrowed from would be pulled down with us,' Kevin glosses.

Ish still seems unconvinced. 'It sounds like putting on a suicide belt so that no one will bump into you on the subway.'

'That is quite a good comparison,' Jurgen agrees. 'We are hoping BOT's high market standing will persuade the other subway riders to fund a particularly large and explosive suicide belt.'

To ensure a quick turnaround, the deal will be done here in Dublin, where at least some of the extraordinarily complicated legal requirements can be brushed under the carpet. Corporate has been assigned extra offices in a building in the neighbouring block; extra staff are being flown in from New York.

On the ninth floor of Transaction House, meanwhile, where until a few months ago a property company had its offices, new doors with code-locks are being hung, expensive new desks and chairs delivered, thrillingly white new whiteboards fitted to the walls. Details are scant as yet, but it is believed that the activity has to do with Porter's other prong: to take BOT deeper into the abstract, developing new financial instruments that will ensure profits no matter what is happening in the so-called real world. Howie's name is on the door of the corner office; he is taking Grisha with him, and a hand-picked team of junior analysts.

'Those guys are going way out.' Kevin is seeking to

alleviate the heartbreak of being passed over for the team by acting as a kind of ninth-floor John the Baptist, making sonorous
prophecies about their work whenever the opportunity arises.
'*Waaaay* out.'

'But what are they actually doing?' Gary McCrum asks.

Kevin shakes his head. 'All I know is that there's some heavy
fucking maths involved.'

'I heard Porter was giving them a hedge fund,' Jocelyn Lockhart says.

'I heard that too.'

'I heard it was a hedge fund, only more counterintuitive.'

'That's one thing you can count on.' Kevin slings his foot over
his knee and swivels in his chair. 'Whatever it is, it'll be *majorly*
counterintuitive.'

'And is Rachael involved in it too?'

'Rachael,' Kevin snorts.

When we are alone, Ish tells me that Howie asked her to be on
his team.

'What? Why didn't you mention this before? What did you say?'

She doesn't reply for a moment; a sudden blast of sun through
the venetian blind throws tiger-stripes of shadow across her face.
'I said no.'

'No?' I am confused: in our world, when an opportunity is presented, you take it. 'I don't expect you to make the slog here for
ever. Howie is the growing star. He will bring you with him.'

Ish shrugs, sips from her water bottle. 'Maybe I'm happy
enough making the slog,' she says. 'Anyway, it sounds like
cobblers.'

'Did he tell you what they were doing?'

'Some sort of a fund all right. He said it was going to transform Western civilization. But it's Howie, Claude. He's a bullshit
artist.'

'Porter doesn't think he's a bullshit artist. Kevin told me New
York's started bringing him in on strategy meetings.'

'That bloke's never had a strategy in his life that didn't involve putting his dick up some poor unwitting bastard's arsehole.'

'Well, in their eyes he is a genius.'

'Yeah,' Ish says disconsolately. 'Who knows, maybe he is.' She turns back to her terminal. 'Bend over, world. Here comes another genius.'

The *Financial Times* posts an article by a former head of the German Bundesbank about the future of the euro. He likens the currency's situation to that of Tinkerbell in *Peter Pan*. There, the fairy is brought back to life when all the children in the world who believe in magic clap in unison. 'In Germany, however, the public and politicians are determinedly sitting on their hands. It is not that they do not believe in magic; rather, they do not believe the other, naughty children should benefit from that magic. They would rather the fairy die, and teach the other children a lesson. Therefore it is not a sentimental judgement to say that the currency may die from a want of love.'

The naughty children in this case being Greece. While the protestors fulminate fruitlessly through the streets, the country's future is being rewritten by the IMF.

'What are they going to do?'

'Sell off national resources. Cut services. I'd guess most public sector workers will be fired. Pensions will be gone, taxes will double, and so on. Until the books are balanced again.'

'Meaning, until the Germans get their money back,' Ish says sardonically.

'The Greeks got huge development grants from the European Union,' Jurgen insists. 'Many billions of euros, which they used to build swimming pools on their roofs and have a ten-year tax holiday.'

'How did they persuade anyone to give them anything?' Kevin asks. 'If their economy's so batshit crazy?'

'Porter Blankly,' Ish says. Kevin looks quizzical. 'The Greek government paid Blankly's old bank Danforth Blaue three hundred million dollars to fiddle the accounts and shift their debts out of sight,' she explains. 'So on paper they looked legit.'

'That was legal?'

'Danforth got their money,' Ish says with a shrug.

'The EU are big boys,' Jocelyn Lockhart says. 'If Danforth cooked the books they should have spotted that for themselves.'

'Didn't the head of the EU also use to work for Danforth?' I remember.

Wheels within wheels; but it's not our place to make moral judgements, only to forecast where this information will drive the market. Right now it resembles an enormous, international game of keep-away, with money taking flight from any company that so much as booked a junket to that side of the Mediterranean. But there is plenty of scope for things to get worse. A bet against togetherness is never a bad option, financially speaking.

I come out of a meeting on Grand Canal Dock that afternoon to see I have missed a call from Paul; after a certain amount of debate with myself, I call him back.

The phone is answered by a high voice. 'Pinaco Sooshin?' it says.

'Excuse me?' I say.

'What?' says the voice.

I realize I recognize it – 'Remington?'

The response is a loud thudding in my ear; then in the background I hear Paul's voice say, 'Don't just throw it on the floor, Remington, Jesus,' and Remington's squeaky apology.

'What is Pinnacle Solutions?' I say when Paul picks up the phone.

'Our conversation the other day got me thinking,' he says. 'Maybe we gave up on Hotwaitress too easily. I talked to Igor and we decided we'd put a few feelers out, see if it was worth having another try.'

So, my worst fears have been realized.

'I should send you a copy of the prospectus. I bet you know lots of people who'd love to get in on the ground floor of something like this – hey,' his voice becomes loud and sharp, 'if that paper clip gets stuck there, I'm not pulling it out. Sorry, Claude, where were we? You were interested in having a look at the prospectus?'

'No, I am simply returning your call,' I say, although now I wish I hadn't.

'Oh, right. Well, listen here, I've been pretty swamped with Hotwaitress the last few days, but I did find time to speak to your waitress friend this morning, and that whole mix-up the last time, that's all been squared away.'

'Squared away?' I stop right there on the street; I feel a surge of omnidirectional gratitude, like a patient being given the all-clear. 'How did you manage that?'

He laughs. 'That's my job, right? Think of it as an editorial intervention.'

'But what did you say to her?'

'It's not important what I said. The point is, if you want to try again with her, you can do it with a clean slate.'

'That is very good news,' I say – and yet a sliver of doubt keeps niggling away at me. 'Although a clean slate – you cannot simply erase her memory . . .'

'I explained it to her, that's all. I went in and casually brought you up and asked if she'd noticed you acting oddly lately. Then I told her you'd just been diagnosed as bipolar.'

I stop again, this time without the all-consuming sense of well-being. 'Bipolar?'

'Yeah, when you think about it it's really the only explanation that makes sense.'

'But . . . but . . .' For a moment I can do little more than splutter. 'But the whole point was to *stop* me from looking like a madman,' I manage at last. 'How can you call it a blank slate, if she thinks I am some kind of lunatic?'

'I said you were *bipolar*, not that you were a lunatic. Everybody's bipolar these days. It's practically à la mode! At the very least, it's not contagious. Or wait – is it contagious?'

This seems to me the exact opposite of a clean slate.

'I'm telling you, Ariadne's fine about it. And from a narrative point of view, it's strong. Gives you a bit of edge, you know? So now we can move on to the next chapter. I've had a few ideas for what we might do . . .'

Can it hurt to hear what he has to say? 'Go on.'

'This time, instead of creating a whole new persona, I think we should work with what's there. Find out your good points and build on them. Now, the fact is that most of the qualities women look for in a man are ones you don't have. Are you tall? No. Are you handsome? I might not be the best judge, but I would have to say no. Are you brave? That would be a tough sell, given that the last time Ariadne saw you, you were fleeing in terror. But you do have one thing that sets you apart: wealth.'

'I told you before, Ariadne isn't impressed by money,' I say, with a certain amount of frustration. 'If she was, why would I need you?'

'I'm not saying you should go in there in a fur coat and stuff a fifty down her cleavage. But nobody's immune from money. It's a matter of how you present it.'

'Present it?' I say, simultaneously suspicious and intrigued.

'Wealth means money, and money means power, and power means transforming one situation into another situation. And waitresses, I've learned from my extensive research, are all waiting to be transformed. This one wants to be an actor, this one wants to be a dancer, this one wants to be a children's book illustrator. While you're sitting there eating your cheesecake and fantasizing about her, she's dreaming of the day someone gives her her big break.'

'Modern life is being somewhere else,' I remember.

'Exactly. Being a waitress is all about not being a waitress.

233

Ariadne's a perfect example. She wants to paint, but she spends her days kowtowing to people who'd burn down the Louvre if they thought there was a buck in it. She's crying out for someone to recognize her talent and set her free. That's where you and your money come in. Suddenly you're not a grasping, malevolent banker any more. You're a sensitive, art-loving, bipolar-but-not-overly-so Frenchman who wants to be her benefactor.'

'Her benefactor,' I repeat, trying out the word. 'How would I become her benefactor?'

'Well, how about you tell her you're thinking of opening a gallery? A gallery devoted to feminist art. You want to exhibit her, in the meantime you're going to bankroll her painting. She can't believe her ears! It's what she's been dreaming about all this time – the regular customer who reveals himself to be the guy with the magic wand. So she goes and paints, and for a while you stay in the shadows, being munificent and mysterious. But then at last you arrange to meet her, and you confess that being around her amazing paintings has made you realize you've got all these other, deeper feelings for her. Which is practically true! You're just tweaking the chronology a little bit.'

'It sounds like I am paying her to love me,' I say, flipping my ID at the Transaction House security guard.

'What are you talking about? It's a classic love story. Two people from different walks of life, who realize they each hold the key to the other's dream. It's straight out of Hollywood.'

'But if your idea is that she will love me only because she feels obligated . . .'

'*Grateful*, Claude. Grateful. What's wrong with that? In many ways it's like a traditional marriage. You protect her financially. She rewards you with love. Everybody wins.'

I decide I can work on the moral mechanics later. The truth is that I am quite taken by his art-gallery idea. But how would it work?

'Don't worry about those details for now. That's all Act Two stuff. Just buy her a few dinners, show her your chequebook, make encouraging noises. See how it goes.'

'Hold the lift!' A tanned arm thrusts itself between the closing doors, followed by a patent-leather pump with a charm bracelet dangling over it. 'Hey Claude! Oh, you're on the phone, sorry.' Slowly but inevitably I feel myself turning bright pink, as though Ish has caught me engaged in some crime.

'Well,' I say to Paul. 'That is most satisfactory. I will proceed as instructed, and revert to you –'

'One more thing,' Paul cuts in. 'She's going away.'

'Ariadne?' I blurt; and then, more quietly, 'For how long?'

'She told me she's going back to Greece for a fortnight. She's leaving tomorrow.'

'Tomorrow?' I blurt again. Beside me, Ish is examining her phone in the way one does when one is pretending not to be listening in.

'Yeah. So, look, I said you might call in, just to put the whole you-being-mad thing to bed once and for all. But it'd need to be – actually, I suppose it'd have to be this afternoon.'

'How can I see her this afternoon?' I demand, feeling Ish's eyes flick on to me and back again and experiencing a wave of irrational fury.

'I don't know, call in for a muffin or something. You don't have to bring the benefacting up yet. Or you could just advert to it.'

'Advert to it?'

'Yeah, you know, mention it in passing.'

'While I am explaining to her that I am bipolar, but in a good way.'

'Yeah, exactly.'

I end the call. The lift eases to a halt and the doors glide open.

'I didn't know you were bipolar,' Ish says as we step out.

'I'm not.'

'There's nothing wrong with it, Claude. My Uncle Nick's

bipolar. For a while there he was convinced he was a koala bear. Used to hang off the satellite dish all day, thought it was a eucalyptus.'

'I'm not bipolar,' I insist, and then, because I am too flustered and irritated to think of a plausible lie, 'That was Paul,' I say.

'Oh, right.' Ish keeps a commendably straight face. 'What did he want?'

'Ariadne's going away. He wants me to go and talk to her before she leaves.' I groan, scrub my face with my hands. 'Aaargh, it is all so ridiculous and embarrassing!'

'You must really like her, to put in this much effort,' Ish says neutrally.

'I do like her,' I say, staring at my shoes. 'I don't know why it is so hard to tell her. I am not twelve years old.'

Ish looks at me for a moment. 'It just is, Claude,' she says. 'It just is.' Then she glances at her watch. 'Tell you what, though, if you want to see her at the café you'd better get your skates on.'

I look up at the clock on the wall of the Research Department. She's right, the Ark will be closing in a few minutes. 'Maybe I should just wait till she comes back from her holidays.'

'No way, Claude, you've got to seize the day with these things,' Ish says firmly. 'Otherwise they drag on and on and on.'

'But I have so much work –'

'You've been mooning over this girl for weeks, just go and talk to her!'

'All right, all right.' With a swiftly deepening sense of unreality – as if it were water pouring into a leaking boat – I pull my coat back on and smooth down my hair. 'Wish me luck.'

'You don't need luck!' she says. But as I am waiting by the lifts I hear her calling my name. I turn and see her hurrying towards me, in her hand a small porcelain jar.

'What's that?'

'I was going through a crate of old stuff last night and I found it,' she says, opening the jar and pouring into her palm a hillock of white powder. 'It's from Kokomoko. They call it *bila*. If you inhale it it's supposed to work as an aphrodisiac.'

'I thought you said I didn't need luck.'

'Go on, give it a go, just for the laugh. What you do is, you blow it in her face like this – oh cripes! Sorry, Claude!'

'Aaargh!' My eyes blaze.

'Oh God! Oh God!' Through tears I see a vaguely Ish-shaped blur bounce fretfully around me.

'I'm fine,' I gasp, feeling my throat begin to reopen. 'Honestly.'

'I'm sorry!' she says. 'Strewth, I must have blown half the jar at you. Are you sure you're okay?'

'I think so . . .'

'Like you don't feel . . . different or anything?' Slowly her face comes back into focus, peering concernedly into mine.

'I'm not sure,' I admit. 'It's hard to tell.'

'Look into my eyes a second, Claude . . . look into my eyes . . .'

'I think I am feeling better now.'

'Hmm, I don't know, you look a bit weird. Maybe you should leave Ariadne till tomorrow.'

'She's going away tomorrow.'

'Oh, right,' Ish says, still holding my gaze.

'I'd better go,' I decide and, turning, stumble for the lift.

In the mirrored wall of the lift I examine myself. *Bila* clings to my lapels and shoulders, glowing faintly like magical dandruff. I brush it away as best I can, though I can do nothing about my eyes, which are red and streaming, and instead of a sophisticated gallery owner make me look authentically deranged. Nevertheless, as I descend, I feel exhilarated, transfigured, as if I have found my way at last into Paul's unwritten book, waiting here all along at an invisible angle to the truth . . .

The café is empty of customers, and in one corner the chairs have been lifted on to the tables. 'We're just about to close,' the blonde waitress tells me.

'I have a message for Ariadne,' I say.

The girl goes to fetch her. A moment later Ariadne emerges from the kitchen, carrot peelings stuck to her hands; what a thing, to envy a carrot peeling. 'Oh, it's you,' she says, in what strikes me as a slightly louder voice than is necessary. Behind me I sense her golden-haired colleague stop what she is doing in order to monitor the situation.

'Yes,' I say, trying to maintain my composure over my pounding heartbeat, the *bila* chattering in my veins. 'I just wanted to . . .' But my attempt at an apology is exploded by a violent sneeze, and my apology for this first sneeze is overwhelmed by a second, even more violent, which ushers in a fit of minor sneezes and sneezelets. With a *tsk* of concern, Ariadne hurries over with a bouquet of paper tissues.

'Thank you.' I dab at my eyes, which are streaming again.

'You have a cold,' she chides, going behind the counter then returning a moment later with a mug of herbal tea. 'You boys are all the same, you don' take care of yourselves.'

'Thanks.' I sniff again, taking the mug. It seems Ish's aphrodisiac has played its part after all: my copious sneezing rules me out as any kind of threat, except as a disseminator of germs. I drink my tea, surreptitiously take in her dark beauty, shimmering against the backdrop of the rain-teeming window. Everything is just as it should be; my line presents itself as if I have the page right in front of me. 'About the other day.'

'Don' worry,' Ariadne says. 'Your Dr Cyrano has come in and explained everything.'

'Who?'

'Dr Cyrano – the psychiatrist?'

I roll my eyes, then realize this makes me look more bipolar. 'Oh yes, of course.'

'He told me about this experimental drug you're taking that makes you act weird around women?'

'Yes, that's right, the experimental drug. However, I have stopped taking it now. In fact, I am completely cured.'

'Oh, that's great!'

'Yes, I wanted to let you know. And also to apologize if I alarmed you.' I pause, looking down at my knees mysteriously. 'There was something else I wanted to ask you.'

'Oh?'

'It relates to your paintings.'

She lights up. 'You want to buy one?'

'It's a bit more complicated than that. If you have a few minutes, maybe we could . . . ?'

She looks intrigued, but the noisy approach of a floor-polishing machine, piloted by her blonde colleague, restores her to reality. 'Ah, but we are closing,' she laments.

'Oh,' I say, then, innocently, 'Maybe tomorrow would be better?'

'Tomorrow I am going away,' she says.

'I see.' I frown, then look at my watch. 'Perhaps a quick drink? Before you go home?'

I can't help being impressed by my own suaveness here; it's as if Ariadne is acting as a kind of catalyst, in whose presence I am transforming into someone half-worthy of her.

Ariadne tocks her tongue thoughtfully against her palate. 'I have somethink to do,' she says. 'But you can come with me, if you want? Is not so far?'

'Perfect,' I say. The scene is unfolding just as I intended – although it is a surprise when she thrusts a large black garbage bag into my hands.

'Buns,' she says enigmatically. She whisks away into the kitchen, then reappears behind a trolley, on top of which sits a large steel vat. 'There's a couple of places we bring what we have left at the end of the day,' she says.

'Ah,' I say, and then, suavely, 'They are fortunate to get such excellent food.'

'I think leftovers is always tasting of leftovers, whatever they are. You coming?'

I jump up and hold the door for her, then thrust open my umbrella and raise it over her head; in this manner, like some strange new creature of feet and wheels and umbrella spokes, we pass over the threshold of the Ark and outside. Outside! Where we are no longer waitress and customer, simply woman and man; where as far as the world is concerned, we could be on a date, or lovers, or ecstatic newly-weds . . .

We make our way over the plaza in the direction of the river. Ariadne is saying something, but I am too giddy to hear. This is happening! This is my life now! As we approach the quays, the rain dies away and we see, shattering the clouds, a glorious sunset strung across the water. 'Oh, how beautiful!' croons Ariadne, coming to a halt. I just smile, as if I had arranged it myself. Ariadne gazes happily at the sky's deep blush, then raises her finger and traces a kind of a benediction in the air. 'You know the artist

Yves Klein?' she says. 'When he is young, he lies on the beach and signs the sky with his finger. He says it was his first artwork.'

'A nice idea,' I say. 'Though hard to fit in a gallery.'

She laughs.

I seize my moment. 'Speaking of galleries,' I begin, and then stop. Ariadne has crossed the road and stepped on to the bridge. 'Where are we going?' I ask, but she doesn't hear me over the rattling of the trolley. She couldn't be taking me to – we're not going to – are we?

But we are.

The squalid tents – fewer in number than the last time I looked – are drenched with rain; rainwater puddles in every available surface. On the improvised fence, rain-bleached posters blare grim statistics of government and bank collusion, with crudely rendered images of pigs in top hats smoking cigars, and fists squashing euro signs. A whiteboard importunes passers-by for 'Things We Need!', followed by a list: tea bags, soap, batteries, and so on. Over the camp a banner hangs, declaring damply, FIRST THEY IGNORE YOU, THEN THEY LAUGH AT YOU, THEN THEY FIGHT YOU, THEN YOU WIN. I feel some of my new-found suaveness escape into the cooling air.

Ariadne opens a makeshift gate and wheels the trolley into the compound. 'Hello!' she shouts, and again, until a dreadlocked head pokes out from one of the tents. His face, painted corpse-grey and decorated with an array of sutures, breaks into a smile when he sees her. He scrambles out and to his feet.

'Ah you're a saint,' he says.

'Just a few bits an' pieces,' Ariadne says to him, handing over a bulging bag. 'Mostly food from today, but there's a jar of coffee too, and some washing-up liquid and other stuff.'

'Fantastic,' the zombie says, beaming down into his trove, then nods at me. 'Who's this?'

'This is Claude,' Ariadne says, adding, to my mind unnecessarily, 'he works in a bank.'

'Oh yeah?' The zombie draws back and examines me with a new attention.

'We are not part of this . . .' I wave my hand at the protest signs, the skeletal ruin of Royal Irish. 'My bank is an investment bank, not a retail bank. And we haven't been given any government money. In fact, we have been punching above our weight.'

'Right,' the zombie says.

'Listen, I'm not here the next couple of weeks,' Ariadne says to him, 'but I tell Riika to keep bringing down something, okay?'

'You're going back to see your parents?'

'Ay, they tell me they are fine, but I can' help to worry. All this craziness, riots, petrol bombs, young people fighting the police every night? No trains, no food in the supermarkets, these lunatics who march around with swastikas – and meanwhile from Europe all they hear is, where's our money?'

As she says this her face quite changes, almost cracks open, revealing a dark, fretful interior I never knew existed. I feel a pang of guilt, having advised many clients over the last year of the dangers of the Greek contagion, not to mention counselling Howie to short Greek bonds for all they were worth, which by the time he was finished was a lot less.

'Europe won't abandon Greece,' I say, as much to reassure myself as Ariadne. 'There are mechanisms in place. People won't be allowed to starve.'

'The mechanisms are only there to make sure the fat cats get their money back,' the zombie interjects. 'All this has happened before. The bankers lose the run of themselves, they bring the whole system crashing down, and then the people who have to pay to get it back on the rails are the ones on the very bottom. Then the CEOs give themselves a big fat raise for a job well done.'

'That's not strictly accurate,' I say.

'Latin America in the 1970s,' he says. 'The banks lend a ton of money to a bunch of gangster dictators, thinking they'll make a packet. Then when all the loans turn bad and the US and Euro banks are on the point of tanking, the IMF steps in with emergency credit so these unfortunate countries can pay them back. But who pays back the IMF? The peasants, the farmers, the factory workers and the shoe-shine boy. That's what happened in Tunisia, Russia, East Asia. That's just what's happening here. It's like this great big circle of debt, with the only result that the people with the very least get poorer and poorer and poorer.'

The heat in his cheeks is visible through the corpse paint. Ariadne gazes at him pityingly, as if he had personally been chased up and down Patagonia by neoliberal economists.

'Look,' I say, feeling my own cheeks turn red. 'It's not a conspiracy. The fact is –'

'In Indonesia they got rid of food supports for the poor,' the zombie interrupts. 'In Madagascar they cut the mosquito eradication programme, and ten thousand people died of malaria.'

'The fact *is*,' I persist, 'that Greece is deeply in debt. It can't afford to pay its workers. It can't afford to keep its electricity on. This is why the IMF is there, to stop the country from completely disintegrating.'

'If they wanted to stop it disintegrating, they'd just cancel the debt,' the zombie says.

'What are you talking about?'

'Write it off. It's all imaginary anyway. Numbers on a piece of paper. So erase them.'

'You have to pay what you owe,' I snap. 'That is the cornerstone of our civilization.'

'Unless you're a bank, right?' the zombie returns. 'Look at this place right here!' He sweeps his hand at Royal Irish's grey façade. 'My grandchildren are going to be paying off the money they blew. My grandchildren are going to be *born into debt* because of them and their incompetence. And still the government's pumping them with more cash!'

Aha: here I have the advantage of him. I feel my anger recede, my suaveness return. 'Not for much longer,' I say. 'The bank will be wound down very shortly. And you and your friends can go home.'

'That's not what I hear.'

'What do you hear?' I say sardonically.

'They're going to keep it open,' the zombie says, throwing back a dreadlock. 'They're going to bring in new taxes so they can dredge up another few billion. They won't stop till we're in administration.'

'The people won't let that happen,' Ariadne comes in. 'They can't.'

'This is Ireland. There's a lot of things people are willing to let happen.' He seems to deflate, gestures gloomily at the rain-sodden tents. 'Half of our lot have given up in the last week. They think there's no point. Nobody's paying any attention.'

'Ay, these guys are paying attention,' Ariadne says, nodding across the street to where, outside the defunct bank, two enormous security guards have appeared, staring at the encampment with arms folded.

'They're there all the time,' the zombie says. 'I think they work for the Centre. So far they haven't crossed the road. Although someone turned a water hose on us last night. All our stuff got soaked, the sleeping bags, the generator. Here, maybe you should head off,' he says quickly, as one of the guards starts speaking into a walkie-talkie. Leaning forward, he kisses her on the cheek. 'I'll see you when you get back.'

We are on our way at last, though Ariadne keeps looking back fretfully: news of the sleeping-bag soaking has given a gloss of martyrdom to the zombie sit-in.

'He's wrong about Royal Irish,' I tell her. 'I just wrote a report for the government, advising them to wind it down. It will probably be announced in the next few days.'

'How will they get their clothes and things dry in this rain?' Ariadne says.

The beautiful sunset has gone, leaving a brooding gunmetal sky from which rain descends in fusillades. As we rattle back over the bridge, I review the situation. The zombie has taken the chapter in completely the wrong direction. I should never have let him speechify like that! I should never have let Ariadne go off-piste with the trolley! How can I get the story back on track? If only I had more *bila*!

We come back on to the IFSC side of the river, rumble northwards past boarded-up doors, broken windows, lowered shutters, roofless houses. We are probably only a couple of minutes from Transaction House as the crow flies, but my surroundings are quite unfamiliar.

'This is where there used to be all the whores,' Ariadne says, seemingly untroubled by the menacing ambience. 'When is call Monto. You know the song?'

'Song?'

'Dave taught it to me. *Now when the Tsar of Russia, and the King of Prussia, landed in the Phoenix Park in a big balloon . . .*'

A fresh wave of paranoia rises up within me. Who is Dave? Is it the zombie? Or some other interloper?

'In the nineteenth century, after the Famine, there was no work and no food,' she is saying, 'so all these women come here and sold their bodies to the British soldiers. They don' have another choice, either they do it here, or they get on the ship' – she gestures back in the direction of the river – 'and sell it in America. Is funny, eh?'

'Is it?'

'Once is the biggest whorehouse in Europe, now is mostly turned into banks.'

'Oh, yes, I see.'

She bows her head, then says in a lower voice, 'My mum told me that since the IMF came, there are all these girls every night at the end of our street. Getting into cars with strangers. Girls I went to school with, some of them.'

'Right,' I say blandly. This avenue of conversation does not seem promising, romantically speaking.

'So there is still money to fuck them, I suppose.'

'I suppose there is.'

'It's so horrible what is happening there,' she says, suddenly passionate. 'There are people starving everywhere you go. People starving! On the streets of the city where I grew up! And the world acts like we deserve it! We didn't drop cluster bombs on Baghdad! We didn't blow up hospitals in Gaza! Now, because we don' pay back some loans, we are the worst in the world?'

Trying to be optimistic, I tell myself that our misfiring encounter can't possibly get any worse. But now we arrive at our destination and I realize I am wrong.

A straggling line of men stretches along the pavement. Some are slouched against the corroded wall, others slumped on the kerb, still others sprawled across the footpath, apparently asleep, so we have to steer the trolley around them. They are young and old, bald and hirsute, corpulent and lean as junkyard dogs. There are Roma men with tragic moustaches and pork-pie hats, gaunt Slavs with chilly eyes, a couple of burly Africans murmuring to each other in French; the majority, though, from their features and accents, appear to be Irish: men with wild sailor beards and bulbous, capillaried noses, cans of beer in toxic colours; skeletal, shiftless men with pinhead-pupils; sheepish men, better-dressed than the others, who chew their gum, clear their throats and study their phones, as though it were a connecting flight they were waiting for.

A palpable quickening runs through the line as Ariadne passes along it; some of the men leer, a few of them address her – not by name, more in the spirit of, 'There she is now,' 'Howya gorgeous,' as well as a less articulate array of grunts and gurns. We make it around the corner without incident, but then in the narrow lane one particularly sordid specimen lurches up and grabs her by the arm. Feverishly I try to remember the

tiger-throw Marco taught us in the Transaction House gym –
then realize the creature just wants to show her an abscess on
his leg, which Ariadne tuts over sympathetically before going
through a door.

We have entered a low, poorly lit hall. Men and the occasional
woman sit eating at rickety trestle tables, or queue with their
trays at the far end, where food sweats unappetizingly under
heat-lamps. A dour fellow in a hairnet comes out from behind the
counter and greets Ariadne. 'Thanks,' he says curtly, taking the
trolley from her and parking it by the hatch.

'How are things, Brendan?' Ariadne asks.

'How are they ever?' this Brendan responds. He pauses, directing an unabashedly hostile look at me. 'You've a new helper?'

'His name is Claude,' Ariadne says. 'I have kidnapped him to
show him how the other half live.'

'This is the Crawley Street shelter,' I say, realizing where I am.
'My bank has done some fund-raisers for you. Raffles, fun runs,
that sort of thing.'

'Of course!' Brendan exclaims. 'It's thanks to you we've been
able to open our East Wing!' He points behind him, though all I
can see is a blank wall.

'Ay, Brendan,' Ariadne scolds.

'No offence,' he says, the choleric blaze in his eyes belying
the words, 'but you people have a lot to answer for. When there
was money everywhere no one wanted to know about this place
because we didn't fit the big success story. Now the country's
broke they tell us there's nothing left for us. Then next thing you
hear they're giving billions to the banks?'

He is trembling now; Ariadne lays a soft hand on his
shoulder.

'Calm down,' she says. 'What's the use to get angry?'

'Sorry,' the hairnetted man says bluntly. Then, turning on his
heel, he mumbles, 'I'll go and get yesterday's vat for you.' He
stumps back to the kitchen, leaving Ariadne and me in a slightly

strained silence, broken sporadically by bloodthirsty cries from the surrounding tables.

'He is not normally like this,' Ariadne says.

'It's fine,' I say. 'As I said, my bank is an investment bank, not a retail bank. So we are not the ones who receive these handouts he's talking about.'

'I meant, I hope he is all right.'

'Oh, yes, of course.'

A noise comes from outside: a chorus of angry voices and a series of thuds. Brendan, who is wheeling out the scrubbed-clean double of the vat we just delivered, thrusts it aside and runs to the door, where a large black SUV has pulled up. Its appearance seems to have enraged the men waiting in line: they have surrounded the vehicle and are rocking it on its wheels, thumping the doors and windows while yelling abuse at the driver, a frightened-looking woman, who has a small child in the back seat. Brendan wades into the crowd, tugging bodies away and shoving them back. 'Lads, lads,' he shouts. With a screech of its wheels, the SUV promptly reverses, and manages to make it back out through the crowd, though not without more kicks and a few gobbets of spittle adorning the shining bodywork.

'What's she doin', comin' here?' a small outraged man demands of Brendan. 'What's she doin' in a fuckin' yoke like that?'

'Go in and have your food and stop annoying people,' Brendan tells him. Then to us he says, 'Her husband went bust. He's done a legger. Bank's kicked her out of the house, she and the kid have been living in that car for two weeks.' He gazes bleakly into the cloud-mobbed sky a moment. 'This place is fucked,' he says, and without further comment returns inside.

We turn back towards the river; I tilt the umbrella against the newly pugnacious wind. Ariadne has fallen silent, although the nature of her thoughts do not remain a mystery for long. 'These fucking banks,' she exclaims, and then, 'Sorry, you work in one, I keep forgetting.'

'No, you're right, some banks acted very badly,' I concur. 'But . . .'

'I know, I know, your bank is an investment bank, not a retail bank.'

'I wasn't going to say that.' In fact I was going to say it, but I also wanted to steer her around to the idea that bankers are capable of doing good. 'Many corporates, as well as creating employment and contributing to GDP, do have significant charity programmes.'

'Right, with the fun runs.'

'Yes, but also we donate a percentage of profits to charity every year.'

'As a tax write-off?'

'Well, that's not the primary reason –'

'Pff, the only reason you do anything is money. Cheap tax, that's why all of you are here.'

'That's a bit –'

But she cuts me off. 'You think if the Irish government turns around and says, "We are putting up the tax, but we *guarantee* every penny can go directly to the people who need it the most, to schools and hospitals and homeless shelters," do you think any of these companies would stay?'

'Well, you see, a business has a legal obligation to its shareholders –'

'Oh yes, just following orders, where do I hear that before?'

Is she serious? Is she genuinely comparing investment banks to Nazi war criminals?

'I'm not saying they are the *same* –' Ariadne's cheeks are pink, and as she speaks she gesticulates vigorously with both hands, so that the trolley is unpiloted and is stopped from crashing off the kerb only by my shins. 'I'm saying that once they have an *excuse*, people will do anything. They do what they are told, and they take their money, and they think it's all okay because it's just their *job*, while their real self is what happens *after* work, when they're bouncing a baby on the knee, or writing poems about snowflakes or whatever.'

The trolley heads for my shins again; I am too despondent to get out of the way. Here I am with the woman of my dreams, and I feel more like I'm having a shouting match with my father.

We push on, silent again save for the metallic yammer of the trolley. There is no food left to deliver, meaning we are on our way back to the Ark. A part of me is glad: Cyrano himself might have trouble reviving this scene. For the sake of closure, however, I say, 'Let's talk about your work.' Ariadne scowls, as if I have proposed we go to the dentist and have all her teeth extracted. Pretending I haven't seen, I go on, 'I must tell you, I admire your paintings very much. I think they are very beautiful. And that they deserve a wider audience. I would like to help you, if I can.' She doesn't respond; the trolley, which I suspect she is deliberately pushing over the bumpiest sections of the pavement, clatters unencouragingly. 'Firstly, I want to exhibit them, in a proper gallery,' I persist. 'Perhaps hire a space that exists, perhaps find somewhere entirely new. Also, I would like to offer you financial assistance, so you can concentrate on painting full-time without having to do menial work.'

'Menial work?'

'The café. Waitressing.'

'Oh,' she says.

For a long time it looks like this is the full extent of her thoughts. 'That's very interesting,' she says at last. 'I am happy you like my paintings.'

'And . . . ?'

'What you are saying, you want to be my patron.'

'Is it a bad thing? The greatest artists had patrons. Leonardo, Velázquez. Today the big banks sponsor a lot of the major art fairs, as well as buying a great deal of the work.'

'Yes, "alternative assets", that's what you call art, isn't it? It's a good source of tax relief?'

I don't reply; what is there to say?

'Did you always want to be a banker?' she asks sadly.

'Not particularly,' I say. 'In college, I studied philosophy. Nietzsche, Foucault, Texier . . .'

As if I have pronounced a secret code-word, her head whips round and she comes to an abrupt stop.

'Texier? You mean François Texier?'

'Well, yes,' I say. 'From Paris, he died a couple of years ago –'

'So, now we can talk,' she says. 'Because you know Texier is my great hero.'

Now it's my turn to come to a halt. Can it be true? Was Paul right all along? 'You have read his philosophy?'

'A little bit. I read what he wrote about financial capitalism. He's very critical, how did you manage to go from Texier to banking?'

'It wasn't something I planned.'

'Anyway, you know he became a painter, late in his life?' Seeing my confusion, she explains, 'When he is quite old, he becomes disillusioned with philosophy. Philosophy, science, religion, they all start by saying they will tell you the truth, and from there they lead only to bigger and bigger lies. But art is different, because art tells you right at the start, "Okay, I'm going to tell you a whole lot of bullshit here . . ." Texier says that in modern times the only one we can still believe is the man who tells us he's lying. And so he gives up philosophy and he starts to paint.'

'I don't think I've ever seen any of his paintings.'

'Oh, Claude, they're so beautiful!' She seizes my arm; her countenance has quite changed, become rapturous and light-filled. 'Strange, you know? And dark? But when I see them, I feel like my heart is gonna explode. One little canvas, this big, makes you remember just how huge and weird the world is, and how fucking amazing it is to be here in it.'

I smile: it has been a long time since I felt like that.

'And he has all these interesting ideas – for example, he

wouldn't ever sell his paintings, he only gives them to friends, because he thinks that when you sell them, the meaning changes? They start to become the false truth that he is trying to escape? But he can't control it: eventually the friends sell them, or they die and their children sell them – anyway, they finish up with the price tag. And in the end he gives up painting too, because he thinks that art is only making things worse.'

'But you?' I say. 'You don't feel like that – do you?'

She frowns, sighs, stops with her trolley in the middle of the path. 'It's very interesting. When I come here first, is because I want to be a painter. I hear there's a boom, Celtic Tiger, and when I get here it's so exciting, so much energy in the air, everyone talking about the future and progress and all that – very different from Greece where, you know, everyone has a name from a myth of three thousand years ago. And the best thing, the art market is so crazy back then, even someone like me can sell paintings. But after a little while, I start to realize the people who come to the galleries, they are not even looking at the paintings. They just in a race with each other to buy it. Paying all this money – you know the most expensive piece always sell the first – so they can belong in this special club.

'An' at the same time, I'm working in the café, I'm coming down here every day, this fucking street –' She waves her hand; I look around at the litter-strewn gutters, the weed-split paving stones, the tenements doomed for the wrecking ball. 'Every time I come here, is a little bit worse. Even with all this money, no one sees it, no one does nothing to change it. And it takes me a time to realize, No one *wants* to see it. That's what this whole boom is about, it's so people don' have to see things. All the fucked-up stuff that is happening, or has happened in the past, they cover it up with money, with talk about the future, with new buildings, with drinking, whatever.'

'But the boom is over,' I say.

'Yes, and now the very same thing is happening again, every-body tries to forget what they did during the boom. Everybody acts instead like they are the victim. You know the Greek word for truth is *aletheia*? *Lethe*, this is the river of forgetting, so the truth, *aletheia*, is that which you don' forget. But here, it's like the total opposite. The truth is what you don't remember.'

'Liffey or Lethe,' I say, recalling the old argument about the Radiohead song.

'It's like this whole country is trying to crawl out of its own skin,' she says. 'And I start to feel that me, with my art, I am help-ing them.'

'But you can paint whatever you want to paint,' I tell her. 'You can paint nothing but these streets, if you want. I'll make sure the whole world sees them.'

'Yes, that's exactly the kind of fucking thing *art* would do,' she laughs, 'and show it in a gallery far away from here, where you can't smell the smell and no one going to stab you with a HIV needle, and people can say, "Oh, how sad, yet how beautiful," then it get bought by some yuppie with a polka-dot tie. Or look at this one.'

We have arrived back on the quays; directly in front of us stands a tall sculpture, depicting, in blackened bronze, six emaciated humanoids and a little bronze dog. 'It's a Famine memorial – you know a million people died, in this tiny little country? And millions more left, on ships that went from right here, and they never come back. So from a terrible thing that really happened, on this spot, we get, a hundred and how many years later, a piece of art, very beautiful, that people can look at as they hurry by with their takeaway lattes . . .'

I don't think I have ever looked at it before, with or without latte. I step up to the sculpture, run my finger down the tortured cheek of one of the gaunt, inconsolable forms. 'It *is* beautiful,' I say, not knowing whether I am contradicting her or not.

'Now look down,' she says.

I do as she says, and see that although the figures themselves are anonymous, names have been printed on the stylized bronze cobblestones beneath their bare feet – names of companies, names of banks, names of individuals: the corporate and private sponsors who paid for the work. Billionaires, businessmen, a disgraced prime minister, a society hostess; others I recognize from newspaper accounts of deals and court cases, corruption charges that were never proved.

'So ask yourself, who does this artwork want you to remember?'

I step back with a chill. The wind pulls and chafes at the surface of the river; on the far side, the night sky is reflected and intensified in the louring windows of the corporate towers, as though they were mining darkness from the air, storing it within them. 'Maybe in a hundred years, some artist will make a sculpture of the old women in Athens looking through the garbage for something to eat,' Ariadne says, resting her cheek against the cold metal shoulder of a peasant. 'And passers-by will stop their rocketpacks to film it with their magic future phones, and they'll think how beautiful, how sad.'

'So you've given up on art,' I say in summary. 'You're turning down my offer.'

'I haven't given up on anything,' she says. 'And you are very kind to make me this offer. But I *like* working in the café. Making a space where people can come together and feel safe and good, for me it's not menial work. Even if they're bankers, maybe if they eat the nice home-cooked food that's made with love, it can change how they think a little bit. And afterwards I can bring the leftovers to the shelter, and at night-time I can paint my paintings, and if anyone wants to buy them they can, they're not very expensive. What does it mean to become a famous artist, anyway? That your paintings cost more money, right? That's all it means, deep down. But why should rich people have all the beauty?'

'Not all the beauty,' I qualify, wistfully taking in her dark radiance, the twin lights in her eyes.

She holds my gaze a moment, then looks away. 'I have made enough escaping. Now I am here, I want to *be* here.'

'Though you are going back to Greece,' I remind her.

'My father is very sick,' she says. 'And everything is so fucked up over there right now that in the hospital there's no food or medicine, so your family has to bring them for you. If you have a family.' She hoists her shoulders, as if shrugging off a cold and sodden cloak. 'Do you go back home often? Are they still in Paris, your parents?'

'No, they died.'

'Ah, I'm sorry.' She has separated herself from the statue and come towards me; she rubs the black cloth of my suit between her finger and thumb. 'It was recent?'

I shrug.

Her hand remains on my arm. In the dusk her green eyes are dark pools in which the reflected street lights swim like lilies. 'So you are alone,' she says.

The wind swirls down the river, the quayside traffic judders like a heavier, earthbound wind; everything seems to liquefy, as if something had broken open.

I realize my story is at a turning point. The subterfuge, the plotting, the misdirection, all of that falls away, and the dull details of my life here too, the whole maze tumbling into itself like panels of scenery. The lie has brought me, as promised, to the truth. 'Look,' I begin.

But that is as far as I get. Ariadne's phone has started to ring. 'Sorry, one second,' she says, holding up a finger to suspend our conversation, like a fairy bringing time to a halt with a twitch of her wand, then unleashes into the phone a torrent of accelerated Greek.

Sequestered within the alien noise, my mind is racing. Am I actually going to do this? Should I talk to Paul first? But the time for Cyranos and surveillance equipment has passed. I have been in a story long enough, trapped on a flat page, delivering lines written by others. Now is the time to step out into the world. How else could this end, but with the hero speaking in his own voice? Ariadne gives me a wrapping-up sign. I take a deep breath, I gird my loins; then into the phone I hear her say, '*S'agapo, Oscar, s'agapo* . . . I love you, baby, I'll be home soon.'

And around me it seems that a hundred doors and windows have been flung open, as in some stuffy room; and all of the potential, the dreams, the imagined futures borne away in an instant, like banknotes thrown to the wind.

'And what did you say?'

'What could I say?'

'Didn't you ask her who it was?'

'No, I simply ignored it, and then continued my pretence that I had approached her only out of an interest in her work.'

'And that was it? Then you just went back to the office?'

'First I bought a painting. *Simulacrum 103*. There it is, by the mantelpiece.' I point to the painting, still in a cardboard box, like a cold, avant-garde pizza. Paul opens the lid, winces, closes it again. At the breakfast bar Igor, who arrived uninvited with Paul, tosses pistachio nuts into his mouth and flips the shells on the ground.

'Let me get this straight,' Paul says. 'The two of you are getting on fine, everything's going according to plan, then she gets this phone call, during which she says –'

' "I love you, Oscar. I'll be home soon." '

'That's all?'

'The rest was in Greek.'

'Well then!' Paul spreads his hands expansively. 'She could have been talking to anybody. Her uncle, her brother. The guy who comes to fix the fridge. You know these Mediterraneans, they're very demonstrative.'

'It wasn't the man who comes to fix the fridge,' I say, recalling the light that jumped in her eyes as soon as she took out her phone. 'She meant what she said.'

'So who is he, then? Who is this Oscar?'

Who is Oscar? Since that moment at the waterside, when my dreams were so casually atomized, I have thought of little else. In my imagination he keeps changing, one moment garrulous and witty, the next silent and serious; right now I picture him as a handsome, athletic type – tanned, stubbled, a pilot for Médecins Sans Frontières who in his spare time writes surprisingly tender poetry. The others have differing opinions: Paul sees him as a brilliant entrepreneur, a wild-eyed maverick making a fortune from imperceptible flaws in the system; Igor proposes that he is a professional sex worker, 'with wang like the extinguisher of fires, who has made her addict to his sex, and she cannot stop sexing him'.

'See, with a high-quality waitress-surveillance system there'd be none of this ambiguity,' Paul says, frowning. 'Without knowing what we're up against, it's hard to work out the best course of action.'

'Only one course,' Igor says. 'Good old-fashioned maiming. Without this monster wang of his, she will soon turn elsewhere for her pleasures.'

'I don't think it will make a difference,' I say. 'The writing was on the wall long before she mentioned Oscar. She hates banks with a passion.'

'But we expected that, right?' Paul says. 'That's why we were pushing the benefactor thing. Didn't she go for that at all?'

'She seemed uncomfortable taking money for her art from someone who works in a bank. She likened us to Nazis.'

He sighs. 'Okay. Well, you're right, once a woman starts calling you a Nazi, it's time to bow out. Frankly, from what you've told me, you may have dodged a bullet. The paintings and the organic food should have been a clear enough warning. Better to get out now, before she starts making you wear vegetarian shoes and call history "herstory".'

'And leave her tampons all over the place,' Igor chimes in wearily. 'This is what happens with my ex-wife. Tampons, everywhere in my house. Then she try to unionize the strippers. Man who says, "We must educate the womens," I say to him, "You think anybody pay to see strippers who have cut off their hair and now dress in boiler suits that they will not take off?" '

'Igor here actually owned his own strip club back in the old country,' Paul explains.

'Happier times, happier times,' Igor says mistily.

'Anyhow, the main thing now is that we put Ariadne behind us and get you back in the game,' Paul says, bending down to his bag. 'If you'll take a look at the laptop here, you'll see the beta version of the new Hotwaitress. We're still updating the database, but there are plenty of options . . .'

'I appreciate your help,' I say. 'But for me, I think the game is over.'

'Over?' Paul looks up from the laptop with a start. 'What do you mean?'

I rise from my chair and go to the window. Uninhabited office blocks blaze with light against the dark sky, a ghost armada sailing the black ocean. 'I suppose I don't feel like I dodged a bullet,' I say. 'I think the bullet went right through me.'

'Then why stop?' Paul says, jumping to his feet. 'We can find out more about Oscar. Maybe there are cracks in the relationship we can exploit. We'll redesign you from the ground up, so whatever Oscar lacks, you have in spades.'

I smile. When I asked him to come over, I still thought there was something he could do; now I can see that the very fact I'm having this conversation shows how hopeless the situation is. Tricks, artifice, the implacable double-agency of money – this is my world, not Ariadne's, and there is simply no way to go from mine to hers.

'Artifice is everybody's world! You think Ariadne gets out of bed looking like that? You think she doesn't put in her time in front of the mirror, getting her beautiful ebony hair to flow just so? Look, you've had a disappointment, I understand that. But a few weeks ago you didn't even know her. What's to stop you having the same feelings for somebody else? Take a look in our database.' He holds the laptop open for me, faces arrayed on the screen like chocolates in a box. 'There are literally hundreds of other waitresses here. Just take a look.'

'No.'

'Look, that's all I'm asking.'

'I don't want anybody else,' I say.

Paul sighs. 'Okay, Claude. It's your decision, of course. But if you don't mind me saying so, you're being awfully naïve about this. Ariadne made an impression on you, and that's great. But life is not literature. Sooner or later, the spell wears off, the romantic feelings disappear, and you're left watching somebody's body disintegrate. You start with a love story, you end up manacled to an hourglass, watching the sands run out.'

'It is true,' Igor concurs in a voice gravelly with regret. 'When I marry my wife, she is filthiest lap dancer in all of Transnistrian Autonomous Region. There are criminals who come out of her stall weeping with shame at the things she has do to them in there. When she choose me, I am joyous as priest in orphanage. But the day we are married, it is like someone steal her away and replace her with her mother. Shoutings, hittings me with rolling pin. Meeting other womens to form terror gangs of feminism. Last time I see her she tell me she want to have breast reduction surgery. I ask her, "Are you mad? God and plastic surgeon have give you best boobs in former Soviet Union, why do you flout this gift?" She will not listen. I cannot bear to see this tragedy, so I come here to begin new life.' He gazes bleakly into his glass. 'She must be fifteen now,' he says.

'What we're offering you here is freedom from that,' Paul says, brandishing the laptop again. 'Don't you understand, that's what Hotwaitress *is*. A way to stay inside the story for ever.'

I understand what he's offering me: a chance to keep paying him a retainer indefinitely. But I am tired of being his mark. 'I think this is goodbye,' I say.

Scowling, he puts the laptop away, takes his coat from the back of the chair.

'Why don't *you* stay inside the story,' I challenge him, 'if everything is better there?'

'It's too late for me,' he says. 'I have a wife, remember?'

'You have an hourglass you're chained to,' I say. 'You've already abandoned your career. If you don't love your wife any more, why don't you leave her too?'

'You really don't understand anything, do you?' he says. 'I read somewhere that money kills your ability to empathize.'

I flinch. He opens the door. 'I do love her,' he says. 'That's the whole problem.' He turns away, repeating to himself, 'That's the whole problem.'

3
Persona Ficta

*In societies where modern conditions of production prevail,
all of life presents itself as an immense accumulation of spectacles.
Everything that was directly lived has moved away into a representation.*

Guy Debord

It's true, Texier said some harsh things about the banks; this, in fact, was putting it mildly. He saw the financial market, with its obsessive will to quantification, as the perfect instance of his totalizing system, his 'eutrophication' or 'veil of Maya' – a web of abstraction so complicated that it asphyxiated what it was supposed to explain before collapsing inevitably under its own weight. The artificial, the *less-than-real*, was once conceived as a kind of hell, he wrote. Yet today the less-than-real is prized more than gold, and the quaint stuff of the tangible – the underlying, as it has become known – exists only as raw material for new and lucrative abstractions. The financial corporation has become a machine for *producing unreality*; why do we desire this unreality? Why do we model ourselves on this machine?

We know that what we call the corporation (Texier wrote) first appeared in Europe's Middle Ages, signed into law by the Pope in AD 1250. It was conceived as a legal *persona ficta* – a 'fictive person' that had many of the attributes of a real person. It was capable of owning property, for example, of suing and being sued; at the same time, it was bodiless, invisible, free from human infirmity and the ravages of time. Conceived as such, the corporation was almost identical to contemporary ideas of angels. According to medieval religious doctrine, angels too were immaterial, ageless, capable of acting like human beings but bound by neither substance nor time; the corporation, an entity which we imagine as a uniquely secular creation, a paragon of reason and common sense, in fact began its life as an offshoot of a Christian myth.

Today, though we no longer believe in angels, we still regard the corporation as a higher order of being. It is composed of ordinary people, but it transcends them; semi-divine, it floats above our messy and contingent reality. Of all the corporations, it is the bank, which produces nothing tangible, which trades only ever in the virtual, that remains closest to pure spirit, and thus sits at the top of the hierarchy, equivalent to the Thrones and Dominions. Whatever it does, we are ready to forgive; or rather we assume that what we see as sins are instead mystical transactions beyond our understanding. We have an instinctive feeling that these dark angels, of us and yet above us, must be protected and appeased – to the extent that we allow them to predate on the material world, feed vampirically off our very reality, leaving us to live among their detritus. We do this because we want to be like them, because we ourselves aspire to the condition of *persona ficta*: free from reality's contingencies and humiliations, insubstantial, unchanging, inviolable, endlessly apart.

Yet how does a person become a *persona ficta*? How can one simultaneously turn fully inwards and make oneself abstract? Perhaps these two operations are less exclusive than we might think. Humans have always used stories to order reality. Now, however, technology allows unprecedented quantities of reality to be turned into story. Reality thereby becomes secondary; just as the banks use the underlying only for what can be derived from it, life becomes merely raw material for our own narratives.

The building block of these narratives is the image. The image operates by delimiting reality, placing boundaries around it, removing its connections and context; in short, by enslaving it. It presents the results, however, as a concentration or apotheosis of reality. The image is the derivative of the self; can it be mere chance that the rise of financial capitalism has coincided with the proliferation and incorporation of the camera into almost every facet of the Western world? The camera's promise is that the moment can be subordinated – deferred, stored, experienced at our leisure. Life and the living of it have, for the first time in history, become separate. In recording our own reality – that is, in simultaneously experiencing and deferring experience – we pass from the actual into the virtual.

Every age dreams of defeating death: this is our chosen method. By hoarding images, we seek to conquer time. Of course, we do not mistake a photograph in a frame or on a screen for the reality as it was. Nevertheless, as Barthes has written, the photograph makes an assertion, and it makes it in a particular mode – what the Greeks called the Aorist, a form of the past tense that is never actually completed but seems to go on indefinitely. Thus, the picture presents us with the past as a continuum which flows parallel to the present, but flows statically, a frozen river, so we may examine it at any point in the future. It is this imagined future self, looking at the pictures of the past, that is the true product of the camera. Although technology has the capability now to record entire lifetimes, meaning that every moment may be pulled from the foaming sea of oblivion to the dry land of perfect recall, the mythic power of the photograph nevertheless relates to the future, and not to the past. Every recording conceals the secret fantasy of a future self who will observe it; this future self is himself the simulacrum, the *persona ficta*. He exists beyond time, beyond action, beyond need; his only function is to witness the continuum of the past, as he might observe the steps that brought him to godhood. Through this fantasy, time is transformed from the condition of loss into a commodity that may be acquired and stockpiled; rather than disappear ceaselessly into the past, life accumulates, each moment becoming a unit of a total self that is the culmination of our experiences in a way that we – biological composites who profligately shed our cells, our memories and our possessions – can never be. And this fantasy self or *persona ficta* is the soul, as conceived by a materialist people; he is the apotheosis of the individual, arrogating reality to himself, just as the bank does with its totalizing abstraction.

Who is with us, in this recursive heaven where time has been defeated? No one: the modern heaven is one of perfect isolation. We are not there either. The transcendental or sempiternal self bends over his screen, in correspondence with a forever-echoing past, leaving a present that is closed off, superfluous, from which (and this is the real meaning of the fantasy) we are exempted. That is our transcendence of death: to achieve a death-in-life, a stasis, a replacement of ourselves with a duplicate whose only function is to relay the past to the future; to conquer loss with a virtual repleteness, to extinguish the present by making ourselves comprehensively elsewhere.

After my father died, I found a cache of old family photographs in the apartment. There were hundreds of them, thousands even; I brought them back to Dublin and, whenever I had an hour free in the evening, began to archive them – feeding them into the scanner, transmuting them into digital form, though I could never decide whether this was to make it easier to look at them, or so I wouldn't have to look at them again.

My father was a blacksmith – with a hammer, an anvil and a forge, just as you might find in a novel of Alexandre Dumas. When I look at his picture, I'm still surprised to see he was not a tall man, nor even especially brawny; close my eyes and he's transformed instantly to the giant of my childhood, the black-browed ogre in his fiery cloud of sparks who thrilled and terrified me even when he was snoozing in his chair.

His father was a blacksmith, and his father before him. That was almost a century ago, when our town was a village and Paris still a murky chimera far beyond the horizon; by the time I was born, the forge lay quiet three days a week and my father had to supplement his income by teaching metalwork at the technical college nearby. He didn't care; on the contrary, he took great pleasure in the idea of himself as a throwback, an obstacle, a mis-shapen stone jamming up the smooth machine of modernity. My father thrived on attrition. In his time he had been a Maoist, a Leninist and a Trotskyite, but this was only so much misdirec-tion. What he believed in was dwarfed by what he didn't believe in. Progress, improvement, the perfectibility of human nature – to him, these were the great myths of our time, used to dispossess the poor and the gullible just as religion had in the past.

Certainly in our town it was easy to disbelieve in progress. It was a ramshackle warren of building sites, warehouses, and shops in which everything seemed already old. The dominant landmark was a disintegrating *magasin général*, a huge concrete grain store overlooking the canal that had lain empty for decades and was now a magnet for taggers, who had transformed it into something iridescent and otherworldly. You could follow the canal all the way into the city, but we rarely did. Paris was the city of modernity, and the home of the greatest of my father's many *bêtes noires*, Baron Haussmann. Before Haussmann came along, it sounded like people in Paris spent most of their time rioting; if they weren't rioting, they were erecting barricades. 'But how can you put a barricade across that?' my father would lament, gesturing at the Boulevard de Sébastopol and its four lanes of traffic.

So we stayed where we were, my father in his smithy, waging his covert war against progress. Perhaps to a blacksmith, this seemed like a war you could win; after all, he spent the day bending things to his intention, taking obdurate, resistant matter and making it obey him; why couldn't he take on the world in the same way, plunge reality itself into the white heat of his will and reform it? And if he couldn't, if the bills mounted up and the bailiffs came, this was just more evidence that the world was biased against us; our poverty was proof of our rectitude, a sign that we were the good guys that those in control wanted to crush.

I, too, regularly found myself subjected to the blast of his will. He didn't want me to be a blacksmith; he wanted me to go to college. This struck me, even as a boy, as a contradiction. Wouldn't I just be lining up with the phonies and the fakes? Why couldn't I stay here with him, learn the family trade? When he heard this he'd laugh, and say the family could only afford one piss artist. But when it came to school reports and parent–teacher meetings, he would not be laughing. There was no question that I would not go to college. By the time I was sixteen, if I so much as showed my face in the backyard he would bellow at me to get back to my studies. And I would dutifully return upstairs to my logarithms or supplementary English, though I wouldn't read; instead I'd watch as he worked or read or played cards and talked about football with Yannick, the boy he hired on the rare occasions he had a backlog.

I knew we were headed for some kind of rupture – in the pictures it seems I can see it, an invisible crack behind the smiles. But I'd thought it would be philosophy that did it. I'd chosen to study it largely in a spirit of revenge: I was too cowardly to defy his wishes outright by refusing to take my college place, and philosophy – demonstrably impractical, infamously unemployable, the polar opposite of my father's own materialist world – seemed the next best thing. As it turned out, though, my father was so proud of me for getting into university that he approved of anything and everything I did there. He dug up an ancient newspaper photograph that showed Texier, Deleuze et al. marching with union leaders in his beloved *événements* of 1968, and stuck it on the wall of his forge; I heard him tell the neighbours that philosophy was France's greatest export.

Instead the rupture came when I took the job in the bank. Having spent a literal lifetime witnessing his anger, I don't think I ever saw him as angry as he was that night. Even though the firm was prestigious, even though the position I'd been offered was lucrative, my father was mortally against the whole financial industry. He was old enough to remember the scandals that emerged after Liberation, the bankers who had collaborated with the Nazis in order to enrich themselves. He accused me of taking the job out of malice; he said I was sticking it to an old man by choosing a career that flew in the face of everything he believed.

I told him he didn't believe in anything, so I didn't see how that could be an issue. 'Oh, you're very clever,' he said. 'There are names for people like you.'

I *was* very clever. He had made me very clever. Now he was annoyed because his gingerbread boy had come to life and run off down the road – *tant pis*, I wasn't coming back. Anyway, the world had changed, hadn't I listened to him proclaim it for years? The money men were taking over, men for whom nothing was real except profits, who sourced their ironwork from China or just used knock-offs made of plastic. In college I could see it all around me: street by street, Paris the working city was being replaced by 'Paris' the stage-set, familiar from the movies, where everyone was perpetually in love and/or carrying a baguette. Hardware stores and laundromats were vanishing, expensive tea shops, sushi restaurants and boutiques of tiny baby clothes arriving to take their place. The Arabs, the Africans, were disappearing too, out past the city limits to the dreaded *banlieues*. Not even our dowdy town was left untouched: the building sites, which for as long as I could remember had been stagnant, began to show signs of activity; developers were throwing up hoardings within sight of the great monument to decay that was the *magasin général*.

Empires fall, that was what he had taught me; the world turns, and people, whole cultures, become obsolete. Progress might be a lie, but it was a lie that swept all before it and so the best tactic was to find high ground.

I took the job, sure that he would come around in time. Why did I think that? This was a man who had chosen, in the 1980s, to pursue the trade of blacksmith. Pig-headed defiance was his *métier*. He loved difficulty, loved it more than he loved me.

And so we played out that first conversation over and over again. Sometimes he would lure me into it, pretending to have a question about the nature of, for example, derivatives, in order to harangue me about the inequities of the global financial system – '. . . so if you wanted to cover yourself, you could then buy what's called an *option* –' 'Which is nothing, am I right? You are trying to sell me thin air?' 'It's not nothing, I am selling you the *choice* to buy something for a specific price at a specific point in the –' 'Why do I need you to sell me the *choice*? Don't I have the choice myself?' 'Well, not in terms of –' 'I'm a free man, last time I looked! Your crowd hasn't managed to sell us all down the river yet!' 'No, but I'm saying, if you wait, the price could –' 'Down with the *collabos*! Vive la France! *Vive la France!*' – and so on, until Maman came in, and told him he must take his medicine.

More usually, though, he launched straight into his jeremiad, calling me a criminal, a parasite, taking me to task for the sins not only of my own profession but those of countless others – of the developers uprooting the city, of the American neoconservative movement, of 'Rat Man', as he termed our president, and of Rat Man's brother Olivier (who was, in fact, a banker). He seemed to enjoy making himself angry – that was the only pleasure either of us found in my visits.

'What does he want me to do?' I said to Maman in the kitchen. 'Become an anarchist and live in a squat?'

'He is old, Claude,' she would sigh. 'He is old and he cannot bear it.'

Eventually I stopped visiting. I told myself I blamed my father for coming between my mother and me; in truth, it suited me rather well. I was busy at work, and there were more enjoyable ways to spend my few hours of leisure. I'd started seeing a girl, a model with a degree in art history from the Sorbonne. I didn't go home for six months. As a result, I didn't find out my mother was sick until she'd been admitted to hospital.

I found my father at her bedside; all the fury I felt at him disappeared in an instant. He sat there, waxy hand on hers; his eyes, blinking uncomprehendingly at me across the white wastes of the hospital sheets, reminded me of the horses that would be brought into his shop to be re-shod, the ones the cabbies drove around and around the Bois de Boulogne for the benefit of tourists – expressive of both resignation and a kind of glacial panic, one that unfolded slowly, over years.

After she died I thought things might be different. I made an effort to see him; for a time I even considered asking him to move into my apartment in Auteuil. But as the shock of her death wore off and bitterness took over, he became more and more impossible. He complained constantly about petty or imaginary things: the postman was opening his mail, the greengrocer overcharged him. He would not eat what I cooked for him; he made racist remarks about the proprietor of the *tabac*; whenever we went for a walk he would light on some new act of gentrification, some cutesy new patisserie or *macaron* shop festooned with love-hearts, and start on a tirade. He discovered plans were afoot to turn the beautiful, collapsing *magasin général* into a hotel. In the artist's rendering online, it had gondolas floating in front of it on the canal. 'Gondolas!' my father spluttered hoarsely. *'Gondolas!'* When the headhunter called me with the offer of a position in Dublin, I didn't have to consider it for long.

I palliated my guilt about leaving by hiring an expensive live-in nurse; and surprisingly quickly, guilt ceased to be an issue. Ariadne was right: Dublin during the boom was custom-made for forgetting. The past, the present, the sins of individuals and multinationals alike, everything dissolved in money and cocaethylene and was borne away by the river. When the crash came, that was better still: the streets were deserted, it was easier than ever to imagine that only the market existed, the numbers that concatenated night and day, and always, always, good times and bad, held within them some means of making money.

I didn't speak to my father often; most of my contact with him came in the form of Skyped complaints from the nurses about his behaviour, or Skyped interviews with their replacements when they quit. It was nurse no. 5, a sweet girl from Martinique, who called me that morning to say he'd passed away overnight; 'like switching off a light', she said approvingly, a good death. Beside me the radio was babbling the market news; through the window I could hear the tram-bell ring. It was six in the morning, I was dressed for the gym. 'Thank you very much,' I said. It was all I could think of.

The line manager arranged for two weeks' compassionate leave. I stayed at the old apartment; I spent most of my time tidying, as if he and she were about to arrive home after a trip away even though I knew that everything would very soon have to be boxed up and taken from the building. I put fresh flowers in the vase on the table; I topped up the bird feeder on the balcony, stood at the door, listening to the whirr of the tiny sparrows' wings, like the riffling of the pages of a book. I kept being surprised by my reflection, the way you might by some minor self-portrait in a neglected corner of the Louvre, having lost your way between masterpieces: tie half-done around my neck, shirt a spectral white that gave my skin a greenish tinge, eyes like those islands of discarded plastic found floating in the middle of the ocean, opaque, polymerized, indestructible.

My father had lost the lease on the yard ten years ago; more apartments had been built on the site of his forge. In a cupboard, I found a trunk filled with old equipment – a heat-mask, various lengths of rubber tubing; at the back of this trunk, thrown there with an appearance of carelessness, I discovered the cache of photographs. It was funny, I couldn't remember him taking them; yet here I was beginning school, here was Maman in a new dress, here were the three of us, visiting my aunt in her little house in Normandy, Maman and me again, at my college graduation; our lives, our family, bound up together in a way that I had never recognized the first time around. I sat on the ancient couch they had never replaced, and went through the pictures over and over. I laid them out in patterns on the coffee table, little coloured squares of time, as if I were playing solitaire, as if there were some perfect configuration that would win the game, retrieve the past in its totality.

Yet the more I tried to retrieve it, the more it shimmered, like a tesseract, into being, the lonelier I felt – as if I were viewing some marvellous planet from a bleak satellite suspended above it. At his funeral, I'd read a line of poetry: *No one is truly dead, until they are no longer loved*; it was from Théophile Gautier, a writer my mother had adored, and initially I found the thought consoling. Now, however, I began to wonder if the reverse also held. If nobody loved you, could you still say you were alive? The few relatives were long gone; I sat there turning over pictures that I didn't even see; I felt a freezing cold, of an order I had never experienced before, as if I were somehow locked outside of the very moment I inhabited, a derivative of something that had ceased to be, and therefore about to disappear too – 'triple witching hour', they call it in banking, when stock index futures, stock index options, options on futures all expire together in a hiss of unbeing . . .

It was the bank that came to my rescue. They called one day, on my parents' phone (I'd kept my mobile switched off) – someone from management whose name I didn't recognize, wanting to know where I was. I was shocked: how long had I been here? Yet when I checked the calendar, everything was in order. I'm on compassionate leave, I told the caller; I still have five days left.

'Yes,' he said, in a tone that suggested he knew this already, and then, rather cursorily, 'I'm sorry.' The line was silent for what seemed a long time. I wondered if I'd been cut off, or put on hold. Then he said, 'Claude, we would like to offer you a 50 per cent raise in your salary.'

'Oh yes?' I said, confused.

'I can also offer you a guaranteed bonus,' he said. He named the amount; it was significant.

'Oh,' I said. It took me a moment to realize he was waiting for a reply. 'Yes, yes,' I said, mostly so I could get off the line.

'I'll courier you over the paperwork right now,' he said.

It wasn't until I was on the return flight that I realized what had happened: that BOT believed or feared that I was using my compassionate leave to speak to banks in Paris with a mind to finding a new and better-paid position. I was surprised, but I didn't suppose it mattered. The plane began its descent; I saw the black river snaking through the city. Liffey or Lethe? That didn't matter either. I found I was relieved to get back to Dublin, where even if I wore black every day for a year no one would ask why, where I was free – free to be a *persona ficta,* free to lose myself in the labyrinth of the present. Or maybe I was imprisoned in the present, in the persona; either way I got paid, and the difference seemed of little consequence.

The zombie was right. The next morning the government announces a further bailout for Royal Irish.

The Minister delivers the news from the steps of the Dáil. 'After a careful study,' he says, 'it is clear to us that Royal Irish Bank is of systemic importance. As its failure would have severe consequences for Ireland and Europe, the government commits to meet all of the bank's present and future capital requirements until liquidity is restored . . .'

'What the fuck?' Ish says. 'He's digging out those dirtbags *again*?'

'Systemic importance, baby,' Gary McCrum says. 'Too big to fail.'

'But the whole point of our report was that it *wasn't* important,' Ish says. 'It's like he went through it and did the exact opposite of everything we recommended.'

'Wouldn't be the first client to do that,' Gary says.

'Perhaps he had information that was not made available to us,' Jurgen says.

'Or he's being counterintuitive,' Kevin suggests.

'He doesn't know what he's doing,' Jocelyn Lockhart says. 'Poor bastard, look at him.'

Still gabbling meaningless statistics into the morning sunshine, the Minister's bleached face is lathered with sweat; the heavy three-piece suit bulges unconvincingly, as if it's filled with straw.

'What's he even doing there?' Ish says. 'Why hasn't he handed over to someone else?'

'Strategic,' Gary McCrum says.

'Nobody without a terminal illness would've been able to get this bailout through,' Jocelyn Lockhart agrees. 'But people feel sorry for him.'

A journalist asks the Minister about possible IMF intervention if Ireland's fortunes continue to decline. The Minister appears irritated. 'I've already made it clear that there will be no third parties . . .' But as he speaks, the camera pans to his left and reveals, in the scrum of apparatchiks behind him, the little Portuguese man again.

'*They're already here* . . .' Jocelyn Lockhart sings.

'Bullshit,' Ish says.

'All over government buildings,' Jocelyn says. 'And I heard they've booked a whole floor of the Merrion Hotel.'

'There's no way IMF'd let him chuck more money at Royal Irish,' Ish objects. 'It's economic suicide.'

The media reaction to the Minister's announcement is apoplectic, terminal illness notwithstanding. The radio waves are clogged with hard-luck stories deriving from the last wave of cuts: grandmothers and children and chronically ill whose pensions were slashed or whose special-needs assistants were withdrawn or whose care was cancelled overnight by governmental austerity, even as yet more billions flow in decidedly unaustere fashion to the notoriously corrupt bank.

Market reaction is divided: bondholders are glad to hear they will be getting their money, but there is an increasing sense of mystery as to where this money will be coming from. The country's budget is running at almost a third of GDP, and any appearance of Ireland in the bond market is accompanied by the financial equivalent of an involuntary shudder.

The market is very, very happy, at the same time, about BOT's takeover of Agron. The incredibly complicated deal, involving literally hundreds of subsidiaries, has been turned around by the Dublin office in record time (the rumour is that three temps were hired just to sign Porter's name on the contracts). At a stroke, BOT has acquired six thousand new employees, ranged all over the world, and from the share price it appears the spectacular gamble has paid off.

'Of course it's paid off,' Ish says. 'The market loves spectacular gambles, it's all bloody men. It's the deals that make sense they get pissy about.'

'What are we going to call ourselves now?' Kevin says. 'We can't really be AgroBOT, can we? Sounds like some kind of android hooligan.'

'That's right up the market's sodding street as well,' Ish says.

She, however, appears to be the only person in the world with any misgivings. As the days pass, the financial world's love for Frankensteinian newcomer AgroBOT only grows, and with it our market capitalization. Message boards fizz with conjecture about Porter Blankly's next innovation, investors battle each other for expensive slivers of the bank's stock – and for holders of that stock, such as the BOT staff, the boom times, as the Irish premier said back in the days of the Celtic Tiger, are getting even more boomer. In fact, the atmosphere in our tiny bubble increasingly comes to resemble that of the Tiger; that is to say, a certain amount of irrational exuberance becomes noticeable.

'Evening all.'

'There's Kev – whoa, check out Kevin's watch, everybody!'

'What – oh, you mean this?' Diamonds glitter from a panoply of unnecessary dials.

'Isn't that the one James Bond wears?'

'Look out, Russkies! Kevin's got the James Bond watch!'

'Aren't you on a temporary contract?' Ish says. 'How could you possibly afford that?'

'I work for BOT, don't I? I leveraged my position, that's all.'

Every evening there is a client presentation or a birthday or a new fat deal to celebrate – and even if there isn't, I find myself drinking anyway, in Life Bar or somewhere more exclusive. In the past, these outings bored me; now, I am glad to eliminate the danger of a few hours on my own, to avail myself instead of the city's many avenues of forgetting.

Tonight we are in the penthouse bar of a boutique hotel, one of the few that managed to survive the crash; a debate is in train over whether a boom or a bust is a better time to be rich, with Brent 'Crude' Kelleher arguing that during a boom there are more luxury goods available, a 'better atmosphere generally', and, although there is a smaller gap between your wealth and that of others, people slightly less rich than you understand exactly how nice your stuff is. Dave Davison, on the other hand, maintains that luxury is debased by being widely available. 'That was why the boom was such a nightmare. You couldn't take a business-class flight without being stuck next to some dishwasher salesman telling you about his 7 Series.'

Jurgen takes us aside to pass on a rumour of another acquisition.

'Another one?'

Jurgen nods. 'Porter is looking at asset management firms, also at one of the large clearing businesses.'

'Didn't he just buy a bank?' Ish says. 'Like, don't we still have a few payments to make on that?'

'On the face of it, yes.' Jurgen lifts off his glasses and polishes them with a handkerchief. 'It comes back to the strategy of counterintuitiveness. As we are all aware, this has been a great success. However, BOT's competitors have started to act counterintuitively as well, meaning that we need to be even more counterintuitive, perhaps even to the point of being counter-counterintuitive.'

'Isn't that the same as being intuitive?'

'That is the question we need to answer. Porter has a team of quants working on it as we speak. For now, he believes that relentless and indiscriminate expansion remains the best policy for the bank. Soon we will be established across the system to such a degree that our future will be secured, no matter what.'

'Unless something counterintuitive happens,' Ish says, but Jurgen has spotted an ex-colleague and bustled away. She turns back to me, laying her hand on my forearm solicitously. 'How are you doing tonight, Claude? Are you holding up okay?'

'I think so,' I say, surprised. 'I have only had two drinks.'

'No, I mean, you know, after your waitress.'

'Oh, that.' I feel my heart plummet, like a lift with a snapped cable. 'I have hardly thought about it.'

'That's good,' she says, but she keeps staring at me sympathetically and patting my arm, as if I were a child with a grazed knee. 'So what's Paul got planned for the Story of Claude now?'

'I have dropped all that,' I say tersely. 'It was a silly idea.'

'Oh, right,' she says. She makes an oar of her finger, scoops it along the inner rim of her cocktail glass, which is frosted with cream. 'No, because I just thought, I mean in a book, when the guy's in love with someone out of his league or whatever and it doesn't work out, what often happens is he realizes he's had feelings for someone else all along.'

'Someone else?'

'Yeah, except, you know, he only realizes now.'

I give this some thought. 'Does that happen in books?'

'It does in the ones I read,' she says, a little defensively.

'To me the scenario does not sound plausible. How does he only realize now? Love is not like an illness, gestating in your body before you begin to feel sick. In my experience, if you are in love, you know it straight away.'

'Yeah, that's true, I suppose,' Ish says.

'Attraction is a conscious thing. If you're attracted to somebody, you are aware of it.'

'Right, fair point,' she says.

'If you have not thought about this person in that way before, it's because you are not attracted —'

'Might just pop up to the bar,' Ish says, jumping to her feet. 'You want anything?'

Actually, I might fit in another drink – but she has already gone!

I wait for her to come back, but after a few minutes there is still no sign; however, I notice Kevin signalling me furiously from the balcony and go outside to find Howie, Grisha and two of their initiates from the mysterious ninth floor, Tom Cremins and Brian O'Brien. With the exception of Grisha, all of them are smoking Montecristos – Montecristos are like Skittles in BOT these days. Brian O'Brien has something in his hand, and his body is wound back as if poised to hurl it over the balcony.

'We're throwing phones!' Kevin squeaks at me excitedly.

'Do it! Do it! Do it!' the others chorus. With a grunt Brian O'Brien whips his arm forward. The little silver oblong flies out of his hand; we watch it twist in and out of the darkness, like a leaf falling from a tree. Then it is gone, into the depths of the river.

'A new winner!' Tom Cremins cheers.

'Let's do watches,' Brian O'Brien says. Kevin suddenly looks alarmed. Fortunately for him, at that very moment a dark shape materializes in the doorway: the Bulgarian, features impassive as runes on a stone.

'About bloody time,' Howie says. The two of them disappear inside.

With the game suspended, there is a silence. Clouds of cigar smoke swirl around the balcony like the atmosphere of some toxic planet, masking and unmasking the faces of my former colleagues.

'So how's it going?' I ask. 'The fund?'

'We can't talk to you about that,' Tom Cremins snaps.

'Of course, of course.' Although it has almost the same name, Agron Torabundo Credit Management is a separate entity to the bank, and the border between the two is strictly patrolled. A key-pad and an iris-scanner have been mounted at the fund's door; the lift's operation has been adjusted so that BOT employees can no longer go directly from the sixth to the ninth floor, but must instead go to the ground floor first, or take the stairs. 'But to speak generally – you are happy? You have found investors?'

Tom Cremins and Brian O'Brien exchange a captured-spy look. Heat beats down from the outdoor lamps. Grisha chomps Bombay mix obliviously in the corner; the crunching from his mouth is the only sound.

'Fund's doing great, Crazy Frog.' Howie's back, visibly rejuvenated by his meeting with the Bulgarian. He stoops to relight his cigar; smoke seethes from the corners of his mouth, curls back over his head. 'Thirty million in investment already, client meetings coming out our assholes, all dying to give us two million minimum stake and a commitment to fuck off and leave us alone to make money for them.'

'Hmm, but it is a hard time to launch a new fund, no?' I suggest. 'With the market so volatile, so much risk . . .'

Howie tokes on his cigar. Behind him Tom and Brian stand tensed, as if waiting for the word to fall on me and beat me senseless. 'Real risk has nothing to do with volatility,' Howie says. 'Real risk is stupid investing decisions. Model we're using, every time someone does something stupid, we make a profit. So we're doing pretty well.'

'What is your model, Howie?' Kevin asks, wide-eyed. 'Is it counterintuitive?'

'Come up with two million euro and we'll tell you,' Tom Cremins says, but Howie checks him with a half-lifted hand. He gazes at Kevin a moment; a thousand tiny fires seem to burn in his fragmented irises. Kevin gulps, and hops nervously up and down, like a flea at a job interview.

'I suppose you could say that,' Howie says, going to the little table and pouring a whiskey for me, then another for himself. 'Your traditional hedge funds exist to make money in poorly performing markets, so as far as that goes, we're a hedge fund. But we'd be taking more of a radical line. The way we see it, investment, in the conventional sense of the word, is finished. Look at the last ten years. We've had a technology crash, a housing crash, not to mention a financial crash that nearly sent the world back to the Stone Age. Oil, gold collapsing, Europe coming apart, even the Swiss franc can't be trusted. Where does the smart man invest if investment doesn't work any more? What's the one reliable area of growth in the twenty-first century?'

'Technology?' Kevin says.

'Inequality,' I say.

'Bingo.' Howie wags his cigar at me. 'You know what the Gini coefficient is, Junior?'

'It's, ah, what they use to measure the gap,' Kevin stammers. 'Between rich and poor.'

'Right. And it's going through the roof. From our undead friends over there' – he tilts his glass at the zombie encampment across the river, where dim lights with coloured halos shine from inside the tents – 'you'll know that a tiny number of very rich people, including fat-cat bankers like us, are sucking up a bigger and bigger percentage of the wealth. And that gap will continue to widen, because with all our extra capital we go and buy up all the assets, so that for instance when Chang working down there in Spar needs somewhere to live, he has to rent his house from me, meaning that I'm getting most of his wages too.' He pauses, puffs on his cigar; the coal glows brazier-bright, everything around it seeming to grow commensurately darker. 'Now, provided you're me and not Chang, that's good news. But if you *are* Chang, then not only is your slice of the pie shrinking, but there are also more and more Changs trying to get a bite of it. Every year there's another hundred million people on the planet, and that is making things very fucking volatile. Look at all this trouble in Oran. We're told it's Islamic fundamentalists. But the real reason is there's been a baby boom, followed by a famine. These people haven't been able to feed their children in six months. No wonder they're getting cranky. And this is just the start. As populations rise, as resources dwindle, as infrastructure's destroyed by hostile climates, we're going to see some really needy folks out there. And that need – not oil, not weapons, not food, even, but *need* – that right there is the last reliable asset.'

'Wait,' I say, as his meaning dawns on me. 'You're talking about debt? Subprime lending? That's what you're basing your fund on?'

'There's not much you can sell to a world full of poor people, Crazy. So instead you make them the product. To be fair, we didn't invent the idea. The real visionaries were the boys on Wall Street. They're the ones who first saw this vast, untapped resource out there, these millions of Americans who were shit poor but who nobody trusted enough to loan money to. They saw that if they could get these deadbeats into the debt market – well, it's like the oil under Alaska, right? Billions and billions of dollars just waiting to be released. I mean, the sheer audacity of it!'

'But they were wrong,' I interject, fighting away the whiskey-fingers tickling the base of my brain. 'Their model didn't work. They brought down the whole financial system.'

'Well, sure, of course.' Howie is unfazed. 'They were working off the Gaussian copula, which was bullshit. But the instrument *we* have is tight as a drum.' He takes a sip from his tumbler and grins at me. 'Lack is the last great gold rush, Claude. The world is poor and getting poorer. But we can turn that to our advantage. When someone's got nothing, does he care how much debt he gets into? When he's walled in, and someone offers him a way out, does he stop to read the small print?'

'And what happens if he can't pay you back?'

'This is what I'm telling you. You work out the correlations and you set it up so the losses don't register.'

'How could they not register?' I'm starting to feel like I'm dreaming. 'How can a loss not be a loss? That's impossible.'

'In conventional terms it's impossible. In conventional terms, two and two is always four and a triangle always has three sides. But there are fields of mathematics where that is not the case. There are fields, largely unknown except in the maths departments of certain obscure Russian universities, where two and two is never four, where a triangle, a square, a circle have the same number of sides.'

Over in the shadows, Grisha's head snaps up. 'Non-Euclidean geometry,' he says. 'Topological, differential, affine. Every level give greater symmetry, more and more figures becomes equivalent to each other. Metric spaces no longer exist, values are translated into their opposite, at this moment we apply providential antinomy, then break symmetries again, return to metric space.'

Leaning against the guard rail, Howie takes this in with the mercenary satisfaction of a carnival barker watching his star turn. 'We've tested the model up and down,' he says, when the Russian has finished. 'Every investor we've presented to has his chequebook out before we get halfway through. This is the new wave. Soon it'll be the only wave.'

Can it be true? The whiskey is making everything swim – or maybe it's the cigar smoke, burning my eyes . . .

'See, you're too cautious, Claude.' Howie's voice seems to come from a distance. 'That's always been your problem. You need to remember they're numbers. They're not real. You can make them do what you want.'

'That's what they said the last time,' I rasp.

'This is different. But for it to work you have to forget everything you know. Such as don't put all your eggs in one basket. That's the first thing they teach you about investment, right? The basket falls, everything's wiped out. The genius of the subprime guys was to realize that if you put in *enough* eggs, and stack them just right, then even if the basket falls, the number that break will be insignificant.'

'But they did break,' I croak, as words, numbers, mathematical functions scroll unreadably before my eyes. 'They lost trillions. They almost destroyed the whole of civilization.'

'Yes. They were thinking counterintuitively, only not quite counterintuitively enough. We're taking it to the next level. We're saying, instead of minimizing the breakages, get rid of the fall.'

'The fall?'

Grisha is muttering something – Russian? Geometry? – from the corner. Beside me, Kevin stands utterly motionless, as if his soul's been charmed out of his body.

'That's what our fund does. The maths is complicated but the concept's very simple. We use non-linear methods so that numerical losses are automatically self-cancelling.' Howie holds up his whiskey glass, as if he is about to toast me. 'Gravity, so to speak, is annulled. Meaning that even if you drop the basket, it never hits the ground.'

He lets go of the glass. For one bewitched instant it seems to hang twinkling in the air – even to float infinitesimally upwards. Then it hits the floor and shatters into pieces.

'Get someone to clean that up,' Howie says to Kevin, and goes back into the bar.

I have had enough. Before leaving, I do one last sweep of the bar for Ish; at my side, Kevin chatters on excitably about how groundbreaking Howie's fund is, how it will revolutionize capitalism, and so on, until I lose my temper and tell him that counterintuitiveness has clearly got out of hand if actual nonsense is now being taken for holy writ.

Kevin looks surprised, even a little hurt. 'It's not nonsense, Claude. It's non-*linear*.'

'Come on. Losses that magically disappear? Risk without risk? This makes sense to you?'

'I'm not a mathematician, am I? It's already paying out at 16 per cent! That's one of the highest returns in the whole industry. And they've got like thirty million in investment – shit, that means Howie's already made . . .' He disappears into a little reverie of calculation. Hedge funds have a different pay structure from banks, a 'two and twenty' model: from the money invested with them they take 2 per cent straight off as their management fee, and then 20 per cent of any profits. Therefore, even if his fund doesn't make a cent, Howie could still walk away with millions.

'It seems to me that he's investing a bit too much with his Bulgarian friend,' I say.

Kevin shrugs. I am the old guard; what I think is not important.

Ish arrives at work late the next day, in what appears to be an even worse mood than me.

'You disappeared last night,' I say.

'Ran into somebody,' she says curtly.

'*Somebody*, eh?' I say, arching an eyebrow.

'Fuck off,' she says.

I throw my hands up in surrender.

'Sorry,' she says. 'Sometimes going out in this place's worse than bloody work.'

'You think?'

'It's all right for you, you're a bloke. You're not spending a small fortune to keep your hair blonde and your pits waxed, for the benefit of some fucking drunk who can't remember your name when he wakes up.' She shakes her head. 'I swear, if I hadn't bought that sodding apartment I'd be so out of here.'

'You could still go if you wanted to,' I say.

'How would I do that, Claude? I'm up to my neck in fucking debt.'

'You could get a transfer. To HQ, for example.'

'New York?'

'No, Torabundo. Then you would be able to visit Kokomoko at weekends. See your old friends.'

She gives me a look that I can't quite decipher. 'Is that what you want?'

'Me? I am talking about what you want. If you are not happy here.'

'Oh, I'm just having a moan,' she sighs, dismissing her own words with a wave of the hand. 'Here, get out the Carambars and tell us a joke.'

I open my drawer, unwrap a couple of toffees and scan the jokes – hit by a flashback from my childhood as I do so, my father chasing me around the kitchen and tickling me – *If it's not funny, why are you laughing? Claude? If it's not funny . . .*

I clear my throat. 'All right. *Quel acteur est une copie de lui-même* – this means, Which actor is a copy of himself?'

'I don't know.'

'George Clon-è.'

Ish looks confused.

'In French, you see, *Clooney* sounds like *Clon-è*,' I explain. 'Like he is the clone of himself.'

'Yeah, I get it.'

'This is actually quite a good joke.'

Ish laughs, lays her hand on my arm. 'Oh, Claude,' she says. 'How could I leave you here on your own? It wouldn't be safe.'

'I don't understand,' I say. But she just keeps laughing.

The conversation throws me; at the same time, I know how she feels. Now that Ariadne is out of the picture, now that chapter is definitively closed, I keep expecting some kind of *change*; instead, life just keeps going, as it always has. I wake a few seconds before the morning alarm; I read the market forecasts as the light begins to break; I analyse reports, brief clients, at night lie in bed and try to decide which is worse, the dream where I watch paralysed as Ariadne walks away, or the one where by some unspecified miracle she is there in my arms and my heart is bursting with happiness, and I know that in the morning I will have to undergo the desolation of losing her all over again. While she is away, I watch all the riot footage I can find, in case I might glimpse her amid the tear gas and flying brickwork. When she returns, I cannot even watch for glimpses; instead, as I walk past the Ark, I force myself to look away. Having her close by only underlines how out of reach she is, giving her up only crystallizes how much I desire her; love loves these paradoxes, love generates paradoxes like this ad infinitum. Perhaps it is no wonder that so many people pursue money instead, possessions, power, goals that are lifeless but at least achievable. Perhaps, after all, that is the true purpose of Business: to replace the shifting, medieval labyrinths of love with the broad, sanitized avenues of materialism, the lightless, involuted city of the self with something grid-like and rational – a reordering in the name of reason, a vast Haussmannization of the heart.

Autumn comes: in our denatured domain we see it in the clenched skies, a new chill edge to the rain. The mood in the city has darkened too. A series of revelations about Royal Irish comes at the same time as leaked details of the next round of austerity measures; the zombie encampment swells with fresh recruits, who sit on the quay, battering pots and pans so relentlessly that even at night when it is quiet we still hear it in our ears.

More significantly, sections of the non-zombie population have also taken to the streets. On the way back from a meeting, my taxi runs into a protest outside government buildings.

'Might be a while,' the driver says, dropping his hands resignedly over the wheel. 'Sorry, mate.'

'That's all right,' I say. In the near distance I hear horns, drums, voices chanting.

'It's them cunts of bankers are to blame.' The taxi driver shakes his head. 'Bad as the paedos, they are.' He thinks about this for a moment, then goes on: 'In fact I'd say most of them *are* fuckin paedos. They have that look about them, wouldn't you say?'

'Mmm,' I say ambiguously from the back seat.

'I'm tellin' you, if one of them thievin' paedo scumbags ever got in my cab . . .' He mashes his fist into his palm, then breaks off, turns to me and asks sunnily, 'What line o' work you in yourself, pal?'

Mercifully, my phone strikes up; feeling rather as Frodo must have slipping on the Ring, I excuse myself to answer it.

At the other end of the line, to my surprise, is Paul; to my even greater surprise, he wants to take me to lunch. 'You have some new scheme for finding me a woman?' I query. 'Because you know this is no longer something I wish to pursue.'

He laughs. 'No schemes, no set-ups, no strings attached. Just two friends, catching up over a good meal.'

I meet him in the plaza outside Transaction House. He looks different – *spruce*, as they say in English. He has had his hair cut, and sports a natty blazer with a thin stripe. 'Have a few meetings lined up later today, got to look the part,' he explains, as we walk across the bridge.

'Meetings – about Hotwaitress?'

'That's right, only it's not called Hotwaitress any more. We gave up the domain name after we got sued, and when we went back a few weeks ago we found someone else had taken it.'

'Someone has used your idea?' I say, trying to sound sorry.

'It's just some joker putting up candids of waitresses in truck-stops. But he's got the name. In fact most of the premium domain names are gone. Hotwaitress.net, Hotwaitress.org, Naughtywaitress, Saucywaitress, Flirtywaitress, Dirtywaitress, Shamelesswaitress, a whole load of others, all taken.'

'How frustrating,' I commiserate.

'Yeah, a lot of perverts out there these days,' he says. 'Luckily, we were still able to get hold of Myhotswaitress.com.'

'Myhotwaitress,' I say, weighing it up. 'Well, this is as good as –'

'Sorry, Claude – it's My*hots*waitress. Hot-*s*, with an *s*.'

'Myhotswaitress,' I repeat dubiously.

'It sounds strange at first, but you get used to it. In fact, it's really grown on me. It's like, these waitresses are so hot that they're hot plural. They're *hots*. Anyhow, that's the reason I wanted to take you to lunch today – as a small thank-you for all you've done in bringing this together. If it weren't for you, Myhotswaitress might still be on the shelf, gathering dust. It was your story, and your faith in me, that inspired me to give it another try.'

'My faith was in you as a novelist,' I say. 'I was hoping to inspire you to write another book.'

'Well, the point is that you inspired me,' he says. 'Whatever direction that took.'

'Where are we going?' I say, as we have been walking for a while and I am getting hungry.

'It's not much further. I have a feeling you'll like this place, Claude. I have a feeling you'll like it a lot.' He permits himself a mysterious smile. 'But what you were saying there, about wanting to inspire me to write a book – in a sense, that's what you've done. I've been thinking lately that Myhotswaitress isn't so different from a novel. Or to put it another way – some people might make the argument that a website like Myhotswaitress is the novel's natural replacement.'

'What people? Igor?'

'Think about it. Why don't we read novels any more? Because thanks to technology, we can turn our own lives into stories. Each of us can be the hero of our own movie. Yet for all the incredible leaps we've made, there are some blank spaces. Things technology can't give us. We've got social media, on the one hand, where we can edit our relationships, control how we appear to the world. We've got porn, on the other, acting out all of our fantasies for us. But between them, in that space between sex and friendship, there's still something missing.'

'Go on,' I say warily.

'What happened between you and Ariadne made me realize we're still waiting for a twenty-first-century way of experiencing love. Even in the digital age, love is something we want and need. But it's tricky. In some ways love is the novel of the emotional world. If you stick with it, and put in the hours, there are wonderful rewards. But it demands a commitment, and today, people don't have time for that. They like the *idea* of it, certainly, but more and more of them are saying about love what they say about the novel: TL, DR – too long, didn't read. So the question becomes, how do we upgrade love? How do we give that deep, rich, novel-like experience in a modern, easily digestible form?'

'By watching waitresses on a spycam?'

'Before you dismiss it, just ask yourself, what do we want from love? We want to be in a story, right? Isn't that how you put it to me? It's like a book: we want to be immersed in detail, pulled along by a narrative, intimately involved with profound or beguiling characters. At the same time, when we're reading a book, we don't actually want to be *in* the story. We don't want a bunch of reanimated dinosaurs actually chasing us around a theme park, for instance. And that's where I realized we went wrong with Ariadne.'

I am confused. 'You think the relationship would have been more successful if I had never tried to talk to her?'

'Exactly!' he says. 'When are we most in love? It's almost always at the start, right? Sometimes before you've got to know the other person at all. There are two reasons for that. First, once you know them better, you realize there're all kinds of downsides and negatives to their personalities you never imagined. They're drunks, they're Nazi sympathizers, they have husbands, whatever. Second, as soon as you get something, you automatically stop wanting it. It's human nature. New shoes, new phone, new love, it's all the same. Think of Marcel in *In Search of Lost Time*. He spends about a thousand pages running around after Albertine. But the minute he gets her, he loses interest.

'You see, when it comes to love, the *relationship* has always been the weak link in the chain. The gap between the person you imagine and the reality that time reveals. In the beginning you're in a story, then you find yourself in the truth, with all of the problems that you were trying to escape in the first place. But thanks to modern technology that doesn't need to happen any more. You can experience the most intimate details of another person's life, without ever having to speak to her. You can preserve the illusion – you can *stay in love* – for as long as you want. It's like your own personalized, never-ending novel!'

'You are saying that your twenty-first-century concept of love does not involve a relationship at all?'

'Well, of course there's a relationship. You're there relating to her, through your computer, feeling all kinds of very passionate and intense emotions – but without the *fear* of those emotions being compromised by the kind of irritating details that derail analogue or legacy relationships. It stays pure. It's actually very romantic! And that's something I only started to realize when I talked to you. Myhotswaitress isn't just for lonely weirdos. Everyone has a secret crush they'd like to get closer to. Men and women, young and old. It doesn't just have to be waitresses either. Already we're thinking about how to carry out surveillance on nurses, air hostesses, shop assistants –'

'Weren't there some legal issues with this?' I say, increasingly troubled by the thought that I have played some part in unleashing it.

'The law will change,' Paul says firmly. 'If it's what the people want, the law can't stand in their way. This is the future. We're not going to stop until we've turned the boring old world into a sexy, fun MyHotsWorld. All we need is a small initial injection of capital.'

His last sentence seems to hang in the air between us, glinting and turning like a fishing lure, and then he says, 'Well, here we are.'

It appears that we have reached our destination; above the portico I see a promising-looking star.

'I asked for a table with a canal view . . . ?' Paul tells the maître d'.

'Certainly, sir. This way.' He leads us to our table and tells us the waiter will be with us shortly. From the window I can see swans drifting lazily through the water; around us, there is a pleasant buzz of well-heeled conversation. I feel my mood lift.

'Anyhow, that's enough shop talk,' Paul says. 'Here, why don't you choose the wine.' He hands me the list, and as I make my

way through the familiar names he sits back expansively, surveying the room.

The waiter arrives and asks us if we would like to order a
drink; I am thinking of a Pernod – but then I see Paul's face. He
is staring at the waiter as if some great offence has been committed. 'What?' he says.

'A drink, sir?' the waiter repeats. 'Or some water?'

'What's going on?' Paul demands.

The waiter, a slender young man in his early twenties, is under-
standably startled. 'Sir?'

'Who are you? Where's the girl?'

The waiter's eyes flicker over to me, but I am equally baffled.
'If you need more time, sir . . .'

'We don't want more time! We want the girl! We want Ludmila! Where is she?'

'Ludmila's not working today, sir,' the waiter quavers.

'But she always works Thursdays!' There is a note of appeal in
Paul's voice now. 'Tuesday, Thursday, Friday, then she does the
split-shift with Michaela on Saturday –'

'Michaela's away on Sunday,' the unfortunate waiter tells him,
evidently too scared to question Paul's seemingly intimate knowledge of the restaurant's work roster. 'So Ludmila's covering for
her and taking her day off today instead.'

This news falls on Paul like a hammer blow; the furious colour
drains from his cheeks, and he slumps back leadenly in his chair.
'Oh,' he says.

'Would you like someone else to serve you, sir?'

'No, no,' Paul says defeatedly.

'We do not have to stay,' I offer, although I still don't understand what is wrong.

'No, it's fine,' he says. 'Let's just get this over with. You go
ahead and order, Claude. I'll have the same as him,' he tells the
waiter, who raises his order pad with a trembling hand.

I duly select for both of us; a moment later, a different waiter arrives at the table with our wine, which he carefully presents and then pours without making eye contact.

'Is everything all right?' I ask Paul, who is listlessly prodding the wicker bread-basket with his fork.

'Yeah, yeah,' he says.

'Who is this Ludmila?'

'Who is Ludmila.' The thought of her rouses him. 'Tall, elegant, refined, with a perfect size-ten figure and distinctive ash-blonde braids, Ludmila Trotyakova is one of the most enchanting figures on the Dublin restaurant scene. Don't be misled by her efficient service; Ludmila is happy to stay and chat with diners about her interests, which include mountain-climbing in Slovakia, the work of the Slovakian composer Ján Levoslav Bella, and the history of the tenth-century duchy of Moravia, later Slovakia.' He shakes his head. 'She would have been right up your street. Damn it, when Igor rang up pretending to be her uncle they told him she'd be here! Now we've come all this way for nothing, and it's going to cost me a damn fortune.'

'So that's what this lunch is about,' I say, as the original waiter scurries past, dropping off our starters with an inaudible blur of words. 'All the talk of friendship and catching up was just a trick. You wanted to dangle this waitress in front of me, so I will invest in your website.'

'No, Claude, no!' Paul reaches across the plates to seize my hand. 'Okay, I admit I wanted to give you an idea of how Myhots-waitress might work. But I also wanted to show you that there are other waitresses out there. You don't have to give up on love just because it didn't work out with Ariadne!'

'I don't think that coming to a restaurant to ogle the staff can be described as "love".'

'Believe me, if you'd seen Ludmila, you wouldn't say that. Ogling her is a transcendent experience, like the piano sonatas of Ján Levoslav Bella.' He presses his lips together contritely. 'Look,

I know I wasn't entirely upfront with you. But try and see things from my perspective. Do you know what it's like out there for the entrepreneur at the moment? The banks are all on the point of going bust, it's impossible to get any credit! All I'm looking for is a little leg-up. If you don't want to invest, the very least you could do is set up a few meetings with some of your clients.'

'I think you will find that I can do a lot less than that.'

'Oh, well, that's lovely, Claude, after all I've done for you.'

'What, exactly, have you done for me? Apart from the incessant lying.'

He goggles at me furiously. 'You know. The, the . . .'

'The attempted robbery? The non-existent book?'

'The advice!' he snaps. 'The advice!'

'It seems to me that your "advice", like your business ideas generally, amounts to little more than a vicarious attempt to sleep with waitresses.'

'Well, let's just drop the subject, shall we?' Paul flashes me a deliberately synthetic smile, and swabs his plate with a hunk of bread. 'Let's just drop it, and concentrate on enjoying this overpriced, pointless meal.'

'An excellent idea,' I respond in kind. 'Let us leave the heavy topics for another time, and simply take pleasure in our long-standing friendship.'

The ensuing silence continues until the waiter returns to relieve us of our plates, when I take the opportunity to add a side of potato dauphinoise to my main course. 'And . . . how are the petits pois today?'

'Delicious, sir. Fresh from our own farm.'

I see Paul glare at me hatefully from the far side of table. 'Perhaps I will have a side of those as well,' I say.

The waiter departs, the silence resumes. Then a machinating smile breaks across his face, and Paul says, 'I meant to tell you – I saw a film last night, reminded me of you.'

'Oh yes?'

'Yeah, it was called *Anal Analyst*. What was the strapline . . . "We've all been fucked in the ass by banks . . . but here comes the biggest dick of all!" '

The couple beside us look at each other in alarm. 'Ah, superb,' I say, as the mains arrive.

'What it is, Rod McMaster is this banking analyst, okay? And in his office there are these two hot girls with really big asses . . .'

He proceeds to give me a lengthy and extremely graphic description of the banking analyst and his associates' adventures at an asset management conference in Luxembourg. If he thinks he is going to embarrass me out of my meal, however, he is wrong.

'On the subject of culture,' I say, when there is a break in the narrative, 'Bimal Banerjee is reading in Dublin tonight.'

Paul recoils violently, as if I had thrown acid in his face.

'They say he will win the Raytheon again this year,' I muse. 'I hope so. *Ararat Rat Rap* is a staggering achievement.'

This time he does not react, other than to continue chewing and then, evidently with some difficulty, swallow.

'You should come,' I suggest. 'It will be exciting to see a real writer, how do you say, in the flesh.'

'I'd like to, Claude,' Paul says, recovering his composure. 'I'm always interested to see what feat of mediocrity the bourgeoisie have canonized now. Unfortunately I can't manage to put out of my head what a vile excrescence that vile excrescence is. So for me, it's like every word is written in pus, you know?'

This impressively unambiguous image brings the exchange to a close, and with it any further desire to eat; I push away my plate. The waiter comes over to clear the table. 'Will that be all, gentlemen?' he asks hopefully.

I have a meeting in less than an hour; nevertheless, out of bloody-mindedness, I order a *digestif*, which Paul watches me drink with unconcealed malevolence.

'Had enough?' he asks sourly.

I give the question some thought. His eyes widen fearfully. I decide to be merciful. Paul motions to the waiter for the bill.

'They always insist on hiding it inside these stupid leather books,' he grumbles when it comes. 'Like maybe you'll mistake it for some magical fairy tale.'

Clearly on this occasion the fairy tale does not have a happy ending. His face turns ashen; he rubs his eyes, and scans the bill again. 'How can this be?' he whispers.

'Let me see,' I say, and take the leather book out of his limp, unresisting hand. Everything appears to be in order. 'Service is not included,' I say, and pass it back to him.

'And Ludmila wasn't even here!' Paul laments.

I sit back and fold my hands peaceably over my stomach.

He thrums his fingers on the tablecloth, then glances up at me. 'Full disclosure. I only have twenty euro on me.'

'Do you,' I say.

'Yeah,' he says.

'How did you intend to pay for the meal?'

'I really hadn't thought that far ahead,' he says. 'I suppose I figured that if I got you to invest right now, in cash, I could pay for it out of that.'

'I see. That is unfortunate, because I left my wallet in the office.'

'You did?'

'Yes.'

'Right.' He looks troubled. The waiter, who is not eager for us to stay, glides close, glances at the still-unaddressed bill, glides on. Paul shoots me an up-from-under look and says in a low voice, 'What if I told you I had a foolproof way for us to walk right out of the restaurant without us paying them a penny?'

I roll my eyes.

'I'm serious. We walk out of here – walk, not run, with our heads held high – and it doesn't cost us a thing.'

'Look, just let me pay,' I say, and reach for the bill.

'I thought you didn't have your wallet.'

'Obviously I have my wallet. I will pay, and put it on expenses.'

'No!' Paul whips it away. 'There's a principle at stake here. These fuckers are totally scamming us.'

'How are they scamming us? We have just eaten an enormous meal.'

'They said Ludmila would be here and she wasn't. I'm not letting them get away with it. All we have to do –'

'I don't want to hear your plan.'

'Listen, it's simple – all we do is, we pretend to have an argument. We have this big flaming row, then I storm out, and then you chase after me, trying to get me back, see? And when we hit the street, *that's* when we run for it.'

'We run for it, with our heads held high.'

'It works, Claude. I've tried it before, in Turkey?'

'I don't care, I am not doing it.'

'Although that was with Clizia – the thing is, it's probably a bit more convincing if it's a lovers' tiff. That way, people are more reluctant to intervene.'

'I am simply going to put the meal on my card. Excuse me!' I call to the waiter.

'Oh, you like the look of him, do you?' Paul declares, yanking his chair back from the table.

'What?'

'All through the meal you were staring at him – devouring him, with your eyes!'

'Excuse me, waiter –'

'A boy, Claude! A mere boy! And you flirt with him right in front of me – like I'm not even here!'

'I have no idea what you are talking about,' I say. At the neighbouring tables the conversation has petered out, and patrons glance over with that combination of embarrassment and glee characteristic of eavesdropping on an argument.

'Don't play innocent!' Paul exclaims. 'You wish you were rid of me, don't you! That's the kind of person you are, you just use people up and toss them aside!'

'Waiter!' My credit card sits conspicuously on top of the leather book, but the staff are now giving us a very wide berth.

'I was once a pretty boy like him,' Paul notes sorrowfully. 'Is it my fault I've got old?'

'Please!' waving my wallet in the air.

'You can't stop yourself, can you? Even now, you can't stop yourself! Well, you can have him! You can have him, you heartless monster!' He jumps to his feet and thrusts on his jacket. I realize that he is going to go through with this, and I will be left here with the whole restaurant staring at me.

'Wait!' I say faintly.

'It's too late for that!' Paul sobs. He turns to go, then momentarily turns back; in a low, husky voice he says, 'You made me love you.'

The staff and clientele look on, appalled; I push back my chair and lurch towards the waiter, proffering my credit card, but he flinches back as if I have just risen out of a swamp. Paul, meanwhile, has flounced over to the exit, a tiny gleam of triumph detectable beneath his ersatz heartbreak – when from a table near the door a man springs up and seizes him by the arm. 'Paul?' he says.

The man is in his mid forties, with curly hair greying at the temples. An array of wrinkles gives his face a kindly, careworn appearance, of a piece with his rumpled suit. Its effect on Paul, however, is Medusa-like: instant paralysis.

'Possibly not the best time,' the man says apologetically, in a tobacco-rich English accent, flicking a glance backwards at me and the roomful of staring diners. 'But I just saw you there and I couldn't, ah . . . I mean, how long has it been? Six years? Seven?'

Paul simply stares back at him, as if pinned to the air.

'I'm sorry, I'm being terribly rude,' the man says, turning to

303

me. 'My name is Dodson, Robert Dodson. You must forgive me for barging in on your, ah, on your meal like this. It's just that . . . The thing is, you see, I'm Paul's . . . I was Paul's editor.'

His editor! A ghost from his former life – no wonder Paul looks so shocked.

'Claude Martingale,' I say, shaking his hand. 'Delighted to meet you.'

'Likewise,' he says. He looks me up and down. 'Yes,' he says.

'Look, Robert.' Paul has begun to revive. 'If it's about the money, I meant to contact you . . .'

'What? Oh goodness, I never – that's all water under the bridge,' the editor says graciously, nodding his greying head.

'And the car, I meant to contact you about that too –'

'Yes, yes,' the editor says placatingly. 'I completely understand. Sometimes things don't, ah, especially when the old, er, artistic temperament's involved – are you an, um, artist, Claude, or . . . ?'

'I'm a banker,' I tell him.

'Ah.' The editor gives me a conspiratorial smile. 'So you pay the bills.'

For a moment I am at a loss as to his meaning; then over his shoulder I see Paul ferociously gurning at me, and I realize what is happening. After witnessing our staged fight, this man has mistaken me for Paul's homosexual lover! 'No, no,' I explain, 'I am just –'

But Paul has grabbed him by the elbow. 'What brings you to Dublin, Robert?' he asks.

'I'm here with an author, as it happens – perhaps you've heard of him? Bimal Banerjee?'

'Hmm.' Paul scratches his head. 'No, can't say I –'

'Bimal Banerjee, author of *The Clowns of Sorrow*?' I blurt over him. 'And *Ararat Rat Rap*?'

'Yes, that's him,' says the editor. 'Do you know his work?'

'Very well,' I tell him, ignoring the withering look Paul is giving me. 'He is truly a tremendous talent.'

'Oh! How kind of you to say,' says the editor. 'He's just over there, actually.' He gestures at a nearby table where a swarthy figure glowers at his cutlery. 'Perhaps you'd like to come over and say hello?'

'We're in a bit of a hurry,' Paul says.

'I could go over,' I say hopefully.

'You're coming with me,' Paul says. 'I haven't forgotten about that waiter, you know.'

'Might be for the best,' Robert Dodson says, thoughtfully twisting a jacket button. 'Caviar didn't agree with him, he's not in the best of humours. But he's giving a reading later, and afterwards we're going to William O'Hara's for dinner – you must know William?'

'Only by his writing,' Paul says. 'Tremendous talent, truly tremendous.'

'Yes, well, his partner's the most marvellous cook. We're staying with them for a few days – I'm sure they'd be only too pleased if you and your, ah, if you and Claude came along?' He looks from me to Paul and back; Paul's ferocious gurn switches on and off in synch. Surely he is not intending that we extend this farce?

'We'd be delighted,' Paul says. The editor beams like the biblical father at his prodigal son. 'I'm so happy to have seen you,' he says. 'Seven years!'

'Me too,' Paul says. 'Well' – he reaches for the door, but then –

'Sir?' The timorous waiter has reappeared beside us. 'Ah, the, ah . . . ?'

'Oh good Lord! The bill!' Paul cries, and pats about in his pocket for a wallet whose very existence I am now beginning to doubt.

'Won't you let me?' the editor suggests.

'No, no, Robert, I couldn't possibly – where did I put that damn wallet?'

'Please, let me,' Robert repeats. 'To celebrate this serendipitous meeting.'

'No, Robert, I won't hear of it, I simply won't – oh, you brute, I can't believe you did that.' Paul's shoulders slump in defeat as the editor passes his card to the waiter, who retreats gratefully.

'You can repay me by telling me about all the exciting new ideas you've been working on,' the editor says, with a rumpled smile.

'Ha ha! No shortage of those!' Paul laughs. 'See you at the reading!'

He pushes through the door, and I follow him on to the street. 'Well, Claude, let the record show, I did technically buy you lunch,' he says. 'I mean, you came for lunch with me, and you didn't have to pay.'

'I suppose that it is true, if you take the word "technically" to its logical limits,' I reply. 'Although, one can say also that technically I did have to pay, by being humiliated in front of a crowded restaurant and then forced to pose as your homosexual lover.'

'Yeah, well, you should be glad you're *not* my homosexual lover, or you'd have some explaining to do after all that fawning. Oh, Bimal Banerjee, he's so terrifically talented! He's so totally titanically true!'

'I am glad I am not your homosexual lover for many different reasons.'

As we set off along the canal back towards the Centre, Paul seems preoccupied.

'Your editor is very charming,' I say. 'Why is it you have not spoken to him for so long?'

He coughs artificially, and squints over at the far bank as if searching for a landmark. 'We had different ideas, I suppose.'

'Different ideas about what you should do with your advance?' I suggest.

'I don't really want to talk about it.'

'Was his idea that you should use it to write your second novel, and your idea that you should sink it all into your Internet start-up?'

Paul doesn't reply.

'What did you do to his car?' I ask, but he doesn't appear to want to talk about that either. 'Anyway, he does not seem to hold grudges,' I say. 'He wanted to hear about your new book.'

'That's just what editors say. It's part of the job, like a priest saying God bless you.'

'To me it sounded sincere.'

'He was just being polite. Anyway, I told you, I don't do that any more.'

I can't understand it: to me the chance meeting seems pure serendipity, but Paul just scowls and stuffs his hands in his pockets.

'So you will not go to the soirée?'

'Oh, I'll go all right. William O'Hara's dinner parties are legendary. Although his books, God, they're like taking a bath in Rohypnol. You fall asleep after a couple of pages, wake up not remembering anything but feeling somehow *violated*.' He turns to me. 'You'll come too, I hope?'

'Me?'

'You're invited, aren't you?'

I would be happy to attend, I say; I have never been to a literary dinner before. 'Although, to avoid more confusion, we should explain to everyone that we are not romantically attached.'

'Why, are you planning to make a move on Totally Tremendous Bimal Banerjee?'

'No, of course not.'

'Do you wish I wasn't here any more, is that it? You're going to use me up and then throw me away?'

'Please, do not remind me.'

'Well, you can have him! You can have him, you heartless beast!'

'I am serious. I found that episode quite traumatic.'

'You made me love you.'

'I assure you, it was quite unintentional.'

The more I think about it, the more I wonder if Paul's apathy at seeing Dodson was merely a front, aimed at covering up a hope he doesn't dare to express. However it unfolds, I have the feeling that tonight will be significant.

The reading is at seven, and I have a lot of work to get through if I'm to make it on time. No sooner have I emerged from my meeting, however, than Ish descends on me.

'Oh, Claude!' she cries, and throws her arms around me.

'What is it? What's wrong?' My first thought is that she has been sacked.

'It's the island!' she sobs.

'What island?'

'Kokomoko.'

'Oh,' I say, relaxing somewhat, then remembering and looking concerned again. 'What's happened?'

Ish tells me that following our conversation the other morning, she decided she would look into the possibility of a transfer after all. In the course of her research, though, she came across a recent Greenpeace report that put Kokomoko near the top of its list of places most endangered by rising seas.

'And every day it's getting worse!' she says, eyes and nose streaming. 'The islanders can't fish because the Torabundo government sold the rights to some European consortium and now there's nothing left in the ocean and they have to buy their food from sodding Australia! But they don't have any money, and the only thing they have to sell is the sand off their beaches!'

They have been exporting sand by the ton, principally to Torabundo, whose success as an international tax haven has led to a construction boom; but the mining of their own coast-line, already at risk from global warming, leaves them perilously exposed.

'They're literally digging their own graves! The report says the next king tide could wipe them out!'

'Who's King Tide?' Kevin says, arriving on the scene.

'It's not a who,' Ish says, and she launches into a complicated account of *perigees* and *perihelions*, alignments of sun and moon that could bring about the twenty-centimetre rise in sea level that would be enough to swamp the island. Her eyes are white, and I think again of that strange conversation a few days ago when she claimed she was just having a moan.

'We have to do something,' she says.

Kevin and I look at each other. 'Do something? Like what?'

'We should tell Porter,' Ish says; then, to our goggling faces, 'BOT's the biggest employer in the whole archipelago, don't you think he'd want to know?'

'But what's it got to do with him?'

'He can't just stand there with his arms folded while they all drown, can he?'

'In fairness, Ish,' Kevin offers, 'it's not like they'd actually *drown*. Obviously, if the island actually started sinking, the UN or somebody would airlift them out of there.'

Ish looks from one of us to the other. 'Christ!' she exclaims, and marches away.

'She's not really going to go bothering Blankly with that stuff, is she?' Kevin says.

'She's just having a bad day,' I say.

'I bet they're wishing now they hadn't spent all their time faff-ing about, swapping shells.'

'Get back to work,' I tell him.

I go to the bookshop alone: Paul has informed me that he won't be attending the reading itself 'as a matter of principle', although he also tells me that if I run into his editor before he gets there I should say he's gone to the men's room.

The shop is packed almost to bursting. A pyramid of *Ararat*s is stacked for sale by the till, but most of the audience are already clutching their own copies to their breasts. No one is talking about asset prices or bond yields or basis points; nobody is promising to crush or rape or dismember some absent third party. Excitement bubbles in the air, and I am just wishing Paul were here to experience it for himself, when on the other side of the room, like an orchid emerging from the thick jungle foliage, I spy Ariadne! She has come directly from work: her hair is tied back, and floury fingerprints smudge the lapels of her parka. In the ecstatic atmosphere my first impulse is to go and talk to her – but then my eyes light on the rangy gaucho by her side, and the happy glow in my heart is extinguished. So this is Oscar. It is little consolation to see he looks exactly like I imagined him: tall, austere, bristling with being. They are not speaking, but his silence is voluminous; in fact his mere presence seems scandalously sexual. I lower my hand and withdraw to the shadows. Maybe I should invest in Paul's start-up after all, I reflect glumly. Watching from a distance is probably as close as a lot of people come to love; if you overlook the exploitation aspect, it is actually a very good idea.

The room is full now; late arrivals are being turned away, and as the clock ticks to the hour, the chatter becomes simultaneously feverish and hushed. Two booksellers arrive at the threshold and, not without difficulty, begin to clear a path through the bodies. Following a few paces behind them – to a thrill of silence from the assembly, like an inverted cheer – come the editor I met this afternoon, a willowy, platinum-blonde girl, a red-faced man with tortoiseshell glasses, and lastly (a rustle of delight now) Bimal Banerjee – short, with a tight, pugilistic frame, a bald head and an air of not suffering fools. Microphones are adjusted, water poured; Banerjee stands to the side, glowering at his feet, as one of the booksellers makes a stammering introduction. Finally, to rapturous applause, the writer takes the podium. He presses his lips together, fiddling with the button on his cuff and darting sceptical glances at the adoring crowd. At last the bookseller raises his hand for silence; the noise abates, the author leans into the microphone and utters: 'Word.'

We, the listeners, nod to ourselves. It is the first word of the novel's first New York section, set in the roiling heat of the summer of 2001, and following the book's rodent narrator, the hip-hop-loving would-be MC Jephot, as he attempts to overcome ratism and master 'flow' in order to take part in a humans-only freestyle battle, which will be the first step on the path to becoming a chart-topping cross-species sensation. There is literally not a sound as Banerjee reads, until very near the end when a man appears in the door and, although there is patently no room for an extra body, proceeds to insinuate himself into the crowd, with a great amount of rustling, and drawing a wake of disapproving mutters from those whose view he has impeded and cries from those whose toes he has evidently stood on.

I deliberately refrain from looking in his direction, but there is no doubt in my mind as to who it is; three or four minutes later he hoves up behind me, smelling of rain and alcohol and still contriving to rustle, even though he is now standing quite still.

'Don't think anyone noticed me,' he whispers heavily in my ear.

'Shh!' hisses a nearby woman.

'Wow, a lot of people here,' Paul murmurs, unzipping his raincoat.

'Will you be quiet?' a man says severely.

Paul holds up his hands pacifically, and we address ourselves to the speaker again – but he has quit the lectern, and the bookseller has retrieved the microphone to thank us for coming. I feel a surge of irritation at Paul, especially when he starts to tell me how 'bourgeois' and 'derivative' Bimal Banerjee's reading was.

'You didn't even hear it! You arrived two minutes from the end!'

'That was enough, Claude. The guy's a hack, a total hack.'

Over the happy din, the bookseller announces that the author will be signing copies of his novel, and the crowd immediately redistributes itself into a long, snaking line. 'You're not going to – oh, for God's sake,' Paul says, rolling his eyes as I join the end. As we shuffle forward, though, he falls silent and his face becomes sombre. This is the life he could have had, or something like it; looking at him sidelong I wonder again if he cares more than he lets on. Has he really just come for a free meal? Or is he hoping that his editor's interest was not, in fact, a formality, that this could be a doorway back into the world he abandoned?

As we draw close to the top of the line, I see that the editor and the willowy blonde girl have gathered by the low table where Banerjee is signing books.

'Here comes the Inquisition,' Paul mutters in my ear. 'Better act like you enjoyed it.'

'I did enjoy it,' I am about to retort – but now, as we step to the top of the line, Paul wrests the book from my hands.

'Towering reading,' he says to Banerjee. 'Truly triumphant.'

'You made it!' Robert Dodson exclaims. 'Bimal, allow me to introduce Paul, an old friend of mine –'

'Didn't I see you come in at the end?' Bimal Banerjee narrows his eyes.

'No, that wasn't me,' Paul says. 'Could you make this out "To Paul and Claude"?'

'Ah yes, forgive me,' the editor says, ushering me into the circle. 'This is Claude, Paul's partner.'

I want to protest, but the proximity of the famous author has rendered me speechless. He passes the book back to me, his black eyes glittering over me like an entomologist's over a bug.

'Thank you,' I attempt to say, but it comes out, 'Pancake.'

The blonde girl is called Ariel. She is Dodson's editorial assistant – very beautiful, with enormous amethyst eyes, though the red rims suggest she has been crying not so long ago. Paul appears quite taken with her – so does Banerjee, who keeps shooting her glances that oscillate from amorous to hostile.

'And this, of course, is William O'Hara, our very kind host for tonight,' Dodson says, as we are joined by the man in tortoise-shell glasses, who is wearing a florid, raffishly under-buttoned shirt that gives him the look of an ageing dandy.

'Oh, what a great pleasure.' Paul clasps O'Hara's hand. 'I adore your work.'

'I feel like I know your face,' O'Hara says, wagging a finger at him. 'Didn't you . . . didn't you write a book once?'

'A youthful folly,' Paul says modestly, though it is clear he is pleased.

'The best kind,' William O'Hara says.

'How many did we sell?' Bimal Banerjee asks Dodson. The editor goes to consult with the bookseller, then comes back with the figure. Bimal Banerjee receives it expressionlessly. 'Cretins,' he says, though whether he is referring to those who bought the book, those who didn't, or indeed to us, is not immediately plain.

From the doorway I see Ariadne waving to me. There is no sign of the gaucho; affixing what I intend as an avuncular smile, I go over.

'Look at you, talking to the famous writer,' she says. 'He is a friend of yours?'

'No, no,' I say. 'I'm just, ah, going to dinner with him.'

'Ha,' she says, eyeing me speculatively.

'Did you enjoy the reading?' I say, adding casually, in the hope that it will sound like a natural extension of the original question, and not make her wonder, for example, how I know his name, 'You are here with Oscar?'

She laughs. 'No, this is not Oscar's kind of thing at *all*. He will be bored after five minutes.' I permit myself a tiny dose of *Schadenfreude* at this sliver of incompatibility, and adjust my position so that the signed Banerjee is on view.

'So how are you? Your father?'

'He is much better, thank you. But I have been thinking about you these days.'

'Oh?' I confine myself to an arch of an eyebrow, although she might as well have set off an atomic bomb inside my head.

'Yes, I want to ask you about something. Last week the landlord has called and said he is going to put up the rent of the Ark. Not just put it up, he's going to double it. The manager has told him, no one's spending money right now, our take is down 30 per cent, there's no way we can pay this much extra. But he just says, first of October, rent goes up. So now we have to . . .'

She looks so sad; as she goes on I find myself lost in a fantasy in which I stride into the Ark with a holdall full of money, which I pour on to the counter to tears of gratitude from Ariadne, while in the sky outside Oscar's Médecins Sans Frontières helicopter explodes in a fireball and drops in hissing shrapnel into the river –

'. . . think we should do?' she says. The iridescent eyes wait on mine expectantly. I jolt from my reverie. What did she ask exactly?

'Ah, um,' I begin. 'Well, that depends . . .'

'Darling?' I am being tapped on the shoulder; I turn to find Paul there, with Robert Dodson beside him. 'We're leaving for William's now.'

'Oh – I see . . .' I suppose I should be thankful to him for getting me off the hook.

'Come along, dear, we'll be late,' he says.

Ariadne is looking from me to Paul and back again with evident confusion. I raise my eyebrows at her in a way that is intended to connote that I am not actually this man's homosexual lover, I am merely pretending in the hope that this will help reunite him with his editor. But this just makes her more confused. I tell her I will come into the Ark next week and talk to her more about it, then hurry after the others.

William O'Hara's house is close by, so we set off on foot. The evening is mild, and the rain has thinned to a fine drizzle, although Bimal Banerjee walks with his shoulders hunched and the lapels of his jacket clutched to his throat, as if it bore him some mortal intent.

'Hey! Claude!' Paul pulls me back into a doorway. 'We need to get this partner thing straight,' he says.

'I agree,' I say, still annoyed with him for embarrassing me in front of Ariadne. 'The fiasco has gone on long enough. Do you want to tell them? Or will I?'

'Tell them what?'

'Well – the truth. Isn't that what you mean?'

'The truth? That I'm a washed-up loser with nothing to show for the last seven years but a mortgage in arrears and a wife who hates my guts? Why would I want to tell them that?'

'Because it is true?'

'Jesus, what is it with you and truth? Can you stop banging that drum for five seconds and just think? Think about the opportunity I have here.' The word arrests me: I lock my eyes on his, and he gazes back at me desperately, before continuing, in a quieter voice, 'These are really influential people, Claude. This could really help me. I promise, down the line, I'll explain everything. But for now . . .'

'All right, all right,' I say, secretly thrilled. 'Although only on the condition you don't talk about our "relationship" unless it's totally necessary. I am not so good at lying as you.'

'Fantastic. I really appreciate it.' He coughs awkwardly. 'There's just one more small thing.'

'Yes?'

'Yeah, I want it to be clear that I'm the one who . . . the one who, you know . . .'

'Who what?'

'Who . . . oh, come on, you know . . .'

'I'm afraid I don't.'

'Well, okay, that I'm the one who, so to speak, goes on top.'

'Who goes on top?'

'Yes.'

'You want it to be clear that whenever we have sexual intercourse, in our imaginary relationship, you are the one who goes on top.'

'Yes.'

'Why?'

'I'd just prefer it. I'd just feel more comfortable if it were made clear that I'm the one on top.'

I roll my eyes and move back on to the path.

'Okay, look, we don't have to tell people, but just so we agree ourselves that that's the way it is. Trust me, even if you don't use the details, it's better to have your characters' backstories fully mapped out. That's an old writing tip.'

We catch up with the others in a beautiful Georgian square, at the centre of which is a small, damply verdant park where cherry trees sway beneath the arms of a magnificent oak and golden light glows from Narnian lamp posts. Even the traffic noise here seems less frenetic, more polite; it is like being in a different city, in a different century, perhaps even on a different, kinder planet.

'How did he afford this place?' Paul murmurs, as O'Hara mounts the steps to a red-brick on the western side.

I shrug. 'He must have sold a lot of books.'

Our host ushers us inside and down a hall until we find ourselves in an exquisite dining room. A chandelier shimmers above us; silver gleams from the sideboard; every detail bespeaks comfort and hospitality.

It is here, nevertheless, that we encounter our first setback. Two more guests are seated at the long rosewood table. O'Hara makes the introductions: the tall, slightly gaunt woman with the scintillating black eyes is Victoria Galahad, a literary agent; 'and this, of course' – he extends a hand to the large, jolly-looking character squeezed not entirely successfully into a wispy ecru dress – 'is Mary Cutlass.'

Mary Cutlass! The same critic who eviscerated Paul's novel seven years ago! She shows no sign of recognition, merely flashes us a quick, heavy-mandibled smile and returns to her conversation; Paul, on the other hand, looks like he is about to faint. I swear under my breath, and on the pretext of fetching something from his coat pull him back out into the hall.

'Are you all right?' I ask him. His face is parchment-white.

'I'm fine, I'm fine,' he insists. 'I've just never seen her in the flesh before. I'm a little surprised she actually *has* flesh. I always pictured her as a sort of floating skull.'

'It's not a big deal,' I say. 'She gave you a bad review, so what? This was a long time ago. You must not let her ruin your night.'

'I'm telling you, I'm fine.'

'Your hands are shaking.'

'You haven't heard the stories I've heard!' he blurts, the façade of indifference crumbling. 'That woman is evil, Claude! Evil! I heard about one writer she did a hatchet job on, he sent a whole package of anthrax to her office. But when she opened it up, the anthrax died! She killed that anthrax stone dead, Claude! With a look! That's the kind of person you're dealing with.'

What can I do, except put my hand on his shoulder and tell him that I'll be here to help him in whatever way I can?

We return to the dining room and sit down across the table from Dodson and Victoria Galahad. 'William and I go back years,' the editor is explaining to Mary Cutlass. 'When I'm in Dublin I often stay with him –'.

'Asterisk saves money wherever it can,' Bimal Banerjee comments, from the far end of the table.

'Who's hungry?' Another man, wearing a paisley apron over a striped shirt, has whirled into the room, bearing a samovar of aromatic soup.

'Ah, *bellissima!*' O'Hara rejoices. 'Everyone, may I present my other half –'

'*Better* half, some would say,' the new man interjects.

'– Crispin O'Connell.'

'*Younger* half, without question,' this Crispin remarks.

'I see you made it out of bed at last, *mia carina.*'

'Oh, I had nothing to do there once the paperboy left,' Crispin rejoins, to a mock-scandalized gasp from O'Hara: 'Oh! *Wicked!*'

'Ha ha,' Paul says. 'My Claude's exactly the same, aren't you, Claude? – Ah, *bellissima!*' as Crispin serves him his soup. Everyone falls to, though Paul still appears on edge, and eats little.

'So tell us, Robert, what does Asterisk have in the pipeline?' asks Victoria Galahad.

'Well, we're publishing the autobiography of Jean-Pierre Lettrefits,' Dodson says, then explains to the rest of us, 'He was CFO at Credit Flanders, then Special Adviser to the Mitterand government, before heading the EU Commission's task force on banking reform. Now he's President of the International Credit Fund.'

'And what's his book called?' O'Hara asks.

'It's called *Who Da Man,*' Dodson says.

'And how is Jean-Pierre?' Crispin says.

'You know Jean-Pierre?' Victoria sparkles.

'I took an economics seminar with him at Oxford,' Crispin says.

'You were at Oxford?' Dodson says.

'That's where we met,' Crispin says, folding O'Hara's hand in his.

'*Bellissima,*' Paul interjects from the edge of the conversation.

'Robert and I were both at Oxford as well,' Victoria explains.

'Though sadly the only sparks were at the debating society,' Dodson adds, to a flick of her scarf. 'And of course Bimal was there too, some years after us – at Jesus, wasn't it, Banerjee?'

'Magdalen,' Banerjee says into his soup. 'Although its homophone would be an apter soubriquet.'

'Ha ha ha!' laughs Paul. 'I hear *that*.'

'Stop interrupting,' I mutter, nudging him under the table.

'What? I'm just joining in the conversation.'

'You're embarrassing me,' I say.

'What about you, William?' the agent turns to our host. 'It's a dreadful question to ask an author, but can we look forward to new work from you any time soon?'

'As a matter of fact, I'm just putting the finishing touches to a novel,' O'Hara says, 'set in the slums of Dublin's inner city. I call it *The Phoenixer*.'

'Oh, bravo,' Victoria says. 'I know you probably hate to talk about i—'

'It's the tale of a boy.' O'Hara rests his wrists on the table and raises his head like a medium at a seance, as though addressing his response to some invisible interlocutor hovering above the door. 'A simple boy named Whacker, who is born into one of those disgusting scabrous tenements, and it's – it's simply his life, do you know, in this dreadful place, as he struggles to get by, with only his penny whistle and his beloved donkey for company.'

'My goodness,' Victoria says. 'It sounds terribly moving.'

'It *is* moving' – O'Hara nods – 'and I say that without arrogance, because I very quickly stopped thinking of it as mine – it's Whacker's book, it's his story, he simply made a gift of it to me, because, I feel, he wanted me to tell people what it was like in these hellholes.'

'Oh God, you're not chewing everyone's ear off about "Whacker", are you?' Crispin comes shouldering his way through the door with a tray. 'Can't I leave you alone for two minutes?'

'I think it's tremendously important that our artists give a voice to these people,' Mary Cutlass avers. 'To remind us that they too have feelings, and hopes and dreams and aspirations –'

'*Feelings*, yes, "Whacker" certainly has no shortage of those,' Crispin says. 'Ever since William began writing this book, it's been, "These pedal-pushers are just the sort of thing Whacker might wear," "This Pot Noodle is all Whacker might eat for a week," "Whacker would understand why those boys broke the antique lantern on the porch –"'

'But he would understand,' O'Hara protests. 'A boy like Whacker simply has no *concept* of antiques.'

'Those hideous pedal-pushers,' Crispin remembers with a shudder. '*That* was the last straw. I told him, "Darling, I have no objection to a *ménage à trois*, if it's tidy, but I will not cohabit with culottes."'

'It sounds like a most worthy endeavour,' Mary Cutlass tells O'Hara.

'There but for the grace of God,' he replies with a sigh.

'The slums of Dublin are like a five-star hotel compared to New Delhi,' Bimal Banerjee sneers.

'Yes, but try getting room service after ten o'clock,' Crispin says. Banerjee has barely tasted his food, although he is making inroads into the wine; instead he occupies himself staring across the table at Ariel, the editorial assistant, who blushes into her soup bowl, as if the bisque were making improper suggestions to her. Attempting to draw him into the conversation, or distract him from whatever episode is unfolding, or not unfolding, Robert Dodson clears his throat and says, 'I should have mentioned before, Bimal – Paul here is a writer too. In fact, we published his first novel, seven years ago.'

'My condolences,' Banerjee says, swivelling his heavy-lidded eyes on Paul.

'Hmm . . .' Mary Cutlass brings her finger to her lip and away again. 'Yes, I think I remember . . . a thing about . . . ah . . .'

Paul issues her a watery smile.

'And what have you been doing since, Paul?' Victoria asks. 'Working on another novel?'

'Well, Victoria, interesting you should ask me that. No, I'm actually in business these days, and as it happens I've been working on a proposal you might fi—'

'Clowns!' exclaims Mary Cutlass. 'Wasn't it about clowns or something?'

'You're thinking of Bimal's first book,' Victoria tells her.

'No, no, it's coming back to me now. Gosh, I think I may even have reviewed it.' She covers her mouth with a beefy hand and twinkles merrily at Paul. 'I hope I didn't say anything too awful.'

Paul offers no response to this, other than the same thin smile.

'You should feel no regret at having failed as a writer,' Banerjee says to Paul. 'It is the dying art of a dying civilization.'

Paul looks surprised, then his eyes narrow.

'You believe the novel is a dying art?' Mary Cutlass presses Banerjee.

'I believe *art* is a dying art,' he says. 'What we are witnessing in twenty-first-century Western society is nothing less than the death of subjectivity. We are in Dublin, so I will quote to you a Dubliner, George Bernard Shaw, who said that man looks in a mirror to see his face, and at art to see his soul. But modern man has no soul to see. He has become little more than a conduit for the transfer of wealth between corporations.'

'That seems a bit pessimistic,' Victoria notes gently. 'Given that modern man has bought several hundred thousand copies of your book.'

'People will always need art,' William O'Hara declares. 'What is it they say? Art exists to keep the truth from killing us.'

'You have to be alive for something to kill you,' Banerjee snaps back.

'I don't think that's true.'

We all turn; Ariel, the beautiful editorial assistant, blushing a deep pink, lays down her cutlery and speaks tremulously to her plate. 'I just mean . . .' Her voice is barely louder than a whisper. 'I think we need art to remind us we're alive. To remind us of the beauty around us. And the people around us. And that they need us. Sometimes we forget. And that's what kills us.'

Hearing this, Banerjee's face utterly transforms: his severe expression disappears, melting into tragic puppy-dog devotion.

'Has anyone read the other books on the shortlist?' Dodson says hurriedly, as the Indian seems on the point of making some sort of declaration. 'I had a look at the Conway Inchbold title, *Antelope Crimes*. Really quite impressive. Built up a genuine sense of menace. The antelope itself was bloody terrifying.'

'Oh yes,' Mary Cutlass agrees. 'The claustrophobic atmosphere, the constant sense of threat – reminiscent of the Russians. Gogol in particular. Don't you adore Gogol?' she says to Paul.

'I'm more of a Yahoo man myself,' Paul says.

Mary Cutlass looks blank.

'Conway Inchbold is a cancer,' says Banerjee.

'All right.' Crispin throws down his napkin. 'I'd like to announce that I've just invented a new rule of etiquette, which is that whoever cooked the meal gets to choose the topic of conversation. And my decision is, no more books.'

'What are we supposed to talk about?' his partner says, looking rather affronted.

'There are several topics available,' Crispin replies blithely.

'Such as?'

'Well, for starters, I'd like to hear more from this mysterious gentleman,' Crispin says, and my blood freezes as I realize he means me. 'Who is he? Who are you? You're not a writer, are you?'

'I'm a banker,' I say.

'Oh, snap!' O'Hara exclaims.

'You work in finance?' I say to Crispin.

'I dabbled, that's all. Anyway, I've retired.' He says this without irony, though I doubt he is even forty years old; but before I can ask what he did, he has pointed his fork at Paul and me. 'And the two of you are a pair?'

Does he suspect? I stare back at him, words dying in my throat.

'That's right,' Paul steps in. 'A pair, that's what we are. A pair of men, two men, in a relationship.'

'And tell us, where did you meet?'

'In a sauna,' Paul says. 'A gay sauna.'

'Which one?' Crispin says.

'Hmm, which one . . .' Paul says, drumming his fingers and contemplating the chandelier. 'Darling, do you remember which one?'

'No,' I say.

'It was in San Francisco,' Paul says, with a flash of what I suppose we must call inspiration. 'I'd gone over for research. Claude was working as a go-go dancer, weren't you, Claude? Claude, weren't you?'

'Yes,' I say, through gritted teeth.

'He was just out of the French navy,' Paul continues. 'They called him the Arse de Triomphe. Our eyes met in the steam room. Next thing, we fell in love.'

'Ah, *che bello*,' William O'Hara says fondly.

'Now we do everything together,' Paul continues; it is like watching a runaway train, a runaway train that is pretending to be gay. 'Holidays to Sweden to buy furniture, London every year for Fashion Week, the opera –'

Crispin pounces on this. 'What's your favourite opera?'

Paul, put on the spot, goes blank. His mouth opens and closes; the runaway train abruptly comes off the track, and with a certain amount of enjoyment I watch it fly through the air, wheels spinning fruitlessly. 'That would have to be . . . ah . . . *Mamma Mia!*'

Crispin and William look at each other in surprise, then dissolve into guffaws. 'Us too!' Crispin squeals. 'It's our terrible secret!'

'And Paul – did you say that you were working on a business venture?' William inquires.

'Yes, William, I did. In fact, it's something you might find inter— ow!' He looks accusingly at me. 'Darling?'

'You promised you wouldn't discuss business tonight, darling,' I say to him.

'I'm not discussing business, darling, they asked what I'm doing and I'm telling them. Actually, I think I may have some brochures here somewhere – ow! Darling, would you please stop kicking me?'

'Darling, I would like a word with you outside, please.'

'What's the problem, I'm just – hey, put that back!' as I snatch away his wine glass.

'I'll give it back after we've had a little word,' I say firmly; grousing under his breath, Paul gets out of his seat.

'Obvious who wears the trousers in *your* household,' Crispin teases.

'I wear the trousers,' Paul rejoins as I bundle him out the door. 'And I go on top!'

Ignoring his protestations, I propel him down the hall and into a darkened sitting room where we are certain to be out of earshot. 'What are you doing?'

'What are *you* doing?' Paul returns. 'I thought you were going to help me!'

'I am helping you. I have spent the last two hours pretending to be gay. But that was because I thought you were trying to win over your editor. I did not realize that you had constructed this charade in order to bilk our hosts out of their money – this is a word, *bilk*?'

'How am I bilking them? I'm just making conversation.'

'Answer this: did you come here this evening with the specific intention to drum up investments for Myhotswaitress?'

'You say that like it's a bad thing,' he protests. 'Myhotswaitress is going to be huge, and I'm giving them the chance to get in on the ground floor! I'm basically thrusting millions and millions of euro into their hands, and you're telling me I'm a bad guest?'

'You told me you had come here to rebuild your relationship with your editor and restart your career.'

'I said no such thing, Claude. I said they were influential people, and they are. Look at the size of this place! I could move my whole family in here and it would take those guys about six months to notice. They're exactly the kind of investor we need.'

'That may be so. Nevertheless, I am informing you now that my part in this deception is over.'

Paul grinds his fists against his temples. 'I don't understand you. You're always on my case about doing something with my life, and then when I try, you're completely unsupportive!'

'Because I want you to write! And everything you do is just a way of avoiding writing! Don't you understand – *you* are the great investment opportunity! *You* have the chance to get in on the ground floor – of yourself!'

'What are you talking about?' Paul exclaims.

It is true, this did not come out quite like I thought it would. 'I am talking about the chance to create a work of art! Instead of merely adding to the transience and the falsity of our times, you can rise above them! Find some meaning within them!'

'Oh, well, that's just peachy for you, isn't it? I'm sure from your perspective it looks like a great idea to crawl up my own ass, or however you put it –'

' "Get in on the ground floor of yourself" –'

'So you and your banker pals can keep merrily turning the world to shit, and then any time you're feeling bad drag in the poor old artist to find some meaning for you! You're like the property developer who spends the year demolishing the countryside, then wants to go on holiday to somewhere *completely unspoiled*. Well, I'm not your meaning-monkey! I'm not here to make you feel better!'

'That's not what I'm saying –'

'I'm living in *your* world, pal. I've got to play by *your* rules. If I've got to add to the falsity to feed my family, then falsity it is. And as for transience, I'll say this for it, at least it's over quick.'

'Ah, young love,' comes a voice from behind us. Standing in the doorway, framed by the light of the hall, is William O'Hara, wine glass perched between finger and thumb like a spheric, translucent butterfly. 'Crispin and I used to fight like that,' he says. 'Now we're like two old maids, making each other tea. But I see you've found it.'

He nods at the far wall. We turn around. Hanging over the fireplace is a painting. In the gloom it appears to be a rectangle of solid black; but now O'Hara switches on a lamp and I can see that the darkness is composed of minute inscriptions, accreting here a little more, here a little less, so that shapes seem to emerge, swim about and disappear again. The effect is surprisingly powerful, and quite beautiful.

'I wanted to bring the guests in for a private viewing, but Crispin thought it would seem like showing off,' O'Hara says. 'He doesn't understand that I don't think of it as *mine*. How could anyone ever believe he owned something as monumental as this?' He gazes up at the painting, as if he were speaking to it rather than to us, drifting across the floor towards it like a strand of inverted smoke pulled backwards into the unlit fire. 'The instant I saw it, I knew I could spend the rest of my life looking at it. Crispin says that's exactly why he doesn't like it. "You never say that about me," he says.' O'Hara smiles. 'He's such a silly old duffer.'

I recognize the painting: after my failed encounter with Ariadne, I spent many nights online looking at this and others, taking some consolation, if that's the word, from their charred and tortured surfaces, like selenographies of some bleak moon.

'François Texier,' I say.

'The philosopher?' Paul is staring up at the painting with a certain amount of misgiving, as if shadowy hands might at any moment emerge from it and pull him in.

'That's right,' O'Hara says. 'You probably know the story?'

Paul shakes his head.

'In the late 1990s he disappeared – dropped out of contact, left his job at the university. He'd been about to begin work on what was to be his definitive statement – he had a title for it, and indeed a contract. But the years went by and the book never surfaced – and neither did Texier. Instead these paintings began to appear in Paris – gifts to his friends, many of them, strange portraits, strange landscapes, strange abstractions. All very strange, and yet in some ways you could see the connection to his thought.'

'And the book?' Paul asks. 'What happened to that?'

'Well, this is the book,' O'Hara says, gesturing to the painting. '*La Marque et le Vide*. The Mark and the Void. If you look closely, you can see –'

'Words . . .'

Words upon words upon yet more words; hundreds of pages of text superimposed one on top of the other, rendering each other utterly illegible – creating instead a cascading darkness that seems to devour the very possibility of meaning.

'He wrote it all out, you see. His book, the unfinished book, on the canvas, in pen and ink. When he had finished he burned the transcript and all his notes, and treated the canvas with the soot. And he stipulated that whoever owned it subsequently would have to expose it to smoke, which it's been chemically designed to absorb over time – that's why we've hung it over a fireplace.'

'What happened?' Paul says. 'He'd had some kind of breakdown?'

'He'd certainly grown wary of the idea of definitive statements,' O'Hara says. 'But in fact the painting fits his philosophy rather well. The mark, "making your mark", this idea that to live in full means to leave some permanent evidence of yourself on the world, he'd become quite suspicious of that. And the corresponding notion that the world is a blank page waiting to be inscribed, a void to be covered up with our doings. No, no. On the contrary. The void comes from inside us, from deep inside us. And the more we try to escape it, the more we turn the world into a mirror. Of that emptiness. That's what he felt he'd done, while attempting to come up with his definitive statement.'

'Dark,' Paul says, his eyes still locked on the painting.

'Well, that depends on how you look at it. You can transform it, you see. That's the point of art, as he saw it.'

'Isn't art about making your mark?'

'In a sense. But art is something you give away, that's the difference. Instead of grabbing up bits of reality for oneself. He became very interested in the tribal cultures of the Pacific – his wife was an anthropologist, he used to travel around Polynesia with her. Anyway, he was very taken with these cycles of exchange they have, whereby objects are passed back and forth through generations, and nothing belongs to anyone in perpetuity. Or rather, that there is no "one" for things to belong to. He used to say that in that part of the world, you wrote your address backwards, that is, first you wrote the country, then your town, then your street, and only lastly your name. Which, when you think about it, makes much more sense. And art for him was an attempt to write his address backwards, so to speak.'

'It's so dark, though,' Paul says, his eyes still locked on the painting.

'Yes, the problem was those very cultures were in danger of being wiped out by all the others busy making their mark.'

'Climate change?'

'Travelling around the Pacific, they could already see it happening. That had a powerful effect on him. Not just the threat of floods and cataclysm and so on, but the fact that no one in the First World wanted to know. And then when his wife died, that seemed to compound everything. This was painted only a few months before his suicide.'

I hadn't known this; I think of Ish and her islanders, and looking at the painting I feel a chill, as if behind the impenetrable black veil I can see drowned faces buried under relentless waves.

'Crispin can't stand it,' O'Hara says, returning his gaze to the painting. 'He says it's depressing. And what it's done to the insurance is just shocking – they're insisting now we install some sort of ghastly alarm system, it'll be like living in a bank vault. But looking at it makes me feel rather hopeful. There's a sort of comfort in the thought of us all swimming around in this void together. The notion that our borders are porous makes me feel oddly complete. Like love, I suppose, isn't it? It's when you forget yourself that you're most who you are. And conversely, as Texier said, there's nothing so selfish as the urge to escape ourselves. Crispin can't stand it when I quote him either,' he concludes apologetically. And then, as a voice calls from elsewhere in the house, 'Dessert!' he says. 'Come.'

Back in the dining room, the conversation has turned to the banking crisis.

'Oh Lord, not again,' O'Hara says.

'When you cook the dinner, you can choose the topics,' Crispin tells him primly.

'That Miles O'Connor is the worst of the lot,' Mary Cutlass says with an access of anger. 'I don't understand how he hasn't been driven from the city.'

'Oh, Miles isn't so bad,' Crispin says, as he portions out cake. 'He helped us out of a hole when all the other banks were being beastly. Who is it you work for again?' He directs this last question at me.

'BOT,' I tell him. 'Or Agron Torabundo, as it is now.'

He is impressed. 'Ever since old Blankly took over, you boys have been raking it in. Funny, he always struck me as a bit of a maverick. It just goes to show, I suppose.' He digs into his dessert.

'And now you've got this hedge fund – what's the chap's name again?'

'Howie,' I say. 'Howard Hogan.'

'This thing's only been going a few weeks,' Crispin informs the table. 'But it's taken off like a rocket. I wish I knew how he does it.' He returns to me. 'I've tried to work out his system, but I can't make head or tail of it.'

'Non-linear maths,' I say, then confess, 'I don't understand it either. There's a Russian.'

Mary Cutlass, who has been looking increasingly baffled by this conversation, breaks in. 'What I would like to know is, when are our writers going to address the banking crisis?'

'I do address it in my new book,' William tells her. 'Whacker's elderly grandmother has her apple cart repossessed by the bank. Of course, those people don't have a clue how to run an apple cart.'

'I mean the whole thing. What it's done to society and so on. There must be a great novel to be written about that.'

'The banking crisis is unrepresentable,' Banerjee says severely. 'These people are not even human.'

'Guilty as charged,' Crispin says with a sigh.

'They've done some terrible things,' Victoria Galahad intervenes. 'Still, I don't know if it's a good idea to go around calling them inhuman.'

'It is their own doing,' Banerjee insists. 'Worse, their vacuous thinking has spread out of the world of finance like an epidemic. Now, people are barely capable of sustaining a genuine emotion, or communicating anything more complex than pictures of cats. Cat pictures and pornography, that is what we have now instead of art. Excuse me.'

With that he gets up and leaves the room.

'Probably gone to hang himself,' Crispin says once the door closes.

'Is he always like that?' William inquires.

'Oh, he's probably just a bit tired, that's all,' Robert Dodson says vaguely. 'Misses his wife.'

Ariel begins to cough, as if her cake has gone down the wrong way. But she quickly recovers, and – perhaps taking advantage of Banerjee's absence – inclines herself over the table towards Paul, rather like a flower bowing under the weight of a raindrop. 'I meant to tell you earlier,' she confides. 'I adored *For Love of a Clown*.'

Paul, who since our conversation in the dining room has been subdued, starts up, blinking in surprise. 'Eh?' he says.

'Your novel,' Ariel, who evidently is used to conversing with writers, explains.

'Oh – what, really?'

'I reread it recently,' she elaborates – she speaks in a soft low voice that makes everything she says sound like a confession of love. 'That line about how we're all clowns in love's circus – *tumbling through sawdust in clothes that don't fit us, waiting for the day we can wipe off our false smiles* . . . gosh, just so perfect.'

'Thank you,' Paul says, seeming to expand before my very eyes. 'Thank you very much.'

'Are you working on something new?' she asks. 'I know you said you'd started a business, but there is a new book on the way, isn't there? I've been waiting such a long time.'

'Hmm,' Paul says, staring into her eyes, which are almost indecently huge and open, like lilies in bloom – petals spread, pollen-flecked pistils exposed to the elements. 'Well, I have been tinkering with something, on and off.'

'Oh!' Ariel applauds softly.

'Really?' Robert Dodson has been listening in. 'A novel?'

Paul looks back and forth, from his former editor to his former editor's sublime assistant: in this instance, at least, beauty defeats truth. 'Yes,' he says.

'Can you tell us what it's about?' Ariel asks.

'Hmm, I'd prefer not to go into it at this stage . . .'

'Just give us an idea,' Dodson encourages.

'What's this?' William inquires.

'Paul's telling us about his novel.'

'Oh, a new one?'

'A word,' Dodson says. 'The bare bones.'

Victoria Galahad, Mary Cutlass and the others are all craned forward on their elbows, as though to catch the words as soon as they appear. Paul looks increasingly panic-stricken. 'It's about, ah . . . it's about, ah . . .'

'Tell them what you told me, that first day we met,' I encourage him.

He looks round at me wildly.

'About the bank. All that.'

'Right,' he says. 'Exactly. It's about a banker, working in an investment bank in the IFSC.'

'Just what we've been talking about,' Mary Cutlass notes.

'So you don't think it's unrepresentable,' Robert Dodson says with a smile.

'With all due respect to Bimal,' William puts in, 'I don't think you can just write off a whole swathe of the modern world like that.'

'Exactly,' Paul says. 'The way I see it, it's the writer's job to try to find the meaning in it, find the humanity in people like Claude here. And if it's not there, to try and understand where it's gone.'

'Hear, hear,' William says.

'Well said,' Victoria Galahad smiles.

Ariel just gazes at him, as though from the bed of a swoon.

'What's it called?' Mary Cutlass says.

'Called?' Paul repeats.

'You must have a title, a working title at least?'

'Of course,' Paul says, a little hoarsely, as the table's eyes swivel on to him again. 'It's called, ah . . . it's called *Anal Analyst*.'

There is a moment of silence.

'*Anal Analyst*,' Dodson says, trying it out.

'*Anal Analyst*,' Mary Cutlass repeats to herself.

'Well, it's certainly memorable,' O'Hara concludes.

'He's a poofter, is he?' Crispin asks. 'Your banker.'

'He's gay, he's been promiscuous, as so many of us have,' Paul improvises. 'But now all that meaningless sex turns out to have a consequence, a terrible consequence. And in his isolated world of money and accumulation, he doesn't have the tools, as it were, to deal with it.'

The heads around the table nod solemnly.

'It sounds fascinating,' Dodson says. 'Has anybody seen it?'

'To be honest, Robert, I'm trying to keep it quiet for now. You know, focus on the writing, get the book finished before the whole market frenzy takes over.'

'That's wise,' Dodson agrees. 'Still, if you wanted to give me an outline, or just have a general chat – Bimal and I are going back to London tomorrow, but we'll be here again for the Black & White Festival in a couple of weeks. William's going to be doing an interview with him . . .'

'I'd like that, Robert,' Paul replies. 'I'd like that very much.'

'You would be better off setting fire to your manuscript and throwing the ashes in the Liffey than publishing it with Asterisk Press.' A caustic voice behind us signals that Bimal Banerjee has returned. 'And if you've been bewitched by the Whore of Bloomsbury here, I should warn you that she can never deliver on her false promises, because she is a creature made entirely of ice.'

'My dear, I don't think you need worry about any of us running off with your woman,' Crispin says, leaning back in his chair. 'But I can't say I haven't wondered if you're going to finish that cake?'

The party winds down shortly after midnight; Robert Dodson explains apologetically that he and his author have an early flight tomorrow. As we leave, William promises to send tickets for the upcoming festival, and Dodson repeats his offer of a private meeting. Walking down the street, Paul seems buoyant. Is it just that he's enjoyed two free meals today? Or something more?

'Well, Claude,' he says after a while. 'We didn't snag any investors. Still, I suppose I should thank you for not letting the cat out of the bag.'

'You're welcome,' I say. 'I enjoyed the evening very much. At the dinner parties I usually go to, everyone just talks about golf.'

'Yeah, writers don't play much golf. Though mostly because they can't afford the green fees. Otherwise they'd never pass up an opportunity to procrastinate like that.'

'Is that right.'

'Probably that's why the clubs keep the subs so high, because they don't want the place clogged up with writers day and night.'

We walk a little further, and then, as it doesn't seem that he will raise it himself, '*Anal Analyst*?' I say.

'It was all I could think of,' he says apologetically.

'Still, it does not seem to have done any harm,' I say. 'I mean, your editor still wants to see it.'

He doesn't reply. I don't understand – why is he so determined to downplay what has happened? 'He wants to meet you and talk about it – this is a big opportunity, no?'

'*Anal Analyst* doesn't exist, remember? I just said that to get him off my case.'

'But it's a positive sign, isn't it?'

'A sign of what? You think he's going to pay big money for a novel that I just made up?'

'Aren't all novels made up?'

Paul rolls his eyes.

'I'm serious,' I persist. 'If you know he likes the idea, why not try to write the book?'

'Books don't pay, Claude. I've got a family to support.'

'How can you say they don't pay? Look at the house we have just been in! With a Texier on the wall worth half a million euro!'

335

Paul comes to a stop, there on the street. 'Half a million? For that thing?'

'More, after the retrospective in New York next year.'

'Half a million euro!' He puts his head in his hands. 'I can't believe you stopped me from bilking them.'

'Aha, you admit it, you *were* trying to bilk them!'

'I was bilking them into making the best financial decision of their lives! With that kind of money behind it, there's no way Myhotswaitress could have failed. We could *all* have been rich, and had hideous paintings in our living rooms. And had living rooms.'

'That's not the point. The point is that it is still possible to support yourself and your family by writing. And now there may be a chance to do so. Why not take it?'

'Haven't we discussed this?'

'Yes, but you have never given me any plausible answer.'

He lets out a gasp of exasperation. 'Because I don't like being reminded I'm obsolete. How about that, for starters?'

'But if you write the truth about our time? How can the truth ever be obsolete?'

'People don't want the truth,' he says, waving a hand at the streets around us. 'They want better-quality lies. High-definition lies on fifty-inch screens. I wrote the damn truth already, Claude. Maybe I didn't write it well, but I wrote it. And not only did no one want to see it, they made me feel like a fool for even trying. They laughed out the window at me as they sped away on the gravy train.'

'That was during the boom. Now the gravy train has stopped.'

'Yeah, well, I can't unsee what I saw. The money poured in, and it was like suddenly everyone in Ireland took off their masks, and they were these horrific, rapacious alien beings who if you fell down in the street would just leave you there to die.'

'Maybe it was the rapacious alien that was the mask. And now they need someone to help them find their true faces again.'

He doesn't reply to this.

I pace alongside him a moment, considering what he has said.

Then, slowly, I nod in agreement. 'No, you're right. It's just as Banerjee said: the world we live in has fallen too far to be saved by art.'

'It's not as *Banerjee said*,' Paul objects. 'It's got nothing to do with Banerjee.'

'Of course not. I only mean that his point was well made, that in this environment you should not feel bad to have failed as a writer.'

For a second time, Paul stops in the street. '*Failed as a writer.* Can you believe he said that?'

'Although in some ways it is a shame,' I reflect. 'Robert was very excited to read your new work.'

Paul mumbles ambiguously.

'And his assistant as well,' I note.

The mutterings take on a more wistful cast.

'*She* certainly seemed to prefer your writing to Banerjee's,' I observe.

There is a turbulent silence, and then Paul blurts, 'Look, I'll be honest, there are times when I wish I hadn't spent seven years playing online poker and stalking waitresses. But to write a book . . . to go back into that world . . .'

'He just wanted to see a proposal,' I urge him. 'It will only be one or two weeks of work. And I can help you – listen to your ideas, check the spelling – whatever it takes.'

'It's not that simple. I'm in debt, Claude. I owe money left and right. I can't just drop everything to go and write a novel.'

'What would you be dropping?' I say.

'The website!'

'Oh yes, of course.'

'If Myhotswaitress were up and running, it'd be a different story,' he says. 'I'd know I had some money coming in. But we're at a crucial stage now. We need to find investors! If I walk away, the whole thing will just collapse!'

How can the same mind that produced *For Love of a Clown*

have come up with Myhotswaitress? How can he not see the difference between the two? Is this simply the artistic personality? But it's true: I have no right to criticize, until I have put some skin in the game. 'If you want,' I tell him, 'I will speak to my clients about investing in Myhotswaitress. And I will personally pledge —' I name a sum. 'But you must submit your proposal to Dodson first. Do we have a deal?'

Paul appears genuinely moved. 'You would do that? You'd really do that?'

'If it means you'll have the freedom to work on your proposal.'

Paul laughs. 'I guess we do. And you know that pledge gets you straight into our Gold Circle of investors.' He bites on a nail. 'Though not our Platinum Circle.'

'I am happy to stay in the Gold Circle.'

'It means you don't get the tiepin.'

'I will live with that.'

The news on Monday morning opens with the story of an elderly couple who starved to death in their apartment; their landlord found them, after calling to see why the rent hadn't been paid. Evidently the couple's daughter had got mixed up with a loan shark; her parents had spent everything they had trying to dig her out. They had been living on cat food, until the cat food ran out. Every day brings another bleak austerity fairy tale like this one, and makes the pot-and-pan charivari of our neighbours the zombies sound all the louder in our ears when we cross the plaza.

'Last week I have called the police,' Jurgen says, looking down through his binoculars, 'and given to them ten different public-order offences these miscreants can be charged with. Still they do nothing.'

'Outrageous,' I say. Although police indifference is perhaps not so hard to fathom; they too have had their wages cut to pay for the failed banks. 'Nevertheless, compared with New York and London it's of little significance, no? There are thousands in the camps over there.'

'One must always clamp down on disobedience before it has a chance to take hold,' Jurgen says; then, still staring out through the binoculars, 'Have you noticed anything odd about Ish's behaviour lately?'

'Odd?' I repeat.

Jurgen lowers the binoculars and turns to me, his colourless eyes scanning my features like an infra-red beam.

'She has been her usual self,' I say.

'Very good,' Jurgen says.

'Why do you ask?' I say casually.

'No reason.' He lifts the binoculars again. 'Porter likes to be sure that all his employees are happy.'

I retreat to my desk, then, lowering my head so I am invisible from the windows, grab Ish by the wrist and pull her towards me. 'What have you done?'

'What?'

'You didn't . . .' A terrible thought occurs to me. 'You didn't say something to Blankly, did you? About Kokomoko?'

Her façade of incomprehension lasts all of ten seconds. 'It was just a short email!' she cries. 'A short, politely worded –'

'I don't believe it.' I bury my head in my hands.

'It's right in his backyard! How's that going to look, if a whole bloody island goes under in his backyard?'

'It's got nothing to do with us!'

'We can help! He's always saying how we create our own reality, isn't this exactly the kind of thing he means?'

Of course it's not what he means. Blankly would drill his mother's own grave if he thought there was oil underneath it. In so far as bankers think about nature at all, it's as the originator of the ruthless survival-of-the-fittest model on which the market is based. If a species becomes extinct, a river runs dry, a civilization is wiped out, by famine or flood or earthquake or volcano, that is usually regarded as reflecting some essential flaw in its business plan. Ish knows that. Why is she acting like this?

'Wait a second.' She turns pale herself, looking at me as if she's just woken from a dream. 'How did you hear about it?'

'Jurgen asked – look, it's all right' – as the enormity of what she has done hits her in a single wave that throws her back in her seat.

'Fuck,' she whispers, and then, imploringly, 'I didn't say anything bad! I just thought he ought to know. What did Jurgen say? What's going to happen to me?'

'Nothing's going to happen,' I say, but then frustration over-takes me again. 'Didn't you think of this before? Why do you care so much about people ten thousand miles away?'

'I don't fucking know, do I? Maybe because no one any closer will let me care about them.'

My phone lights up; I am grateful for the reprieve.

The caller is a man – a reporter. 'My name is Ron Hallissey, I work at the *Record* – Mr Martingale, your name has been given to me as one of the authors of a recent report on Royal Irish Bank compiled by Agron Torabundo for the Department of Finance. Is that correct?'

'Yes, but –'

'I just wondered if you could expand on some of the recom-mendations your report makes. You advise government to inject a further eight billion euro of direct liquidity to Royal Irish –'

'I – what?'

'I wondered, given the cuts that've already been made –'

'Wait, I advise them to what?'

'– to, for instance, palliative care, cervical cancer vaccinations, back-to-work schemes, rehousing for at-risk minorities – whether you had specific ideas where the next cuts should come from, in order to pay for this latest bailout –'

'Wait, wait,' I interrupt. 'I didn't recommend any bailout . . .' I break off: someone's tapping my shoulder. It's Rachael's secretary.

'Can you come upstairs?' she says.

'I'm on a call,' I tell her.

She reaches over to the phone station and pulls the plug. The red light, and all the other lights, dwindle instantly into darkness. 'It's not actually a question,' she says.

Rachael is standing in her office with her back to me, gazing out the window. 'Sit down, Claude.'

I do so. On her desk, festooned in red crêpe paper, is a bottle of Irish whiskey, with the government harp on the label.

'The Minister's office sent it over by way of thanks. They were extremely pleased with your work.' She looks back at me over her shoulder. 'Perhaps that surprises you.'

'From the press conference it sounded as if they had ignored most of my suggestions.'

'That's because we rewrote them,' she says.

A gull swoops down to land outside her window; it scrutinizes the office with an eye the same livid corpse-green as the river below.

'After speaking to you, Jurgen had some concerns about your report's content, so before releasing it I called it up here and went through it with him. What the Department saw was the revised version.'

'In which you advised them to continue the bailout?'

'In which we advised that Royal Irish had a short-term liquidity issue, owing to the ongoing outflow of corporate deposits and overnight funding. Nasty, but fixable.' She steps away from the window and takes her seat opposite me, regarding me impassively for what seems a very long time.

'My figures were accurate,' I say slowly. 'The evidence is there. Royal is finished. No amount of money will fix it.'

'So you advised it should be wound down and its bondholders go unpaid,' she says.

'Why should public money be used to pay off private business debts?'

'And did you wonder at all who those bondholders could be?'

'That did not seem pertinent.'

'Claude,' she says – at that moment, the secretary's voice issues from the phone, and Rachael roars a single, terrifying 'No!' before returning affectlessly to me – 'Claude, we have some extremely important clients who bought heavily into Royal Irish. How do you think they would feel if they discovered that we had advised the government to let the bank go down and their investment with it?'

I begin to say that most of the original bondholders sold on at a loss some time ago, but she cuts me off. 'No, Claude. I want you to think about this. What would *our* clients think if *we* were responsible for them losing millions of euros?'

I clear my throat. 'I take your point, but the Irish government is also our client.'

'The Irish government commissioned a single report.'

'Yes, but to avoid a conflict, surely best practice is to –'

Rachael beats her fists on the desk. 'I told you, Claude! The best outcomes for the key players, that's what I asked you to find, can't you read between the lines?'

'But to pretend the bank is still alive, when clearly it is not –'

'What is wrong with you people?' she exclaims. Her eyes hold mine, as if she is genuinely seeking an answer; for a moment she looks terribly young, like a teacher at her wits' end with an intractable group of infants. 'Do you know what we are to a man like Porter Blankly, Claude? We're nothing. We're irrelevant. We're a godforsaken rock in the middle of the ocean. If we sank under the waves tomorrow, he'd barely even notice. Now, I've been trying to change his mind. I've been trying to put this place on the map, prove to him that our office can be a serious contributor to the company. And then I have one of my analysts advising government to burn our biggest client?'

She blinks at me as if inviting a response. But I have nothing to say. She takes a deep breath, unknots her fists and, in a more controlled voice, says, 'Walter's built up a 25 per cent stake in Royal Irish.'

'Walter?'

'Walter Corless. Dublex. When the share price started to fall, he took the opportunity to double down. Then he doubled down again – indirectly, through a broker, so nobody knew it was him.' She pauses. 'From your reaction I'm guessing it wasn't your idea.'

I'm speechless; in fact, my whole body has gone numb. At a certain level of success, it's not unusual for major clients to imagine they achieved it all by themselves; they'll dismiss their advisers, start making decisions led purely by their gut, keep going until their empires are in ruins. But Walter always seemed too smart for that; or rather, he seemed such a monster in every other regard that I assumed he must be possessed of a sterling business sense to balance it all out.

'When your report came in I called our major clients on spec before submitting,' Rachael says. 'That's when he told me.'

'How could he even afford it? A quarter of a *bank*?'

'It's in CFDs. He only needed to put down the margin. But that means now the bank's in trouble, his losses are amplified. It's already been making loans to him to cover the margin calls. If the share price falls much further he'll be wiped out.' She locks her eyes on me again. 'I don't need to tell you that if Dublex went under, there would be major consequences for AgroBOT. Cash flow, legal – I don't even want to think about it.'

And that would be the tip of the iceberg, for us and for Ireland. Dublex employs thousands of people; whole towns are built around its operations. Its implosion would make the crash to date look like a day at the races.

'The government can't prop up Royal Irish indefinitely,' I say. 'There isn't any money left.'

'Not indefinitely,' Rachael says. 'I thought it might give us some time. Only now it appears someone in the Department of Finance has leaked the report to the press and they're starting to ask questions.'

'Yes, someone called me only a few minutes ago.'

'Well, you can call him back and confirm that you stand by every word,' she says. 'After careful analysis of their accounts you concluded, blah blah blah.' She swivels in her chair; her face is recast in the greenish light of the terminal, giving it a submarine chill. 'Be thankful we got your report before it was sent, Claude. Otherwise we would be having a very different conversation. Take your gift.' She points to the bottle of whiskey on the desk. 'And send up Ish.'

344

Ish isn't here: she has just left for a meeting in London and won't be back until tomorrow. I think about texting to warn her of what's in store, then decide she's better not knowing. There is nothing she can do; at least this way she can get a good night's sleep.

Three more journalists call that afternoon, as well as the man from the *Record*. I do as I'm told, telling them that the report's recommendations are sound, and that the question of how to pay for them was not part of my remit. By four o'clock, a picture of me taken at a conference two years ago appears on several news websites with the caption *Martingale: Cold* or *Martingale: French*. Later, a story runs in one of the tabloids with the headline *Fat-Cat Banker Who Thinks We Haven't Suffered Enough*.

'This fat-cat thing is such bullshit,' Kevin opines. 'Since when are bankers fat? We're in the gym like every day.'

'Criticize if you want, but at least be accurate,' Jocelyn agrees.

'When you think of what they could have said – you know, *Crazy Frog Says, Let Them Eat Cake*, that kind of thing.'

'It's just lazy journalism,' Jocelyn says.

Coincidentally, Walter calls too, in order to rant about some regulatory hold-up or other. I can't concentrate on what he's saying: it takes all of my restraint not to break in on him and bellow, 'You told me you didn't have a holding in Royal Irish! You told me!' But maintaining these charades is what professionalism means; and anyway, when I investigate, I find that the arcane derivative he used to make the investment means that he didn't actually own anything, but instead was making a kind of leveraged bet on shares held by a broker-dealer, so technically he was telling the truth.

The market's lending to the government, the government's lending to Royal, Royal's lending to Walter to cover Walter's own stake in Royal, pulled ever-downwards by the market . . . I draw a diagram on a scrap of paper, trying to work it all out, but very quickly it turns into a self-devouring incomprehensibility, an uroboros of debt like the black twin of Ish's kula ring . . .

I ask Jurgen what will happen next.

'Rachael is trying to persuade Walter to get rid of his holding, before the market finds out about it and the Royal Irish black hole becomes a much larger and more dangerous Royal Irish-Dublex black hole,' Jurgen says. 'The problem is that Walter is still under the impression that Royal is about to bounce back.'

Magical thinking: an invaluable quality for an entrepreneur, until it isn't. But Walter!

Jurgen shrugs. 'Walter is a person. People do irrational things. They act according to the story they want to hear, instead of the reality.' He cocks his head, a mechanical bird. 'Where is Ish?'

I leave the office early. Ariadne waves to me from the window of the Ark. I remember she wanted to speak to me about her problems with the rent, but I feel contaminated after the Dublex revelation, so I just wave and pass on. At home I turn on the news, only to find myself faced, as though the broadcast were coming directly from my conscience, with the Minister again – haggard and worn, reciting the findings of the faked report like some poisonous spell whose consequences he has no conception of.

When the phone rings, my first, dreadful thought is that the journalists have somehow got my mobile number. But this time the caller is Paul. William O'Hara has emailed him to confirm our place on the guest list for his public interview with Banerjee at the Black & White Festival. 'It's two weeks on Thursday,' he says. 'So time to get moving.'

'Excellent,' I say.

'Excellent, so when are you coming over?'

'You want me to come over?'

'I thought you said you were going to help,' Paul returns, a little sharply.

'Yes, although I meant in the way of providing background detail, moral support, that sort of thing.'

'Oh, I see, so basically you're saying I have to do it all by myself.'

'Aren't novels usually written this way?'

A sigh crackles from the receiver. 'This isn't a novel, Claude. It's a *proposal*. I've got a few ideas, but I want to bounce them off someone first.'

Bounce them off someone: the phrase reassures me. It suggests there will be little more required of me than a physical presence. I can be a presence; and a bout of artistic creativity might be just the kind of activity I need to purge the noxious taste of the day. I set out, trying not to think about Dublex and its shaky foundations, trying not to see in the streets and faces I encounter a reality that has been secretly changed, the first imperceptible marks of a new and lessened future; I concentrate instead on novelistic details: fruit stacked in the grocery, the stooped old woman casting breadcrumbs to the pigeons, a convoy of robed priests climbing aboard a bus.

The rain has been falling all day; it seems a whole sea must have spilled from the sky. The swollen river lours like a drunkard disturbed from his sleep; clogged gutters quickly become filthy lakes, over which pedestrians skip and dance and hop with grim grey faces, as in some totalitarian musical. On Paul's street the weather has driven almost everyone indoors, though a couple of men make do with a sheet of polyurethane beneath which they share a dog-end, like doughty Tommies in a Passchendaele trench.

Paul, when he answers his door, has a twitchy demeanour I haven't seen before. 'Let's get to it,' he says. 'Clizia's going out in a minute, so we'll have a couple of hours totally free.'

'Volleyball?'

'Yes, they're in the quarter-finals. Nearly there, eh?'

'Good for them,' I say ingenuously, while a surge of rain strikes the window in a mocking minor chord.

'Okay, down to business,' he says, directing me to sit at the kitchen table.

Instantly, Remington detaches himself from the television.

'What are you doing, Daddy?'

'We're writing a story,' Paul says. 'Now be quiet.'

'Is it a story about an ant?'

'No.'

'Is it a story about an ant who goes all around the world and then he comes back and he lives in a matchbox and his name is Roland?'

'Go and watch your cartoons,' Paul says, gripping the boy by the shoulders and shunting him back towards television. 'That's an order.'

With a little sigh, Remington picks up the remote; a torrent of explosions, strobes and rainbows fragmenting into hissing diamonds blasts from the TV, like ECT with product placement.

'Okay. Okay.' Paul seems considerably tenser than usual. He picks up a plastic biro, chews the end, then sets it down again. 'The thing is,' he says, 'I don't think this is going to work.'

Clearly my role here is going to be more involved than I'd expected. 'It's just a proposal,' I tell him in a calming voice. 'And you already have most of it, in what you told Dodson at the party.'

'But that's just it, Claude.' He looks up at me with eyes that are flashing vortices of anxiety. '*Anal Analyst*. What *is* that? You know?'

'Well, it is just as you said, a working title. Obviously you will not use *Anal* in the actual book.'

He shakes his head vigorously. '*Anal*'s not the issue. *Anal* is fine. The problem is *Analyst*. Who wants to read about an analyst? Who knows what an analyst even *is*?'

'I know what an analyst is. I can tell you.'

'You've already told me. You've told me what you do ten times, and I forget it straight away. It's like it's too boring to be retained by the human mind.'

'Can't you make it interesting? Isn't that your job?'

'Within reason. But I need some kind of story. I need something to *happen*. Today, for example, tell me what you did today.'

I flinch inwardly. His eyes fix on me, enormous, gibbous, like the eyes of some nocturnal animal peering out of the forest; in them, as if from a hidden camera, I see myself at Rachael's desk, promising to lie about the phoney report . . . 'I developed a financial model of a notional amalgam of the three main Irish banks,' I say.

'That's what I mean! No one wants to read about some guy going around developing financial models.'

'Dodson wanted to. He said it sounded bold.'

'*Bold* is code for *no one's going to buy that*. Look, I've made my decision, the analyst's out. So what we're left with is *Anal*. Igor and I talked through a few ideas earlier today. See if anything jumps out at you.' Placing a pair of reading glasses on his nose, he frowns down at the notebook. '*Anal Amateurs*. The comic tale of two medical students as they attempt to raise the money for college by opening their own unorthodox proctology clinic. *Eighteen and Anal*. The battle of an uptight young man to shake off his authoritarian upbringing. *Twenty-Four-Hour Red-Hot Anal*. In Finland, the land of the midnight sun, a local blacksmith's decision to open a colonic irrigation centre causes tension in the old community –'

'I will be honest, I think you are going down the wrong path with these anal themes.'

'But we told Dodson that it was called *Anal Analyst*,' Paul remonstrates. 'That's the idea he wanted to hear about. We've already scrapped the analyst. If we chuck *Anal* too, what's left? You want me to hand him a pile of blank pages? Publishers won't pay money for blank pages, Claude. I've tried it and they won't.'

Before I can reply (what can I possibly say?) the bathroom door flies open; like a goddess emerging from a volcano, Clizia steps out in a billow of steam. She is wearing boots of white patent leather that climb up above her knee, leaving perhaps twelve scandalous inches of thigh exposed between them and the hem of her mini-skirt, which is also white and also patent leather. 'I am going to volleyball,' she says deadpan, but then, raising her voice abruptly, 'Vot is this?'

'What's what?' Paul turns to follow her pointing finger. 'Oh, for God's sake – Remington, what's in your mouth?'

'Uh-igh,' comes the unconvincing reply.

'Is that the plug from the TV?'

'I was trying to make myself electric,' Remington explains in a small voice.

'Can't you even take care of him for five minutes?' Clizia rails. 'How can I go out, if I can't trust you to watch him?'

'He was chewing a plug, that's all,' Paul protests. 'It's not like he had his fingers in the socket.'

'Is like the less you do, the lazier you get,' she says.

'You'll be late for your game,' he says shortly.

'Huh,' she says. She goes to the door, where, rather desultorily, she slings over her shoulder the worn nylon sports bag. 'I am leaving,' she says.

'Okay, fine.'

But she doesn't leave; instead she hovers by the door, examining us where we sit at the table. 'Vot are you doink?'

'Nothing.'

'Chasing again the waitresses?'

'Yeah, that's right.'

'Daddy's writing a story!' Remington sings from the floor.

'A story?' She looks from me to her husband and back.

'You didn't tell her?' I say to Paul.

'Tell me vot?'

Paul flurries a hand impatiently. 'It's nothing. We ran into my old editor last week and we're trying to put together a proposal for him. It probably won't come to anything.'

'He was very interested in seeing something new,' I tell her.

'Oh,' she says. She looks surprised.

'Have a good game,' Paul says.

'Yes,' she says. Her imperious façade seems to waver, then she gathers herself.

'Bye, Mama,' the little boy calls. The door closes, and we hear her clop away down the hall.

'Why didn't you tell her you met Dodson?' I ask.

'Oh God, Claude, she's been through that wringer so many times, what's the point of putting her through it again? When we don't even have anything concrete?'

'So let's make something concrete,' I exhort him. 'I think we dismissed the alienated banker too quickly. Think about it: the reasons you want to throw it away, aren't those in fact its strengths? He's boring, his life is boring, isn't that the point? Isn't that what makes his story true? He's the modern man, he lives to work, he has everything anyone could want – or rather, he has enough money to buy anything anyone could want – yet his life is empty. And then he meets this beautiful waitress –'

The key turns in the door. Clizia, grimacing, comes limping into the apartment.

Paul jumps up, hurries to assist her. 'What happened?'

'Ach, I come out of building, my foot slip on kerb.' She sinks into a chair, massages her ankle. 'Ugh, all these stairs, I think I never make it.'

'You should have called me,' Paul reproves her, bringing some ice from the kitchen. 'You think it's sprained?'

She sighs stoically. 'I'm sure is fine. Maybe I rest him for a little while.' She casts a sidelong glance at the notebook on the table. 'How is story going?'

'Oh Christ, don't ask,' Paul says.

'It's actually going quite well,' I tell her.

'You should use this green crayon, Daddy,' Remington says, proffering a box. 'It's a better colour for stories.'

'Have you had your bath yet?' Clizia says.

'I don't need a bath.'

Paul protests that she should stay off her feet, but Clizia insists that she already feels better now that she has taken her boots off. She leads Remington towards the bathroom.

'But I want to show Daddy the other good crayons,' he says.

'Daddy's working,' she replies, and the ghost of a smile crosses her lips.

It takes all evening, but at last I persuade him to give the banker another shot. We draw up a list of supporting characters; he promises he will call me early next week, when he has a rough idea of the plot, the basic mechanisms by which our Everyman is brought together with the woman who will transform him.

Ish is back in the office the following afternoon. She is in good humour, cracking jokes, flirting with clients, apparently with no idea that her fate hangs in the balance. But she's the only one. Bankers, beneath the façade of reason, are as superstitious as sailors, with a preternatural sensitivity to bad luck. Her colleagues might not know what exactly she's done, but they can tell something's up, and the whole Research Department gives her a wide berth. Eyes track her from behind every terminal, then vanish as she draws near; when face-to-face contact is unavoidable, they try to keep at least one dividing wall between them, and wince anticipatorily, as if a bolt of lightning might descend and incinerate her at any moment.

But the lightning bolt doesn't come – not that afternoon, nor the next morning. As we slip into afternoon with no word from the Uncanny Valley I begin to allow myself to hope. Maybe Rachael changed her mind? Or maybe I imagined the whole thing? Maybe she doesn't know about the email to Blankly, maybe Jurgen was just making a general inquiry?

'Hey, Claude, you're on TV!'

I look up. There I am on the plaza, explaining to a journalist why it is a very good thing that the government is giving the last of its money to a failed bank.

'I never noticed how big your head was before,' Jocelyn Lock-hart says.

'Or your fucking accent,' Gary McCrum says. 'It's so *French*.'

'Oh shit,' Ish says. She is looking into her computer; it's as if I can hear her go pale. She turns to me with eyes like moons and says in a hoarse whisper, 'Just got a mail from Rachael. She wants me to come up for a chat.'

'Oh?' I try to sound casual.

'What do you think it means?'

'Hmm,' I stroke my chin. 'Well, probably, she just wants to see how you are. Talk about life generally. You know. A chat.'

'That woman's never had a chat in her life,' Ish says. Her face is like a ghost's; the fake tan somehow makes her look paler still. 'Christ – you reckon it's about the email? Am I going to get canned?'

'Of course not,' I say firmly. 'You are a valued member of the team.'

'Oh God,' she says, and covers her face with her hands.

As soon as the lift door closes over her I run to the department head's office.

'I don't fucking know, Claude,' Liam English says. 'She dropped the fucking ball in a major way. We're in the middle of not one but two giant takeovers, and she's writing the CEO *letters*, like my fucking eight-year-old asking Santa Claus to save the rainforest?' He tugs furiously on his electronic cigarette, sends coils of vapour ghosting over his head. 'It's not just the fucking impudence of it. We've borrowed up to our tits to pull these deals off. We don't want anything happening that'd give our backers the heebie-jeebies. And here's Ish, trying to get us to carry the can for global fucking warming! What if the press got hold of that email? *Bank Drowns Primitive Island Race* – how's that going to fucking look?'

'Isn't it possible that helping Kokomoko could bring some good publicity?' I plead. 'You know, banks have had a lot of bad

354

press, but here's one doing something positive? Ready to act ethically?'

Liam sits back in his chair, looks at me square in the eye until I feel my will buckle and collapse. As I return to my desk, I catch Kevin tracking me: calculating what's just happened, how much it's damaged me, the best means of taking advantage.

'Fax for you, Claude,' Kimberlee says, clipping in from Reception.

I take the paper from her hand. There is no text; it is a solid block of blackness. 'What is this?'

'That's how it came out,' she says, shrugging. 'But with your name on the top.'

I stare at the page. It reminds me eerily of the painting I saw in William O'Hara's house, some deathly message coiled just beneath its surface.

'Looks like someone's marked your cards, Claude-o,' Gary says, without looking away from his screen.

'Bollocks, it's just some student trying to use up our ink supply,' Jocelyn says.

'Look out, capitalism,' Gary says.

The lift doors open. I spin round in my chair just as Ish emerges. No security guards with her: that's a good sign. Yet she looks shell-shocked – grey as ashes, her eyes wide but focused on nothing.

'Are you all right? What happened?'

'I'm not sure.'

'You're not sure?'

Ish begins to speak, then, glancing up, realizes that everyone in the office is staring at her – with a kind of appreciative mystification, as if five minutes previously they'd seen her jump out the window. Tugging my sleeve, she leads me into the lobby.

'Rachael was livid about that email,' she says. 'You'd think I'd sent Blankly a photocopy of my arse.'

'But she didn't . . . you're not . . . ?'

'She was going to, I have no fucking doubt. But then in the middle of everything – Howie called.'

'Howie?'

'Yeah, he phoned down and insisted he be put through to her, there and then. So she listens to him for a couple of minutes, barely says a word herself. Next thing you know, she's sending me back downstairs, telling me in the future to keep her in the loop.'

'What loop?'

'From what she said it sounded like the island was part of some ATCM investment strategy.'

'ATCM? Howie's fund?' The more she tells me, the more confused I am.

'She says if I'd clarified that with her, none of this would be an issue.'

'Wait . . . Howie's fund is going to invest in Kokomoko?' This is like hearing that Hitler has deployed the Waffen-SS to build an owl sanctuary.

'That's what he told her. I mean, I presume he just made it up, to get me off the hook.'

She is calling his mobile but there is no answer. 'Fuck it,' she says. 'I'm going to find out what's going on.'

'What about the Chinese wall?' I say. But she has already charged off up the stairs to Agron Torabundo Credit Management.

The factotum who answers the door is not pleased to see us. 'You can't be up here!' he scolds.

Ish just pushes past him; the factotum throws his hands in the air, then promptly vanishes, leaving us to find our own way.

Life is very different here on the ninth floor. There are paintings on the walls, and fresh flowers on every flat surface; operatives zip back and forth in loafers and chinos, exuding an air of easeful mastery that is a million miles from the feverish hamster-wheeling of the research area, to say nothing of the bellowing chaos of the traders' den. The only discordant note is struck by the two men sitting squeezed into a comically small and ornate chaise longue – burly, lumpen characters with a single eyebrow between them, furrowed menacingly at anyone who happens to look their way.

'Ish!' Howie is standing in an office doorway, waving his arm at us as if from the top deck of a yacht. To one side of him, an astonishingly tall and beautiful woman is helping a stubby, moustachioed man into a camel-hair coat. Whatever has happened in the office, the stubby man seems very pleased about it. He shakes Howie's hand and takes his leave; the burly men rise and button their jackets.

'Make yourselves at home,' Howie says, beckoning us in. The office is enormous, with an enormous monitor and an enormous view of the mountains. On the enormous desk sits a holdall filled with banknotes.

'Are we interrupting something . . . ?'

'New client,' Howie says. He zips the bag closed; a moment later the beautiful woman returns and takes it from his hand. She looks a little like one of the dancers from Velvet Dream's; her attire – extremely high heels, metallic micro-skirt, huge hoop earrings – might comfortably be described as *unsecretarial*.

'Zenya, babes, I'm not taking any calls for the next few minutes, okay?' Howie tells her.

She trembles doubtfully on the threshold then turns away, pronouncing his words silently to herself as if trying to keep them in her head.

'*Sex alphabet,*' Ish mouths to me.

Howie slides into his seat and smiles expansively. 'So the two of you have practically given Rachael a prolapse,' he says. 'That deserves a drink.' Fishing under his desk, he produces a bottle and three glasses. 'You heard the Secretary of the US Treasury was on to her about Royal Irish?'

'The US Treasury?' I repeat. 'In Washington?'

'Very, very concerned that nobody loses money,' Howie says, pouring out three-finger measures of single malt and passing them to us.

'Meaning Walter?' I say.

'Meaning Danforth,' Howie says. 'Danforth's deep into them.'

'What's Royal Irish got to do with the US Treasury?' Ish says. 'And what's Walter got to do with Royal Irish? And Danforth?'

'Ask Crazy Frog here. His report was all set to nuke the lot of them.'

Ish turns to me questioningly, but I don't reply. I have no idea how Danforth could be involved in Royal Irish; I'm feeling increasingly like the whole day is one ongoing dream.

'I don't know what they're getting so riled up about,' Howie says. 'The Minister's not making the decisions any more, so your report's pretty much irrelevant anyway. But you know the Americans, they want every box ticked – cheers.'

We return the toast circumspectly. The exuberant burn of the whiskey seems exactly wrong for this time and situation.

'So I just met Rachael,' Ish says.

'Yeah!' Howie yelps with laughter. 'Jesus, Ish. Asking Porter to save a bunch of cavemen in the middle of the Pacific! What were you thinking? Did you have your period or something?'

'How did you find out?' Ish asks, in a small, flat voice.

'Blankly! You should have heard him! *Who does this little bitch think she is? I'll piss those fucking monkeys underwater myself!*' He laughs to himself. 'Well, anyway. I managed to sort it out. Just don't send him any more emails. Seriously, even if the Earth's about to crash into the sun.'

'Thanks,' Ish says meekly, chafing her legs together like a little girl.

'No problem,' Howie says.

'What did you say to him?'

The opulent smile again, dripping diamonds. 'I told him you were irreplaceable. Which is the truth.'

'Rachael said something about you investing in Kokomoko.'

'Yeah,' Howie chuckles.

'That was BS, right?'

'Nope, that was true too,' Howie says, and then, 'Well, well, look who's out of his box.'

Grisha is eyeing us warily from the doorway. He's lost weight, and gained deep rings around his eyes; in his filthy clothes he looks like a defrocked Rasputin, chained up in some dungeon of the mind.

'What are you doing here, Ivan? Smell the pretty lady, did you?'

Sticking close to the wall, Grisha sidles in and hovers behind us, a blurred darkness like an unexplained shadow.

'I'm just telling Ish about Phase Two,' Howie says to him. Grisha only grunts.

I take the bait. 'Phase Two?'

'It's still in development. We haven't thought of a name for it yet. Probably Gaia or Ecofund or something like that.'

'What's it got to do with the island?' Ish asks, and only some-one who knew her well would pick up the trace of dread in her voice.

'To get Porter and Rachael off the warpath' – Howie stretches back, putting his arms behind his head – 'I had to persuade them you were doing a nixer for me, and that this island of yours had something to do with the fund. Which, let me tell you, was not easy. I mean, it's got no infrastructure, no exports, no educated workforce. Plus there's the small matter that it's about to be buried by a tidal wave. Very difficult to pass it off as a business venture. But then it hit me: maybe that's the point.'

He pauses dramatically, and it strikes me, just as it did on the hotel balcony that night, that this is a performance. But I can't tell what kind; I can't tell whether he believes what he's saying, or even whether he wants us to believe it.

'How is it the point?' I say at last.

'I'm glad you asked me that, Crazy. Now, you two might want to hold on to your seats, because this is some heady stuff. So I told you before about how our little fund here operates. That by using a lot of very, very complicated maths, Grisha's established a financial instrument that can essentially reverse the polarity of losses, meaning that if you invest with us, you're guaranteed to make money. Which in today's uncertain investment climate is an attractive proposition. And we've been doing pretty well for a couple of greenhorns, haven't we, Grisha?'

Grisha doesn't reply, just blazes darkly by the door.

'Until now, we've been using the instrument defensively, as a safeguard. This losses-to-profits operation isn't just a matter of changing minuses into pluses, after all. It's a difficult process. But for a while now we've been looking at other options, other ways to maximize our returns. None of them seemed quite right. And then you came along with your island, and everything just fell into place.'

He drains his whiskey, pours himself a fresh measure. 'This is actually very good,' he notes.

'The island,' Ish presses.

'Oh yeah. So I thought to myself, what if, instead of using the instrument as a backup, we used it *offensively*? You'll remember Wall Street did that with credit default swaps – first they used them to insure their own loans against default, and then they started using them to bet on other people's loans defaulting. What if we started deliberately targeting losing propositions? Sank our money into investments we knew were going to fail, that no one else would touch – could we use providential antinomies to turn those losses into profits? So that the worse something did, the more we'd make?'

'Wait,' Ish says, in a high, strained voice, 'are you talking about investing in the island . . . *because* it's going to sink?'

'I'm talking about going beyond the counterintuitive.' Howie's voice shrugs off its ironic mantle, takes on an oracular resonance.

'I'm talking about *monetizing failure*. If you could do that . . . what would it mean?'

'But that is pure alchemy,' I say. 'Monetizing failure – it's completely irrational. I can't understand how such a thing could be possible.'

'Of course you can't. You're not a mathematical genius. And much as I like you, Claude, you'll understand if I don't tell you our secret formula. You know what something like that is worth? As it is we've got to keep Grisha here under lock and key. Good thing he doesn't like going outside, right, Grisha?'

The Russian smiles an empty smile. Ish shakes her head, wilts back in her chair like a flower sprayed with a toxin.

'Genius or not, no one's going to invest in something they know will lose money,' I say. 'It's like asking them to throw their savings in the fire.'

'You're right about that, Crazy.' Howie commends me with the whiskey glass. 'Getting people on board, that's the drawback. But say to start out we don't pick something utterly hopeless. Instead we come up with something that could theoretically turn a buck. For instance, we put a golf course on the island, and a five-star hotel –'

'A *golf* course?' Ish repeats in a half-shriek.

'Well, sure. It's all right there in your email. The rolling meadows, the sand dunes, all that. It's perfect.'

'But the island's tiny,' Ish protests. 'And the meadows are where the islanders graze their goats.'

'In fairness, people aren't going to travel thousands of miles to see a bunch of goats,' Howie says. 'Anyway, the point is that this time round it's the investment proper that's the insurance. See? If the big wave never comes, we can make money from the hotel – a conventional return, call it. But if the wave *does* come, as seems statistically likely, and if the island goes under with our investment – that's when we really cash in. Call that' – with a bow to me – 'your *irrational* return.'

Neither Ish nor I speak. She is pinned back in her chair, eyes huge, as if she has witnessed an atrocity.

'Come on, guys! Show some enthusiasm!' Howie half-laughs, half-shouts. 'Don't you see the bottom line here? Even when it all goes tits up, you still get paid! Profit is finally liberated from circumstance! It's the Holy Grail! It's the singularity!'

'It's madness,' I say.

'The investors don't think it's madness, Claude.' Howie shakes his head. 'That last meeting I had' – he gestures towards the door the stubby man with the moustache recently exited – 'he's putting a million in it. A million of his own money, for something that doesn't even have a name yet.'

'Then he is mad too.'

'Maybe it sounds mad now. But that's because you're ignoring the existing information. The smart investor knows that in a few years from now there aren't going to *be* any more conventional profits. What's on the cards for Ish's little island isn't a one-off. This is just the beginning.'

'You're talking about global warming.'

'I'm talking about the whole fucking shooting match, Claude. Seizures in the electricity grid, degradation of ecosystems, the spread of epidemics, the disintegration of the financial system – they're all part of the same phenomenon. Civilization has become a bubble. When it pops, it's going to be very, very messy. Even in the best-case scenario, no one's going to make a cent for three hundred years – unless they can work out how to make loss pay.'

'But that means profiting from human misery!' Two bright spots have appeared on Ish's cheeks.

'Profiting from conditions we did nothing to create,' Howie says. 'What's wrong with that?'

'Obviously it's fucking wrong, Howie. How's anything going to get *better* if your stupid fund pays out every time there's a humanitarian disaster?'

'I don't understand why you're getting so emotional,' he says.

'It's maths, that's all. It's a new mathematical model, according to which capital will no longer be adversely affected by developments in the non-banking world. How can that be a bad thing?'

'Because we *live* in the non-banking world! The non-banking world is the *world*, don't you get it? What's the point of making millions if in a few years the whole planet will be underwater?'

Howie just looks at her, with the dumb, bestial eyes of a lamb; Ish emits a furious gurgle, then jumps to her feet and stamps out of the room.

'You're welcome,' Howie says. Grisha chuckles approvingly. 'Okay, Ivan, off you go,' Howie tells him. Still chuckling, the Russian lurches out.

'Christ, he gives me the fucking creeps,' Howie says. 'I don't think he's washed once since he got here.'

I take a last sip of my whiskey and rise to my feet. 'I should get back too,' I say. 'This has been very entertaining. Between ourselves, though, you don't honestly believe it can work, do you?'

Howie laughs. 'I'm just giving people what they want, Claude. That's all I've ever tried to do.'

'You think this is what they want? To invest in catastrophe?'

'Of course it is. A great big flood's coming, we've got the lifeboat? An Ark for the chosen few, where they can relax with a martini, watch everybody else drown? It's exactly what they want. It's what they've wanted their whole lives.'

'But this' – I gesture around me at the computer, the office, the rooms and staff beyond, the external manifestations of the fund – 'it's not an Ark. It isn't anything. It's a fiction. A fairy tale.'

'We're in the business of fairy tales, Claude.' He swirls his glass a moment, then says, 'Did you know I started in stats? That was my undergraduate degree. In my final year, I did a paper on salaries-to-performance ratios in the City of London. One of the Big Five banks let me and a couple of friends come in and analyse the track record of their best traders. We spent a month going through five years of figures: the stocks they'd picked, the hits, the misses, the money they'd made and the money they'd lost. What we found was that a random selection would have given better results than their picks. One year one guy might be lucky, another year another might be lucky. But year-on-year consistency was close to zero. Meaning that if you'd pulled the stocks out of a hat, or had a monkey pick them by throwing darts at a board, in the long run you would have done better.

'Anyhow, we go to the bank's Chief Financial Officer with our findings. We're expecting they'll cause a stir. If there's nothing more to it than blind chance, then the bank's whole trading operation is a sham! So yeah, we're pretty excited. And the CFO listens and says it's a very interesting study. That night, he has one of his minions take us out on the piss – cocktails, strippers, the whole bit, and then we go back to college and that's the end of that. Except that when I finish my degree I find I can't get a job in London for love nor money. No one in the Square Mile will touch me, not to clean the fucking toilets. So it's back to the Emerald Isle with my tail between my legs.'

He smiles up at me; I gaze back at him, not understanding.

'It's meaningless, Claude. All of this,' he says, flicking a hand at the window, 'and all of this,' tapping the Bloomberg, 'and everything you do and everything everyone like you does all day long in cities around the world – it's meaningless. You don't have the information to predict what the future will bring. Yes, you think you can make an educated guess. This whole trillion-dollar industry is predicated on the belief that clever men can make educated guesses. But it's an illusion. In actuality, your educated guesses are just pissing in the wind. Statistically speaking.'

He rotates his tumbler on the glass-topped desk. 'I guess the good news for us,' he says, 'is that people like illusions. They like strong narratives, they like good stories. The one about the brilliant CEO who makes tough decisions and turns the company around. The one about the clever man in the very expensive suit whose penetrating analysis can tell if the share price will go up or

364

down. Even now, when everybody's out for our blood, they still want to believe that we've got the answers. That *someone's* got the answers. They'd rather believe that than the truth.' He tosses back his whiskey. 'In fact that's about the one sure bet you can make. If it's a choice between a difficult truth and a simple lie, people will take the lie every time. Even if it kills them.'

Halfway down the stairs I find Ish sitting on a step; from above, I can see dark roots growing through her blonde hair. I'm about to tell her what Howie more or less admitted – that Phase Two is a mirage, a trap for unwary investors, that nothing will come of it. But was that what he said? When I revisit the scene of only a moment ago, I find it has already become shifting, elusive, uncertain, as though the conversation had contained some hidden application, some proprietary software that now acts to shut down any memory of it, every detail, large and small, vanishing out of my mind even as I watch . . .

She wipes her eyes perfunctorily. 'What's this about Walter?' she says.

Reluctantly, I tell her about the concealed stake in Royal, the rewritten report.

'Fucking hell,' she says, shaking her head.

Outside, night is setting in: across the river, the floors of the unoccupied office blocks fluoresce, a thousand cold fires blazing for no one.

'I wish Rachael had fired me,' Ish says. 'Then I wouldn't have had to find out about any of this. I would have felt like I'd done something noble. Instead of helping Howie turn the end of the world into a cash cow.'

'It's not as bad as you think.'

'It is. It's worse. Actual people are going to be affected by this. People who don't know what a derivative is. People who don't even have bank accounts. They're going to wake up some morning and find they're not able to buy food, because some genius

365

five thousand miles away has found a new way to game the system.'

'It won't work. It can't. It doesn't make any sense.'

'Nothing we do makes any sense. Doesn't seem to stop it.' She turns to look at me. 'What kind of people are we, Claude? Like – what kind of people are we?'

'None of this is your fault.'

'I don't know about that.'

'If Howie hadn't thought of it, someone else would. You were trying to help, that's all.'

She snuffles, blows out her cheeks, then lets out a single bark of a laugh. 'I did have my period,' she says.

'Excuse me?'

'When I sent the email to Porter? And Howie was saying I must have had my period, to do something so emotional and mad? I did have it.'

'It is not emotional and mad to want to help people,' I tell her, but she doesn't reply, just gazes out at the scraps of light on the river as they glister and disappear into the blue-black opacity of the night.

4
King Tide

This sucker could go down.

George W. Bush

The Minister dies next morning. I'm taking a call when I see the news flash up on the terminal. Reflexively, I stand to check the big screen mounted on the wall; all around the office my colleagues do likewise, popping up over the dividers like so many Italian-suited meerkats.

The announcement is followed by a lavish package of biography and tributes, clearly put together weeks before: pictures of the Minister as a child, sitting on a donkey in knickerbockers; rasping footage of him as an ambitious young TD; fellow politicos voicing the usual saccharine platitudes.

'Poor cunt,' Jocelyn says.

'Maybe now they'll appoint somebody competent,' Brent 'Crude' Kelleher says.

Jurgen watches, arms folded, from the back of the room; even when the obit comes to the Royal Irish scandal, and the controversial report, he remains utterly impassive.

The market is equivocal about the Minister's death. The financial news is dominated instead by yet another banking scandal: a trader in a Parisian bank has embezzled an as-yet-unknown number of millions from a client account.

'He was on the Delta One desk at Pécuchet, but he'd started out in back office and he knew all the security codes,' Joe Peston says. 'Sneaked in at night when all the drones had gone home, forged a whole load of documents signing the client's money over to himself.'

'Wow, old school,' says Kevin. On the screen a bewildered-looking man in a black suit and black tie is being led in handcuffs to a police van.

'The French press are calling him "Pierrot",' Joe says. 'Because he's all in black.'

'The famous French sense of humour,' Jocelyn says.

'How much did he take?' I ask.

'Not a huge amount originally. Ten million or so from some mutual fund. They hadn't even noticed, it was the crazy trades he was making with it that got him busted when Internal Compliance finally woke up.'

'Ten million euro!' Kevin nudges me joshingly. 'That'd buy a lot of frog's legs, eh, Claude?'

The news lifts everybody's spirits – partly *Schadenfreude*, partly bankerly superstition, the belief that at any given time there are only a limited number of Bad Things that can happen, which if they've already happened to someone else therefore can't happen to you.

I try to use it to break the ice with Ish, who ever since the Howie episode has been monosyllabic. 'This rogue trader will hurt Pécuchet,' I say.

'Good on him,' she says. She is glowering into her computer as if attempting to destroy it telepathically.

'Good on him for stealing ten million euro?' I repeat.

'Yeah.'

'And losing it all on futile bets?'

'Yeah.'

'Money that was enough to build a whole school, that instead goes up in smoke?'

'Oh yeah, like they were going to use one cent of it to build schools.'

'Well, they were not just going to throw it away.'

'You're right, Claude. They were going to use it to add a few more inches to some squillionaire's fucking money mountain, so he could stand on top of it, waving his dick at everybody below. That's what they were going to do. That's all any of us ever do.'

I think about this, rocking gently in my chair. Ish hammers at her keyboard, ignoring the lights on her phone. 'Is everything all right?' I say.

'I don't know what I'm doing here any more,' she blurts. 'I feel like a prostitute – worse than a prostitute, I mean, at least prostitutes have the excuse of really needing the money.'

'But you do need the money,' I say. 'For your mortgage.' I intend it as a consolation, but that is not how it sounds.

A little later, Jurgen appears, descending in a kind of hail of false heartiness. 'Claude, Claude, Claude,' he says, clapping me on the shoulder. 'How is everything, Claude? What are you working on at the moment?'

I explain that, in anticipation of more fallout from Pécuchet, I'm changing from a Neutral to a Sell recommend on several Continental banks – then tail off. Jurgen is not listening; instead he is merely nodding vacantly while staring over my shoulder at my terminal.

'Are you looking for something?' I ask.

'Hmm? Me?' he says innocently, now scrutinizing the documents on my desk.

'Are you . . . are you *spying* on me?'

'Of course not,' he says, and then, 'What areas, specifically, did you think I was spying on?'

'What's going on?' I snap upright in my chair.

'Nothing,' Jurgen assures me. 'Except that HR has confirmed you used to work in the back office, like Pécuchet's rogue trader did.'

'That was years ago,' I protest, 'in a different bank, in a different country. I have never even been in the BOT back office.'

'Exactly,' he agrees. 'So it is safe to say you are not embezzling funds from your present clients.'

'Are you seriously asking me this?'

'It has come down from Compliance,' Jurgen says apologetically. 'Everyone with a back-office history is being checked, across the whole bank.'

'That's ridiculous,' Ish says. 'Claude's as straight as a die. He won't even take sugar home from the canteen.'

Jurgen's interrogative gaze swivels on to her. 'Sugar sachets are company property,' he says.

'You have my word, I have not been embezzling, forging or making unauthorized trades,' I say.

'That is good enough for me, Claude.' Again he pats my shoulder. 'However, we will need to take your hard drive, just to make sure.' He motions over two men in black T-shirts, who set about detaching plugs and cables, and finally lift my terminal off the desk.

'Is this absolutely necessary?'

'Phone,' one of them says to me, holding out his hand.

'How am I supposed to work?'

'It won't take long,' Jurgen promises.

'This fucking place,' Ish says when they have finished. 'I swear, as soon as I get my next bonus I am *gone*.'

'Right,' I say.

'I mean it this time.'

I dig out some old paperwork and spread it over my denuded desk, but am too furious to do anything. I turn to the TV: it is showing a report from Oran, where an airstrike on rebel positions is believed to have secured the region at last. A clip of the Caliph and the British ex-PM smiling together, ringed by Imperial Guards, is followed by shots of smoking wasteland, weeping women, charred body parts. Oil prices have stabilized following the news, a voice tells us.

I get up, go to the window. The rain is pouring down interminably, turning the world into thin, shifting vertical bands like monochrome ribbons, as if the whole day's been fed into the shredder. Where is Ariadne? I think with a pang. And where is Paul? Has he given up on me? Did he decide the banker was unsalvageable after all, even in fiction?

'Call for you, Claude,' Kimberlee says.

The voice on the line is heavily accented, and sounds upset. It takes me a moment to identify it as Clizia's.

'He got a review,' she says.

'Paul?' I'm confused. 'For the proposal?'

'For *Clown*,' she says. 'Some idiot on Apeiron. He is going crazy. Please, Frenchman, you must come!'

I fetch my tablet from the apartment so I can read the review in the taxi. Posted last night by someone styling himself Wombat Willy, it is headed 'A Fiasco Is Not a Circus' and consists of a long list of criticisms, which includes, though is not limited to, the unfunniness of the clown, incorrect inspection procedures followed by the health and safety officer, the implausible ending (in which Bobo saves Timmy from a subdural haematoma by performing a one-man show that keeps him laughing until the ambulance arrives ('SHOW ME ONE MEDICAL TEXTBOOK THAT SAYS THIS!!!')) and a misleading comparison on the jacket copy to Bimal Banerjee's *The Clowns of Sorrow*. He also notes that the book was delivered two days late and that he got a paper cut taking it out of the box, before giving it a rating of two thistles and a swastika.

Strange bestial noises can be heard as I come up the corridor.

'Daddy's writing his book,' Remington tells me as he lets me in.

'Is that right.'

A loud crash issues from somewhere behind him.

'I'm writing a book too. Look.' He hands me a sheet of paper, on which he has scrawled REMINGTIM REMNINGTONTON REMEMINSON and other variants in crayon.

'Very good! Is your mother . . . ah.'

Clizia, in a dressing gown, comes out of the nursery with a phone to her ear. 'Because I can't,' she is saying. Her expression is anguished and there are tears in her eyes. 'I just can't. Maybe next week. I have to go.' She rings off, looks up at me exhaustedly.

'Thanks for coming,' she says. 'I didn't know who else I can call.'

'That's all right.'

A bellowing comes from the bedroom, followed by a series of thuds.

'When did he see the review?'

'An hour ago. But this whole week, he is acting strange. Not sleep, not eat, walking around talking to himself – then he sees this Internet, and . . .'

'All right. Don't worry.'

I knock on the bedroom door, then enter. A Louis Quatorze chair lies on its side; many of the towers of books are now scattered over the floor.

'What's the point, Claude?' Paul cries on seeing me. 'You work and you slave for years, you make sacrifices and put your family through hell, just to get it in the neck from some guy calling himself Wombat Willy?'

Clizia is right: he looks quite disturbed. His hair, clothes, even eyebrows, are askew, as in some allegorical figure of Frazzlement.

'Why should you care what Wombat Willy thinks?' I cajole. 'This is just one person, who we know nothing about. He could be a fanatical racist, or a chronic masturbator – or maybe he is a she, and enormously fat, and for years she has not left her house, which she shares with her eight cats, also enormously fat.'

'Pretty sure it's a he,' Paul says morosely. 'I looked up his other reviews. He gave a lightning bolt and a Buckingham Palace to the Phillips For Him BodyShave. He called it the gold standard of ball-hair removal.'

'That just proves my point,' I say. 'You're an artist. You can't be dictated to by the market. Do you think, if he were writing today, Shakespeare would care if he got only one and a half pineapples for *Hamlet*, or three smiley faces for *Romeo and Juliet*? Do you think James Joyce would rewrite *Ulysses* because some Internet wombat said there's not enough story? All of these books' – gesturing at the volumes that now litter the floor – 'how many do you think would never have been written if the authors gave up because of one man who spends his time writing anonymous essays about ball hair?'

'That's easy for you to say. I need readers, Claude. I need those scumballs to feed my wife and child. Now everybody who comes to the website to look at my book is going to end up buying a stupid multi-head razor instead!' He rights the chair and flumps down in it. Behind him, in the half-light cast by a fallen lamp, I can see a long dagger of damp blackening the flowery wallpaper.

'How is the proposal going?'

'Terribly,' he says.

I feel a surge of frustration. 'I thought we worked everything out. We have a hero, a heroine, a good idea of the plot. What's the problem?'

'The problem is *writing*, Claude. The problem is writing, and writing is the problem. Coming up with an idea is just like the entrance ticket into this enormous fucking labyrinth of – oh, what now?'

The door opens and Remington marches in, holding out his sheet, to which he has added ERMIINGTREM in blue crayon. 'Dad, my story has a new bit.'

'That's great, buddy, I'll read it later.'

'Read it now.'

'I'll read it when it's finished.'

'Now!' Remington says.

'Fuck!' his father exclaims. He jumps up, goes to the door. 'Clizia!'

'I'm on the phone!' the voice comes back.

'For Christ's *sake!*' Paul says, stamping out to find her.

'I'd like to hear your story,' I say to Remington.

The boy turns to me seriously. 'It's about a boy called Remington,' he says.

'And what happens to him?'

'He goes away with his mama.'

I start. 'Where does he go?' I say – but before the boy can answer, Clizia comes into the room. She appears shaken, as though after some tumultuous passage.

'Who keeps calling you?' Paul demands, following after her.

'The captain of the volleyball team,' she says.

'Can't she take no for an answer?'

Clizia affixes a bleached, perfunctory smile. 'Now, little one,' she says to Remington, and she picks him up and carries him out of the room.

Paul sinks back in his chair, drapes his wrist over his eyes. 'God, I'm so tired,' he says.

'Let's get moving with this,' I say, rousing him. Clearly there is more riding on this proposal than money, even if he can't see it. 'Where exactly are you stuck?'

'I'm stuck where I've always been stuck, with this damn unintelligible banker! I can't make sense of a single thing he does!'

'Forget about his job for now. You were right, it's too complicated and will only bore people. Stick with the love story. The girl who rescues him from the bank.'

'But that's just it!' Paul pounds his palm on the armchair. 'Why does he get the girl? What does she see in him?'

She sees the person he could be, I begin to say – but that notion, so perfect on the sixth floor of Transaction House, here seems hollow, pallid, woefully naïve.

'It's one thing trying to get you a date with a waitress in real life.' Paul is pacing back and forth now over the shoals of books. 'But in a novel there needs to be some kind of logic. There needs to be some kind of justice. He can't just *buy* her.'

'He is not buying her. He is in love with her.'

'So what? There could be umpteen people in love with her. There could be some sweet, idealistic, totally broke young painter that completely adores her. Why should the banker get her?'

'Why shouldn't he?' I say, feeling a glow of anger rise from my stomach. 'She redeems him.'

'How is he redeemed? What does he sacrifice?'

'Maybe he quits his job.'

'That's it? He waltzes off into the sunset with his pockets full of money and we're all supposed to cheer? That's fucking lame, Claude. He's never done a good thing for anyone, give me one reason why he should get the girl too.'

'Because that's how life is,' I snap.

'Well, no one wants to read that story, believe me.'

'You're the expert on what people don't want to read,' I return, but he doesn't hear. He's storming back and forth, berating himself in the same deranged manner I heard when I came in.

'Banerjee was right,' he is saying. 'It just can't be done. It just doesn't work any more.'

My anger fades, and I feel a pang of guilt: have I done this to him? Have I infected him, and his wife, with my own misplaced hopes? Or is there some way forward?

'Didn't you tell me once' – I am embarrassed at the desperation evident in my voice – 'that at some point in his life everyone finds himself at a crossroads? Where the clock strikes thirteen, and he must make a choice who he will be, good or bad? Can't we find that moment for the banker?'

Paul looks down at his hands; I have a strange sense of impending dissolution, like an actor at an audition who has delivered his lines and now stares into the darkness, waiting for his invisible judges to dismiss him.

'What were you saying a minute ago, about listening to the market,' he says, with his head bowed.

'I said you shouldn't do it.'

'No, I think you were on to something. Maybe that's the angle we need to take. Work out what people want, and go from there.'

'Work out what Wombat Willy wants?'

'He buys books, doesn't he? I've got to make some money from this, Claude. I'm on the fucking ropes here. The whole industry's on the ropes. It isn't the time to be precious.' He kneads his scalp distractedly. 'So what is it they want? Strong narratives, right? Exciting stories, characters you remember. Drama, violence, murdered prostitutes. A serial killer is on the loose, that kind of thing.'

'That sounds like the kind of stupid *scénario* the world is already full of.'

'Well, we can spin it, right? Tweak the formula. The murderer's the detective, the murderer's the narrator, something like that. The first thing we need to do is think of a fresh angle.' He brings his fingertips to his temple, as if he were trying to tune in a radio. 'You said something interesting there about *Ulysses* not having enough plot. So how about . . . how about we *give* it a plot? We use the characters and the basic set-up – but with a high-octane, twenty-first-century story!'

'Are you talking about . . . ?'

'A sequel to *Ulysses*!' A feverish light dances in his eyes, sickly sweat burnishing his forehead. 'Think about it! It's the most literary book there is! And yet it ends on this completely inconclusive note. That's why for generations readers have been crying out for a follow-up. And now here it is!' He seizes his pen, writes with such vigour that he tears the page. 'It's ten years after the last book ended. Leopold Bloom is divorced from Molly. He's hit the bottle, he's bitter, he's jaded, he's working as a cop in New York City. A rash of murders has broken out across the city. The killer's leaving obscure literary references written on their bodies . . .'

Pornography, the word pops into my mind. I am still hoping he will break off, crack a grin, tell me *Gotcha!*; but on the contrary, it only gets worse.

'Jesus, Claude, I think I've got it. How about this for a twist. When you get to the last page of the book, Bloom goes, "I can now reveal the murderer was . . . YOU!"'

'What?'

'"YOU!"' he says again, pointing his finger at my chest, almost beside himself with excitement.

'Me?'

'You, like, whoever's reading the book. Think about it, who's the very last person the reader will suspect of committing the crime? Herself, right? Imagine how she's going to feel when the detective says, "It was YOU!" And we could have like a 3D finger pointing out of the page!'

'How can the reader have committed a crime in a fictional world to which she has no access?'

'That's a minor detail,' he says. 'Anyway, why should the reader get off the hook? She's as guilty as anybody. Don't you see? This turns the whole crime genre on its head! It'll be huge!'

He returns to his scribbling, giggling to himself all the while; he doesn't notice as I slip out of the room.

In the kitchen, I find Clizia placing a bucket under a drip. 'You have a little leak?' I say, though the leak is more of a stream, descending steadily from a grey mass in the ceiling.

'Oh, this old place!' Clizia says gaily. Then, glancing at the bedroom, with the same false smile, she says, 'He's forgotten about the review?'

'I think it's given him some interesting new ideas!' I say. We both laugh, though I am not sure why. 'And you?' I inquire. 'Your ankle, it is better?'

'Vot?' she says, still smiling.

'When you spoke on the phone earlier, to your coach, I thought . . .' Clizia looks at me uncomprehendingly. 'Never mind,' I say.

'Bye bye, Claude,' Remington, now drawing a large multicoloured R, sings from under her feet.

'Goodbye, my friends,' I say, in the kindly fashion of the family doctor in a nineteenth-century play. 'I will see you both very soon, I'm sure.'

I am halfway down the corridor when she catches up with me.
'Frenchman!'

I turn. The smile is gone; her fingers are tight around my flesh.
'He will write the book this time – won't he?'

What can I tell her?

'Of course,' I say.

A dark-skinned boy runs into a crystal-blue sea. A man in a suit hands his passport to a ticket agent. The boy leaps from the water with a shell in his hand, a plane lifts into a powder-blue sky. A young woman sits cross-legged on the sand, boring a hole in the shell. More shells lie in a pile at her feet. She and the boy turn at the sound of a motor. It is the man in the suit, speeding over the waves in a powerboat. The boat runs up on the beach. The boy leads the man to the spot where the woman sits. The man opens his briefcase and takes out a thread. The woman smiles, and begins to string the shells on to it.

Agron Torabundo, a voiceover says. *Not global. Planetary.*

'It's testing really well,' Skylark Fitzgibbon says, folding closed the screen. 'In European and American markets.'

Be careful what you wish for, isn't that what they say? Ish has got what she wanted: plans are in motion to 'save' Kokomoko. Already sea walls are being constructed, sand imported to replace what's been taken; this Skylark Fitzgibbon, who emerged from the Marketing Department last week like a kind of Barbie-shaped Erinys, sends us regular updates on the golf course, now to be located at the northern end of the island in an area she refers to variously as 'almost uninhabited' and 'effectively uninhabited'.

'One last thing: what do you think those shell necklaces would retail for? I know they're not for sale, but if they were, does eighty-five dollars sound right? Ballpark?'

A paranoid mind might suspect that all of this had been put together specifically to torture Ish. Every email, every peppy chat with Skylark, visibly reduces her, as if some verdant last fragment of her own simpler, happier past were being surgically excised. But there is nothing she can do.

My computer has been returned; getting back to work, I find the world in its customary state of turmoil. The impending investigation of money-laundering by a major British bank is causing havoc on the FTSE. In Greece, a bomb in an Athens bank has killed three tellers, one of them a pregnant woman; investors respond by buying up German bunds. The euro is in crisis, America is in crisis, the market is on the brink of meltdown yet again, like a hysterical ex-lover who keeps calling you up, threatening suicide.

Ireland, on the other hand, is weirdly calm. Economically, the situation is worse than ever, but the Minister's death seems to have functioned as a kind of pressure valve. Thousands attend the state funeral, and as the encomiums keep coming, public anger is diverted to other, less disruptive emotions: pity, guilt, a kind of defanged, non-specific regret. The marches peter out; awkward questions about the Royal Irish report dry up; the abusive calls and sinister black faxes, which I had been receiving in a steady stream, dwindle almost to nothing; and one morning I arrive at work to find Jurgen standing at the window with a mug of coffee and a contented air, like a man surveying a pile of freshly chopped logs. At first I can't see what's giving him so much satisfaction. Then I realize. The quay is bare; the zombies are gone. It looks as if the pavement has been scoured to ensure not a trace of them remains, though down in the water, fragments of placards, bottles and items of clothing bob forlornly.

'Police?'

'Local people taking matters into their own hands.' His smile is as sheer and white as a cliff face. 'The Irish understand what needs to be done.'

I think about Ariadne's friend with the dreadlocks, try to summon up some spark of triumph. Nothing comes. Instead I feel as if she's been banished too, scrubbed away from my world, even though I can see her, just about, through the dawn-dazed glass of the Ark.

AgroBOT rampages on. The acquisition of clearing house Parsifal is completed, that of TerraNova asset management almost. Kevin points proudly to a *Wall Street Journal* article calling the bank 'omnivorous'. An inspirational memo from Porter notes that 'a stitch in time saves nine'; our subsequent long position in Time Warner, where in a shock move Bastian Stich is appointed CEO the following week, pays off handsomely. Our stock rises; people revise their bonus expectations upwards; there is talk of moving into a new premises. Champagne is drunk, cigars are smoked, lap dances enjoyed; the rain-logged sky is a rag soaked in chloroform, pressing relentlessly down on the city.

Then everything changes.

'What's this shit?' Gary McCrum says, staring at his terminal.

No warning, no explanation; just a small but noticeable decline in our share price.

Liam English plays it down. 'Regression to the mean, that's all. Market valuation's been increasing for six months straight, there was bound to be an adjustment sooner or later.'

'This isn't an adjustment, it's a nosedive.'

'It's not a nosedive,' Liam says irritably. He looks off into space, tugs on his tie as though pumping it for information, then concedes, 'Look, there's a certain amount of rethinking going on out there about counterintuitiveness. It's the usual story – you do something new, everyone else piles in, there're some bad deals, the market panics. As the originators we might be carrying the can for more than is fair. It'll pass.'

He huffs back to his office and closes the venetian blind; but through the apertures we detect, or imagine we detect, the blue glow of an electronic cigarette.

'He's stonewalling us,' Jocelyn Lockhart says.

'You think something's happening?'

'There's rumours going around.'

'What sort of rumours?'

'That we over-borrowed to pay for the Agron takeover. That our core assets are overvalued. That we're broke, essentially.'

'But . . . it's not true, is it?' Kevin says.

'It's just some hedge fund taking shots in the dark,' Gary McCrum says. 'Standard trash-and-cash. Liam's right, it'll burn itself out.'

Jocelyn shrugs. 'We'll see.'

I spend most of the day taking calls from clients and counter-parties, listening to casual but pointed inquiries about trades and investments; I assure them that there's nothing to worry about, that this is simply an anomaly, that by tomorrow everything will be back to normal.

On the contrary. Overnight, the temperature becomes a fever, and the next morning the calls begin before I even leave my apartment, slowly but inexorably rising in volume and anxiety over the course of the day, while the bank's share price slowly but inexorably falls. We field the queries, we soothe the qualms, we placate and mollify to the best of our ability – but as our superiors aren't telling us anything, this doesn't amount to much.

'Word is we're over-leveraged.'

'It's mid-quarter, everyone's over-leveraged.'

'I heard we couldn't make good on a deal.'

'That's bullshit.'

'Don't yell at me, I'm just telling you what people are saying.'

'Come on, if we'd DK'd on a trade we'd know about it. It'd be all over the place.'

'It *is* all over the place.'

'I had a customer ask me today if we were still solvent. This is a guy I've traded with for years. I said yes but I'm not even sure we are.'

We are not sure of anything, except this: AgroBOT is under siege – a strange, metaphysical siege, in which lies beset truth.

The question of who began the attacks very soon becomes

unimportant. In the market, it does not take long for rumour to become self-fulfilling. Spread a story, no matter how wild; if even a handful of shareholders believe it and sell their stock, a notional drop in value becomes an actual drop, the false narrative supersedes the true, people panic, the sell-off intensifies, the share price collapses, the hedge fund or whoever was behind the initial short makes a killing.

If a company's fundamentals are strong, as ours are, this won't happen; the rumours won't stick, the attacks will abate, the short-sellers will give up, look for an easier mark elsewhere. It's only a matter of time: that's what we tell ourselves, that's what we tell our clients. But we can feel the market as never before, a palpable entity, delving into our terminals, our trades, our collective past – an invisible hand, tapping the walls, looking for the weak spot.

I'm in the office till close to midnight, trying to talk away client jitters; I'm back again at 6 a.m., doing the same. As the minutes tick towards the opening of the market, the fear mounts, the pressure becomes almost unbearable, a hissing force that pushes against the eyeballs. Events roll silently in a band across the TV, messages ping on to my computer screen, Joe Peston and Dwayne McGuckian and Mike Purzel iterate numbers into their headsets, the telephones ring and ring and ring. The effort of defending the bank is visible on every face, and although the floor is as noisy as ever, it seems we can hear the silence beneath it, oceanically deep, oceanically cold.

And the loudest silence is Porter's. In our hour of need, he seems to have vanished, leaving us with only more conjecture.

'I heard he had another heart attack.'

'I heard his wife tried to commit suicide.'

'He wouldn't stay out of the office for that.'

'If you'd stop whining like little girls for a minute,' Dave Davison's bored baritone rises up from behind a divider, 'then you'd realize the reason we haven't heard from him is that he already has it covered. We've got an open line of credit with his buddy the Caliph. More than enough to carry us through some market hissy-fit.'

That's true, but there is a hitch. Following his merciless quashing of the rebellion, the Caliph has been removed by his Imperial Guard to an undisclosed location while the last dregs of the uprising are mopped up.

'It's a delicate situation,' Jurgen explains. 'They are purging his ministries of any suspected sympathizers. For security reasons, the Caliph prefers to monitor this from a distance.'

'And what about us? He can't even pick up a phone?'

'It is only a matter of time,' Jurgen says.

Others are less optimistic.

'Someone knows something,' Howie says, watching the screen. 'Someone's got something on us.'

Business on the ninth floor has stalled. Howie's investors, spooked by the sudden dip in our fortunes, refuse to believe his assurances that the bank and the fund are two separate entities; some of them are even demanding their money back.

'I tell them, how can I give you your money back? I *invested* it. That's what you paid me to do. It's not like I put it a suitcase and buried it in the back garden.' He has been down here most of the morning, Chinese wall notwithstanding; he claims he is trying to contain the contamination, though he spends most of his time kicking furniture.

'What are the hedge funds saying?' I ask him.

'They're saying we're fucked, Claude. It's not like it's a secret. People are climbing over each other, trying to ditch their stock. Some crowd in California are betting a fortune we'll be gone in less than a week.'

'Less than a week?'

'Why not? Bear went under in less than a week. Lehman went in less than a week. They were both much bigger than us.'

A chill of silence sweeps through the room, as if a door had been blown open by some soundless storm.

'But why is this happening?' I say. 'What is it they think they know?'

'They know AgroBOT's a pissant operation run by people who don't have a bull's notion what they're doing,' Howie returns.

'If it did go under . . .' little Terry Fosco pipes up, 'would that mean our shares'd be worthless?'

'It won't go under,' Dave Davison insists. 'I'm telling you, they won't let it. They can't.'

'Though if it does,' Gary McCrum says with a kind of bitter relish, 'we won't get a penny. We'll be at the end of a long, long line.'

'Where's Porter?' Kevin cries. 'Why doesn't he say something? Why doesn't he do something?'

The same questions, the same unsatisfactory answers, hour after hour, like a torturous carousel; and in the background the edifice we thought indestructible is being steadily and invisibly dismantled, as if by ghosts. By now, most of the calls have dried up: clients no longer want reassurance; instead they seek to put as much distance as they can between them and us. New business is non-existent.

'We're like lepers out there,' Howie fumes, sending another wastebasket flying. 'We're like Greece.'

One man remains unafraid of infection. Around lunchtime, Walter's car pulls up outside. He doesn't look like someone whose empire is on the brink of collapsing. Instead he looks like he's swallowed it whole; he's grown so bloated that to fit in the limo I have to sit with my knees practically up to my chin. I'm expecting an inquisition about the bank's current performance, or a furious command to liquidate his investments, but he doesn't even mention AgroBOT's travails, just hands me the usual bundle of cheques. Hasn't he heard? Or doesn't he care? Maybe as Walter Corless he believes himself immune to the flying grit of circumstance; he writes his own story, which intersects with the wider world's only as and when he desires it. Or maybe he, too, knows something we don't.

'Most of our lenders have rolled over the loans we need to keep operating today,' Jurgen says. It is morning, just about; outside, first light struggles against twisting cords of rain; Jurgen has a curiously antic quality about him, that maniacal energy that comes with lack of sleep. 'However, in return they are seeking significantly more margin, which is proving problematic. We could sell off some bonds in order to raise the cash, but the fear is that this might be interpreted as a sign that we are in trouble.'

'The market seems pretty clear that we're in trouble, Jurgen.'

'Yes, however, they don't know yet how much trouble,' he says.

Panicked eyes meet in momentary panic-embraces.

'One of our hedge-fund clients has requested we return the cash they have given us to administer,' he explains. 'This will leave a serious hole in the bank's balance sheet.'

'What about the Caliph? The line of credit?'

The Caliph remains incommunicado. 'His secret service is reporting a security breach, presumably some handful of militants that escaped the bombing. There is no threat to the Caliph himself, but personal access is limited to his Imperial Guard.'

'We don't want to *access* him. We just want him to give us some money.'

'We are monitoring the situation,' Jurgen says.

After the briefing there is nothing to do. All our meetings have been cancelled: no one wants to trade with us. In limbo, people start acting strangely. Some leave without explanation for long, fugue-like breaks, return muttering to themselves, attended by unfamiliar smells. Others throw their feet up on the desk and make long-distance calls, or sit motionlessly for hours, staring at online poker hands. On the way to the toilet I encounter Kimberlee the receptionist emerging furtively from the handicapped stall with Dave Davison, the back of her skirt snarled up in her tights.

Who could blame them? As the share price falls, and our lives are hollowed out proportionally, I yearn for something physical – the touch of a hand, a smile, anything that could deliver me from all this abstraction. But it feels like the physical world is ever less available, like we're trapped in a car that's plunged into the sea and we can't get the windows to roll down . . .

Then a cry goes up. 'Porter's making a statement!'

Instantly a crowd gathers under the big screen, weary faces burnished by hope. Banking being essentially a confidence trick, to insist publicly on your solvency is a risky move: unless it's pitched exactly right, it could be taken as an admission that the game is up. But this is Porter Blankly! Of course it will be pitched right! Porter will explain everything, and we will come back bigger and better than ever.

'. . . beleaguered bank,' the news anchor is saying, 'amid mounting fears of a debt downgrade . . .' At the bottom of the screen, the crawl reads, *11 per cent drop in twenty-four hours . . .*

'Eleven per cent!' someone behind me moans.

'Shh!'

'Don't shush me, I took out a *loan* to buy those shares!'

'Shut the fuck up!'

'. . . failed to calm a hostile market, causing an escalating series of margin calls, amid speculation that at least one Wall Street firm has refused any further trade with Agron Torabundo and that restructuring is becoming unavoidable . . .'

'Fuck you, bitch, Porter's going to restructure your ugly face!'

'. . . go live as these questions and others are put to the bank's Co-Vice President of Global Equities, George Death.'

The crowd in front of the TV falls silent. 'What?' someone says.

The picture cuts to a conference room where a very small man is crossing a stage to a lectern.

'Who the fuck is this guy?'

'Did Porter shrink in the wash?'

The man has begun to speak; however, only the top of his head is visible over the top of the lectern, and it quickly becomes evident the microphones are too far away to pick up his voice. An aide runs on and frantically begins adjusting the mikes; the Co-Vice President, apparently unaware of any issue, continues to read inaudibly. Muttering can be heard from the unseen press corps. There is a crunch of static. '—iderable upside,' the top of the Co-Vice President's head says. 'That is all I have to say at this time. Thank you, gentlemen.' He stumps away from the lectern in a fusillade of flashes and hollering.

For a moment, silence. Then:

'Christ, that's not going to help.'

'Couldn't they have found someone more than four feet tall?'

'Couldn't they have found someone whose *name* isn't *Death*?'

'Actually, I think it's pronounced *Deeth*.'

'Oh, great, call the *Wall Street Journal*.'

'Shares have just dropped another two points,' Gary reports.

The room churns with exclamations of gloom, until Rachael appears in the doorway. Clapping her hands in a teacherly fashion, 'You heard the Co-Vice President,' she says. 'The bank is fully capitalized, so please concentrate on your —' She pauses, as her secretary clatters in at top speed to whisper in her ear; then, turning pale, she rushes back to her office. A minute later, the news comes across Bloomberg that AgroBOT's long- and short-term credit rating has been downgraded to junk.

The grumbling of a moment ago resolves into a single, consensual moan: it might be the bank's death-cry.

'What's going on?' Kevin asks, tugging my sleeve.

I explain that the big institutional investors, the pension funds and so on, are prohibited from putting their money in anything with a rating of BB+ or lower, and so the downgrade means that at the stroke of a pen we have lost most of our lenders, and with them the money we need to do the things we do. It seems I can feel a physical snap, a breaking-away, and I go to the window, half-expecting to find Transaction House now floating down the Liffey. But of course everything is where it always is.

In the lobby the lift doors hiss open. Brent 'Crude' Kelleher, who to judge by his jubilant expression has not heard the latest news, saunters into the office bearing two large paper bags. 'They're giving away muffins at the hippie place!'

In the general indifference, I feel like an icicle has stabbed me in the heart.

'Some sort of closing-down thing,' Brent says, then, clearly troubled by my reaction, 'I got one for you, Claude.'

I push past him, jab the button for the lift, almost immediately think better of it and crash down the stairs.

Rain is falling again, in dense needles that seem to surround and isolate the people dashing across the plaza, like some ingenious, ever-shifting force field, the ultra-fine bars of some immanent cage. After weeks of downpour, floods have beset Dublin; the underground rivers that criss-cross beneath the city's foundations have come to the surface and found the plains where they would in the past have dissipated now occupied by the tax-relief malls, car parks and apartment blocks of the boom. And the Liffey's rising, too: on the far side of the plaza, trash laps the mossy tops of the quays, jackals feeding on the slimy corpse of some enormous beast.

In the Ark, it looks like the end of the world is expected any minute. Rain-soaked consumers jostle past each other, deliberately avoiding eye contact, arms loaded with pastries, crêpes, organic prune juice. At the counter, the staff have a besieged look. With some difficulty, I elbow my way through to Ariadne.

'Claude!' she exclaims when she sees me, but in an instant her delight turns to sadness. 'Where have you been?' she says, with an unconcealed note of accusation.

'Busy,' I say guiltily, and then, 'What's happening?'

'Special deal,' she says. 'Buy anything, get two other things free.'

'Some special occasion?' I am praying that Brent has got it wrong. She shrugs fatalistically. 'We are closing.'

Nothing changes, but everything does: I feel like an extraterrestrial in a comic book, who, looking up at a blank square of sky, knows that his home planet has exploded. 'I see.'

'I have told you the landlord wants to put up the rent, right? So we went to see the bank, but they say there's nothing they can do.'

'I can't believe it,' I say softly.

'Today's our last day, that's why we get rid of everything. If there's anything you want, just take it. I don't charge you.'

'What's in there?' A florid woman beside me points suspiciously at a wicker tray of buns. I wait while Ariadne explains that these are cinnamon, these pear, these raisin; the woman, still glowering mistrustfully, throws a couple in her basket, then stalks off. Outside the rain rattles from the overflowing gutters like gunfire.

'The Ark is leaving just when we need it most,' I say.

'Ay, what can we do? We don' want to close, but is impossible. I don' know who does the landlord expect to move in and pay his crazy rent. Or does he jus' want to force us out?'

I start to explain the logic of the upward-only rent review – that the value of a building as an asset is based on the rent that *could* be charged for it, meaning it often makes more sense to keep that rent high and the building unoccupied than to lower the rent and have to mark down its overall . . . I tail off. Ariadne is gazing at me with a mixture of bewilderment and horror. All I can do, even now, is parrot the lines of the enemy! What is wrong with me?

'What will you do?' I say quickly. 'Where will you go?'

'I don' know yet,' she reflects. 'Everything happens so quickly. I'd like to stay, but it's hard to find work here, and is so expensive, and . . .' She lets out a heavy, troubled sigh. 'Is people just going to let this happen?'

'You mean the rent review?' Though I know she doesn't.

'I mean *everything*.' She casts a sallow hand at the window, the waterlogged, debt-laden nation outside. 'It gets worse and worse, and still people just shrug their shoulders. In Greece, in Spain, they're out on the streets. Here, if you go on the streets, they think you're a fool or a criminal and you deserve whatever you get. What's everyone so afraid of? Why don't they do something? If they care?'

As she says this, her eyes swing directly up to meet mine, their challenge so violent that I take an involuntary step backwards. I begin to ask her about her friend the zombie, then realize that the answer, whatever it is, will probably not reflect well on me, so instead I change the subject. 'Oscar will go with you? If you leave?'

'Of course,' she says, it seems to me curtly; and then from behind me there comes a crash, and we look over to see that someone has knocked a box of pasta from the shelf. Ariadne groans, and fetches a dustpan and brush. 'Mother of Christ, these people,' she murmurs, kneeling down to sweep up the spilled linguine. 'If any of them have come before today, we wouldn't need to close.'

'Why don't you give the food to the shelter?'

'Because it close too. Last week. Brendan says the government won't give any more money. You know, they have all this bullshit with the banks.'

'Yes,' I say faintly, and with a flush of shame.

The door opens and closes, opens and closes; the beginnings of the lunch crowd join the pandemonium, a fresh stream of shoulders and elbows bruising their way by.

'I must go back to work,' Ariadne says defeatedly.

She takes a step into the melee, and it hits me, like an axe blow, that this is the last time I will see her. There will be no sunsets, no hooting train whistles, no valedictory speeches: I have not earned any of that. She will simply leave the frame and be gone and never be replaced, that's how it works in the real world –

'Wait!'

She turns, looks at my hand on her sleeve.

'Maybe I can do something,' I say, with a dry mouth. 'For the café. Find a backer, negotiate with the landlord for a couple of months' extension. Buy some time, at least.'

'Thanks, Claude,' she says gently. 'But I think it's too late.'

'I know people,' I insist, still clutching her arm. 'I should have thought of it before. I'll go back to the office and make some calls.'

'Thank you,' she repeats. 'That's very kind.'

Investors are always looking for a good opportunity, I tell her, forecasts for the service industry are strong, then take into account footfall in the Financial Services Centre, and the growing market for specialist foods – on and on I babble, with less and less idea what I'm saying, just to keep the conversation alive, to keep her here with me for a few seconds longer, until at last the words run out and I am left gaping at her in silence. Ariadne doesn't move away. Instead she looks down again at my hand on her forearm, then up again at me: some invisible veil falls away, and in that instant I see that she has understood everything. Nowhere to hide now; all I can do is pretend I haven't noticed she's noticed, find some trivial remark that will give us both an escape route. But my powers of dissembling have deserted me; instead I hang wretchedly in the lamplight of her gaze, like an abject, sodden stranger who appears on her step in the middle of a rainstorm and throws himself on her mercy.

Someone is calling her name from behind the till. With a supreme effort I manage to relinquish her arm, but she stays where she is a moment longer, holding my gaze with strangely liquid eyes. 'Goodbye, Claude,' she says at last. Leaning forward she kisses my cheek. And then she is gone, devoured in the churn of lunchtime vultures.

The rest of the day is an unremitting agony. Never has the office seemed so toxic. The bland pastel shirts, the veined mock-leather of the desks, the swirling screensavers and bright glowing spreadsheets: these are merely lesser darknesses in a vast and opaque and airless night, a lesson in entropy that is repeated and repeated until it has drummed its emptiness into every cell of my being.

The scale of the pain catches me off-guard. I thought I'd reconciled myself long ago to being without her. Now I realize that instead of giving her up, my heart had concocted a future in which we would go on, if not together, at least in parallel – that I might continue to love her from a distance, and she would continue to live her life with that love wrapped around her, an unseen protector, like an angel's wing . . .

I do my best to keep my promise to her, but with the bank in its current state of public disintegration, pitching an investment is like a poisoner trying to sell cookies door-to-door. At this stage most of my contacts don't even answer the phone. There must be something I can do! In a novel, the café's rack-renting landlord would turn out to be one of our wicked clients – Walter Corless, maybe, who for all these years has harboured an irrational hatred of macrobiotic foods, and plans to convert the café into a car park; I would confront him, and gloatingly he'd reveal to me all of his sinister and illegal business dealings, only to discover that I'd recorded the conversation, and thus brought down his whole Babelian empire.

But in the real world, which is the world of business, there are no stories like this – with heroes and villains, motives other than profit. The 'landlord' isn't a person, just the name given to an investment portfolio; the decision was made in the void eye of another hurricane a thousand miles away, a Canadian pension fund, a German reinsurance firm, an asset management company in Tokyo or Sydney or Lahore. No one working there will ever have seen the Ark or know anything about it, except as a figure on a spreadsheet; the lease is doubtless administered by someone just like me, wishing he was elsewhere, sending off the rote email while dreaming of another waitress in another café . . .

Day turns into night. There is nothing to do, but we stay at our desks until the New York market closes, in the hope that some magical buyer might appear, pay off our debts and let us keep our jobs. That doesn't happen, so we move our operations to Life, where we sit in anxious silence around a table, nibbling trail mix; then somehow it is morning again, and cleaners in orange uniforms are hoovering about my feet.

The day does not start well. Excelsior announce they will not roll over a hundred-million-dollar loan due to be repaid tomorrow; in New York, two sets of lawyers move into AgroBOT HQ – one drafting documents for any potential third parties that might come forward with a rescue plan, the other preparing papers for bankruptcy. 'And that's the good news,' Gary McCrum says.

Word from Oran is that the Caliph has been overthrown.

'Overthrown, dismembered, and fed to his own dogs,' Gary clarifies.

'But . . . how? Wasn't he in some hideout with his bodyguards?'

'It was the Imperial Guard that did it,' Jurgen explains. 'Apparently they were unhappy about the extent of the coalition's bombing campaign.'

'And this has been verified?'

'See for yourself,' Gary says. He takes out his phone and shows us a video of a bearded man weeping in terror as a carving knife is brought to his neck –

'Turn it off,' mutters Ish.

'We have not spoken to the bodyguards,' Jurgen says, 'but our sense is that the line of credit is no longer on the table.'

'So what are our options?' Jocelyn Lockhart asks.

'We don't *have* any options,' Gary McCrum says grimly. 'We're finished.'

'But we've done nothing *wrong*,' Brent protests. 'A whole bank can't go down because of a bunch of unsubstantiated rumours, it doesn't make any sense!'

'Ordinarily I would agree,' Jurgen says. 'However, the thing about these unsubstantiated rumours is that they are true. We have learned that among our recent acquisitions is several billion euros of now-worthless Greek debt.'

Stunned silence, then, as Jurgen seems content to leave it there, someone does the necessary: 'Why . . . would we buy . . . several billion euros of Greek debt?'

'That is an interesting question,' Jurgen says, like a medical professor discussing an anatomical curiosity in a textbook. 'The answer seems to be that we did not know we were buying it. In a spirit of counterintuitiveness, it appears that due diligence was rushed through. Furthermore, this debt had been carefully concealed within several layers of shells, swaps, special purpose vehicles, like a computer virus that waits inside another file.'

'Concealed by who?' Jocelyn says. 'The Greek government?'

They have always seemed too inept and lazy to come up with this kind of machination.

'Not exactly. If you remember, just before they joined the EU, the Greeks hired Danforth Blaue to cover up the enormous holes on their balance sheet.'

Another silence. Jurgen smacks his lips together, as if he has just enjoyed a particularly delicious snack.

'So . . .' Slowly Ish puts it together. 'Danforth Blaue took this toxic debt and hid it away, and then we came along and bought it?'

'Someone else bought it, and then Agron bought them, and then we bought Agron,' Jurgen says.

'All that glitters isn't gold,' Kevin says, shaking his head. 'Porter's memo,' he explains, seeing our baffled faces. 'That must be what he meant.'

'Buying Agron was *Porter's idea*, you fool,' Gary snaps.

'So?'

'So, if he had actually known it wasn't gold, surely he would have just *not bought it*, instead of sending everyone some unintelligible riddle about how we shouldn't buy it and then buying it.'

'Maybe he was testing us,' Kevin says. 'You know, like God.'

'Wait a second,' Ish says. 'Porter was CEO of Danforth Blaue. If Danforth's responsible for us buying a bunch of toxic crap that looks like it's going to drag us under – doesn't that mean that Porter's just pulled a huge con on Porter? He's basically bankrupted himself?'

'Fuck.' Jocelyn Lockhart rubs his jaw. 'Poetic justice.'

'The great genius,' Gary says sardonically. 'No wonder he's keeping his head down.'

'It is true that the takeovers have not worked out exactly as planned,' Jurgen says. 'However, it would be a mistake to write off Porter's strategy too soon. The very scale of AgroBOT's impending collapse means that it cannot be allowed to happen. Thanks to his expansions, we are so big now that if we go down, an untold number of trading partners and counterparties will be pulled down with us, bringing the entire global banking system grinding to a halt. In a matter of hours, money will stop coming out of ATMs. In two or three days, there will be no food left on the supermarket shelves. By the end of the week, petrol will have run out, followed shortly by electricity. Within a month, the very fabric of civilization will have totally collapsed. We have seen in many movies what the consequences will be. Gang of cannibals will rove the ruined highways. Families will shiver in the darkness of sewers. Strange, millenarian cults will perform human sacrifices to artefacts once taken for granted by us and now worshipped as gods. Ordinary public sector workers will now wear dog collars and Mohawks, and drive futuristic, weaponized vehicles powered by paraffin. An endless metaphorical night will swallow the Earth, although in practice the current diurnal system of sunrise and sunset should continue unaffected.'

Somewhere in the middle of this we have forgotten why it constitutes good news.

'Because it means that the market has no choice but to refinance us!' Jurgen says, with a shrill, falsetto laugh. 'Porter's acquisitions policy has been underwritten by nothing less than civilization itself! So you see, this is no more than the storm in a teacup! What is everyone so worried about?'

He glides away, repeating this last phrase to himself like a mantra.

'He's putting an awful lot of faith in this too-big-to-fail thing,' Jocelyn Lockhart says slowly.

'Did I ever tell you about my Aunt Nelly?' Ish says. 'She was always bragging that her tits were too big to fail. Every Saturday night she'd go out without so much as a lick of lippy on. "Don't need it," she'd say. "Got these." Then one day she was leaning over her fishpond and she fell in.'

'She drowned?'

'No, but when they brought her to Emergency, that's where she met my Uncle Nick.'

The morning grinds on, white-bitten and slow as a glacier. We sit stiff-backed at our desks, row upon row, like children in some terrorized classroom, and whenever the lift doors open, we all whip round in unison, each expecting, though we don't admit it, to see a cohort of security guards troop out: Reinaldus, Esteban, Timoleon, the same surly men we've nodded to as they sat slouched in Reception on so many mornings, now transformed – stalking through the office, distributing boxes, rousing us from our desks, like stuporous, torpid jungle cats who one day find the door to their cage left open and instantly reassume their true natures, the contempt in their eyes telling us everything we need to know . . .

'We have enough capital to trade till the end of the day.' Liam English tries to make this sound positive.

'And after that . . . ?' A circle of chalky faces, like some ghostly Greek chorus.

'After that, ah, we'd be looking for either a buyout or a government intervention.'

'Except nobody wants to intervene,' Jocelyn says.

'But what about civilization?' Kimberlee asks. 'The apocalypse? Don't they care about the apocalypse?'

Liam explains that the market consensus is that AgroBOT is not too big to fail after all, only *almost* too big to fail – a crucial difference.

'So nobody's going to die,' Gary says.

Liam shakes his head.

'But tomorrow's Casual Day,' Kimberlee says sadly. 'We can't close on Casual Day, it's always such a laugh.'

'Casual Day would be one of the less significant movers in global capitalism,' Liam tells her.

'And where's Porter, in the middle of all this?' Brent Kelleher erupts. 'Hasn't he got anything to say? Shouldn't he give some bloody account of himself, before they send him off into the sunset with his fifty-million-dollar severance package?'

'There's not a lot Porter can do,' Liam says. 'If there's going to be a rescue, it'll have to come from outside.'

So it's back to the wait. Dave Davison reads the racing pages; Thomas 'Yuan' McGregor arranges pebbles on his mouse mat. Knots of panic become interfused with a weird, blissed-out lethargy, the kind of light-headedness you get when the oxygen is running out. From the window, I can see the shutters are down on the Ark, making it look like a sarcophagus; I keep imagining Ariadne is trapped inside, have to stop myself from running to help . . .

'Three feet high and rising, eh, Claude?' Ish says.

'What?'

'The river.' Below, filthy water is frothing ever closer to street level.

'The Liffey has never burst its banks.' This is what I hear people telling each other in supermarket queues.

'Yeah, well, banks have been known to fail, haven't they?' She doesn't sound overly concerned; in fact, she's been quite blithe since the prospect of AgroBOT's imminent destruction emerged, possibly because Skylark Fitzgibbon and all mention of golf courses disappeared around the same time. This seems disloyal: I feel a surge of anger, but before I can say anything Kimberlee appears and hands me a piece of paper.

'Fax for you, Claude.'

'You don't have to keep bringing them,' I say. But she's already gone.

'Someone still loves you, eh, Claude?' Ish says, pinching my arm.

Mike Purzel comes running in. 'Barclays is looking into a buyout.'

Everyone jumps out of their seats and crowds around him; then Liam English comes out of his office, and they leave Mike and gather around him instead. Liam confirms that Barclays has made contact. Cheers resound through the room. 'Talks are at a preliminary stage,' Liam warns, but he doesn't object to following further developments from the pub.

'Are you coming?' Ish is halfway out the door.

'In a minute.'

I remain at the window, looking at the fax in my hand. At the top, somebody has carefully printed, *FAO Claude Martingale.* Then follows the now-familiar block of assiduous blackness. It occurs to me that instead of an attempt to use up ink, you could read it, if you wanted, as a story – the story of Claude, the real one, with which the version I'd hoped for, Ariadne, love, adventure, all that, has been overwritten. Because even if a buyout materializes and the bank is saved, the Ark will still be gone, won't it? And Ariadne with it? Leaving me with nothing but the present, the never-ending present, on which to inscribe myself over and over, in letters that are skyscraper-high . . .

A man is standing in our office. Stubby, moustachioed, he stares directly at me. Where have I seen him before? 'Looking for Howard Hogan,' he says. He speaks in an even, courteous tone, but specks of sweat glisten on his temples, and the brilliant-white collar of his shirt digs deep into his pink neck. It is the man we saw when Ish and I visited Howie's fund, I realize – the chortling fellow who left the bag full of banknotes.

'Upstairs,' I say, jabbing at the ceiling. 'Ninth floor.'

'Doesn't seem to be anyone there,' the man says. His tone remains steady, but his eyes boggle at me, seize me by the lapels and shake me.

'I'm afraid I can't help you,' I tell him. 'This is Agron Torabundo Bank. Agron Torabundo Credit Management is a separate enterprise.'

He stares at me another moment, then seems to wilt: a merchant prince stripped of his belongings, lost among savages. A door opens and in rush the two burly men who accompanied him on the ninth floor that day. He raises his eyebrows; they shake their heads. He emits a low gurgle as if inside him something were being throttled. Without another word he turns on his heel and heads for the lobby, phone pressed to his ear.

When he is gone, I climb the stairwell to the ninth floor. A fire extinguisher has been used to break down the door. Inside, the beautiful artwork is gone, as well as most of the furniture. None of the staff seems to be here either, though a residue of panic remains etched in the air, conjuring images of rushing bodies, boxes hastily filled . . .

On Howie's desk, an empty bottle of whiskey sits by a sticky glass. One edge of the keyboard is sprinkled with powder. I touch a key and the screen comes to life: a game of Tetris, coloured blocks piled claustrophobically all the way to the top. The ledgers that line the shelf on the back wall are all empty, the drawers likewise, except for a pair of pink panties and a biography of Steve

Jobs. I find myself thinking of Paul's red notebook, page after page filled with cartoon penises.

Hearing a noise, I leave the room and turn a corner to find Tom Cremins and Brian O'Brien hard at work, one feeding documents into the shredder, the other smashing up hard drives with a hammer. They look up momentarily but don't speak to me. Beyond them is a wall safe, empty; beside the safe is another door. No one answers when I knock; in fact there is no sense the room has ever been occupied. No files, no phone, no stationery or computer clutter the beautiful maple desk; the softest veil of dust lies over everything, like a protective covering. In the corner, however, is a large cupboard. On a hunch I turn the handle.

'Go away,' Grisha says.

'What are you doing in here?' The closet is just big enough for a mop and bucket, on the latter of which the quant is sitting.

'Maths. You are not understanding.'

'On the walls?'

His shoulders snap up and down. I gaze around me at the algorithmic scrawl that covers the cupboard's interior. Even the ceiling has been inscribed with tiny pinched print, and with a shiver I think again of the Texier painting: the proliferation of minute brushstrokes, tiny bricks in a huge altarpiece to Nothing.

'Everyone's gone,' I say. 'Howie, everyone.'

He ignores this, continues his calculations.

'The fund's finished,' I tell him, and when he doesn't respond to this either, push a little harder: 'It was all a fraud. A Ponzi scheme. I imagine the money Howie paid out to the investors was the money he was getting from new clients. Everything else he took for himself.'

Scritch-scratch goes the pen, filling the wall with infinitesimal signs.

'He didn't use your model,' I say gently. 'Do you understand? You, your providential antinomies, you were just props. None of it was real.'

'None of *this* is reality!' Grisha rejoins, with an impatient wave at everything outside the cupboard. 'Only *this*!' He taps vehemently on the walls with his pen.

'The instrument?'

He scowls, scrubs his shaggy head, muttering under his breath; then, twisting quickly, as if he is about to rise and strike me, he says, in a high, querulous voice, 'You peoples are thinking you can use maths like slave! Do this, do that – I laugh at you, ha! ha! ha! You are like shadows who think they can direct the sun!'

He stops, looks over my shoulder. Someone is standing in the doorway. It's Howie's Bulgarian dealer. In his hand is an ice pick. We don't move; we don't even breathe. He has lost his sunglasses; for a long moment he stares at us with incomprehensible eyes. Then he turns away. A moment later, from down the hall, we hear rampaging noises, terrorized cries.

'Come to Life,' I tell Grisha. 'It's not safe here.'

'*Life*,' Grisha repeats mockingly.

'Everyone's down there.'

'Dance while you can, little shadow,' he says softly, returning to his equations. 'Dance in the light.'

AgroBOT staff are the only customers in Life Bar; the semi-darkness and sticky floor seem a better fit for us in our degraded state than Transaction House.

'Claude, Claude . . .' Liam English, far drunker than their short time in the pub would seem to allow, half-stands to greet me. '*Asseyez-vous*, Claude. What'll you have?' Pulling a wad of notes from his pocket, he stumbles off without waiting for an answer.

'Check it out, Claude.' Jocelyn Lockhart points at the plasma screen on the wall. 'Miles has been taken in for questioning.'

The screen shows the silver-haired head of Royal Irish jauntily strolling into a police station, where, the newsreader informs us sonorously, he will be questioned for up to thirty-six hours.

'New minister making his presence felt,' Dave Davison comments.

'Bollocks,' Joe Peston says. 'Miles is sat in there watching *Home and Away* while the coppers bring him fish and chips. It's all just a show for the little people.'

'I can't believe that that fucking clip joint is still trading and we're going under,' Gary McCrum says darkly.

'Maybe Porter should have moved the HQ to Ireland,' Jocelyn says.

'Fuck Porter.'

'Here, Claude, have you seen Howie?' Ish asks me. 'There were some people in here looking for him.'

I shake my head, ask what's happening with Barclays.

'*Nada*,' Gary says. 'They're still in talks. I'm not holding my breath.'

'I heard Porter's not even there,' Dave says. 'It's that little guy again. The co-global head of whatever.'

'I'll say this for Porter, he's a cool customer.' Jocelyn sighs, topping up his beer. 'His bank goes down the tubes and he doesn't break a sweat? I mean, he must have a ton of preferred stock, right? What's that going to cost him? And still he's nowhere to be found.'

At this, Ish starts; then she sinks slowly back into her chair, her expression somewhere between perplexity and horror, as if she's struggling with some demonic conundrum whose solution leads straight to the charnel house. On the TV over her head, the news cycles on: a car burning in a street in Oran, the new Irish finance minister announcing four new jobs at a toilet-brush factory, floods in Bangladesh, in Prague, in Cork, the AgroBOT press conference again, with the caption *Death: look at the upside.*

The sun begins to set. More bodies appear in the doorway's pocket of golden dusk and, with the same half-ironical, half-hopeless smile, make their way over to our table. Traders, analysts, salesmen, back office: people I've never spoken to, people whose names I don't even know. The eschatological atmosphere, the sense that beyond our little ring of survivors – illuminated now by candles the barman has set down on the grouped tables – darkness prevails, brings to mind those medieval books in which a small band of travellers, fleeing plague or disaster, take refuge in a waystation and pass the night exchanging tales.

'Remember the time the fire alarm went off, and then when we went back inside, it went off again?'

'Remember that intern Howie kept giving extra accounts to? And he took all that meth, and tried to jump out the window?'

'Remember the time the fire alarm went off?' says Torquil Quinn, just arrived, taking off his scarf. 'And then when we went back inside, it went off again?' He is surprised by the muted reception this gets.

'Well, lookit,' Dave Davison sums up, 'whatever happens, we can't complain. We've had a good run of it.'

'AgroBOT is a great bank,' Liam English concurs emotionally, prodding the table with his index finger so the glasses shake. 'A great bloody bank. And if it goes down because we had the guts to take a chance and do things counterintuitively, there's no shame in that.' Then, noticing through his whiskey fog that this hasn't had the galvanizing effect he intended, 'Though it won't go down,' he adds.

'I've been thinking about moving on anyway,' Joe Peston says. 'Maybe it's time to give something back.'

Heads nod, and the conversation turns to restoring old boats, teaching underprivileged children, other long-cherished dreams whose hour may at last have come. Then Liam English's phone rings. Instantly silence falls across the table. Liam makes a show of indifference, looking at the number, appearing to think it over. 'Rachael,' he says, picking it up at last. 'Yeah . . . okay . . . right . . . okay, grand. I will, yes. Okay.'

He puts the phone down, lifts his glass, sips, gasps with satisfaction. Finally he becomes aware of the many eyes staring at him. 'So Barclays have passed,' he says.

There is an audible, collective gasp, followed by a long, wintry nothing.

'So that's it,' Jocelyn Lockhart says bitterly.

'I just bought a Jaguar!' Brent Kelleher moans. 'Now I'm going to be one of those people who go around the supermarket checking which is the cheapest muesli?'

'There could still be a buyout,' Terry Fosco pleads. 'Like, by someone else.'

'Who's going to be dumb enough to buy eight billion dollars' worth of radioactive Greek shit?'

On the TV screen over the bar, the new Minister for Finance, toilet brush in his hand, perorates soundlessly from a podium.

Around our table, too, silence reigns. No one mentions the underprivileged or boat restoration.

'Fuck it!' Dave Davison exclaims. 'We can't spend our last fucking night sitting round feeling sorry for ourselves!'

'You're right!' Gary McCrum joins in. 'We're AgroBOT! If we're going to go down, we should do it in style!'

'VD's?'

'Let's roll!'

In the blink of an eye, we are in our coats, the prospect of one last blowout on expenses lending us superhuman speed. I catch Ish's eye; she shrugs, not wanting to go home any more than I do, and gathers up her belongings.

Gary waves his hand superfluously at a long line of static cabs and topples into the one at the top; Ish and I pile into the back seat of the next one, Kevin into the front. 'Follow that car,' he says, pointing. The driver, African, heavy-set, regards me questioningly in the mirror, but doesn't speak.

As soon as we're off, Ish grips my arm, leans into me and says in a low, urgent voice, 'Something about this isn't right.'

'Eh?'

'Think about it – if *we* didn't know we were carrying all this Greek debt, how did anyone else find out?'

'Eh?' I say again.

'The rumours, where did they come from? Someone spread this story around to drive down our share price. But if Danforth had parcelled up the Greek debt and hidden it so cleverly that even our own due diligence didn't spot it, who could that have been?'

Alcohol sloshes around my brain, and weariness, and grief, all of them crying out against yet more abstraction. But Ish is insistent. 'It would have to be someone who *knew* what Danforth had done, right?'

'Such as who?'

'Such as, for instance, Danforth's former CEO.'

This wakes me up. 'What are you saying? Porter started the rumours?'

'Doesn't it make sense? He knows Agron's unwittingly carrying a ton of toxic securities. He buys them out for fuck all and sends our share price through the roof. Then he puts it about that we're carrying the debt. The whole deal is set up for one colossal short.'

'That would be insider trading.'

'I'll say. It'd be the greatest insider trade of all time. What would he make from it? Tens of millions? More?'

'Porter wouldn't bring down his own bank.'

'Wouldn't he? For a hundred million dollars?'

'He's got ten times that in stock options.'

'Maybe he did it for a billion dollars, then. Or,' a fresh thought strikes her, 'maybe he's got a plan to save the bank, once he's pulled off his short. Meaning he can cash in twice.'

'You're crazy,' I tell her, and turn to the window. Porter makes billions, someone else makes billions, it's legitimate, it's not – who cares? Who cares about any of it?

We continue in silence for a moment. In the passenger seat, Kevin is telling the taxi driver how much he enjoys black music.

'I heard the Ark closed down,' Ish says.

'Yes. Weird coincidence.'

'Probably for the best,' she says, placing her hand on mine. 'Don't you think?'

'You mean because of my unrequited love.'

'I mean, it feels like all of this – maybe it came at the right time. We have a chance to get out now, while we're still young. Do something with our lives.'

'Restore old boats?'

'Something that actually helps people.'

'Personally, I'm sceptical about the helping-people thing,' Kevin pipes up from the front. 'The whole "Look at me, I'm such a good person" bit. We could all spend our lives scrubbing oil off fucking seagulls, you know? But where would that get the world, ultimately? If everybody was altruistic, there literally wouldn't be anyone left to help. And meanwhile all the stuff that needed to be done wouldn't get done.'

'I take it you're planning to stay in banking,' Ish says.

'Society needs selfish people,' Kevin says. 'We're the ones who keep the whole thing moving forward. Anyway, you can't change who you are. If you're a boa constrictor, there's no use trying to be a sheepdog. There's no sense in saying, "I'm tired of choking small animals to death, instead I think I'll round up sheep for a living." It just won't work.'

There is a honk: from the taxi in front, Dave Davison and Mike Purzel are mooning us. Kevin chortles, gives them the finger.

'I don't think of you as a boa constrictor,' I tell Ish.

'Thanks, Claude.'

'Though what about your mortgage? If you are planning on helping people.'

Ish considers this. 'Sometimes I wonder if I just got that mortgage so I didn't have to ask myself why I was working in some shitty bank.'

The car inches through the traffic in fits and starts. Rain deluges the windscreen, rain slicks the streets; rain has taken over this town, like a Mafia gang rolled in from some nightmare metropolis.

'What about you, Claude?' A street lamp in the window gives her a momentary, rain-diffused halo. 'What will you do?'

I don't know what I will do. I don't have a plan, or an ideal to pursue. My love story is over; after tomorrow, the bank will be gone too, and I will probably never see any of these people again, and there will be no sign that the last two years ever happened. Apart from the money, of course; the money will still be there, piled up in my account, like those towers of hoarded newspapers they find in old people's houses after they die.

'I suppose I will look for another position,' I say. 'I hear Goldman are looking.'

I am conscious of her disapproval, but for a moment she doesn't speak; the back-seat silence is filled by the slur of the tyres on the wet street, the muffled thrum of the city.

'On Kokomoko they have this legend,' she says at last. 'Of a tribe that left the gift circle. And this tribe, every time they go out in their boats they catch a full net of fish, and every time they dive to the seabed they find the most beautiful shells, and every time they fight in a battle they win. And if you're starving, or you need allies for a war, or a necklace for a dowry, in the middle of the night these tribesmen will appear at your bedside, and they'll offer you whatever you want. But the thing is, once you take it, you'll never be able to pay them back. Your food, your possessions, the clothes on your back – they'll keep coming and coming, in the middle of the night, and sooner or later they'll take your mother, your daughter, your whole family – carry them away to their island, that no one ever returns from.'

Shff shff, go the wipers on the windscreen; traffic-light red dazzles over the glass.

'The anthropologists think it's got its roots in history. The slavers used to sail out from Torabundo around the archipelago, trying to get the islanders to take on loans. Particularly if the fish catch was down. The islanders didn't really understand what loans were – they were used to just giving each other what they needed, so they fell into these enormous debts. The slavers would take their children as "security" until they paid them back. And their parents'd never see them again. So these legends arose sort of like warnings. If you leave the gift circle, if you take the zombie gold, then you're already dead.' Leaning forward, she taps the driver on the shoulder. 'Let me out here, please.'

I do not conceal my dismay. 'Aren't you coming to VD's?'

She shakes her head. 'Have a lap dance for me, eh? See you tomorrow for the grand finale.'

She steps out into the rain; the door shuts, and the taxi shrieks back into motion.

Kevin cranes his head around. 'I'll tell you one thing I won't miss, that's stories about those sodding islanders. Some bunch of oddballs who don't even wear trousers, telling us we're dead?' He turns back to the front. 'When I'm dead, you'll know all about it,' he says. 'You can expect a very volatile market that day, my friend.'

From the basement door red lights flash, and a deep percussive rumbling issues. 'All right, mate?' The bouncer checks me with his hand. 'Where ye comin' from?'

'Life,' I tell him.

'Oh yeah?' He scrutinizes Kevin and me with pale hobgoblin eyes.

'Our colleagues are inside,' I say. 'Agron Torabundo.'

His eyes narrow; I wonder momentarily if he is one of our shareholders. 'Tell your pals in there to cool it,' he says.

The whole of AgroBOT seems to be downstairs, sweat rings under their armpits, faces simultaneously grinning and aghast, like soldiers on furlough from some terrible war. Kevin prods me, points to where Jurgen is waving at us from a table. 'You have made it at last!' he hollers as we stumble out of the melee. 'I am thinking you will never be coming!'

He appears oddly relaxed, even jovial, as if we were at our Christmas party; he shunts along the banquette so we can squeeze in beside him, orders us drinks from a passing nymph. Chris Kane is at the table as well, telling the fire-alarm story to some people from Sales. Around us, the mood has intensified from gloom into a kind of morbid bacchanal. Champagne bottles pack the tables like skittles; suited figures process continuously to the bathroom in twos and threes, while others are led away by silver-knickered houris to the cubicles at the back of the club. House beats pound at my body. I take a bottle from the nymph's tray, debate interiorly as to whether or not I should stay. And then –

'Something wrong, Claude?'

'I thought I saw . . .' It feels almost too absurd to say out loud;

but as the mass of bodies around us reconfigures itself, just for a second the face re-emerges.

'Who?'

'Porter.'

'Porter?' Jurgen's laughter is more kindly than mocking. 'I think perhaps in Life Bar you are drinking many Jägerbombs.'

He's right, I think; and then the crowd kaleidoscopes again, and once more I see him, by a little door in a distant corner, as if on his way in or out. The light is dim, and people keep getting in the way, but how can it be anyone else? The snow-white hair, the golden skin, the famous jawline that has triumphed in innumerable boardroom battles? And the man he is deep in talk with, don't I know him too – small, spry, silver-haired, a gleam in his eye – isn't that Miles O'Connor?

'Hmm, I am not seeing either of them.'

Pushing Jurgen aside, I jump from my seat and hurry towards the corner. As I get closer it seems other figures flicker out of the darkness – the little Portuguese man who had haunted the Minister – and there, isn't that Howie? And, and *Walter*? But my way is blocked again and again, colleagues stepping in front of me to clasp me in beery embraces or take my picture with their phones, and by the time I reach the corner, neither Porter nor Miles nor any of the others is anywhere to be seen.

A trick of the light after all. Shoulders slumping, I come to a halt. Around me, fragments of conversations flurry, memories jousting with each other in loud, unhearing voices. Down the stairs men continue to come, surveying the scene with identical expressions of childlike avarice; the nymphs thread through them, bearing order pads and trays of drinks, pushed-up breasts and intoxicating smiles. A dark-haired dancer has come onstage, the girl who looks like Ariadne; I pause to watch her grind her crotch against the pole, a mechanical Siren delivering her one-note song.

It was a mistake to come here; the night has nothing more to offer. I decide to cut my losses, make my way to the exit.

And then I see someone indisputably real. So: at least one mystery has been solved tonight. I follow at a distance, watching the figure weave through the crowd, then come to rest in a niche close by the warren of private booths, where thinking herself unobserved she sighs, arches her back and rolls her head. Marching briskly up to her, I tap her on the shoulder. 'No volleyball tonight?'

She spins around – and I recoil. An enormous contusion, a swollen rainbow of purples and greens, adorns one side of her face. 'Vot are you doing here?' The words come in a gasp. 'Is he here too?' She casts desperately about the room, her hands frenetically hopping up and down over her bare flesh, as if they could cover it up one piece at a time.

'It's just me,' I assure her. 'I'm here with my work colleagues.'

Her breathing eases; her eyes lift to scan mine. 'So you do not go to festival,' she says.

'Festival?'

Clizia waits, puffed eye louring at me, then lightens sardonically as she sees the realization hit me. Of course: tonight is the first night of the Black & White Festival. William O'Hara is interviewing Bimal Banerjee as we speak, and Robert Dodson is waiting in the wings to discuss Paul's book proposal . . .

'Oh,' I say. Trying to gauge from her expression what he told her, what I need to say here. 'Yes, ah, I was going to go with him, but there has been a crisis at work . . .'

She flaps a hand at me dismissively. 'Don't bother, Frenchman.'

'He could have gone by himself,' I point out. 'I've been too busy at work to get in touch with him. He told you he was going? To meet Dodson?'

'Oh, he tells me lots of things. Wonderful things. This very morning, he says that tonight he does something big. A new plan that will change everything.'

'Well then! That must be what he meant!' I tell her I have not seen him for a little while, but that I know he's been working hard on the proposal, and it must be nearly finished –

'It will never be finished, Frenchman,' she says, cutting me off. 'There will never be a book. I have fooled myself with this hope a hundred times.' She looks at me dully. 'All this week he does not even look at his desk. Does not lift up a pen. Just drinks with that idiot Igor.'

'But then why would he tell you . . . why . . .'

'Because he's a liar.' The bitter smile drops, and it seems that her whole face is suffused with the shadow of the wounded eye. 'That is what he does, Frenchman. He lies. If he wrote his lies down, he would have enough for fifty books. But he is too afraid to lift the pen.' Her face becomes stone. 'All of this time, I have been the fool who believes him. No more.'

Her tone is bleak, final; I cast about desperately for some means of defending him. 'What about you?' I say. 'When is the last time you told him the truth?'

Clizia shrugs her beautiful shoulders. She has stopped looking at me, instead scans the crowd for customers, as the crowd, simultaneously, slows to appraise her. Most men recoil when they catch sight of her black eye – but not all of them do.

'Where have you told him you are tonight?'

She doesn't reply, directs a salacious smile at a corporate type who has paused at the edge of our conversation; he gulps, takes out his wallet, fingers through it, moves on. Her smile inverts, her brow becoming thunderous. She insinuates herself into the throng, with me bumbling after. 'How long have you been working here?'

'Leave me alone.'

'Who did that to your face?'

'It's not important.'

'Was it . . . ?'

'Don't be ridiculous.'

'But he's seen it? Doesn't he know? Hasn't he guessed?'

'I believe his lies, so he believes mine.' She turns and looks at me straight on. 'That's how it goes at the end of love.'

She walks away. I grab her elbow. Instantly a bouncer bristles mastiff-like from the shadows. At some imperceptible signal from Clizia, he withdraws again.

'You are costing me money,' she says coldly.

'*Alors*, how much?' I reach into my pockets. 'How much does it cost to be alone with you?'

'Private dance fifty euro.'

I hand her a note; she takes it without comment. Jocelyn Lockhart and Gary McCrum spot me from the bar and cheer. My cheeks burn; I do my best not to look at her as she leads me back to the booths.

The room is small and cramped. A red light comes on as she closes the door. She backs me into an uncomfortable chair, stands over me like a robot Amazon. 'Five minutes. Vot do you want me to do for you?'

'Tell me the truth.'

'Vot for?'

'I want to help you.'

'I don't need your help.'

'It looks like you do.'

'This is just temporary.'

'Who did that to you?'

'Club boss.'

'Why?'

'Because I borrow money, then I don't come to work.'

'When Paul was writing his book proposal?'

'You are wasting your fifty euro, Frenchman. The truth is the least interesting thing about me.'

'Why did you come back to the club?'

'You have seen how we live.'

'You had a job.'

'I lost it.'

'But this – dancing – you hate it. He told me.'

'Is commercial transaction. Very soon I have enough to leave.'

'Leave the club?'

She smiles; she knows I know that is not what she means. My heart plunges in a spiral. 'Where will you go?'

'Home.'

'With Remington?'

'Of course.'

I prop my elbows on my knees, scrub my head with my hands. 'I wish you'd told me about this before. I can help you. I have money. It's the one thing I do have.'

'Oh, Claude . . .' She stops short, brings her slender fingers to her heart. 'Would you really do that for me? You are special man, very special man.' She draws closer, till her breasts are hovering inches from my nose. 'Maybe I can think of special way to repay you,' she whispers. 'A secret, just between us two?'

'Stop,' I mutter.

She reels away, with a leer of barren triumph. 'The hero with his shining wallet,' she says. 'This club is full of men who want to *help* me, Frenchman.'

Exasperated, I rise from the chair; she flinches back theatrically, as if I had moved against her. I sit back again, say carefully, 'I know you have made many sacrifices. And I know your husband has failed you many times. But I am asking you to give him just one more chance. I'm sure that this time, with a little help, he can finish this book –'

'The book!' She throws her hands in the air. 'You are the same as him! I don't care about the book! I don't care if he writes another fucking word! I just want him to be here in the world with me! Be here with his son! Instead of walking around like the dead man!'

'He loves you.'

She flicks her hand as at some insignificant noise.

'He does!' I insist. 'He told me!'

'He loves me, and he drinks our money!' she exclaims. 'He loves me, and eviction notice comes! He loves me, and I listen to my little boy's tummy rumble all the night long!' She draws back;

the bruised flesh around her eye pulsates with loathing. 'What do you know about it anyway? Little lonely Frenchman, with your sad dreams of true love, what do you know about love or truth? You sit in your palace of death buying and selling human souls, you don't even look out window to see the world you make us live in.'

'You are wrong. I do look out. I see what you have, and I envy it. The cliché is true, there are some things money can't buy.'

'Money can buy anything real,' Clizia says.

'You have not always believed that.'

She pulls up, looks at me aslant with an ironical smile. Even in silence the force of her rage hits me like a gale. 'It is true. Perhaps in each of us there is a little Frenchman who sighs and knots his fingers and gaze at sunset. When I was young I have lots of dreams. I dream of escaping my shithole town. I dream of marrying an artist and never think about money. I follow my dreams and I end up on a stage showing my pussy to drunks.' She pulls indifferently at a banknote that still protrudes from her G-string, looks up at me with false merriment. 'That is how it goes, Frenchman. We dream our dreams, and we take our pay, and the world turns to shit.'

There is a click, and the lights come on. 'Time's up,' she says.

I gawp at her, floundering, then fumble out my wallet. I have no cash left. She looks at me coolly, as she might at any other of her clients, priapic, in love with her, desperate to prolong the fraudulent moment. 'Please,' I entreat her, 'you must promise me that before you do anything, you will let me talk to him.'

'I have to go,' Clizia says.

'You can't give up yet! Just wait a little bit longer!'

Standing in the doorway, shot through by shafts of light from the dance floor, she appears fissiparous, disintegrating. 'Go home, Frenchman,' she says. 'This is not your story.'

She turns away and is swallowed instantly by the nebular

darkness. I hurry out after her, but at the door I'm seized by Gary and Jocelyn and Dave Davison. 'Have you heard, Claude?'

'There's a rescue package!'

'We're still alive!'

Their faces swing about me like carnival masks, repeating the same words – 'government', 'last minute', 'Royal'. But I'm too addled to make sense of them. All I can think is that I must find Paul at once. To the sound of champagne corks popping, I climb the stairs and out on to the street.

Just as I flag down a cab, though, I remember that I gave the last of the cash in my wallet to Clizia. I search about my pockets frantically and at last dig something out – and freeze there on the side of the road.

'Are you getting in or not?' the driver wants to know.

'Sorry, sorry.' I wave numbly; he swears and pulls away again. I remain at the kerb, staring at the paper in my hand – not a bank-note, but the fax from earlier today. It nests in my palm, a sheet of perfect black; and Clizia's words resound in my ears. *This very morning he tells me that tonight he does something big. A new plan that will change everything.*

A terrible thought springs out of the darkness. What if this time he was telling the truth?

The road and footpath have almost disappeared, reduced by the downpour to islets of grit in a black lagoon of water. The rain is coming down heavier than ever – in its frenzy and force hardly like rain at all any more, but rather the bodying forth of something awful, until now hiding out in the abstract, gathering strength there, awaiting its moment to hurl itself into the actual. A sense of impending doom is unavoidable; I break into a run, splashing past nightclubs and pizza restaurants, then leaving the waterlogged street for the shadows of the square, where I instantly spot –

Nothing. In the decorous Georgian enclave, all is calm. The cherry trees cast their blossoms softly against the night; silence turns about the solemn axis of the oak tree like the moon through the houses of some rarefied, red-brick zodiac. My dash slows to a jog, then a plod; my heartbeat does likewise, and I see my fears for what they are: absurd, too absurd for words. Clearly the events of the day have taken their toll on me. Not even Paul would attempt a plan so outlandish – except for the plot of one of his unwritten books, maybe! I laugh out loud, there on the leaf-strewn street, am answered with a murmur of reproof from a covey of pigeons lodged in a dripping magnolia . . . and then the unmistakable sound of breaking glass.

Dread thuds back into my ears; at the same moment the grey boulders of the clouds roll away from the moon, and in the interval of light I see, amid the Benzes and Jaguars parked around the square, a large and anomalous white van. KGB EXTERMINATIONS, runs the legend on its side, with a picture of a terrorized mouse fleeing a man in a trench coat. I start to run again.

William O'Hara's house is almost entirely dark, save for a dim glow from deep within. The garden is deserted, the front door undisturbed. It's still possible I've got it wrong – but then a gate leading to a side passage opens, and a masked figure appears.

'What the –?' he says. 'What are you doing here?'

'What are *you* doing here?' I return, with a sense of déjà vu.

'Dad?'

'*Mon dieu* – what is *he* doing here?'

'Look, Claude, I don't mean to be rude, but we're sort of in the middle of something here –'

'What is about, this racket-making out here?' A third figure comes shambling out of the shadows – dressed, like Paul, in black, with a stocking over his head. 'What is this fucking Frenchman doing here?' he demands when he sees me. 'It is not enough you bring your son? Who else is coming? Your wife? Your mother-in-law?'

'I didn't bring him,' Paul hisses back. 'I don't know why he's here! What the hell are you doing with that window? You could hear it a mile away!'

'How I can concentrate with you people jabbering like *ba-bushkas* out here?'

'You said you knew what you were doing!' Paul jabs his finger at his accomplice.

'That was before I found out that as well as art heist I must be babysitting!' Igor shouts. I grab Paul's arm and point: a light has gone on in an upper floor of the house next door. Reluctantly, he stifles his retort; Igor, with an air of vindication, turns on his heel and disappears back into the black shadow of the house, from which a moment later further shattering noises ensue.

'Oh, that's great, Igor. Why don't we send up a few flares while we're at it? Or put it on Facebook? *Current status: breaking into William O'Hara's house.*'

'Dad?' The boy pulls at his hand until Paul hunkers down.

'Again?' he says incredulously. 'Didn't you use the toilet in Igor's?'

'Igor's toilet is scary,' Remington says sorrowfully.

'Well, you'll just have to hold it in until – aha, here we go!' Above us the front door swings open, a panel of deeper black in the tenebrous façade of the house, as if the night were a series of nesting darknesses into which we were tunnelling. Paul's son has already scampered up the steps, and his father after him.

'Wait!' I hiss after them. 'Are you crazy?' They are already out of sight. For a moment, I remain hovering in the garden, then with a curse hurry inside.

The house, so convivial and warm before, is as cold as a tomb. I pursue Paul's dim ghost down the hall as he shepherds Remington, who is clutching his bottom with both hands, into the bathroom. Depositing the boy on the toilet seat, he turns to me sternly. 'What are you doing here? Why do you have to keep sticking your nose into my business?'

'Because you are about to make a terrible mistake! If you steal that painting, you will never again have peace in your life.'

'Oh, you mean like the fantastically wonderful peace I'm enjoying now? Getting into my own home by the fire escape to avoid the bailiffs? Is that the kind of thing you mean?'

'I know you have problems,' I say, as he wipes the boy's bottom. 'But this isn't the way to solve them!'

'Fuck you, pal. If you were so concerned about my problems, why didn't you help me with the website?' His eyes bore into me. 'You promised you'd pitch it to your clients. Did you tell anyone? Did you tell a single person?'

I gape back at him dumbly.

'See? With friends like you, no wonder this is what I'm reduced to.'

'It's been busy . . . and my investors – it's not as simple as just calling them up . . .'

He grunts disgustedly, refastening Remington's trousers and scooping him into his arms.

'But what about your proposal?' I say. '*Ulysses II*?'

He grimaces. 'Let's just say I came to my senses.'

'What do you mean?'

'I mean, if I'm going to prostitute myself with some idiotic idea, I at least want to make some money from it.'

'But there would be money,' I call after him. 'Dodson would pay! Look at this place! Doesn't it prove a writer can still have a good life –?'

He rounds on me so sharply I almost crash into him. 'What are you, a child?' His eyes flash at me through the darkness. 'You think O'Hara paid for all this with his crappy books? Don't you know who Crispin is?'

I have no option but to gape again.

'He's one of you! He's on the board of the bank that gave me my loan! Every time I open one of their eviction notices there's his name in the small print on the bottom of the page!' He turns away again. 'So you'll forgive me if I don't shed any tears.'

'What about Clizia? You think she wants a thief for a husband?'

'I'm hardly going to tell her, am I?'

'So what will you tell her? That you're still working on your book? You're going to lie to her for the rest of your life?'

He spins around again. 'Jesus, will you get off my case? You're not going to make me feel guilty about this. If I was some big bank going bust I'd have governments around the world throwing money at me. Instead, because I'm just some ordinary defenceless Joe Schmoe, I'm left to rot. Society has given me no choice but to steal this painting. So will you please get out of my way.'

I want to tell him what I learned in the club: that alone might make him think again. But the words stick in my throat. Somehow Clizia's secret career seems much more damning than infidelity; and even if he knew her intentions, he has missed his chance with Dodson, so what could he do to make things right?

A door flies open; Igor barrels out like a methylated Sasquatch. 'What is delay?' he rasps. 'Hurry, hurry!'

I follow them into a room I recognize from our previous visit. Over the fireplace hangs *The Mark and the Void*, its myriad darknesses sparking blackly; my skin prickles in response, making me shiver.

'Dad, can I help steal the painting?'

'We're not stealing anything. It's a trick, remember? We're just playing a trick on Daddy's friend. Now why don't you sit down there on the couch and watch the TV.' Paul goes over to the corner and switches on the set. Remington sits down dutifully.

'A child at an art heist,' Igor grumbles again. 'Who has heard of such a thing?'

'Who's heard of getting a babysitter for an art heist?' Paul rejoins. 'Plus do you know how much they cost these days?'

'That's a false economy!' Igor bellows – but Paul holds up a hand, cutting him off.

'Wait a second,' he says.

A familiar voice is issuing from the TV. 'We live in a civilization in the late stages of necrosis,' it is saying. 'What we take for life is in actuality its decomposition.'

'Dad?'

'Shh.'

'Technology is the noose that mankind swings from.' A bronzed, austere face fills the screen. 'Too in love with its own erection to notice it is being asphyxiated.'

'Dad, this isn't cartoons.'

'Shh, be quiet.'

'And the writer, where does he fit into this?' prompts another, more diffident voice – belonging, I realize, to the man whose living room we are currently standing in.

'The writer is the most tragic figure of all,' Bimal Banerjee says. 'The parasite that does not realize its host is dead.'

'Speak for yourself, pal!' Paul tells the TV. 'Can you believe people actually pay money to hear this guy? It's like getting a civics class from Charles Manson.'

'Hey! Let's get to work!' Igor claps his hands.

'All right, all right . . .'

In the faint glow of the television, the Texier radiates a strange and not entirely wholesome lustre, a kind of paradoxical dark-light that as they draw near it makes the two men look shadowy and insubstantial.

'What we call progress is in fact a vast and unprecedented project of dissociation,' Banerjee intones from the television. 'A separation into individual units, technologically cocooned.'

'You are sure it's not alarmed?' Igor growls, studying the back of the canvas.

'That's what he told me. Though that was a couple of weeks ago.'

'Right,' Igor decides, and in unison both men raise their hands to the frame.

'No!' I cry – but it is too late: they have lifted the painting away from the wall and lowered it to the floor.

'Where nothing is at risk, what need is there for art?' Banerjee says.

'Ach, I leave knife in van!' Igor says. 'Hold on, I return.'

He clomps out of the room. I turn quickly to Paul. 'There is still time to stop this. Think! Even if you get away with it, what does it bring you?'

'If Igor's buyer comes through, twenty-five thousand euro.' He looks down at the painting; laid out on the carpet it resembles a fissure, a personalized abyss we are about to tumble into.

'And you genuinely believe this will solve all your problems?'

'No, but it'll solve twenty-five thousand of them,' he says.

'But people still want stories . . . ?' On-screen, William O'Hara is looking bewildered.

'Oh yes, they still want stories,' Banerjee replies. 'But increasingly those stories are coming from the Third World, from the past, from the lives of people who have not yet sold their souls to machines. More and more, art resembles a kind of narrative colonialism. That is why I have come to my decision.'

'What decision?' William O'Hara asks.

'What decision?' Paul echoes.

'To stop writing,' Banerjee says.

'Ha!' Paul exclaims.

'Stop writing?' On the TV screen, William O'Hara is agog.

'I do not see my art as a consumer product,' Banerjee says. 'Therefore I am removing it from the marketplace.'

'Can't take the heat, eh?' Paul jeers at the TV, evidently without awareness of any irony.

'But surely the writer has a duty.' William O'Hara takes off his glasses and rubs his eyes. 'That is, we can't simply abandon the world to its fate . . . ?'

'It is only when it has ceased to beat that the world will realize literature was its heart,' Banerjee says. 'But that is no longer my concern.'

This revelation has clearly stymied O'Hara, who's turned a dangerous-looking shade of pink; the Indian places a hand on his knee, and says, 'Don't worry – for those who are willing to sell themselves, there is still plenty of money to be made.'

At this the older man's face goes from pink to brick-red – but how he responds we do not find out, because now, from behind us, there comes a long, strangulated cry. Igor has returned from the van; he is crouched over the painting, gazing at it in horror. Following his eye down, we see, newly emblazoned in large green letters across the black canvas, REMINGTON.

'It wasn't me,' Remington pipes up pre-emptively.

Paul emits a cry of his own. 'Oh God, Remington . . .'

'I spelled it right,' Remington points out.

Igor kneels over the desecrated painting in a convulsion of rage and grief, like King Lear over Cordelia. 'No,' he whispers, dabbing at the green letters without effect. 'No, no . . .'

'Maybe they won't notice,' Paul ventures.

'Not notice?' Igor's eyes flick up balefully. 'Not notice?'

'I mean . . .' Paul says, backing away as Igor rises to his feet, 'they might think it's just . . . you know . . . modern . . .'

'I give you something to notice!' Igor howls, lunging after Paul, who dodges behind the television, where interviewer and interviewee are glaring at each other in silence – and it has just occurred to me to wonder whether the broadcast is live when the door flies open and the light blinks on, and there in the threshold, as if he has escaped from the screen, is Bimal Banerjee.

For a long moment he gazes down at us; then, with a malefic grin, 'So!' he exclaims. From his tone it is plain that even if he does not understand the full significance of the scene, he sees, with a torturer's instinct, an opportunity to inflict pain. 'So!' he declares again, with relish, and hands on hips he swaggers into the room. But almost immediately, he comes to a stop; then he crumples to the ground. Curiously, it is only after the fact that I realize what has happened – namely, that I have hit him on the head with a bronze statuette of a faun. Now he lies on the ground, utterly motionless.

'Jesus, Claude, what have you done?'

'What's wrong with the man, Daddy?'

'Claude's killed him,' Paul whispers, then looks up at me. 'You've killed Bimal Banerjee!'

Without a word, Igor dashes to the window, throws up the sash and jumps out. We should probably think about doing the same – but already another figure has appeared in the doorway: Paul's editor, Robert Dodson. Now it is his turn to take in the scene, piece by piece: the curtain flapping at the open window; the painting on the floor, with scissors, Stanley knife, plastic sheeting arranged about it; Paul, stocking rolled back over his head, and me, still clutching the sexually explicit sculpture; and lastly the celebrated author himself, lying prostrate on the carpet, although, I am glad to see, still breathing. Nobody says a word; then, from the TV, the pre-recorded Banerjee pronounces, 'The problem with British publishing is that it is run by dinosaurs whose whole intelligence is absorbed in avoiding evolution.'

Robert Dodson frowns gently, sampling this thought just as one might the bouquet of a fine wine; then, stepping over Banerjee's prone body, he shakes his umbrella into the fireplace, turns to us and says, 'So I take it you've come to talk about the book?'

Thinking about it, it strikes me that this could be the best of all possible outcomes. To have stolen the painting would have been a disaster, the beginning of a new and unending story of guilt, paranoia and pursuit; to have bungled it in any other way than we did would have meant disgrace and very probably prison sentences. Instead, Robert Dodson takes care of everything; it's as if he's been tidying up botched art heists his whole life. 'Might just stick this back on the wall,' he says as if to himself, picking up the Texier.

'It, uh, fell down,' Paul says gruffly.

'Oh yes, yes, they'll do that,' Dodson agrees. 'A friend of mine works in the Tate, it's a real problem – hullo, who's this?'

From behind the curtain Remington steps out, his mouth smeared with the same green pigment with which he recently augmented the painting.

'This is my son,' Paul says reluctantly.

'Ah – oh,' Dodson says. He looks at the canvas, then at the boy. 'Might his name be Remington?'

'It might,' Paul confesses.

'Right, right. Hmm, well, if you could just give me a hand to get this chap back into place . . .'

The defaced painting is surprisingly heavy: we stagger over to the mantel and, gasping, hoist it back up on to its hooks. Dodson steps back and considers it. REMINGTON blares expensively back at us. 'Tell you what,' he says, and then, without elaborating, bends down, scoops a handful of soot from the fireplace and smears it judiciously over the sprawling letters. 'I mean, it's intended as a dynamic sort of a piece, changing over time and so forth,' he says to me.

'Interaction with the environment,' I agree. 'This is exactly the kind of thing Texier intended.'

As he makes a few more minor adjustments, he explains that William and Crispin are still at the festival, but that Bimal Banerjee had contracted a migraine after the interview. 'He said it was probably the high concentration of mediocrity,' he tells us, deadpan. 'But I'm glad, because it means we can finally have a chat about *Anal Analyst*.'

Paul, hearing this, looks guiltier than he did when apprehended stealing the painting.

'I must say, ever since you mentioned it that night, I haven't been able to stop thinking about it,' Dodson says. 'Perhaps I could tease a few more details from you? Characters, a rough idea of the length, and so on?'

Paul lets out a long sigh. 'Look, Robert, there is no *Anal Analyst*.'

'There isn't?' The editor looks confused. I am confused too. What's he doing? He's been offered a lifeline, why doesn't he grab it? And then, almost simultaneously, it hits me. Paul doesn't want a lifeline; he has never wanted a lifeline. The real goal of the heist and his other ludicrous schemes isn't to haul himself out of the water – it's to scupper the ship, to find rock bottom, to rid himself once and for all of any last vestiges of hope. The failure of his last book crushed him so thoroughly that he would rather steal a painting, be caught, disgraced and imprisoned, than write another one and see it fail too.

But this time I am not going to let him sabotage himself.

'What he means,' I interrupt, 'is that since we saw you, the book has been significantly changed.'

'Oh yes?' Dodson's interest is piqued anew.

'And improved,' I say. Paul is glaring at me, but I ignore him. 'Instead of a promiscuous gay man, the book now tells the story of a banker who . . . who falls in love with . . .' I trail off. The implausibility, the unwritability of a love story set in the IFSC suddenly seems incontrovertible. But what to put in its place? Fragments of abandoned narratives float surreally about my mind's eye: detectives, wombats, James Joyce firing a revolver. My mouth opens and closes. Dodson considers me doubtfully; Paul's glower transmutes into a smirk – and then, in a moment of perfect simplicity, it comes, or rather it has been there all along.

'It tells the story of *two* men,' I say. 'The first is a lonely banker, who spends his days making money, and his nights searching for something to spend it on, a perfect circle of meaningless consumption. He has no friends, no family. Maybe he is running from something in his past, or trying to fill some loss with possessions. Or maybe he works simply so that he doesn't have to think. But then he meets a writer who says he wants to put him in a book. For the first time the banker begins to come out of his ennui. In reality, though, the writer is planning to rob the bank.'

'Ha!' Dodson barks appreciatively, while Paul twists his mouth up and mutters under his breath.

'At first, the two men seem very different. The banker is successful, solitary; his life is dominated by money. The writer has a family, but struggles to make art in a time when everything is defined by its price tag. Beneath the surface, though, both men are driven by the same urge to escape. The writer hides behind failure just as the banker hides behind wealth. They have lost faith in the world, and in themselves.' I avoid looking at Paul when I say this, though I can hear his ever more irritated sighs. 'For this reason, even though his book is just a trick, the writer and the banker become friends. And with this friendship, they begin to bring each other back to life.'

'So it's a love story,' Robert Dodson says with a smile.

'I suppose you could call it that,' I agree bashfully. 'Through

434

the banker, the writer is inspired to start writing his book for real –'

'Yes!' The editor brings his hands together. 'I can see it. It's all about giving, isn't it? The writer gives the banker companionship, the banker gives the writer faith, the writer begins a new book, about the banker, the same man he once believed was nothing more than an empty shell – and he gives that to us! We realize it's the very book that we're now holding in our hands!'

'Yes, yes!' I listen to this, grinning, with a sense, joyous as it is inexplicable, that everything has come together, all problems solved.

Then Dodson looks back at me and says, 'And the banker?'

'What?'

'The banker, what happens to him?'

'What happens . . . ?'

'He can't just go back to the office after all that, can he?'

'No, no, of course not . . . no, the banker . . .' He can't go back to the office, I can see that, but as to what he should do instead – 'The banker . . . ah . . .'

Dodson slowly nods his head, willing me on, but it's no good, my mind has gone blank, and no matter how I try, all I can see is the banker at his desk, obediently tending to his work, his terminal full of numbers. 'The banker has to . . . he has to . . .'

'That's enough,' Paul says.

I slump, gaze back at him wretchedly.

Paul turns to the editor with a stony countenance. 'He's just trying to cover for me. The truth is that when I said, "There is no book," that's exactly what I meant.'

'There's no book?' Dodson's kindly, clever face puckers in incomprehension.

'There's no book, Claude is not my life partner, we've never been to Sweden. I don't write any more, Robert. I haven't had a saleable idea in seven years. I didn't come here tonight to talk to you about a manuscript. I came to steal that painting.'

'Oh,' Dodson says. His brows furrow and knead together, as though masticating this information – then once again the door opens, and William O'Hara enters in a state of panic.

'The window in the alley's smashed!' he exclaims, then notices our presence. 'Hullo,' he says.

'Bumped into these boys out for a walk,' Dodson breezes. 'Asked them in for a minute – hope that's all right?'

'Out for a walk?' William O'Hara repeats, rainwater dripping off his coat into a pool at his feet.

'Yes, babysitting this little chap here. Can't sleep, poor thing – anyhow, they wanted to say hello.'

'We were very sorry to miss the interview,' I chip in.

'Count your blessings,' William O'Hara says.

He steps back, inspects us thoughtfully. Remington is chewing on his crayon; the rolled-up stocking is still perched on top of Paul's head, like a tiny beige beret. O'Hara clears his throat. He appears on the point of asking a question, a question that I suspect will prove very hard to answer, when he is distracted by a groan.

'Who's that?' he says, and then, peering over the couch, 'What's Banerjee doing on the floor?'

'Touch of migraine,' Robert Dodson says.

'Oh,' William O'Hara says. He sounds cheered. He takes another look at the felled author and says brightly, 'Well! Who's for a drink?'

'We should bring this little boy home,' I say.

'Suit yourselves,' O'Hara says. 'I'll let you out.' He turns for the door – then, as if it has yanked at his sleeve, turns back again and stares at The Mark and the Void. He remains staring for what seems like a very long time. 'You know,' he says at last, 'I don't mean to sound like I'm bragging, but every time I look at that painting I see something new.' He shakes his head proudly. 'That's a real work of art,' he says.

Igor and the van are long gone, and neither of us has any cash, so there is no choice but to walk back towards the river. The rain has restarted, and descends on us in enormous drenching globules. The mood, it need hardly be said, is low.

'You should not be disappointed,' I tell him. 'From what I have read, art theft is a very hard crime to pull off.'

Paul nods morosely. 'It's Igor I feel bad for,' he says. 'He was going to buy a hot tub.'

'Dad . . .' Remington is rubbing his eyes with his fists.

'Okay, buddy, we'll be home soon.' He hoists the boy up, letting his small head fall on his shoulder. 'Listen, Claude. I appreciate what you were trying to do back there, with Dodson. For the record, though, if there's one thing people want to read about even less than a French banker, it's a novelist struggling to write his new book.'

'If I ever pretend to submit a book proposal again I will keep that in mind.'

'Seriously, I know you mean well, but you're box-office poison,' he says. Then he adds, 'I'm sorry it didn't work out.'

'Me too,' I say.

We reach the quays. The wind batters us as we cross the river; below us, the water foams seawards, throws spume up over the walls to deluge the bronze figures of the Famine sculpture and their modern-day doubles a few yards away, the city's cadaverous addicts, huddled in the negligible shelter of the trestle bridge, while from the roof of the Custom House the golden statue of Commerce looks over the city.

'What will you do now?' I say, when we get to the far side.

437

'I'm not sure,' he admits. 'I'd go back to Myhotswaitress, but right now I need something that'll bring in money, like, tomorrow.'

'How much is it you're looking for?'

'More than you've got, Claude.' He says it with a smile, as if he wants to reassure me, as if I might have felt compelled to pay off his mortgage for him, had I the funds, though this isn't something that really happens, is it, even between friends? Not in the real world?

'We'll muddle through somehow,' he says, 'we always do.' At that moment there comes a bleep from his pocket; with his free hand he takes out his phone. 'Well, there's some good news,' he says, reading the message. 'Clizia's won her volleyball game. That means they're through to the final.'

'How wonderful,' I say, as my lungs fill up with cement.

'You know, win or lose, I think she'll be glad when it's finally over. All these late nights?' He chuckles to himself. 'And the other night she got an elbow right in the face, swelled up into a massive shiner.'

'Yes,' I say, betraying no emotion.

'The point is, I suppose I should look on the bright side. I might be unemployed and broke and about to be evicted, but I still have my family, right? I mean, in some ways I'm probably the richest man you know.'

'Definitely,' I say, looking away to where the river, gorged with the night's rain, charges triumphantly, like an army putting its enemies to rout.

We shake hands, make vague promises to meet again; then Paul turns, child in his arms, towards the north. I stand and watch him disappear into the waves of rain – seeming to walk right out of the world, as if there were no more of his story left to play out.

Continuing down the quay, I discover a Carambar in my pocket. The joke on the wrapper is the George Clooney one again. On my phone, a baffled message from Ish, asking if these crazy stories about AgroBOT buying out Royal Irish are true; several humorous texts from co-workers, increasingly incoherent as the celebrations go on; a long voicemail from Walter Corless, ranting that the Caliph still owes him money. He makes no mention of AgroBOT's death and resurrection, as if the events of the last two days had never happened. Maybe, from his perspective, they never did.

I delete the message, turn the phone off.

What happens to the banker? Nothing happens to the banker. The banker is paid to be a person to whom nothing happens.

Walking across the plaza, I see an A4 page in a plastic protector taped to the metal shutter of the Ark, thanking the café's customers for their loyalty and wishing them well. A customer: that's all I amounted to in the end. Her customer, Paul's customer, someone who pays his money, takes his goods and then walks away.

Now the glass citadel of Transaction House rises before me, shimmering through the rain like a ghostly privateer; I think about Ish's tribe, scouring the waves for souls to make away with. Tomorrow we will be back in business: I can hardly bear to think about it.

As I pass the door, though, something stops me, pulls me back. What is it? The security desk is unmanned, the lights are off, all is in darkness. Yet some strange energy emanates from within, tugs at me with invisible fingers. Without knowing why, I push the door and find that in all the excitement it has been left ajar.

Inside, the strange pressure only grows; and as I climb into the lift I feel the same tension a surfer must feel, stalking barefoot over the shingle while a storm brews above the waves – still hidden in clear skies but there to touch, an electricity that crackles along the surface of the water, a blanket of static beneath which every drop buzzes.

I step out on to the sixth floor.

No one is here – no Asia team, no frantic interns, no midnight strategists building some invincible trade; I walk through the

desks feeling like a visitor from the future, a tourist in some bur-
eaucratic ruin. On my desk I see Walter's cheques and bank
drafts, the ones he gave me a couple of days ago, still sitting there,
uninvested. I never did anything with them; with the bank going
down, there hadn't seemed a point.

Is there a point now?

Am I going to do this?

Somewhere out in the night a clock strikes thirteen.

The next day the storm has lifted; the office is filled with sunshine. It slants through the windows in great radiant sheets, burnishing white shirts to such a brightness that from certain angles the room appears to be filled with angels, floating about their heavenly station, reciting beatific litanies of numbers.

'I still don't get it,' Ish says. 'I thought we were going bust. How can we buy a bank if we're going bust? And why would we want to buy Royal Irish?'

'Optics,' Gary McCrum says, sucking a choc ice, leafing through a watch catalogue. Now that we're being rescued, everyone's acting like they expected it all along.

'Okay, for the last time,' Jocelyn says heavily. 'Everyone knows Royal Irish is dead in the water, right? But the government's been afraid to let it go under, because the whole world'll hear about it and no one'll ever put their money in this country again. So a buyout like this suits them perfectly. They can proclaim the bank's been cleaned up enough to sell on, Royal's absorbed into a well-respected firm, its name is never spoken again, everyone gets on with their lives.'

'But what's in it for us? Why would we buy Royal, if it's such a basket case?'

Because we're not really buying it, is the answer. The doomed investments, the enormous book of bad loans, the copious lawsuits as well as Walter's festering 25 per cent stake have all been quietly parcelled up and transferred to a government agency. 'Basically, all we're buying is the name, and the HQ building there.' Jocelyn jabs his thumb at the monolithic edifice on the far quay, presently invisible behind the window-dazzle.

'And we're getting it for practically nothing,' Gary adds. 'The site alone's worth twice what we're paying.'

But still. Isn't AgroBOT broke? What about all that Greek debt? Well. This is the clever part of the deal. At the heart of its extremely complicated mechanics is a swap: in return for taking the PR millstone that is Royal off their hands, the government has agreed to exchange all of AgroBOT's toxic waste for guaranteed state bonds.

'They're just going to take it from us?' Ish says incredulously.

'I'm not sure they know what it is,' Jocelyn says.

'They know,' Gary contradicts him.

'Then why would they take it?'

Gary lifts up his watch catalogue, puts his feet on the desk. 'Not their decision any more, is it?' he says, rolling the stick of his choc ice with his tongue.

Whose decision is it? The IMF, the EU, the ECB? Some other conglomeration of acronyms? That is not for us to know. The bottom line is that our balance sheet will be clean again and AgroBOT made whole; and the Irish people – along with their unstaffed hospitals, their potholed roads, their overstuffed classrooms, medieval prisons, dying pensioners – will become the proud owners of six billion euros' worth of, as Jocelyn likes to call it, radioactive Greek shit.

This doesn't go unremarked upon. Though the government tries to spin it as a happy ending for Royal Irish, many commentators see the AgroBOT bailout for what it is, and are asking why Ireland has been lumbered with rescuing a bank that is not itself Irish, nor European, nor, when it comes down to it, in the northern hemisphere.

A more pressing point is that Ireland simply cannot afford to take on AgroBOT's debts. The deal, if it's voted through, will effectively bankrupt the country. So why are they doing it?

'My surmise is that taking on AgroBOT's debt is the condition of Ireland receiving aid from higher up,' Jurgen says.

'So they're deliberately bankrupting themselves so they can get a handout from Europe? How does that make any sense?'

'You are perhaps making the mistake of judging Irish actions by an external standard.' Jurgen's smile has the same brilliant opacity as the sunlight in the window. 'You must remember that unlike the French, the British, the' – with a little cough – 'Germans, the Irish have never commanded their own empire. For the greater part of their history, they have been the subjects of foreign powers. Of course, we must go through the motions of equality *und so weiter*. But the fact is that the Irish are at root a slave race. We have seen this during their brief period of good fortune, when they are acting like the servant who has found the key to the wine cellar while his master is away. Even then it is clear they are not fit to be rulers of themselves. And they do not wish it either. This is why, although it seems to you and me the terrible injustice, they will carry their new debt without grumbling, even with gratitude.'

'They'll be . . . grateful? For paying off AgroBOT's debt?'

'Exactly so. Do not forget, Claude, this is a country until very recently ruled by priests. Thanks to them, the Irish already believe they are born in debt, a terrible debt of sin which they can never pay in full. A people like this is more comfortable wrapped in chains. For this reason, I am believing the deal will pass through parliament without issue.'

Nevertheless, we must take no chances. 'As we have seen in the last weeks, the public mood is unpredictable. Prior to next week's vote, it is more than ever important that the contents of your original report on Royal Irish are forgotten. The IT Department has taken the liberty of destroying all related material on your hard drive and on the AgroBOT servers. You will do the same with any files on external drives or your own machine.'

'All right.'

'I must tell you, Claude, you have impressed a lot of people with your handling of this matter. Yes, with the initial report you have badly miscalculated. But after that, you have made the case to the media very convincingly.'

'You mean I lied.'

'Sometimes for the greater good it is necessary to bend the truth a little. For a society to prosper, it's the strong, not the weak, that must be protected. The journalists will not understand this, of course. But those who know are not forgetting your contribution. You have a bright future here at AgroBOT, very, very bright.'

He returns his gaze to the window. Across the water, the white sky glows in the unfinished windows of the Royal HQ, blind eyes shining through a concrete mask. 'Beautiful, isn't it?'

I am too surprised to reply.

'True, it does not look like much now,' Jurgen considers. 'But in a few years, the housing market will recover, unemployment will fall, and the Irish will be clamouring once more for high-interest loans to fund their four-wheel drives and shopping trips to New York. At this point I am predicting our new acquisition will prove very lucrative.'

'You mean the whole thing will happen all over again.'

'Yes, it will happen all over again. But this time we will be prepared.' He looks out at the river, the static cranes, the office blocks, as if any moment all of it will turn into money . . . 'Life is so fucking beautiful,' he says.

The market loves the *coup de théâtre* of the Royal Irish buyout: although the Irish government hasn't yet signed off on the deal, AgroBOT's share price has already begun to climb. In the days that follow, the bank's credit rating is upgraded, and then upgraded again; the *Wall Street Journal* runs a feature on Porter Blankly, with a picture of the CEO smoking a fat cigar and the quote, 'When they say you're over-leveraged . . . that's when you buy another bank.' According to this article, the deal was clinched over a round of golf with Ireland's political elite, in which Blankly, who flew in directly from New York and had not slept in thirty-six hours, made a par 5 in two shots before sinking a putt for an eagle 3. The rumour within AgroBOT is that Howie and Grisha were responsible for the details; although investors are demanding an investigation into the collapse of their ninth-floor fund, word is they've already been spirited to New York to sit at Porter's right hand. None of this may be true; still, visitors to the Uncanny Valley report that Rachael spends most of her time these days by the window, gazing out towards the sea, like a lonesome maiden waiting for her sailor to come home.

Does it need to be said that nobody follows through on his vows to leave banking and take up shoemaking, orphan husbandry, semi-professional paragliding, whatever else? Kevin is given a permanent contract; a solicitors' firm specializing in liquidation opens an office on the ninth floor; Skylark Fitzgibbon reappears in the form of a barrage of publicity pictures from Kokomoko, showing the first shipments of topsoil arriving onshore, rich loamy mounds that will become the greens and fairways of the golf course, smiling islanders beside her in blue Agron Torabundo T-shirts.

'So Blankly got away with it.'

'Got away with what?'

'Cashing in twice.'

'Not this crazy conspiracy theory again.'

'I'm just saying.'

No one else is saying; everyone is just grateful to be back to work. And within a very short time, a matter of days, life is just as it was. Or almost.

'Who is that man, Ish?'

'What?'

'The man, there, coming out of Liam's office.'

'Oh, the dude in black?'

'He's a new employee?'

'Hmm, I think he's from Compliance.'

'Compliance?'

'Yeah, I heard there's been someone snooping around the last couple of days, asking questions.'

'What about?'

'Beats me. Wouldn't reckon it's got anything to do with us.'

'No, no, of course not.'

'You going somewhere, Claude?'

'Yes, I have a, um, meeting. If anyone's looking for me . . . ah . . .'

'Don't worry, I never saw you.'

The door doesn't open so much as implode at my knock, giving way to a seething mass of small children, who run back and forth and bump into one another in an exemplary display of Brownian motion.

'Thanks for coming,' Paul says, wading through them with me to the relative safety of the kitchen table. 'Sorry about the short notice. We weren't going to do anything, but then Clizia's game got cancelled, so . . .'

'It's my pleasure,' I say. 'It's not every day that someone turns five.'

'Thank God for that. Here, let me see if I can . . .' He cranes over the swarm and plucks out his son, who is panting with excitement and partially covered with a recent meal. 'Look who it is, Remington! It's your Uncle Claude!'

'Happy burp-day,' I say, handing him my present.

'What is it?'

'It's an ant farm,' I explain. 'Where ants live.' I help him remove the wrapping paper to reveal the plastic window through which ants may be seen running up and down tunnels with small objects in their mouths, occasionally stopping to flail antennae with other ants. The resemblance to the Financial Services Centre seems to me indisputable.

'Is Roland in there?' Remington asks.

'Hmm, there are certainly some ants that might be related . . .'

'Let's take them out!'

'Maybe later,' his father says hastily, removing the box from the boy's hands and putting it on a high shelf. Remington shrugs and rejoins the anarchy. 'So I have news,' Paul says to me.

'Oh yes?'

'Yeah. Dodson called.'

The first thing I think of is Banerjee. 'He's pressing charges? Or – my God, he's not dead, is he?'

'Relax, Banerjee's fine, they're all fine. No, he was calling about the book.'

'What book?'

'*My* book. He thinks it's got legs. He wants to publish it.'

'He wants to –?' I feel a soar of elation, though also a certain amount of confusion: there do seem to be a number of loose ends to this news, for example that there is no book.

'There's no book now,' Paul corrects me. 'But after hearing our proposal that night Robert says it's all right there.' His voice takes on a loftier tone, adding, 'He says it's the book I was born to write.'

'He says *Anal Analyst* is the book you were born to write?'

'He's not 100 per cent sure about the title,' Paul concedes.

'Well,' I say, attempting to take this in. 'And you don't . . . that is, in the past you have had some doubts about writing. The modern audience, competing technologies, that kind of thing.'

'Cold feet, that's all that was,' Paul says dismissively. 'Does the blackbird sing for an audience? Does the sun rise in the hope that some douche'll take a picture of it on his phone? I just needed someone to believe in me. That's what I've been waiting for, all this time.'

'I believed in you,' I remind him.

'I know, I know.'

'Clizia believed in you.'

'Yeah, well, someone who's professionally qualified to believe in me, I mean.'

It strikes me that Robert Dodson believed in him the last time, and he just never submitted the book, but I decide not to press the point. 'And he will give you some money, as well as belief?'

'He needs a couple of pages first – just the basic set-up, to

448

show the finance people. But once that's done, he's pretty sure he can scrap the previous advance and set up a whole new deal.'

'Debt forgiveness, eh?'

'They won't pay much. But get this. Just a few days after I saw you, I got an email from this investment company, asking about buying the apartment for cash.'

'This apartment?'

'Yes! I told them straight up it's got structural problems. They didn't seem to care. Cyrano Solutions, you ever heard of them?'

'No, but there are all kinds of foreign investors in town, buying up property.'

'I couldn't find anything about them online. It sounded kind of shady to me. But then the next thing I know we get this huge whomp of money into our account! I mean just like that! And these people say we can wait and move out whenever. Isn't that crazy? Like I wouldn't say our troubles are over, exactly, but I'll be able to keep writing full-time, at least till I've got a first draft. After that maybe I can get a few gigs on the side, reviews, that kind of thing – you know, now that I've got my bona fides again.'

'That is wonderful.' I clink his plastic glass. 'Congratulations.'

'Thanks. We were sailing pretty close to the wind this time. Sometimes I even thought . . . well, why dwell on it. Suffice to say, it's nice to have some good news for a change. And a lot of it's down to you.'

'Me?' I say, through a mouthful of butterfly cake.

'You assaulting Banerjee did me no harm at all. He didn't say it, but I got the distinct impression Dodson's been wanting to hit him with a sculpture for a long, long time. I reckon I could have given him the ABC after that and he still would have published it.'

'*Au contraire*, it is your talent.'

'So the question now is how to end it,' Paul says, as in a far corner of the room a synthesizer polka starts up and the children dance around. 'Dodson thinks he's got to rob the bank.'

'The banker?'

'He says it's the only ending that makes sense. After everything that happens.'

'I see,' I say, a cold spiral of metal coiling up from my gut.

'So I wanted to run something by you. I know you said robbing an investment bank was basically impossible. But I've been reading about this guy in France, this Pierrot – you've heard of him?'

'Of course.'

The children are jumping up and down now, the noise so thunderous it almost drowns out the music.

'He breaks into the back office in the middle of the night, forges some papers, transfers his clients' money into his own account. Couldn't that work here?'

The music stops abruptly: the children freeze.

'Pierrot got caught,' I say.

'He got greedy. He did it over and over. What if our guy only does it once? And he takes the money from some really evil client, so it wouldn't seem so much like stealing?'

I stroke my chin; my fingers feel like ice. 'It's true, if he put the money into a third party's account it would be almost impossible for the bank to get back,' I say, forcing the words through numb lips. 'And maybe, if he was lucky, the client wouldn't find out till their end-of-year returns. Still, it would only be a matter of time.'

'In theory, though, you could have it so that by the time the client finds out they've got away?'

' "They"?'

'The banker and the waitress.'

I feel a curious jolt, as if the world has slipped from its wheel. 'What about her boyfriend?'

'She doesn't have a boyfriend,' Paul says, erasing him with a single wave of the hand. 'Maybe the banker *thinks* she has a boyfriend. And that's what makes his sacrifice authentic? But then he finds out the truth, using a bespoke waitress surveillance system. Although Dodson's not 100 per cent about that part either,' he confesses.

'Dad, we need you for pass-the-parcel . . .' Remington appears at his father's elbow.

'Oh, right – but in principle, that'd work? The back-office thing?'

They get away; a happy ending. 'Yes, I think that would work very well.'

'Dad.'

'All right, all right. Hey, try the dinosaur cake, Claude, it's unbeatable!'

He is pulled away. Left by the table, nibbling on dinosaur cake, I think about what he said. Could they really escape, the banker and the waitress? Is there still somewhere in the world the bank wouldn't find them?

'You look like one of the musical statues.'

I turn around. Clizia has materialized beside me. 'Just day-dreaming,' I tell her. 'Enjoying the party?'

'I should get back to the office. But I'm worried that if I move I will stand on somebody.'

'They're tougher than they look,' she says with a laugh. Her hair is tied back, and instead of her usual micro-skirt she wears a tracksuit, liberally adorned with food smears and tiny finger-prints; the bruising around her eye has faded almost to nothing.

'Things are better?' I say.

She shrugs. 'If he finishes book.'

'What about you? How are your . . . travel plans?'

She shrugs again, though not without a smile. 'We'll see. For now, everything is good.'

'No more volleyball.'

'I pay off boss.' She waits a moment after relaying this infor-mation, then says, 'Don't you want to know how?'

'Hmm, Paul mentioned that you've sold the apartment?'

She looks amusedly into my eyes, and for a moment our gazes

criss-cross, glancing off one another like bright swords in a duel. Then she takes my hand. 'Come, before you leave, there's someone I want you to meet.' She scans the partygoers, then locates the one she is looking for, beside the refrigerator: a small, olive-skinned boy, with a blue stripe on the bridge of his nose and pink daubs on his cheeks.

'This is one of Remington's friends from school,' she says. 'Tell Claude your name, darling.'

The small child looks up at me. He does not speak: he does not need to. His eyes are a brilliant, luminescent green, like light through the trees of some Olympian forest.

'I think maybe you know his mother,' Clizia says innocently. 'She works in a café near your bank?'

'Ah – oh – is that right?' I stammer.

'It closed . . . but then it opened again.'

'I see.'

'Someone gave them a whole lot of money.'

'Is that so? Good for them.'

'But they don't know who he is.'

'Well, that's the business world, so impersonal . . .'

Clizia touches my arm, leans in to me and says, 'You're a good man, Claude.'

'Me? Oh, you mean the ant farm?'

'There are not many good men. So few that sometimes we forget even to look for them. We are too busy trying to pick out the best of the bad men.'

I continue to make fish-out-of-water gestures of incomprehension, which Clizia continues to ignore.

'Oscar's mother will be coming to collect him in about half an hour,' she says absently, stooping to pick up a little girl who has collided with the dustbin. 'If you are still here, you can all walk back together?'

Ariadne? Here? With no more tricks, or ploys, or misunderstandings? For an instant it seems that life and story are merging at last into one, everything I hoped for coming true . . . but then my phone begins to ring, and I remember it's already too late for that.

'Where are you, Claude?' Rachael's secretary is at the other end of the line.

'I had a meeting.'

A compact, merciless hammering of keys. 'I can't see anything in your diary.'

'Yes, it was . . . unscheduled.'

'You're needed back at the office.'

'With regard to something in particular . . . ?'

'Just get back here,' she says.

I step out of the lift to find the office submerged in a kind of silent panic, a frantic gloom that envelops everything like a fog. Through windows, around corners, senior management can be seen having agitated conversations, then hurrying off in different directions. I go to my desk, moving calmly, as if I am being watched.

The man in black is in Liam English's office, interviewing staff.

'One of the accounts got tapped,' Gary McCrum says in a low voice.

'Whose?' Jocelyn Lockhart says. 'How much was taken?'

Gary McCrum shrugs.

'What's going to happen?' Kevin asks.

'They're talking to everyone,' Gary says. 'But I reckon they already know who it was.'

'Who? And . . . how?'

'And how's he supposed to've done it?'

'I heard there was some security fuck-up the night of the margin call,' Brent 'Crude' Kelleher says. 'A bunch of doors got left open. Including back office.'

'They think someone went in there?'

'They found something on the floor the next day.'

'I heard that too,' Terry Fosco joins in huskily, spinning round in his chair. 'I heard they found a Goldman Sachs business card.'

'I heard it was a USB key,' Dave Davison says from the water cooler, 'and on it there was a virus the IT people had never seen before.'

'It was a sweet wrapper,' Thomas 'Yuan' McGregor says. His eyes are bleary: he has been summoned from his bed.

'A *sweet* wrapper?'

'What, back office don't eat sweets?'

At that moment, the office door opens and everyone falls silent. An apparatchik from Sales emerges, looking pale and traumatized. He glances at us, then steps quickly away, fingering his collar. Liam English comes to the threshold with Rachael and the man in black. Rachael is holding a clipboard, in a cursory way that makes it look like a prop. The man in black looks over the room; his eyes, quite without life or expression, pause on me . . .

'David Davison,' Rachael calls.

'Fuck,' Dave mutters, getting to his feet.

'You think it was him?' Kevin says breathlessly, once the door closes. 'Dave?'

'They're talking to everyone, you tool,' Gary says.

'Well *someone's* in for it,' Jocelyn says, then rolls back to his desk.

The others follow suit; I turn to my terminal, where the numbers scroll across my screen, twittering among themselves like birds, amidst a general silence so taut you could punch a hole in it –

The lift doors open. Ish bounces across the floor, autumn air clinging to her coat. 'Hey, guess what! The Ark's reopened!'

'Oh yes, I saw that,' smiling at her queasily.

'Want to come and have a look?'

'I don't think anyone's supposed to leave.'

'They're interviewing *alphabetically*. They won't get to us till midnight. Come on, Claude, a coffee at least . . .'

My limbs are heavy as stone; I don't think I have the strength to go anywhere, except maybe to hide under my desk. Ish, however, won't take no for an answer.

'Pretty mental, isn't it?' she says in the lift. 'You think it's true? Someone's pulled a Pierrot?'

I shrug, burble nothings.

'I heard it was the Dublex account,' she says, and then, 'Where'd you go earlier?'

455

I tell her about the birthday party, and Paul's good news.

'For real this time? He's not trying to knock the place off again?'

'I don't think so.'

'Sounds like someone's beaten him to it, anyway,' Ish remarks.

I thought I'd feel better once I got into the fresh air. Instead the dread only seems to intensify, sparking in my hair and teeth and fingertips.

'Claude!' Ariadne throws her arms around me when we step through the door. 'We're back! Can you believe it?'

'Yes, it's very good,' I stammer at her weakly.

'An investor comes out of nowhere, give us everything we needed. We don't even know who he is! I thought maybe it's someone you called?'

'One of my clients? Hmm, no, no, I don't think so . . .'

She seats us, gives us menus, scampers away again. Ish gives me a long look. 'All coming up roses for your mates today, isn't it?'

I wrinkle my forehead perplexedly. ' "*Coming up roses . . .* "?'

She laughs. 'All right, never mind.'

The Ark is aglow. The light seems warmer, the smells sweeter than ever before; the waitresses beam at each other as they pass with their trays. Even the customers seem enlivened, swiping their phones with a flourish, adding winks and grins to their presentations, treating themselves to an extra sachet of artificial sweetener. But the celebratory atmosphere only makes me feel more remote, like I'm a hole that's been cut out of the page.

'So tell us about this book, then,' Ish prompts. 'It's the same set-up as before? All about you?'

'Well, about a fictional Everyman,' I say. 'Working in a bank.'

'And what's the story?'

'Paul has not decided yet,' I say with difficulty. 'But he is thinking that perhaps the banker . . . ah . . . robs the bank.'

'Robs it?'

'Yes . . .' On the tabletop, my phone flashes awake a moment, then darkens again. 'Yes, only . . . only . . .'

'He fucks it up,' Ish says.

My eyes snap up. Ish looks back at me expressionlessly.

'He leaves something behind,' she says. 'They're on to him straight away.'

I gulp, cover it up with a sip of coffee that makes me gag in turn. 'That seems to be how the story's going,' I admit.

Ish's kind eyes study me with concern. 'Bit of a downer, eh? As an ending?'

'It's probably more realistic,' I say stoically.

'Couldn't there be a twist or something?'

'What sort of a twist?'

Ish looks down at her hands for a long time. 'How about he's got a mate?'

'Who does?'

'The banker. He's got a mate, and his mate's got – she's got something the bank doesn't want anyone to see.'

'Like what?'

'Like a report,' she says. 'On a flash drive.'

Everything freezes. I feel my mouth drop open, my eyes stare like they're going to pop out of my head.

'He told her to get rid of it, but she didn't,' she continues. 'And the day the government's about to approve the bailout, she sends it to the newspapers.'

A shaft of sea-light tumbles through the window, flashes from the last blonde streaks in her hair. The strangest sensation steals over me, as if an invisible sun, hidden for decades behind an eclipse, were for the first time coming into view.

'If people knew what the bank had been up to, might be tricky to justify bailing it out, mightn't it?' she muses. 'And without the bailout . . . well, it's goodbye bank.' She glances over her shoulder in the direction of Transaction House, as if half-expecting to see it crumbling into dust here and now.

457

'She'd lose her job.' I am barely able to speak.

'She'd lose her job of being an arsehole,' she says. 'She'd probably be grateful.'

I flop back in my chair. The space around me has taken on a wild, kinetic feel, as if it's gained an extra dimension.

'Why?' I say.

'Eh?'

'Why does she do it?'

'Why did *you* do it?' she returns. My cheeks flare; she softens. 'Some things are too big to fail, aren't they?'

Outside, the rainbow flag cracks in the wind; the blue air seems to tinkle, as if with secret chimes. 'Thank you,' I say.

'Just seemed like a better ending,' she says.

'So what would you do next?'

'It's not me, is it, it's the character.'

'Okay, what does the character do? In the epilogue? I can tell Paul.'

'I don't know ... maybe she takes up anthropology again. Goes back to the island, lives with the tribe, tries to help stop them being washed away.'

'That would work.'

'Then she meets a handsome island chieftain and falls in love.'

'Yes.'

'He's tall, has a nice body.'

'Of course.'

'And he's really good at racquetball.'

'Let me write this down.'

'What about you, Claude? What happens to you?'

Before I can reply, Ariadne appears at the table with a plate of baklava. 'You want to try?' she says. 'I have changed the recipe.'

She waits while we dig in with our spoons.

'Fuck,' Ish says. 'This is incredible.'

'*Nostimo*,' I agree. 'Very *nostimo*.'

'That's because this time I use Greek honey,' Ariadne says;

458

then adds, looking at me, 'Once you taste it, always you will be coming back for more.'

With that, she dances away again. Ish raises an eyebrow.

'What?' I say.

'You need to ask her out.'

'In the book, you mean?' I say. 'Or in real life?'

Ish grins at me over her cup.

'That's up to you, mate,' she says. 'That's up to you.'

Acknowledgements

Thanks to Simon Prosser, Mitzi Angel, Anna Kelly and Caroline Pretty for their invaluable editorial work; to Natasha Fairweather for her support and insight; and to all at United Agents. Thanks to Donna Tartt for her inspired early reading. Thanks also to Anna Ridley, Cliona Lewis, Patricia McVeigh, Neil Stewart, Mark C. O'Flaherty, Tim Jarvis, Ronan Kelly, Jonathan Hanly, Jon Ihle, Stephen McGovern, Adam Kelly, Sarah Bannan and Linda Fallon. A big ευχαριστώ to Viviana Miliaresi for all of her help. Thanks to the Arts Council of Ireland, An Chomhairle Ealaíon, for their financial assistance. Miriam and Sam – for real life, my love and gratitude to you always.